DAVID PARRY
AND PATRICK WITHROW

The Jacamar Nest

An M&S Paperback from
McClelland & Stewart Inc.
The Canadian Publishers

An M&S Paperback from McClelland & Stewart Inc.

First printing May 1992

Published by arrangement with Macmillan of Canada

Canadian Cataloguing in Publication Data

Parry, David, 1941-
The jacamar nest

"An M&S paperback."
ISBN 0-7710-6931-6

I. Withrow, Patrick.   II. Title.

PS8581.A77J3 1992   C813'.54   C92-093542-7
PR9199.3.P37J3   1992

Cover painting by Heather Cooper
Cover design by Kong Njo

Printed and bound in Canada

McClelland & Stewart Inc.
The Canadian Publishers
481 University Avenue
Toronto, Ontario
M5G 2E9

To Doreen and Lynne

PROLOGUE

Watkins Glen, New York, August 7.

Staedtlander blinked. He was sure he had seen the easel move. There it went again: the legs buckling in protest, or maybe even trying to walk out from under the ugliest painting it had ever been asked to hold.

He shook his head and stared at the thing again: a gloomy confusion of blue and ochre oils. Could anyone with even one working eye have mistaken this for talent? Did the rich man— the filthy rich man, Staedtlander suspected—really believe that Staedtlander would drive all the way up from Philadelphia to examine a painting in progress, pronounce it a work of genius, and rush back to his gallery to break the news?

He did. And Staedtlander had already cashed the rich man's cheque.

He could hear them in the kitchen, stirring drinks, opening and closing drawers. Any second now they'd be out, studying him with expectant smiles: she with the pretty dark eyes and the paint smudge on her cheek; he with a confident grin, both of them waiting for Staedtlander's pronouncement. The rich man had been vague about his relationship with the girl. Staedtlander didn't think he was her father.

"Your beer." The man handed him a bottle and a glass. "You sure that's all you want? We got nice scotch."

"It's a long drive back," Staedtlander said. "Beer's fine." To himself he said, that settles that. A father wouldn't refer to his

1

daughter's scotch as something "we" got. Wouldn't it be something to throw the smug bastard a curve: tell him that, with all due respect, this is one rat's ass of a canvas, and why didn't the young lady take up word processing or nuclear physics instead?

Then stomp out the door, just like that.

Staedtlander savored the thought. But as he poured his beer he knew what he had to do. The man's donation had been generous and, while it might not save the gallery, his cheque could draw more philanthropists out of the woodwork.

"Well, what do you think?" The man spoke to him, but his eyes were on her.

The girl waited, dark eyes wide.

Staedtlander set the beer bottle on a table and lifted his glass. The man had told him to milk it out a little, look as if he were taking his time, so she wouldn't suspect that anything had been arranged. He took a long sip and examined the canvas. He smiled at the girl. "Incredible!" he said. "Absolutely incredible!"

Then he threw up on the painting.

The girl dropped her glass, smashing it on the hardwood, liquid trickling away through the cracks. She ran from the room in tears. The man stared at Staedtlander in disbelief, then hurried out, calling her name.

By this time Staedtlander was doubled up in pain on the floor. Neither of them heard him when he coughed out, "The beer. There's something in that beer."

CHAPTER 1

Miami, Florida, August 12.

Harry had never seen house numbers like this, bouncing all over the neighborhood. Find two or three in the order they should be in and the next one would be out by ten. Number 118 sat across the street from 79, while 51A stood beside a leaning shack called 51½. That one was next to a three-storey pile with eight doorbells that was numbered 51. Some places had no numbers at all. Harry wondered how the postman found his way with the welfare cheques.

He gave up checking numbers and started looking for a house whose garage had blown up. Two blocks later he found it.

Harry climbed out of the rented air-conditioned Plymouth and began to peel off his worsted suit jacket. Then he decided no, even in this heat, even in this neighborhood, he looked more professional with it on. Harry knew that in this part of town that would matter. There would always be eyes on a white man, eyes like those of the old black guy on the porch across the street.

Harry walked up to the charred leftovers of the garage, just as though he knew what he was looking for. He tried to piece together what had happened. The car's gas tank had blown up. The tar paper roof had caught fire, and then the dried spruce beams. The fire department must have gotten here quickly to have saved anything at all.

The reports agreed that the victim had been under the car when the tank blew up, and that the explosion had lifted the car off its cinder blocks and set the left rear leaf spring down on his head. After the firemen had got the blaze under control they had to jack up the car to get what was left of him out. Harry didn't know how you would ever get used to a job like that.

He poked a shoe at the debris and moved a board. He saw brown slime and hoped it was dog shit.

Harry took out his handkerchief and wiped his hands, although he hadn't touched anything with them. It was just as the report had said it would be; he wasn't finding out anything new.

The problem was, liquid gasoline doesn't blow up: it burns. Gasoline has to be in a gaseous form to explode. Blowing up a gas tank is tough. Harry knew this; he had tried.

The old black man across the street who had gone into the house for a moment was back out again, sitting in the shadows of the porch on what looked like an old bus seat. Harry had guessed he would come back out with a friend and maybe start giving him a hard time about being on private property. But he had come back out alone and sat back down on his bus seat with a can of beer. He was having some trouble with the pull tab.

Harry knew he was going to have to talk to the old man. He just wished there were a way to do it without mentioning insurance. It didn't seem to matter that he was an investigator, not a salesman. People's eyes glazed over as soon as they heard who he worked for.

What would Biff do in a situation like this?

Sometimes Harry resorted to barefaced lies, telling people he was with a state senate inquiry or doing research for Mike Wallace. Last week he had told a woman that he'd been retained to undertake a discreet inquiry by someone whose name couldn't come into the picture. "There's talk of divorce, and when you're doing a project for a young man who's been in *Fortune*'s last three billionaire annuals . . . " That had worked well, a little too well. The woman had been impressed, asked him in, poured tall drinks, and tried her damnedest to get him into the sack. Harry, who didn't get many offers like that, had nevertheless declined; and had kicked himself every day since.

He smiled at the old man on the bus seat. "Warm enough, isn't it?"

The old man thought it over. "Especially for walking around in a coat made out of a horse blanket. I guess it'd be especially warm then." He took another try at the can tab and it finally opened. Foam shot out the hole. "Be especially warm then," he repeated.

"Harry Bracken, Hanover Casualty." Harry stuffed his hand into the pocket of his jacket to find a business card. But the old man had already put out a trembling hand to be shaken. Harry pulled out the card and tried to switch it to his left hand, but by then the old man had assumed that Harry didn't want to shake his hand at all, and pulled it back. Harry put out his right hand again and the old man looked at it carefully, then shook it. Harry tried to give the man his card while he was still shaking his hand and the old man reached for it, forgetting that he was already holding a beer. A rush of foam washed onto Harry's jacket. That was one of the problems with changing careers at forty: the little things could drive you crazy.

Harry nodded toward the garage. "You see it happen?"

The old man shook his head. "Didn't see it happen. Talked to him just the day before, though. Came over to borrow a plier. Foreign boy. That's what he called them, a plier."

"What did he want the plier for?" Harry knew the answer already.

"Said he had to do some work on his car. Said he always did his own car repairs, didn't want to pay somebody else to do his car repairs."

Not with what he was paying in life insurance premiums every month, Harry said to himself. To the old man he said, "You ever do any car repairs yourself?"

"Got to have money to have a car. Even if they give you a car free like they do on the television, you're going to need money to run it. I've done some repairs on cars though. My brothers, they had cars. One time, I could do brakes. Some of the electrics. Like that."

"Not many jobs you could do with a plier, though," Harry said.

"Not many jobs you could do even if you had a pair of them.

Especially these new cars. You look under the hood and there ain't nothing there you'd recognize. You want a beer? You look like a man who'd like a beer, running around in that wool jacket. Where from up north are you from?"

"New Hampshire. I'd like a beer, if you've got lots."

The old man nodded and pulled himself out of the seat and headed into the house.

Harry stared across at what had been Georges Hassan's garage. The Coroner's verdict and the police reports that were stapled to the claim had agreed with each other that the victim had been working on his car. Hanover Casualty received a small but statistically predictable number of claims on people who blew themselves up while working on their cars, just as it received a small but statistically predictable number of claims on people struck by lightning or drowning in their baths. What put this claim out of the ordinary was the size: six hundred thousand dollars, including the double indemnity for accidental death. It had been filed by a sister in Beirut.

But before a cheque was issued, Hanover's computer had pushed out a day-glo pink alert card of the kind that landed routinely on the desk in Harry's cubicle. Over the past eighteen months more than eighteen million dollars had been paid to beneficiaries in third-world countries, and a disturbingly small percentage of these had been in the major statistically predictable categories, such as death by jogging, driving drunk, or eating too much fried food. Not only were the deaths themselves unusual, it was common knowledge that at least two—some said three—of last year's decedents had staged resurrections miraculous enough to have excited the Twelve Apostles.

It was also common knowledge that half a dozen other "third worlders," as they inevitably came to be known in Harry's department, were not only still living but living in more than modest comfort.

So the bright young programmers at Hanover Casualty had instructed their machines to flash "tilt" on any death claim involving a third-world citizen whenever the amount exceeded a quarter million dollars.

"Want to know what I thought?" the old man asked, handing out a beer as beaded with sweat as he was. "What I thought was the guy was a jerk. Anybody with a half-assed idea of what was what, he'd use a socket set, box wrenches, anything but pliers. Pliers, they take the knurls off the nuts, round 'em right off."

Harry opened his pull tab.

"And he didn't bring the pliers back. I used to use them to open the pull tabs with. Arthritis."

"Did you mention to the police that this guy borrowed your pliers?"

"Those boys? They were being too busy trying to look like television show police. They all wear the sunglasses now, even at night. Probably wear them to hump in. They roll out a lot of snappy questions they've practiced on each other, and they don't wait for the answers. If I told them my name once, I told them a dozen times: Jackson Andrews. Like the seventh President, only backwards. But those boys don't listen to anyone. Too full of themselves. And I'm not just talking white boys here. I'm talking people who ought to know better. I maybe told them about the pliers, but I can't say if they listened. Don't have the pliers now, anyway."

"And you didn't see it happen," Harry said.

"Didn't see it happen. I was at my sister's. She has arthritis, same as me. Nobody else seen it either, far as I know. Nobody around here cares about the welfare of the community any more. You see that green house down there? There's a woman in there who's fucking three cab drivers. Anybody watching out for that? No. Nobody cares. Three cab drivers. All different companies, too."

Harry drained his beer and set the can down quietly so the old man wouldn't take it as a hint that he wanted another.

As soon as Harry announced who he was at the hotel, the fat kid behind the desk did a double-take. Harry wondered if he'd been mistaken for a celebrity. He had never been able to get used to watching American television again after being away for so many years, so he had no idea who was hot on the talk shows. "Guy says it's life and death," the fat kid said. He reached around to the room slot and pulled out a small pile of pink message slips. "Sounds really very anxious, very angry. Really very angry. Says you should call immediately. He was very, very insistent."

Harry guessed that the kid wanted him to return the call so he could get back to his copy of *Vanity Fair* without frequent interruptions. He took the message slips and headed for his room. He didn't have to read them to know who was bothering the kid.

The air in his room smelled processed. He walked across to the air conditioner and turned it off. It took a while for him to get the window open, as if no one had opened it before. He saw some kids splashing in the pool, thought about going down and jumping in with them, but decided on a shower instead. He took a long one, starting with the water on hot, then gradually making it cooler until finally he was standing under a stream of cold water. He wrapped himself in a towel that wasn't as fluffy as it looked, poured three fingers of Hundred Pipers into a plastic glass, and telephoned Penzler.

"Harry, you're not supposed to be there. You're supposed to be here. I've had my secretary leave three messages telling you that. I myself have left a couple of messages. Pretend for a moment that I'm your immediate superior. Just pretend that I'm the man who can have you out on the street picking your ass. Then do what I tell you. Pack up your swimsuit. Come home."

"Good to talk to you, Bill."

"The travel-arrangements people tell me there are dozens of flights out of there each day."

"Bill, I've only been down here a day and I can almost guarantee that we won't have to pay. The cops and the coroner never even came close to what really happened."

"You want to talk close? You're this close" —Harry could picture Penzler holding up a thumb and a forefinger to show the telephone how close— "to looking for another job. That's bad news for you, Harry, because they don't make a lot of jobs for people like you. Besides, who told you to go to Miami? You're supposed to be in New York."

"I finished in New York. That's a clean one. But there was an alert card on this Hassan claim, and since I had somebody for Fleur to stay with, and since I was at the airport—"

"Ah, you know how to get to an airport. Good. Get to one. Come home. Now."

"What's so urgent? Can't you use Brock?"

"Jeff Brock is less than competent."

"Bill, Georges Hassan wasn't under the car. It was somebody else."

"I don't care if Saddam fucking Hussein was under the car. I care deeply that you get home. Now. You're going to Buffalo."

"Send Brock. He's used to getting buffaloed," Harry said.

"One of our clients has a problem there. The Kohl Brewing Company. Makes beer. Needs you."

"What I'm saying, Bill, is that the guy under the car wasn't our client. We don't need to pay the six hundred grand."

"What I'm saying is, you shuffle off to Buffalo now."

"Buffalo will still be there next week."

"Your job won't. Harry, I know you have trouble interpreting instructions that leave themselves open to interpretation." Penzler emitted low sighs between each phrase. "So. I'm going to ask you to disregard the balance of today's conversation and focus only on the next two words. Are you with me so far?"

Harry let the line carry static for a while.

"Harry?"

Harry drained the last of his drink and started flipping through the pull-out index of "local services" attached to the bottom of the phone.

"Harry, I know the game. Not only do I know the game, I've had men shot for trying it on." That wasn't quite true, but Penzler had started to believe it. In combat situations he had threatened to have men shot, and it had always had the intended effect on junior officers, most of whom had no idea that colonels don't have the authority to do that sort of thing. Penzler had resented not having the authority.

Harry flipped open the index at "Dance Instruction—Ballroom." Rudolph & Vera's on Collins Avenue were offering "new friends and a whole new sense of self-worth, with Visa or MasterCard welcomed."

"Two words, Harry. The only two words I want you to remember."

Harry wondered how they charged for the self-worth. Was it on some sort of graduated scale?

"The two words, Harry, are 'Come home.' Now."

Could you get self-worth on an introductory basis? Maybe Rudolph and Vera would let you wheel it around the dance floor first, see how it looked before you took it home.

"Harry? Harry? Do I have an affirmative on that?"

Was Georges Hassan the kind of guy who would invest in self-worth? How much could he buy for six hundred thousand? Harry quietly replaced the receiver. "'Come home now' is three words," he said to his empty glass.

He took the phone off the hook, folded a pillow around the receiver, and rammed it into the drawer in the bedside table. Then he poured three more fingers of scotch.

The black man, Jackson Andrews, had said that Hassan had come around to talk just the once. Harry figured that just the once was enough. Hassan had borrowed the pliers to establish that he liked to work on cars. When he, or a reasonable facsimile of him, was found in the wreckage, no one would have trouble believing his death was an accident.

And it looked as if he was going to get away with it. Harry guessed that with all the crime and cocaine in the city, the police were not going to look too deeply into something they could get out of their homicide files by agreeing to call it an accident.

He finished his drink, put on clean underwear and a clean shirt, and stepped back into his humid suit.

Then he drove to the coroner's building, where a technician made it clear that he wasn't crazy about taking up the taxpayers' time to screw around looking for files that the office had declared closed. Harry slipped a twenty under the edge of the technician's desk calendar. It didn't improve the man's disposition, but it did shake loose a set of dental X-rays.

On his way back to the hotel, Harry stopped at a bottle store and bought more beer. At the cash register he paid and put his change away. As an afterthought, he pulled out a hundred-dollar bill and told the owner to deliver however many cases of Budweiser that would buy to Mr. Jackson Andrews. He wrote down Andrews's address for the man, and made a hundred-dollar entry in his Daytimer under "laundry."

Back at the hotel, the plump kid looked bothered. "Your Mr. Penzler's been calling, but I told him you were on the phone. I didn't know you were out. Your phone must be off the hook."

Harry told the kid he didn't think he was still on the phone, so maybe the phone was off the hook. Back in his room he closed the door and walked to the bedside table. "No wonder your phone's not working," he said to himself. "Some asshole's stuffed the receiver in the drawer."

A look through the Yellow Pages showed him that the section for dentists was smaller than the section for escort services. But that was only because the dentists weren't running quarter-page ads promising "hot conversation" and "cuddly encounters." There were hundreds of numbers he was going to have to call if he was ever going to find a dental X-ray for the real Georges Hassan—one that he could compare with the X-ray he'd been given today—and prove that the corpse in the garage was someone else. Harry knew that he might phone them all and still end up drawing a blank. There was a good possibility that Georges Hassan had never had his teeth fixed in Miami, at least not under his own name.

A day and a half later, Harry knew that was the case. After dialing every dentist in the area, he learned that the only guys named Georges Hassan—"that's Georges with an 's,' ma'am"—who had ever had dental X-rays taken in or around Miami were under fifteen or over fifty-five. At the front desk, meanwhile, the pudgy clerk was sullenly piling up message slips, each more profane than the one before.

Harry poured a drink and swung his feet up on the bed. He

spilled Hassan's file across the blanket and picked at the papers, studying each one, front and back. Everything seemed to be in order, all neat and tidy. He noticed the change-of-address notification that Hassan's sister, the beneficiary, had sent in a couple of months ago, informing the company of her move to Beirut. Previously, she had lived in Atlanta, Georgia. Harry mulled that over. If she and brother Georges were close enough for her to collect this kind of money, wasn't there a chance that Georges had visited her in Atlanta? And if he had visited her there, maybe he had stayed awhile. Possibly long enough to have done some business with a dentist.

So Harry drove to the telephone company, asked to see the Atlanta directory, and persuaded a woman with gray hair and kind eyes to photocopy another five pages of dentists' numbers for him.

Back in his room, he started dialing Atlanta numbers. This time he got lucky right at the top of the second page. A woman at a South View dental clinic told him that a Georges Hassan had been treated there twice. The address she gave was the one that Hassan's sister had written on her change-of-address form.

Next morning, Harry was holding two sets of X-rays up to a light, telling the woman at the South View clinic that he didn't know as much about teeth as he really ought to, but he'd bet a month's pay that he was looking at pictures of two completely different sets of teeth. A few minutes later a man in a white smock with a small patch of blood on the front said yes, he thought so, too.

Harry smiled, a big broad game-show smile. This would teach Penzler not to try and pull him off a case.

"Ever considered having that incisor capped?" asked the man with the blood on his smock.

CHAPTER 2

Paris, France, August 13.

Waiting for the message, he sat at a window table and savored the strong black coffee. He knew he could get a better and cheaper brew at one of the Algerian cafes or at one of the new Lebanese restaurants that were being built with exiled money. But it wasn't the coffee that had brought him to Les Halles. It was the chance to look across the square at the new American restaurant, the one in the chain that was their target.

Ismail Gezmis held the cup to his cheek and felt its warmth. His dark eyes were fixed on the famous neon trademark as he thought about the months of planning.

He had made a point of attending the restaurant's official opening, when a gaunt-cheeked French actress had cut the ribbon and a dark-suited American executive had delivered a brief address. "Unlike its American cousins," the executive had intoned, "this location will, of course, serve wine." And serve wine it did, a plonk as consistently indifferent as the food that it accompanied.

Gezmis had seen the quarterly earnings of the chain reported in the *Herald Tribune* and he had been unable to believe the figures. So he had sat for two hours and counted the customers, and multiplied that by the number of hours in a business week and the number of weeks in a quarter. He had multiplied that number by what he guessed to be the average amount spent per customer. Then he had multiplied all that by the 9,878 restaurants that the *Herald Tribune* had said the company owned worldwide. And then he knew that the figures had been correct.

So had Qatar. Taking their war to America had been Qatar's idea. Qatar had studied in California and witnessed firsthand the monumental indifference of Americans to the struggle of the Palestinian people. The average American, Qatar believed, had no idea of the grief their government was causing by spending fully one quarter of its foreign aid to support Zionism.

Now, thanks to his group's partnership with Iraq, also lusting for revenge against America, they would soon have the enemy's attention.

Gezmis watched the young people with knapsacks and designer jeans filing into the restaurant. In another hour, he guessed there would be line-ups into the street.

He had read how well the chain adapted to new surroundings. In Germany and Scandinavia, they served beer. In Japan it was tea. The next one was going up in Jerusalem, in sight of the Jaffa Gate, not far from the YMCA and the King David Hotel. Gezmis wondered which of the religions there the menu would salute. Would there be kosher burgers? Spare ribs for Christians? He knew the restaurant would have done its research. They would choose food designed not to attract the wrath of Moslem fanatics or Orthodox rabbis, or to offend the Christian Arabs.

Gezmis's earliest memories of Jerusalem were faraway sounds and faint smells and the warmth of a breast against his cheek. There were other, more confusing recollections: his mother filling up jars of water, knowing that the mains would soon be cut; his father filling sandbags. The faraway sounds were the single cracks of the Mausers that both Jews and Arabs had used to snipe at each other. The deeper sounds were the Arab Legion's field guns shelling the Jewish quarter of the old city day after day. The faint smells were of burning and of rotting garbage piled in the streets. Gezmis dimly remembered being taken in his father's green Buick Roadmaster to the West Bank when they had heard the Jewish trucks rumbling down the street and the loudspeakers telling them to leave.

He thought that he remembered these things but he knew they might just have been stories that his father had told him. His father had loved Jerusalem and had been bitter about leaving. But he had also been prepared, better prepared than the hundreds of thousands who ended up in the camps. Dr. Gezmis had been a Palestinian in the classic mold: he knew that money had no country and he kept his where he could get it when he needed it.

Ismail Gezmis drained the last of his coffee. Across the square, young Americans were sitting on the steps of the restaurant, sipping milkshakes and letting the empty containers fall into the gutter.

They were a friendly enough people, the Americans. Gezmis had met many of them during his three years in Paris. Individually, they could engage in thoughtful and earnest conversation, often surprising him with their candor and open disapproval of their government's stand. But as a group they were loud and inconsiderate.

Gezmis reasoned that Americans had no traditional sense of honor, no unifying bond, no sense of history to protect. If there were any national vision at all, it seemed to grow more ragged every day.

But he could not really disdain them, any more than he could disdain the Zionists. How could one disdain Americans when, after a mere two hundred years they effectively ruled the world? How could one—in all honesty—disdain the Zionists, who had brought to life land that had lain fallow and fruitless for thousands of years?

He signaled for more coffee and ordered a brioche. How on earth could those young Americans across the square prefer hamburger to this?

The answer to that, of course, was marketing, something at which the Americans excelled. His father had wanted him to study business in America, as Qatar had done. But on his way to sit for his *tawjihi*, the matriculation he would need to enter the American college, a group of young Israeli soldiers had waylaid him and beaten him up. They had laughed and told him that the world did not need more educated Arabs. Then they warned him that if he planned to take his *tawjihi* again, they would be waiting.

He had found his way into el-Fatah instead, and the terrorists had given him a different education, at training camps in Syria and Lebanon.

Those had been days of prosperity for the PLO and most of its factions. Oil money was flowing at its fastest, Qadaffi was handing over bonuses to those who perpetrated the greatest outrages, and Lebanese businesses were paying millions to Arafat's people merely for the privilege of being left alone.

Gezmis had distinguished himself quickly, not by acts of violence, an area in which there seemed to be plenty of talent already, but in strategic planning and problem solving. For example, to allow their hijackers to circumvent security checks at airports, he had suggested that the PLO buy its own duty-free shop—the one at Dar es Salaam International Airport in Tanzania was available. Since duty-free goods were picked up after passenger inspection, it would be a simple matter of handing over the right shopping bags containing the right selection of weapons to the right travelers. From Tanzania they could connect to almost any flight and airport in the world without passing through another security check.

The chair beside him clattered as the messenger sat down and followed Ismail's gaze to the restaurant across the square. "They are all here," the messenger whispered. "I haven't told any of them where the meeting is. But they seem very anxious to begin."

Gezmis nodded. They would be anxious, but no more than he. It had taken, in all, more than eighteen months to put the program together: the first thirteen months working with Qatar, then, since his friend's tragic death, working with the Englishwoman who had lived with Qatar and who was now determined to keep his dream alive.

And now, with the Iraqis on their side, the final missing pieces had dropped into place.

To Ismail Gezmis, opening up a front on American soil was a

stroke of brilliance. In Baghdad, the leaders of the Revolutionary Council had been at first incredulous, then jubilant, when Gezmis had explained the plan and shown them how easily it would work. It would raise hundreds of millions of American dollars to help his people crawl from the camps and start on the road back to Jerusalem. And by then their message would have penetrated the thick-headed consciousness of the American people.

Gezmis stood and paid the bill. He added five francs more to the service charge, his generosity a small prayer for success.

Before he left, he took a final glance at the restaurant across the square. Soon, Qatar. Soon there will be a return to Jerusalem, where the Prophet took off to heaven on a white horse and where my father took off to the West Bank in a green Buick Roadmaster.

CHAPTER 3

Hanover, New Hampshire, August 15.

Harry wrote his report in longhand on the flight home. He recommended that the company press charges for criminal fraud and, as an afterthought, suggested a press conference to let everyone know that Hanover Casualty was not a company to fuck with.

"We can't do that," William Penzler said when he reached the end of the report.

"Can't do what?" Harry asked. "Can't press charges or can't charge off to the press?"

"We can't do either. If you were more of a team player, Harry, you'd have known this three days ago. You'd have come home when I asked you to and you'd have found all this out."

"Found all what out?" Harry's stomach was starting to turn the way it had once turned when he'd been holding the winning ticket on a five-hundred-dollar daily double, and the "inquiry" sign had flashed on at the end of the second race.

"That we've already paid the claim." Penzler folded his fingers and snapped out his locked hands in a move that he hoped conveyed finality.

"So let's go and get our money back. It wouldn't be the first time."

"Our money is in West Beirut, Harry. Are you volunteering to go into West Beirut to bring our money back?" When Harry said nothing, Penzler said, "No, I didn't think you were." He walked to his desk and slid Harry's report to the bottom of the single small pile of papers there. He tapped the pile until the edges were straight.

Harry watched. Finally, he asked, "Why did we pay, Bill?"

Now Penzler was straightening the pile so that the edges were parallel with the edges of the desk.

"Jesus, Bill, how am I supposed to do my job if I don't know what's going on around here?"

Penzler started to say something but cut himself off. He walked to the window and stood looking out, hands clasped behind his back. He was a military man who could return to the military with the first scotch of the day.

"When I got up this morning and saw the fog I remembered the Chinese bugles. They always played the bugles before they attacked. And they liked the fog. They really liked the fog, Harry. It meant we couldn't call for air support."

To Harry, other people's wars were about as interesting as other people's golf games. But he knew better than to interrupt and Penzler knew that he knew.

"It was a question of mechanics really," Penzler went on. "Simple mechanics. They decide to throw nine thousand Chinese at you. You have four hundred men. For simplicity's sake, let's call it twenty-five Chinese for every man. Can you picture that, Harry? Now, the Chinese become visible out of the fog at about a hundred and fifty yards. On that sort of terrain a Chinese soldier can cover a hundred and fifty yards in something under a minute. So your kill rate per man has to be one Chinese every two seconds. That's assuming they don't kill any of yours and that you don't kill any of your own."

Harry decided to wait him out. He knew that when Penzler got started on mechanics he could keep it up long enough to make you forget the question he was trying to evade.

When Penzler finished, Harry said, "What are you saying, Bill? That you can't tell me why we paid a six-hundred-thousand-dollar claim that we didn't have to? I mean, shit."

"Your trouble, Harry, is that you've seen so much in your young life you think you have all the answers. But you, more than most, should know that things are not always as they seem."

Harry mulled that over. "It has something to do with my old pals at Langley, doesn't it?"

"I'm not saying it does or it doesn't. Now about this brewery business—"

"Come on, Bill, I put in a lot of years—"

"Which is why you should understand why I may not be in a position to tell you." He was proud of not being in the position: there was power in it, the same kind of power that was implicit in being an undisclosed source.

"Sure. CIA wants someone dead, only not really dead. Am I close?" Harry persisted.

"I can't say."

"In theory it would work, though, wouldn't it?"

"That is merely conjecture."

Harry thought for a moment. "Okay, conjecture this one. Suppose Langley had a guy over there, a local. A good one. How do they keep him working for us good guys? Money? Money's no good to him if he can't spend it. And as soon as he starts to spend it, somebody's going to put two and two together and figure out where it came from. So he can only use any money Langley gives him after he retires and moves away. But if he's retired he's no use to the good guys, right? So let's say, in the abstract of course, that our hypothetical Georges Hassan is persuaded by God knows who to pull one of the third-worlder tricks that have been keeping our claims people busy. Instead of going home in a box, he shows up alive, but with all the proper paper proving he's dead. Maybe even a death notice from the *Miami Herald* for them all to chuckle over. More to the point, he goes home with six hundred grand and everyone knows it came from the Great Satan's insurance fat cats. How am I doing, Bill? As a conjecture, I mean."

Penzler sat.

"Here's something else," Harry pressed on. "He not only gets the money to spend without anyone worrying about where it came from, but the fact that he's officially dead in the U.S.A.

makes it highly unlikely that he could be working for the United States Government."

Penzler closed his eyes and folded his hands on his desk. "Harry, I would like you to promise me that you won't discuss with anyone else what you and I have just discussed. Even in the abstract."

Harry grinned. "Cowboys. Even though Uncle's paying this one, if word gets out how easy it is to get their hands on that kind of cash, you're going to have all kinds of greedheads pulling the same crap. Costs a lot to keep a terrorist operation going these days. Hope you haven't opened any doors."

"Harry, I would like you to open the door over there, walk through it, and go to Buffalo. Try to get there for Monday morning. Wolf Kohl, the principal owner at Kohl's Brewing Company, seems very anxious. He thinks someone is tampering with his beer."

"That *would* make a brewer hopping mad."

"Goodbye, Harry," Penzler said.

Harry made a right turn onto East Wheelock at the Hanover Inn. Across the road, some of the students dressed in light sweaters and jeans were tossing Frisbees on Dartmouth Green. As he so often did when he passed Dartmouth College, Harry found himself thinking back to his own school days at a less prestigious institute of learning in New York City.

He had received his invitation to serve his country in the tidy living room of a very untidy professor. Harry had been recruited by his penis.

"It's about your dick," his history professor had told him. "What I want you to do is keep it out of my daughter. At least until she finishes her semester."

Harry had said nothing at first, so the professor had continued. "I'm not objecting on moral grounds, Harry, but her grades are slipping and they were never that good to begin with. I want you to promise me you'll stop. At least with my daughter."

Harry, too startled to say anything else, had agreed that he would stop—until the end of the semester.

"Good, good." The professor had walked to an old wooden icebox whose insides he had replaced with a refrigerating unit. He pulled out two bottles. "I make this myself, all by myself. Can't get Smithwick's here, so I try to come as close as I can." He eased off the caps slowly and presented one to Harry with a quiet reverence.

Harry took a tentative sip. It tasted like pureed bread.

"Now that we're drinking partners who have reached an understanding about my daughter," the professor said, "I hope you'll permit me to make an observation."

Harry dared another sip, and nodded.

"It's about your brain, Harry. The logical part of it isn't very developed. That may be because for the past little while you've been thinking with your dick. But from the papers you've handed in, I'd say that the creative part of your mind is quite agile. Frolicsome. Damn close to childlike. All of which makes you eminently unsuited for a great many careers. You're not very well organized. You couldn't run a gas station or manage a bank. Hell, you couldn't stage manage a bun fight in a bakery. You're also ill disciplined and badly kempt. So what I have in mind for you is a career that makes the most of these advantages. Something in the military. More or less."

The professor paused to pour beer down his throat. "Now traditionally, the military takes people and molds them. Makes men of boys. Gives them character. The problem is that the military tends to make the same character out of every boy it molds. It makes them logical, which is lovely when they're up against another army, because the other army has molded its boys too. Both sides can then be fearsomely logical against each other and the slaughter goes along according to plan."

Harry started to say something, but the professor waved him quiet.

"The trouble these days is that we're starting to fight groups here and there who haven't been molded. Some people are putting their war into the hands of amateurs, who just go around killing people and blowing things up with no training whatsoever. And the military doesn't know what to do about that. So we"—the professor waved his hand airily to indicate a group that hung cloud-like somewhere—"have put together a group of unmolded people at the request of governments here and there. To fill up this group, we occasionally draft young persons to do this and that. I wondered if you might consider an internship, getting some things done for us."

"It's really not a very defined sort of offer, Professor."

"Exactly the point. Exactly. Clever of you to pick that up. And now that you're no longer putting your thing in my daughter, perhaps you'd call me Biff."

That had been years ago, before God had invented real pain for Harry. Before hangovers, before mucous buildup, before Rachel died and left him with Fleur, before twinges in the knee. And before Harry had been confronted by the awareness that he was not the king of the world and never would be.

In the meantime, he had survived a seventeen-year career, the end of which had come about abruptly and, in Harry's view, unfairly. William Penzler, at Biff's urging, had rescued him by summoning him to New Hampshire and a job that Harry was still trying to adjust to six months later. "It's a sordid little job: poking and prying. It'll take advantage of your unique talents, Harry. And keep your hand in," Biff had promised.

On a day like today, as he drove through streets filled with pretty young women who were taking the summer courses at the college, his life astonished him. He started inventorying its components. The further away he got from the center of town, the more he got into the suburbs, the longer the inventory became and the more astonished he was. He was working for an insurance company. He was living in a house with a microwave oven. He had a mortgage. Fleur, his daughter, was about the same age as those girls he was finding so attractive on this sunny Friday afternoon of his first New Hampshire summer.

He had a green Plymouth. He had a car phone. He had a driveway with a carport. He had a rose bush that needed pruning before fall. He had brass numbers on his house and a matching brass mail box. (They'd been put there by the previous owners, but he'd polished them the weekend before last, which meant there was complicity.) Harry opened the door and walked to the kitchen through the sunlit dust motes dancing in the hall. There was a note on the counter. There usually was: do all daughters of a certain age communicate exclusively in writing? Fleur was out. She was babysitting the Mastersons' cats. She'd be back later. There was some cheese and some wine in the refrigerator.

Fleur would call.

He hoped she would. No one else was likely to, and it struck him that he'd already read every book in the house.

CHAPTER 4

Paris, France, August 14.

A man and woman were suspended in a net, both of them naked. Below, patrons took nervous sips from drinks that cost the equivalent of eighteen U.S. dollars a glass.

A pudgy Englishman with a gin and tonic turned his gaze briefly from the net to glance at three Arabs in white robes and burnooses striding quickly past his table. "Bloody Arabs and their forty-dollar oil," the Englishman said to his wife, who was still gaping up at the net where, with just a hint of boredom, the girl had begun to give her partner a blow job.

The disappointed Englishman jerked a thumb as a door at the rear of the club closed behind the Arabs. "That's where the good show is. Back there, they're probably doing it with donkeys."

Ismail Gezmis watched on the television monitor in the manager's office as Salim, Majeed, and Gamil Rashid joined Felix Tidyman in the adjoining room and looked around warily. It was clear from their expressions that Salim and Majeed had been offended by his choice of meeting place. Their God demanded women in veils, not in nets performing public sex.

But Gezmis had wanted them to be offended. He wanted to drive home the point that there were different worlds, with different rules from their own, and that in the following months many things would happen that they wouldn't understand; they were going to have to trust his judgment. Most of all he wanted them disoriented, off-balance. Keeping them waiting would remind them that he was in charge.

He watched the monitor as Gamil Rashid wiggled slightly in his chair. Gezmis knew that Rashid had reason to be nervous. For two years his faction had been weakening, wounded by lack of funds and driven to more desperate atrocities to keep up morale. Their latest attack on an Israeli beach near Ashdod had ended in disaster, with four of their commandos killed and eleven taken prisoner.

Rashid had scraped together enough cash to buy his men new camouflage trousers, tightly fitted and attractively patterned. The trousers had cheered them for a few days. But now the men were looking at their antique SMGs and comparing them to the newer, more effective weapons of Arafat's people.

Next to Rashid sat Abu Salim, head of Black June. His group had none of the PLO's 130 mm guns or Soviet-made B-21 rocket launchers. But the men were certainly brave enough. For the moment, Gezmis needed the name of Salim's group more than he needed the group itself. The Palestinian and Iraqi students he was recruiting in America would be impressed by an invitation from Salim to join in the American jihad.

Then there was Majeed. Majeed was there simply because Majeed needed money—Gezmis had met the man's Eurasian mistress—and because he controlled an excellent document-printing facility.

Ismail Gezmis remembered the arguments he had used to win them over. He had shown them that the source of America's wealth was also its Achilles' heel. He had patiently described in great detail the vulnerability of corporate reputations. He had explained how sales had declined at McDonald's Restaurants with the rumor that earthworms had been ground up in their meat; how the makers of Tylenol had suffered when crackpots had tampered with the product on the store shelves. "America is a brand-name society," Gezmis had told them. "They spend billions creating their trademarks. They will gladly pay millions to protect them."

Through the monitor Gezmis shifted his gaze to the American, still standing, still making the most of his considerable height. Qatar had been right about their needing an American. And in Felix Tidyman, Gezmis felt that they had chosen well. Tidyman, a former CIA operative, had managed one of the agency's proprietary export agencies and made himself wealthy in the process. With the money he had bought land, a lot of land, around the dirt-poor Texas farm where he had been raised. His undoing had been an arms shipment to Libya, which came to light during the Iran-Contra scandals, when scapegoats were in high demand. Tidyman had served only a short term in prison, but the loss of his land was a wound that would not heal.

Gezmis looked at his watch and switched off the monitor. It was time. He reached into his jacket pocket, pulled out the telegram from Marjorie Brooks, and opened the door to the adjoining room.

Gezmis cut off the mandatory round of greetings and small talk as quickly as decency permitted. "My friends." He waved the telegram in the air. "The Jacamar program is showing every sign of success. We will soon be in a position to proceed to our next phase."

This met with cautious murmurs of approval.

Gezmis held up his hand and smiled at Felix Tidyman. "If I were Mr. Tidyman, I might be inclined to suggest a toast at this point. Given the nature of our program, a round of beer— American beer—would be appropriate. But since the Prophet denies us that pleasure, I suggest we move on to the business at hand."

CHAPTER 5

Buffalo, New York, August 16.

Harry had always remembered the hills of upper New York State as looking picture perfect, a backdrop that might have been put together for a movie. These were hills that had been rounded by glaciers, vivid with a remarkable range of greens in summer and with colors more vibrant than the tropics in autumn. Driving four miles an hour above the speed limit with the windows down, Harry was pleased to see that nothing had changed.

He had left the afternoon before, a Sunday. Fleur had been invited to someone's cottage "for the parasailing," and her excitement had reminded him of Rachel's the first time he had taken her skiing. He hadn't wanted to sit around the house thinking about Fleur parasailing. He didn't want to think about her ever being in danger again. Driving would keep his mind off it. It would also allow him more time off the interstate, so he could take in the landscape.

The landscape itself was pretty, but the French would have done a better job of decorating it. Over on that hill there would have been a village with creamy stone houses topped with red tile roofs instead of a microwave tower. The road would have been lined with poplars, rather than the shards of steel-belted radials thrown off by trucks. On this kind of Sunday in France, Harry, you would have stopped at a restaurant, sat with Rachel on the terrace, eaten oysters, drunk some wine, and talked some simple nonsense.

Here and there he was encouraged to see remarkably neat farms with houses from the 1850s, small brave structures that might have been built by North American hobbits.

Harry thought about how many cords of wood it would have taken to heat one of these houses in the 1850s. Who would have cut the wood and how did they haul it? What was the average per-person consumption of water for baths, and where did it come from, and who hauled that? What did the people who first lived in those little huddled houses smell like? And what did you do on a Friday or Saturday night when the nearest neighbors were half a mile away and the roads were clogged with snow? Did anyone ever have an affair here and if so, how, and on what days of the week? Where did they have it? And what happened then?

Harry wondered how people got along without Jacuzzis, satellite phones, or lemon-scented dish detergent. Think of it, Harry, a world without oat bran, without sugar substitutes, sometimes without sugar. How many of those things could you give up? Could you give up rock and roll, Harry? Could Fleur? Could you give up two-ply toilet paper? Name five things invented in the last two decades you would be happy to go without.

Every so often a band of suburbs indicated the approach of a town. The brick and clapboard of the country gave way to aluminum and colored vinyl. What would the canal men of the 1850s have thought of vinyl siding and above-ground pools? What would the farmers have thought about freeze-dried coffee and garlic-flavored croutons? What is this mental masturbation, Harry? Keep this up and you'll end up in a seniors' home with a blanket on your lap.

He spent Sunday night at an old hotel on Seneca Lake, close enough to Buffalo to give him time for breakfast and still make the brewery by Monday mid-morning. He dreamed of teams of Clydesdales hauling fat wagons full of calorie-reduced pasta with tangy sauce and above them, Fleur, flying.

*

Wolfgang Kohl stared through the window of his office at the red brick walls of his brewery. He saw a green Plymouth that he didn't recognize pull into the visitors' parking lot. That was when he noticed that another of the four-foot-high, hand-carved letters in the KOHL'S BREWING sign was missing. This time it was the "O." Every fraternity house in New York State must have one of those letters by now. Looking down behind the loading dock he saw two of his truckers sharing a joint. Pigeon shit covered his windowsill.

"Fuck 'em," he said. "Fuck 'em all."

Kohl walked over to his rosewood desk and stabbed a finger at the intercom. "Find out which dink meeting my son is in and tell him to haul his ass up here."

In meetings that his father did not attend, Matthew Kohl referred to him as "the old gentleman." To the uninitiated this conjured a quiet, polished person in a starched shirt and vest. But Wolfgang Kohl was profanely unquiet, studiously unpolished, and partial to open-necked shirts and expensive sweaters. He also slept with better women than his son did. To his face, Matthew Kohl called his father "Sir."

"You wanted me, sir?"

Wolfgang Kohl pushed a piece of paper across his desk. "That the best you can do?"

Matthew picked up the paper just long enough to recognize his own name at the bottom.

"Yes."

"You want to pay them off. What does O'Connor think about that? She got any more guts than you?"

"I've approved a security retainer. You said it was to be my decision."

Wolfgang Kohl shook his head slowly. "What do you think your forebears would think of that decision?"

"I really couldn't say, sir."

"They're the reason you and I are here, Matthew. Your great-grandfather fought all the other motherfucker breweries, smashed more of their barrels than they smashed of his. That was back when there were twenty-five breweries in Buffalo. Your

Grandpa fought the U.S. government and Prohibition. He was reduced to making malted milk and ginger ale, Lord have mercy upon us. I was two years younger than you are now when I took over. That was 1959, and the first problem I had to deal with was the Teamsters. They wanted to organize the staff. I told them the staff was as organized as it was ever going to get, and when they didn't take my word on that, I beat the shit out of them."

He smiled at his son, but Matthew was looking out the window at the sky.

"Then in the sixties, we had those bright young fuckers who wanted me to turn out pasteurized beer. Longer shelf life. I threw the bright young fuckers out. The other regional breweries hired them. Where are those other regionals now? Sucked up by the nationals. Because they were making the same dull beer as the nationals, and the nationals could out-advertise them twenty-to-one. That was a decision I had to make. The same way I asked you to make this one."

"Yes."

"And your decision is to pay them off."

"Security retainer," Matthew said again.

"I don't know if I'm doing anything for you by sticking you with that decision."

His secretary, a frail, gray-haired woman, appeared at the door, not certain if she should interrupt. When it seemed clear that the young Mr. Kohl was not going to reply, she coughed and said, "Mr. Bracken is waiting."

Harry walked in and found a man in his sixties who looked more than mildly pissed off. Beside him was a younger man who had the facial bones of the older man. But where the old man looked as if he might be somebody worth drinking beer with, the young man looked as if his shirt had been stuffed by a taxidermist.

The young man spoke first. "I'm Matthew Kohl. This is my father, Wolfgang Kohl. I'm sorry to have brought you all this way for nothing, Mr. Bracken, but we're really at a state now where we don't need your help. The matter appears to have been resolved."

"Resolved?"

"Under control."

"Maybe—it's Matthew isn't it?—maybe what you should do is explain to me how things have been resolved and what kind of control they're under."

"Frankly, the matter is not one in which Hanover Casualty has any further involvement."

"I'm still having trouble understanding you," Harry confessed. "Have these people who threatened you told you that they're not going to do what they said they were going to do? Or have you decided to pay them off?"

A young woman entered the office without knocking. She walked straight up to Wolfgang Kohl and said, "We've got another one."

William Penzler had once told Harry that when everybody else is jumping up and down in a troubling situation, the way to get yourself noticed is just to sit still: simply shut your mouth until everybody else runs out of steam. Harry sat still and shut his mouth.

So did the others for a long twenty seconds. Harry tried to guess which of the three would break the silence. At first, he thought it would be the older man; he could see blood rising up above his open collar. Then he thought it would be the woman. She had an "Oh shit, what have I done?" look on her face. He changed his mind: it would be Matthew. The eyes were giving him away.

"Miss Alex O'Connor," Matthew said finally, with a lavish lack of enthusiasm, "this is Mr. Bracken. Mr. Bracken, Miss O'Connor. Miss O'Connor is the product manager in charge of our King Kohl brand. Mr. Bracken is an insurance investigator, whom I believe is just leaving."

"Oh, I'm pleased to meet you, Mr. Bracken." She looked angry. She looked embarrassed. And with her slim build, dark blonde hair, and chocolate brown eyes, Harry thought she looked quietly pretty. But she did not look pleased: her lips were tight.

"Maybe you could leave us for five minutes, Bracken." Wolfgang Kohl had taken charge.

"Oh I really don't think we'll be needing Mr. Bracken at all, sir," Matthew said.

"I think we should discuss that, Matthew."

Harry smiled his best Boy Scout smile. "Maybe I could have a beer while I was waiting."

They looked relieved.

Harry paused at the door. "But I'd like to know whether the beer will kill me, or merely make me miss a few days' work. I'm sure that most of the folks who drink it will be asking the same question soon."

"I've told you, it doesn't concern you." Matthew's face had the same look he probably wore when other golfers caught him doctoring his scorecard.

"She just said, 'We've got another one,'" Harry reminded them. "I'd like to know, another what? Another one getting diarrhea? Another one drinking ground glass? Some of my best friends are beer drinkers, so I'd kind of like to know."

The three stood like figures in a seventeenth century court painting, rigid and uncomfortable. The woman broke the silence this time. "Actually, what it is, there are isolated cases of vomiting." She made her mouth very small as she said it, pursing her lips. Harry wondered if she knew that she was doing it. He wondered how long it would take him to get annoyed with the habit if he ever got to know her. He wondered if he'd ever get to know her.

Matthew looked about to interrupt, but the old man made a gesture—a hand slicing air—and cut him off. He made another gesture—a beckoning sign—to tell the woman to continue.

"Because it's just vomiting, we've been able to keep it quiet," Alex continued. "But we can't figure out how they've done it to us. We've tested the lines, the vats, the bottles—everything. We know the chemical they used: ipecac. Hospitals use it to induce vomiting in poisoning victims. If it comes into contact with alcohol, the alcohol takes on the ipecac's power to induce vomiting. Not all our beer was affected, but we can't isolate the problem to any single batch." Her lips were still tight as she spoke.

"You said bottles. Any problems with the cans at all?" Harry asked.

Alex and Matthew looked to Wolfgang, expecting him to field it.

He did. "No cans in my brewery, Mr. Bracken. Never had them, never will. Kohl's Beer is worth a bottle. With metal cans you get too much fluctuation in temperature. There's no protection good as glass. Kohl's Beer is worth a bottle."

Harry felt properly chastised. "So what was your next plan?"

Matthew took back the floor. "The next part of the plan is, as I keep repeating, no concern of yours. We have been informed that the situation has ended."

"Except for a few poor suckers out there vomiting."

"We have been assured that there will be a few more isolated incidents but that the vomiting will be relatively mild," Matthew said. "It could be argued that the vomiting may prove beneficial. One never really knows about these things. It may lead some heavier users to examine their habits. As for ourselves, the experience has also been beneficial. We ended up re-examining all of our purchasing and manufacturing techniques and our equipment. Because of that we'll doubtless make a superior product in the future. But as I say, the incident is closed."

"But paying off this group—"

"Nobody has stated that anybody has been paid off. However, were that the case, it should be remembered that we pay off a lot of groups. So does your company. Hanover Casualty offers kidnap insurance: quietly and under the counter, but it offers it. And consider our tax monies. They're spent on slum dwellers, on convicted felons, on drug addicts, on helping terrorists turn other countries into dictatorships and to help rich monarchs win back their countries so they can continue being rich monarchs. If indeed we were paying anyone off, I think we might regard it in much the same way as the other taxes we pay."

"But you're being coerced."

"Would you pay your income tax if there were no coercion?" Matthew shot back.

"Do you know how much you would be paying, if indeed you were paying? I'm asking as a beer drinker. Every time I lift a glass am I going to buy one bullet for this group? Two bullets? Or are they putting it all into milk and vitamins for the needy, or new vending machines to launder their money?"

"Interesting point," Alex O'Connor cut in.

Harry smiled, grateful for even the slightest hint of encouragement. He hoped she thought it was a charming smile. "Look, here's what I'm going to do," he decided. "I'm going to check into that large white hotel just off the interstate."

He paused for alternative suggestions. None was offered.

"I'm going to check in there. And I'm going to wait for you people to call me. I believe I can help. But there's a limit on how long I'll wait. It's the time it takes to drink a six pack. Of Schlitz."

It had made an effective exit, but lying on his hotel bed, with three empty cans already on the telephone table, Harry knew he should have given them a definite time to call.

And if they do call, Harry, what do you do then? Promise to—without fail—track down these wretched malefactors?

Perhaps it's the Irish; the IRA has succeeded against one of the world's best intelligence services, but would even they have the nerve for something like this? Maybe it's some radical consumer group. A Chinese triad? A temperance bund? Dissident Samoans? Disaffected Americans? Affected Arabs? You don't know who's doing this, Harry, and you have no idea where to start looking. You don't even know how they're doing it. Harry, you don't know shit.

He thought about the woman. He could never figure out why a certain kind of very American woman would look taller than a French woman of the same height and proportions. Or why, if you put a French woman and an American woman in the same dress, the French woman would somehow seem more desirable and the American woman more wholesome. Why were French women's mouths more animated? Rachel's had been very animated. Was it a difference in per capita wine consumption? If so, was it a difference in the per capita male wine consumption or the per capita female wine consumption? Or did it have to be shared wine consumption?

The phone rang.

It was Alex O'Connor.

"Look, Mr. Bracken, do you actually know what you're doing?"

"Of course I do. I'm a highly trained insurance investigator. I have seventeen years of international experience."

"There are a lot of guys with seventeen years' experience; often it's one year's experience repeated seventeen times."

Tough woman. "I'll bet you a dinner."

"A dinner on what?"

"That you've got braces," Harry said slowly. He realized immediately that he shouldn't have made the bet. The silence on the phone told him that, and so did his experience: you should only confess a certain amount of perception to a woman.

"So?" she said, finally.

"I was demonstrating my perception. And my lack of grace."

"Nice job with both. Where do you want to eat?"

Harry asked her if she knew somewhere that served regional cuisine. She asked what region he had in mind. He said the regional food of western New York State would be fine. She told him that the dining room at his hotel served a fine example of what was eaten by the locals rather than the sort of thing handed out to the tourists. "The tourists get trout and fresh berries in season, but what the locals seem to like is overdone roast beef and a sort of gray-green bean."

Harry wondered aloud if there wasn't a way to grow the green beans gray and save all the trouble and non-renewable resources it took to change the color.

"I'll meet you there at seven," she said.

Over drinks, he said, "It would really help if I knew why you were here."

"You said you could help."

"Yes, but it would help if I knew if you are here with the

blessing of Mr. Kohl and Mr. Kohl. Or because you don't agree with what's been done."

She looked at him and wondered if she had ever seen such an average-looking man in her life. He was of average height, average weight or near enough to it, had mouse-brown hair, and—when it was at rest—an average face as well. The eyes were blue and were pretty well where they should be, the nose was of normal length and breadth, and the mouth might have established a norm for North American forty-year-old male mouths.

The problem was, the face was seldom at rest. In front of her, Harry seemed to have little control over it. He smiled more broadly than normal people smiled, furrowed his brow more than was acceptable in a man whose profession should have taught him to keep a poker face, and twinkled when most men would have set their faces in a more macho pose.

"I'm here because I market a product that's been making people puke. Ultimately, my career depends on how this turns out. I've put a lot of work into this job. I don't want to end up in the marketing casebooks as 'the dumb broad who watched her market get poisoned,'" she said.

"So I'm talking to you. That's you, Alex, not you, Kohl's Brewing."

"So far, yes. Although Mr. Kohl—senior—expressed a keen interest in . . . " She hesitated uncomfortably.

"Go on," Harry encouraged.

"Mr. Kohl, you understand, employs the vernacular." Her lips were still pursed.

"And in the vernacular, what would he like to do?"

"Ram a red hot poker up their ass."

"It's good to have objectives."

"So what are you going to do, Mr. Bracken?"

"I thought I'd put myself alongside of danger. Get on with the adventure. Go to the black rabid heart of the mystery. I thought . . . I'd order two cold beer." He paused. "King Kohls."

"Good Christ, not . . . King Kohls." She lifted her napkin to cover her mouth; her eyes swept the room.

"We must meet the enema face to face," Harry said.

"It isn't an enema: it causes vomiting."

"That would make a nice slogan."

"What if we got sick?"

"Then we'll have to find ways to comfort each other. I'll put cold cloths on your fevered brow, while you hold my head at the toilet."

"You sure promise a girl a good time."

"Two K.K.'s," Harry said to the waitress.

They came in frosty mugs with generous heads.

He took a sip and resisted the temptation to fall on the floor faking spasms. He could tell she was waiting for something like that.

The roast beef was delicious: seared on the outside, pink and finally red in the center. The green beans were crisp, having been stir-fried rather than boiled. The horseradish was potent enough to start Alex's eyes watering, and the potatoes had been mashed with butter. There was a bottle of Bully Hill red something.

Harry decided he was having a very acceptable evening. He toyed with nine different ideas, seven of which had nothing to do with their problem.

"We should talk a little business, Harry." He was "Harry" now: remarkable progress.

"Exactly my thoughts. Do you want coffee?"

"I want another bottle of wine."

"Ah, yes."

"But I'll have coffee. Decaffeinated."

"Well, yes. Business." Harry said. "Let's start with what we know. Which isn't much. First, somebody did the deed. We'll call this person X."

"Let's call them the Jacamar Corporation. That's the name on their prospectus."

Harry was swallowing the last of his wine. He started to cough. A minute later he finished. "Prospectus?"

She bent down to a large purse and pulled out a slim leather portfolio. "I don't know what else you'd call it." She handed it to Harry. "Please don't tell the Kohls I let you see it."

Harry turned to the first page and squinted. "I think I need a little more candlepower. Perhaps we could adjourn to my room." Between the wine and the lack of practice, he wasn't good at this.

"It's okay. You can keep it till morning." Not missing a beat but keeping her voice light and friendly, not wanting Harry to feel put down.

Harry didn't. He put the portfolio on his lap so he wouldn't leave without it. "Everything you've told me suggests they had help from one or more of your employees. Not everyone would be able to do a thing like that."

"How do you mean?"

"I mean not everybody would be mentally equipped to do it. Someone came into the beer factory—"

"We prefer the term brewery," she said.

"Right. Came into work and took the top off the jar of ipecac and dropped it into the beer. Not everyone can do that. Perhaps someone who believes that he's serving a cause."

"Why do you say 'he'?"

Harry considered the question. "Point. But whoever it is, it's someone who wakes up in the morning, showers, gets on clothes, takes the jar of poison off a shelf, puts it in a pocket, has coffee, pops out the door, drives to the beer factory—brewery, sorry—goes to whatever post he—or she—goes to, takes the drug out of his or her pocket, and drops it into the beer. That takes a person who is different from most of us. I hope."

Alex nodded but said nothing.

"What you could get for me," Harry said, "is a printout of your personnel records. Pay special attention to any employees who have quit recently. Pay even more special attention to anyone who joined the company for only a short period. If your personnel records mention anybody with shifty eyes and damp palms, put a big red X beside the name. I've also got another problem."

She lifted an eyebrow, waiting for more.

"Only some of your customers are retching their guts up. But you say the beer they were drinking didn't come from any one batch. And other people drank beer from the same batch and didn't get sick. If you gave me the names of, say, half a dozen of the people who have been complaining, I'd go visit them and maybe find out what they have in common."

"We'd go, Harry. You and I. If you visit my customers I go with you."

"They all from this area?" Harry asked.

"One of the gentlemen called us from an art gallery in Philadelphia. He was most upset. Said he drank one of our beers when he was visiting someone in Watkins Glen, I think it was. Said he not only suffered severe pain and humiliation, but also a considerable financial loss. Some people really lay it on pretty thick, don't they? Anyway, Matthew Kohl is going to talk to him. But everyone else is from around this area, so we could visit some of them tomorrow if you like."

"Okay, let's go calling," Harry said.

"Nine a.m.?"

"What shall we do till then?"

"We could have a shower. I'm going home for mine. You could have yours here. I'm sure they have cold water. And then you could read the prospectus."

She smiled. It was a galaxy of stainless steel: railroad tracks, top and bottom. Then she called for the bill, pushing a gold-colored card at the waiter. She smiled again. The woman had stars in her mouth.

He watched her through the lobby, watched her get into a low sports sedan, and watched it leave with just the tiniest chirp of protest from the fat tires. Then Harry walked back through the lobby and considered his options. He could go up to his room and read the prospectus. He could have a sensible sleep and read it in the morning. He could get into his own car and see what delights were offered to strangers in these parts. Or he could go to the hotel bar and upset the purists by ordering a bloody Caesar at this hour of night.

His guidance system found the bar. He took a stool well away from everyone else and ordered from a sullen man whose name tag said he was Gus.

The population of the bar, like that of most hotel bars, split neatly into two components: those who were there to have fun and those who were there to have a drink. Those who were there to have a drink all appeared to be Harry's age or older. These were the men—all males tonight—who roamed America selling communications systems, toxic waste facilities, and video courses for motivating the sales force. The other group consisted exclusively of twenty-two-year-old men and women in heat.

Sipping on his beer, Harry considered how the large chains made money from the North American mating ceremony. In hotel bars across the country, people were doing exactly what these people were doing: dancing, telling ethnic jokes, lying to each other about what happened at the office, and trying to come to some sort of arrangement. Had this chain done research into this? Did it know the profitability of each court-ship? Did someone stand up at meetings and say, "According to these three thousand psychographically correct respondents, we could increase profitability an extra twenty-six percent by cut-ting the light so the man and woman look better to each other?" Less reflection off the braces? Perhaps they had a special depart-ment for this? The Department of Recreational Lust? Harry wondered how they referred to it in memos.

And how about their Department for Wandering Engineers and Video Salesmen All by Themselves at Night? Harry waved for his bill and pictured someone addressing their meeting: "Right, we know they drink more when they're despondent. Ideas? More depressing bar snacks? Very good. A mirror at each seat? That could do it. Just a second, hold on, I think I've got it. Let's clone that bartender we have in Buffalo, you know the one: that sullen old bastard named Gus."

The portfolio contained forty-seven typewritten pages on meth-ods of contaminating beer: eighteen different ways in all. It explained how each of the eighteen ways could be applied to the products of Kohl's Brewing Company. It told of methods to render every bottle flat, of infusions that would turn the hoppy odor noxious, of interesting bacteria that could live in beer, of chemicals that would turn the drinkers' urine red, and of additives that could kill a person in three minutes flat. The study also described how the pure spring water in which Kohl's took such pride could be contaminated at three separate stages, how the female hop blossoms imported from the Okanagan Valley to give Kohl's its distinctive aroma could be poisoned, and how the stainless steel draft kegs could be made unfit for re-use. It gave precise details on how the large copper kettles could be treated to induce nausea, and how an adjustment to the Krausening containers would change the flavor of the lager to that of rotting cabbage. All this information was offered in flat, technically credible prose, complete with a table of contents, flow chart, and index. It had all been bound inside a leather cover from Mark Cross. Accompanying the study was a letter typed on stationery emblazoned with the logo of a little long-beaked bird. Above the bird were the words "The Jacamar Corporation." There was no return address.

The accompanying letter did not refer to the contaminant study. It simply asked whether the president of Kohl's Brewing Company would give an hour of his time to meet with a Mr. Felix Tidyman to talk about matters of security and quality control.

CHAPTER 6

Beverly Hills, California, August 16.

The stockings that hugged the contours of their faces made them seem aged and grotesque. But their moves were those of young, athletic men.

There were three of them at the rear of the Beverly Hills mansion, guns lowered to their sides. They were breathing quickly and shallowly. Looking back, the leader saw that they had left footprints on the closely mown grass. The security guard would be by in less than three minutes. The leader raised his hand, then dropped it in a fast chopping motion. The shortest of the three, a man built like a stump, swiveled and kicked, aiming his boot heel at the door lock. The second man's boot finished the job and, an instant later, the group was through the door. One rolled across the terra cotta floor of the kitchen, another stationed himself immediately inside the door, while the leader ran across the room, screaming and grabbing at the young woman. Eight seconds after the stump-like man had first landed his boot on the lock, his leader had an arm around the young woman's neck and the flat black muzzle of his gun jabbing into her breast.

"Up, up, up, up, up, up!" His voice was high-pitched, thickly accented and, Marjorie Brooks decided, remarkably void of self-assurance.

She turned to look at the man with brief disdain. Then she studied the others, who were working up their own confidence by kicking over chairs. Marjorie Brooks took a long breath, and when she spoke it was in the voice of an English headmistress. "All right." She let the last word linger. "Quite enough, you two. And get your pistol out of my breast, you incompetent bloody yob. And quit breaking up the furniture."

The man who had jabbed her removed his arm. He pulled back his gun and stared at it, as if trying to confirm its authenticity. The men who had been tipping chairs looked nervously at each other. The stump-like one went to the last chair he had knocked over and placed it back upright.

In the room that the previous owner of the mansion had called his studio, Ismail Gezmis, dressed in a light gray summer suit, decided he had seen enough. He turned off the monitor, opened the door, and walked down a long hall to the kitchen. He paused in the doorway, and straightened his blue silk tie. "Gentlemen, good afternoon. My name is Ismail Gezmis."

The three nodded respectfully but made no move to identify themselves.

"I believe that Miss Brooks is quite correct," Gezmis continued. "These premises have been purchased with hard-earned funds. They must be respected."

Yesterday had been Gezmis's first visit to the Jacamar main base. He had expected to find spartan quarters in a working-class neighborhood. When the taxi pulled up in the circular driveway of a fieldstone house in Beverly Hills, he insisted he'd been taken to the wrong location.

"That's the address you asked for, sunshine," the driver replied.

While they argued, Felix Tidyman, the former CIA operative, appeared at the front door, grinning over his little surprise. "The neighbors think the kids are young sheiks," he said.

Weeks ago, Tidyman explained, when he had been searching for potential recruits, he had visited the Los Angeles chapter of the Friends of Palestine. A letter of introduction from Ismail Gezmis asked for their fullest cooperation. Tidyman left with the names of everyone who had donated funds to the group over the past fifteen years.

He recognized a few of the donors as minor show business figures. But one name almost jumped off the page. Tidyman couldn't believe it. Here was one of America's most enduring celebrities: an actor who appeared on television every Wednesday evening, the father figure to a multi-colored group of precocious orphans. The man had once made a discreet but substantial cash donation to the PLO.

Tidyman asked around at the Friends of Palestine and learned that the actor had made the gift after a long and bitter fight with the chairman of the network that carried his weekly program. The chairman was Jewish and a vocal supporter of Israel.

Tidyman recognized an opportunity. He was unable to make contact with the actor but, by persistent badgering, he arranged a meeting with his agent.

The agent quietly explained that the actor had since settled his differences with the network president and that the gift had been a one-time donation, more an indication of his anger than his ideology. The agent sighed and said, "Of course, you understand," as if that were the end of it.

Felix Tidyman had listened politely, then said that, since the first gift was to be the only one, he would take immediate steps to thank the actor publicly for his singular act of generosity.

"Shit, no," the agent exploded. "Don't you *dare* do anything like that. You know how much future he'd have in this town if something like that got out?" He hunched his shoulders and gave his head a series of quick shakes, affecting a shudder.

Felix Tidyman didn't react, just sat smiling through the outburst, waiting for the agent to settle down again. When he did, Tidyman gave himself a little slap in the side of the head, and said, "Hey, what am I thinking of? Of course, if we did anything like that it would really put a crimp in your man's career. Yours too, come to think of it."

The agent, who had been thinking all along in terms of a single-level disaster, sat bolt upright as a fresh crop of consequences occurred to him. He made a soft gagging sound and waved for Tidyman to continue.

"Well, I'm kind of new to this whole business," Tidyman

said. "But the way I understand it, a lot of folks wouldn't take kindly to the idea of your man supporting the PLO. Or the idea of your giving him that kind of advice."

"Oh, hey, now I had no hand in—"

"Sure, I know, you're just the guy's agent. Just acting under orders."

"He saw the pictures of those Palestinian kids in the camps," the agent protested. "Heard they were eating dogs and cats. He just wanted to help the kids, was all."

"Do you think there would be any kind of spillover onto your other clients? You know, people getting on their case 'cause they have you as an agent?"

"Jesus Christ ... " The man started to speak, then let his voice trail off, realizing his objection had nowhere to go.

Tidyman kept his thoughtful expression. "You know what else I've found about this town? It's a bitch to find a place to live."

Tidyman told the agent about a story he'd read in *People* magazine that mentioned the actor's three homes, one of them a large fieldstone house in Beverly Hills. "We'd like to put an offer on the place," Tidyman told him. He pulled a piece of paper from his pocket. "You'll understand that if we're going to help keep those kids in the camps from eating cats and dogs we can't spend a whole lot of money on real estate. But if you could see your way clear to recommend this offer ... "

The agent stared at the paper and looked up at Tidyman. The message was starting to sink in.

Tidyman waited for a moment. "And we were hoping he might sell it to us furnished."

Ismail Gezmis had been astonished to learn of the bargain Tidyman had struck for the beautiful home. And he had been delighted to see how much progress had been made in converting it into a working base, with training rooms, dormitory, even a computer room, where two young hackers were working on codes to gain access into company computers.

The only thing that Ismail Gezmis hadn't liked about the house was the casual attitude of the students.

"The main purpose of this kind of exercise," he was telling them now as they removed the stockings from their faces, "is to coordinate our movements when we take a mission into a public place. Remember, the objective is not to indulge ourselves, nor to inflict ourselves upon attractive women."

Mahmoud, the student who had pressed his automatic into Marjorie's breast, lowered his head slightly.

"The objective, my young friends, is to terrorize. And what I do not sense is any real *terror*." He shot the word out with such force that Mahmoud jerked back in alarm.

Marjorie Brooks watched in knowing anticipation. She had seen him make this transition before, and each time it left her perspiring slightly. Ismail Gezmis was about to change from an eloquent and well-dressed Arabian gentleman into something more feral from the desert edge.

"What I have encountered here are three young men who have taken our organization's time and our organization's money, and have done nothing in return except go through the motions—"

"Hey, no, really." Mahmoud, at twenty-five, was still picking up the intricacies of electrical engineering and California English. He was so determined to press home his innocence that he missed the knife-edge of anger in the eyes of Ismail Gezmis. He also failed to see the hand that shot through the air until the side of the fist collided with his upper lip, drawing blood and sending the young man staggering into the wall.

Gezmis kept talking as if nothing had happened. He was a schoolteacher; this was his classroom. "I sense the presence of young people who are supposed to study our enemy's ways to better understand his weaknesses. But instead of such weaknesses being studied, I now learn that they have been . . . emulated." On that word, Mahmoud, who had just collected himself away from the wall, took a backhanded blow from Gezmis that sent his head cracking into the door jamb.

"As a student, you should learn two things today, Mahmoud."

Mahmoud shook his head and struggled to his feet.

"Point one. Despite your youth, despite your health, despite your alleged dedication to our cause, you are incapable of protecting yourself from one angered man twenty years your senior. Point two, my friend, is that you have allowed yourselves to degenerate to such a degree you can count on no help at all from your . . . friends."

Marjorie thought she knew what would happen next. She watched with her mouth slightly open, lips moist. On "friends" Gezmis leaped with both feet straight out and hurled himself into the other young men who had been huddled together watching Mahmoud's beating with a mixture of sympathy and glee. Gezmis and the pair spilled over the actor's marble-topped coffee table. Seconds later, Gezmis was back on his feet, holding the other two students by their collars.

"You are the reason that the Jew has seized our homeland." Gezmis dropped his hand from their collars. He shrugged, turned, and walked from the room. Marjorie gave the young men an oblivious smile and followed him out. She knew their humiliation had been all the more devastating for her having been in the room. Ismail Gezmis had planned it well.

It was his ability to plan that set Gezmis apart from other terrorists she had known. And that included Qatar, the man who had been her lover for six years and Gezmis's best friend for many years before.

She had met Qatar in Paris, where she had taken a one-week spring package holiday from her teaching job in Birmingham. A friend of hers studying the history of the Middle East at the Sorbonne had introduced them. At first Qatar had hidden his true vocation from her—a reflex action geared to survival. The Mossad was reaching an alarming number of his colleagues through female agents. Even after she had returned to Paris for her summer holidays and moved in with him, he had kept the myth alive. He and Ismail Gezmis were in the travel business, he told her, increasing tourist traffic to the Holy Land. Their odd hours were related to the needs of travel agents and clients from abroad.

Back in England, her friends had begged her to see reason,

and to keep to her own kind. They had no way of knowing that their efforts only supported Qatar's repeated claim that an Arab's struggle was made more severe by the steadfast refusal of the rest of the world to understand him.

Qatar, at odds with the dour Moslem image she had once accepted as reality, loved big red wines and good whiskey. He laughed loud and often and through the whitest teeth that she had ever seen. Despite the Arabs' reputation for selfishness in bed, Qatar had been the most gentle, most thoughtful lover she had known.

As their conversations grew longer and deeper, Marjorie Brooks had felt that her eyes were being patiently and lovingly eased open for the very first time.

She had known better than to debate fundamentals with Qatar, but soon formed her own views on the wisdom of their endless war. She had difficulty accepting the catechism of Arab grief, aware that the Israelis too were dedicated fighters who had also suffered in an uncaring world. But she knew that the rage consuming Qatar and Ismail and their friends was linked to the rushing sense of helplessness they felt at the suffering of their people.

For five years Marjorie Brooks shared Qatar's pain, lived his fear, knew the joy of an occasional triumph, but never really experienced his life herself, and never felt she fully understood the roots of his struggle.

Qatar had been killed on his way to negotiate a ransom for a kidnapped Israeli arms broker. The media reported that he was gunned down by what appeared to be a team of well-trained assassins: four quiet shots from a .22 calibre pistol at extremely close range.

"The Mossad." She still remembered Ismail Gezmis choking on the words.

After Qatar's death, Marjorie had returned to sunless Birmingham. But she found no comfort in the clumsy ministrations of her parents, who were not at all sure how one went about explaining her affair to relatives and friends.

Her own friends had long since married. Following a few

awkward reunions, when she watched without feeling while their children were cuddled, fed, and changed, she realized that her life was going to have to be with the friends of Qatar. Not as someone's moral support this time, but as a full-fledged participant. Vengeance on the animals who had ripped her world apart was a secondary aim, but it would never be far below the surface.

In time, her relationship with Ismail Gezmis grew closer. In some ways he became the brother she had never had. Because a man alone sometimes raises the suspicions of police and security forces more rapidly than a man and a wife, she and Ismail had often traveled as a married couple. Yet they had never slept together, despite the proximity and the opportunity.

But Abdel Saddam had refused to believe that the relationship with Ismail wasn't sexual and he'd set out to prove that a few days ago. Saddam, a twenty-six-year-old fluently bilingual Iraqi student who had been recruited into the Jacamar project, had been sharing a one-bedroom apartment with her across the Canadian border for a few months earlier that summer, not far from Kohl's Brewing. During the days she'd been checking the local operations of a multinational restaurant chain, and he'd taken the blue-collar job that would allow them to launch the first part of the first Jacamar project in North America. But during the nights Saddam had taken the pretense that they were man and wife too far.

On the day they moved in, while Marjorie hung second-hand curtains, Saddam had gone out to buy Chinese food and rosé wine. Through the meal he had leered at her as if it were a foregone conclusion that she would be dessert.

"That wine's not too bad, huh?" He held the empty bottle up to the light. "I could use a little more. What do you say?"

Marjorie had finished one glass to Saddam's four. She said yes, she'd have more if he wanted to open another bottle. Saddam took that as a promising sign. He carried the empty into the tiny kitchen, placed it on the counter beside the stove, and quietly walked back behind Marjorie's chair.

Reaching over her shoulders, he plunged both hands down the front of her blouse. "Mmm, nice."

Marjorie took hold of her paper plate filled with chow mein noodles and jumbo shrimp, and lifted it back above her head and into Saddam's face, pressing it in and regretting that the sauce was not hotter.

Saddam's subsequent overtures had been less direct. He restrained himself to verbal propositions once or twice a week, usually when Marjorie announced that she was turning in, and just before she headed for the bedroom.

"Why don't you join me tonight?" Saddam would pat the pull-out couch. "Be a nice change, I promise."

And Marjorie would disappear down the hall, hoping the cretin would keep the volume down on the Carson show.

But last week, on her last night in the apartment, he had tried something new. He had switched off the television and put a tape in the stereo. It was The Mighty Arrow, a Caribbean singer whose pounding socca rhythm Marjorie Brooks despised. He turned up the volume and waited.

In seconds, she flung open the bedroom door and made straight for the stereo. Saddam sat grinning on the couch while she punched at buttons on the machine. When that had no effect on the volume, she yanked on the cord and pulled the plug.

Still smiling, Saddam gave his head an amused little shake and jumped from the couch. He pushed the plug back in. By this time, Marjorie was almost back to her bedroom door.

"Raise your hand if you want to jam," screamed The Mighty Arrow.

Marjorie Brooks, legs driving determinedly under her knee-length cotton nightgown, stomped back into the room and reached for the cord again.

Abdel Saddam grabbed her arm just as she got there.

Marjorie swung her free arm around to smash it into the side of his head, but Saddam got his own hand up just in time and gripped that arm as well.

She let go of the cord and brought her knee up sharply toward Saddam's crotch. But he had been waiting for exactly that move; he stepped lightly sideways, yanking her left arm up behind her back.

Marjorie cried out as Abdel smiled wider and twirled her around. He fell backward onto the couch, bringing her down on top of him, both arms now pinned to her side.

She screamed, a chilling counterpoint to the cheery socca sounds still throbbing from the speaker.

Saddam, surprising her with his strength, shifted his weight and rolled her around underneath him. She kicked out with both feet and the nightgown hiked up to her waist. He smiled again; she was naked underneath.

He jerked her hands up above her head and gripped both sleeves of her nightgown with one hand. With the other he unzipped his fly.

"Saddam, you bastard, you rotten bloody bastard, so help me, Christ, I'll kill you."

He was breathing faster now. He forced her legs open with his knee. Then he gripped his penis in his hand and rubbed the tip along the inside of her thigh. "See how nice that feels? Is this what you been waiting for?"

She tried to pull her arms free but his grip on her sleeves was rigid. She kicked her legs against his back.

"Ooh, a little massage, that's nice. That's good. Here, little girl, you ready now? You ready for old Abdel now?" He pushed inside her. Then he let go of her arms and used his hands to shove her nightgown all the way up. He buried his face between her breasts, his eyes out of reach of her nails. "Hey look, your little nubbies all nice and perky. You like this, huh? You like old Abdel?" He gripped her buttocks with both hands and drove in deeper. She pulled at his hair and almost immediately felt him come inside her.

Marjorie Brooks let go of his hair and dropped her fists to her side, as he eased himself from her, damp and limp. Breathing heavily, she smiled at the ceiling. "That was your last time, lover," she said in a barely audible whisper. "The last six strokes you'll ever take."

Marjorie knew that with one word to Gezmis, Saddam would pay dearly. She wondered if she ought to give that word, knowing the anger it would raise. And would it change the way that Ismail felt toward her? Had Saddam, the cunning swine, taken that into account, guessing that she would be reluctant to report to Ismail the dirty little details of what he had done?

Had Saddam guessed right?

And if he hadn't, why had she not yet told Ismail anything about it?

CHAPTER 7

Buffalo, New York, August 17.

Harry didn't want to knock on the door. Every time he knocked on a door and started asking questions people lied to him. He was an investigator, true, but he had never got used to the idea of people deliberately telling him lies. In his old job people had told him lies, but usually in other tongues, and Harry had found that more acceptable somehow. When his own people had started lying to him, Harry had guessed that his days there were numbered. And he had guessed right. Now he preferred those parts of his jobs that were more abstract.

He liked going over papers in the office: forensic results, the findings of fire inspectors, police records, credit checks, resumes, backgrounders, evaluations. He felt that his talent lay in seeing not what was there, but what was missing: the gap in employment, the vagueness about loan repayments, the "I-forgot-to-tell-you-about-my-ex-wife-Yvonne-and-three-sons" sort of thing that turned an ordinary fire into arson because the policyholder had a large demand loan due and an industrial property that could be turned into money if first it were turned into ashes.

But the face-to-face interviews were painful. He disliked asking personal questions ("Did your late wife have any history of depression or was suicide just a sudden whim?"), especially since he knew that, as often as not, the answer he would get would be a lie.

Harry and Alex walked up the three porch steps and through the Moorish arch that was the entrance to the porch. Harry had a case of beer under each arm.

"Okay," she said, "I'm going to introduce you as one of our chemists."

Christ, Harry thought, even she was embarrassed to be seen with a guy in insurance.

As if she was reading his mind, she said, "If we tell them you're with our insurance company, some of these people might start seeing dollar signs."

That was fine with Harry. He always liked a chance to lie to people before they lied to him.

The doorbell of the pseudo-Spanish mission sounded like the first four chimes of Big Ben. Harry had half expected mission bells. There was no other sound for half a minute, until a hacking cough came closer to the door. A large black man opened the door just a little, then all the way. "You're Miss O'Connor?" She nodded and he stood aside to let them in.

Harry put the beer down, and noticed that the hall had polished oak floors, gumwood trim, and rough plaster that was either freshly painted or freshly cleaned.

The man showed them to chairs in the living room.

"Yes, I'm Miss O'Connor and this is Mr. Bracken, who is one of our chemists at the brewery. He'd like to take away your empty bottles to check for contamination. We've also brought two new cases of King Kohl for you."

"I don't know if I ever want to drink that beer again."

"Tell you what: before we go, Mr. Bracken and I will have a beer from each of those cases. We'll drink them right here, so you'll know they're okay. Okay?"

"Guess so. The stuff worked pretty fast on me." The black man smiled. "Maybe you could try them out on the porch. My wife keeps a nice clean house, but she didn't much like cleaning up that mess. Whatever it was, it hit me like a kick in the stomach."

Harry rubbed his lip. "Perhaps you could show me the empties?"

"Only but one empty, and that's the one that emptied me. You could certainly take that fellow away. And all the full ones, too." He heaved himself up from his chair and showed them to the kitchen, a tiny room that seemed out of scale with the rest of the house. A small stove stood only inches from the sink. And the cabinets were so narrow that the man had been forced to shove the beer carton in on its side. "I guess these cupboards were made before people could afford a couple of dozen beer all at one time. Marci—she's the wife—wants new ones. But you put the full-size cabinets in here, you're going to have to hire an anorexic to do the cooking. Here's the beer, man. Now let's go out on the porch and try some new ones."

The second place was on the eighth floor of a highrise condominium building. Empty windows suggested that a lot of the units still hadn't been sold despite a sign that promised squash courts, an indoor pool, and "the unique lifestyle of a vertical community."

"I'm not sure I should be talking to you without my attorney present." The man had a thin face and gold-colored wire rims. His handshake was light.

They were shown into a room that might have been brought intact from Finland. The couch and chairs were trimmed in steam-bent laminated wood and the upholstery was a dramatically bland shade of cotton. Harry surprised Alex by opening the conversation. He had less trouble talking to the upwardly mobile, armed as he was with a reservoir of considerable disdain. For the occasion he borrowed a thick New York accent.

"Mr. Heinchuk, a guy like you knows the score. Every company has complaints like this from time to time: the rat's ear in the soup can, the cockroach droppings in the frozen dinner. I don't think we have to go through that kind of thing with you."

Heinchuk looked visibly relieved that Harry wasn't going to go through that kind of thing with him. "I know what you mean," he said quickly. "But I sure don't think much of what happened to me. I take a swallow of the beer and I hurl my oats all over the rug. You can see the stains."

"Exactly the situation." Harry was warming to his role. "And we're concerned about it: deeply concerned. You're the kind of customer we want. We're doing one of America's rare natural beers—unpasteurized, pure, additive-free. We won't even package it in cans because in this part of the country temperature fluctuations can bruise the taste. It's like we say back at the shop: 'Kohl's beer is worth a bottle.'"

"Exactly, that's the reason I buy it. You were selling a good, honest product there with King Kohl. There's only one problem: it made me puke all over the rug."

Harry frowned and gave a Nixonesque shake of the head. "It's got our brewmasters very upset. Two of them handed in their resignations yesterday. Men who have been with us nearly two decades. Good Christian family men, both of them."

"A real shame," Heinchuk murmured. He was buying the story as easily as he had bought other stories on the merits of oat bran, BMWs, and two-hundred-dollar walking shoes.

"I want you to show me where you keep your beer," Harry said. "I want you to give me at least one bottle—make that the case—to take to an independent laboratory. And I want you to tell me any nuances of taste you encountered before the ah, incident."

"Sure, glad to help." Why did these people always like to feel involved, Harry wondered. "Come on down here. I keep the beer in the wine cellar. All these condos come with four-by-four-foot wine cellars. If you're going to live you may as well live right, I like to say."

Harry went with him through the ceramic tiled kitchen and stopped when they came to a closet. Heinchuk pointed out the temperature control dial on the wall outside; then he opened the door. There was the beer, stored as carefully as the man's La Cour Pavillion and Mouton-Cadet.

"Must be nice having a wine cellar," Harry observed. "Saves you from keeping your rooms at room temperature."

*

The third call took them to AAA Abco Auto Body, where a sign said, "We pay the deductible on windshields." The lot was littered with the kind of vehicle used by male teenagers to parade in front of burger stands. Some were spotted with primer paint the color of acne cream.

It took Harry back some years. "Like, later on, you want to pick up some Johnnie Walker Black Label and go cruising?" he asked Alex.

"I'm washing my hair."

"Like, after you wash your hair?"

"Then I gotta dry it."

The door to the shop was stuck, so Harry gave it a thump with his shoulder. "What is it, my zits? It's my zits, ain't it? You don't want to go out with my zits."

"Well, maybe after my hair dries you could take me out to San Antoine for dinner. It's dark in there. No one will see your zits. Or my braces. And they do a nice spinach salad."

Harry liked the way she took the body shop in stride: the sound of the rasp, the smell of body filler, the ozone from the battery charger.

"My dad ran a place like this," she said. "A little neater, but a lot like this."

Harry turned to give her a look of surprise. That was when he noticed the coveralls protruding from beneath a battered Chev. He bent down and yelled over the noise. "Do you have a Laxdal here? A Jerry Laxdal?"

"Who's asking?" a voice called back.

"We're from King Kohl beer."

A body rolled out on a dirty wheeled tray. A man about forty, still horizontal, looked up at Alex, then at Harry, then back at Alex. "Both of you from Kohl's?"

Harry said, "Yes."

"I'd rather talk to her."

Alex knelt down. "Perhaps you'd care to do it face to face?"

The man hauled himself quickly to his feet. "I'm Jerry." He pulled an orange cloth from his coveralls pocket and wiped his hands.

Alex introduced them. "My father used to have a body shop."

Jerry looked her over and decided against making the most obvious remark. "Yeah? Well, maybe he could tell me how to make some money out of this one."

"Claims adjusters," she said. "Get on their good side any way you can. We used to have them over for dinner. I'd cook steaks. Once they start recommending you for estimates you can't go wrong. A few small favors now and then. Christmas. Canadian Club. I don't know what they're drinking now. Last insurance guy I saw was heavily into Bully Hill wine."

Jerry wiped his nose with the rag and scowled as if he were going to start giving his views on insurance guys. Instead, he said, "You're here about the beer?"

"Yes. We'd like to know how it happened. Were you eating anything with it at all?"

"I wasn't eating anything. It was morning and I don't like to eat on an empty stomach. Like to have a beer around ten-thirty. It sort of settles my stomach and flushes out the Bondo dust."

"It wasn't the Bondo dust that made you sick?" Alex wondered.

"Shit, no. I breathe that stuff all day. And paint fumes. And solvent fumes. Every day. I figure I got enough chemicals in my body, I won't have to pay for embalming when I go. That should please the old lady no end."

"Where do you keep your beer at home?" Harry asked.

"At home? I can't keep beer at home. Keep it at home and the kids drink it. They're twelve and fourteen so they got no money to buy their own."

"Boys will be boys," Harry said.

"Yeah, right." Jerry scowled. "But these boys are girls. Little buggers. The point is, I keep my beer here."

"Where?"

"Over in the old Coke machine. We all put in three quarters when we take out a beer. Slows the drinking down a bit so we can get some work done."

Harry walked over and looked at the Coke machine.

"Fixed it up myself," Jerry said. "Keeps them Kohls real

cold, you know, like your jingle says: 'A cold King Kohl makes a merry old soul.' "

They thanked him and left. Jerry was still singing the tune when he crawled back under the car.

The salad was not what Harry had expected. The spinach was fresh, with slices of broiled tomato on top, and on top of the tomato was a carpet of crispy bacon bits in a hot vinaigrette.

"Secretary food," Alex said. "My dad called it secretary food. He thought lettuce was for rabbits and secretaries. My mother served him a Caesar salad once and that's what he said, secretary food."

"He gave up the body shop?" Harry asked.

"Sold it. Retired." She looked up at him. "I was a late kid. They thought they'd never have one. Spoiled me rotten. Always very concerned about my being able to take care of myself. Or maybe that was just his excuse for us to do the things he might have done if he'd had a son. He taught me to shoot when I was twelve. Made me keep it up too. Pistol range at least once a month. I used to be able to arm wrestle, too, until I found it was putting muscles in the wrong places."

Harry looked. Everything seemed to be in the right place.

"Piano lessons. Scuba. Everything but braces. He thought they were sissy. Or he thought they'd make me look too pretty. Or maybe he didn't want them because they'd hurt me. Anyway. It all made me want to make something of myself. I finished school and started at Kohl's. I bullied poor old Mr. Kohl into giving me a chance to show what I could do. Met him at the pistol club. Outshot him. The job was working well until . . . "

Harry thought that might be a cue to get back to business. But he wasn't sure. He coughed nervously. "You say you've done checks all along the bottling line?"

She put down her fork. "Two thousand bottles at random. Checked them all. Seven people checking the water—three of them brought in from New York City. Did you know that a brewery our size spends more money on water purification than a city of fifty thousand? Bet you didn't know that, huh?"

She gave him a smile; lots of steel. Harry winked back.

"Then we checked our hops. The malt. The barley. We did our own checks first, then sent samples to two outside labs. We flew four guys over from Germany to look at the equipment. They said our stuff was good as new and our product could stand up with the best in the world, by which they meant the best in Germany. It isn't the bottles. It isn't the water or the hops or the barley. And however they're doing it, it isn't affecting all the beer we put out. Just a few bottles here and there. The only way you could make that happen is to put something into the occasional bottle right on the line. But our bottles are all filled out in the open where we have inspectors watching everything that goes on."

"You've covered it all," Harry said.

"So where did we go wrong?"

"What'll you give me if I tell you?"

"I don't know. What do you want?"

Harry gave her what he thought was a hearty leer.

"Oh, is that all?" she said. "What a deal. Want the Brownie outfit to go with the braces?"

"Maybe all that plus a nickel. I'd hate to think I went cheap."

She picked up her purse, found a nickel, and held it up. "Just what can I get for a nickel here, mister?"

She flipped the coin out and Harry snatched it from the air. "The first guy, the guy with the narrow kitchen, he stored his beer on its side. The second guy, Mr. Condo, he had his bottles stored in his wine rack. Also on their side." Harry paused.

Her face lit up. "And Jerry at the body shop, he had his bottles in his Coke machine. On their side. So. Then. Well. In that position the beer would be in constant touch with the bottle caps. So then. It's something on the bottle caps. Or on some of the bottle caps. Likely just a few, to keep us guessing."

"My room number is 1607," Harry reminded her.

"Good. I'll pick you up tomorrow, right after breakfast. Our supplier is Canada Caps, just across the border up in Ontario.

We'll go and see what they know, see if we can't nail this thing down. What I have to do tonight is phone Matthew Kohl. Then I have to phone those people whose beer we've replaced and tell them that if they've stored any of it on the side not to drink it. The best idea would be to phone them tonight."

Harry ended up back in the bar. "You're the bloody Caesar," Gus remembered.

The Buffalo chapter of Wandering Engineers and Video Salesmen All by Themselves at Night decided to adjourn just as Harry was draining the last of his third bloody caesar. He checked to see what was happening over in Recreational Lust and saw a guy who looked as if he should have quit drinking thirty dollars ago. The guy was moving in on two women. Harry guessed that the women had both had face lifts and tummy tucks somewhere along the line. He also guessed they had taken those pains in the hope of ending up with something better than the bozo who was breathing over them now. One of the women fished for car keys, while the other made a production out of checking her watch, unable to believe the time. It was time for Harry to call it a night.

He heard his phone ringing before he got his key in the door. "Where have you been? I've been calling you for an hour and a half." Clearly ticked off.

"Hey, I'm sorry, hon, I clear forgot this was my night to stay home with the kids. Jesus, twelve years we been married and I still can't get it straight—"

"Harry, shut up. This is fucking awful."

That stopped him. "Hey, I'm sorry. What's the problem?"

"Matthew Kohl. Jesus, Harry, I can't believe it. I called him as soon as I got home. I thought he'd be really pleased that we— that you—solved this thing in what, a day? Day and a half? You know, after he'd spent all that money, after he'd brought in all those experts—"

"After he'd told whoever that he'd pay them off."

"Well, yes, that's exactly what the idiot's done. Said he'd come to a contractual understanding with the Jacamar people regarding security matters. It stinks, Harry, it really stinks."

"What's Kohl Senior's position in this?"

"I can't believe that he's sitting still for it. I guess he respects my opinion, but Matthew is the only son he's got. Someday Matty's going to have to run the place and make the decisions. Maybe Senior thinks Junior should get in a little training now."

"And Matthew has decided that the case is closed."

"Well, yes. He says he'll have a quiet chat with the people at Canada Caps and that should be the end of it. I thought I'd better call and let you know."

"Right, okay, fine. I guess."

"Because I won't, well, I won't be stopping by in the morning, you know, to pick you up, go to the cap plant."

"Sure." Harry was used to being pulled off cases.

"So I guess that's that."

"I've had a good time here," Harry said.

"I've had a good time too, Harry." She said it as if she were patting him on the shoulder.

"Well, I hope it all works out. For you, I mean."

"Thank you, Harry. Thanks for everything."

"Goodbye." Harry hung up the phone and headed straight back to the bar. He half-hoped the guy who had been putting the move on the two women would come over, maybe give him a hard time, or just talk too loud, any excuse to whonk the bastard in the face. But the bastard was gone. So were the two women. Harry sat at the bar by himself, hoping Gus would be his usual surly self, or maybe just look at him the wrong way so he could whonk Gus in the face. But Gus came over and told him that when he was there earlier he'd left a twenty under his glass when a ten would have been more than enough, and did he really mean to do that?

Harry felt cheated: how the hell could he whonk an honest man? He bought Gus a drink and had a couple more himself. Then he went back to his room and lay down on the bed with his clothes on. "Thank you, Harry. Thanks for everything," he said to himself, and fell asleep.

At six o'clock sharp, the phone rang again.

"Morning, Harry. I know you're a man to bleed the most from a morning so I thought I'd call before you broke from the gate."

"Hnnh?"

"I'll come right to it, Harry. Just got a call from Matthew Kohl. Comes from good stock. His father was with my battalion, did you know that?"

Harry started tuning in. Old-sounding voice, talking army. Penzler. Harry had begun to notice he was always updating his war stories. Next they'd be about sandstorms in Kuwait.

"Morning, Bill."

"You made a real impression on the Kohls, Harry. Young man said you talked straight from the shoulder and he respected that. Not easy to get respect from the young these days, but you did it, Harry. And the Kohls—Senior and Junior, as I understand it— are grateful."

"I'll be back this afternoon, Bill." He knew the bastard wasn't listening.

"But they also apparently feel that your further cooperation might be just a whisker on the counterproductive side."

"I'm leaving right after breakfast. Should be there by two this afternoon."

"Seems they're a mite skittish about publicity, and since they have the whole thing under control, and since the company isn't making any claim, well it more or less precludes our continued strategic or tactical involvement."

"If I don't stop to eat, I could make it by one-thirty."

"So he asked if I'd invite you home, and I told him there were one or two missions here that you should be looking after. So before you feel the urge to screw up a good relationship I just want you to know that you'll be expected here by o-nine hundred tomorrow."

"Jesus, Bill, that's rushing it." If the guy's not going to listen, you might as well play it all the way, Harry reasoned.

"Tomorrow morning, Harry. Be here." This time Penzler hung up first.

Harry found his way into the shower and let the water run hot and long. Then he switched it to cold. He felt better when he stepped out. But he didn't feel good. In a world that had finally gone stark raving mad, she would have made a good friend.

CHAPTER 8

Los Angeles, California, August 17.

Alistair Duffy, silver-haired and tanned, was wearing the smile of a man who has just finished surprising himself. Curled into his arm on the bed in a suite at the Hotel Bel-Air was the good-looking Englishwoman he had met in the lobby. The woman had been a little surprised herself.

But all warm feelings aside, when the telephone rang on the table beside his bed, Duffy's first thought was that it had something to do with her. Perhaps some kind of shakedown.

Cuthbertson, who handled the restaurant chain's press relations, had warned him it could happen if he kept leaving himself wide open. But Cuthbertson's idea of an enjoyable time was getting Duffy and his senior executives to stand around talking to crippled kids, while assholes with punk haircuts poked at them with light meters and microphones and tried to get them on the eleven o'clock news.

Fat chance of that. The only thing you saw these days on the eleven o'clock news were detectives pointing to bullet holes over liquor store cash registers and surly black men walking into court holding yesterday's newspaper up to their heads. Which just went to show that Cuthbertson didn't have all the answers either.

But Duffy had to admit that this call could be a problem. He knew he had taken a chance, bringing the woman to his room. Certainly no one in his organization would have dared to disturb him at 2 a.m. Nor would his wife.

He let the phone ring until he felt the woman stirring against his arm. He switched on the lamp and grabbed the receiver.

"Yes."

Marjorie Brooks blinked at the light and sat up on the pillow. She wondered why so many American executives answered their phones with "Yes" instead of "Hello," or "Hatcher here." Perhaps it was because "Yes" let them punch a little extra hiss into the *s*, to remind you that you've just interrupted someone more important than yourself.

She noticed that Alistair Duffy was already giving her a rather odd look. And he hadn't yet heard what Felix Tidyman was about to tell him. Now Duffy was holding out the phone so she could hear the conversation while Duffy watched her eyes.

"Who is this?" Duffy asked.

Marjorie pushed her hair away and angled her head nearer to the earpiece.

"Who I am is not terribly relevant at present."

Marjorie liked the way Tidyman gave each word a careful, almost artificial, quality that made it more foreboding. She wondered where he'd learned that trick.

"Of considerably greater importance is the plight of nine thousand restaurants," Tidyman continued.

Duffy sighed into the phone. This was going to be something more than a typical shakedown. *Plight?* Who the fuck used words like *plight?*

But in one sense he was relieved. The wacko on the phone quite obviously had nothing to do with the girl. Duffy realized that he had totally misread that situation. The guy wasn't calling for something personal: this was strictly business. The company took a lot of calls like this. Usually the people in security looked after them.

Duffy thought of a couple of wise-ass things to reply with, but they didn't have quite the bite that the situation—or the lateness of the hour—demanded, and he was unable to think of anything better.

So he hung up the phone.

He snapped off the light and turned back to Marjorie. Earlier that evening the girl had unlocked a reserve of stamina he hadn't felt in years. He wasn't deluding himself about the kind of woman she was but he guessed that, whatever it was, she was better at it than anyone he'd known before.

"What do you do at that place?" she had asked him earlier when the name of the restaurant had come up. She was straddling the erect old soldier that would soon be working double shifts, one right after the other.

"Well, I more or less run the company," Duffy had told her. "I'm CEO and chairman."

"Chairman? As in chairman of the board?"

Duffy had smiled and nodded from the pillow. Marjorie had made an admiring comment about the size of his plank and said, yes, she could tell that he knew a thing or two about running a board all right.

And then she had set out to prove it, remembering things she had done with Qatar and feeling a pervasive wonder at it all.

Now Chairman Duffy wondered if he could recapture that moment. He leaned over and kissed her worried eyes.

Marjorie Brooks responded by tightening an arm around his waist and moving herself in on his leg. Already she had been startled by the strange man's energetic double-header. Now it was her turn to smile—at the thought of someone his age going for the hat trick.

She moved her hand to help him along and was just beginning to get results when the telephone rang again.

Duffy yanked the receiver off the hook and let it rest on the pillow beside his head. Marjorie stopped her hand. He nudged her elbow, urging her to continue.

"Mr. Duffy?" Tidyman's voice called from the distant earpiece.

"Yes."

"Mr. Duffy? I'm afraid I can't hear you very well. You sound as if you might be some distance from the telephone."

"I would very much like to be some distance from the telephone," Al Duffy said. He suddenly realized that Marjorie's efforts were going to be in vain.

"Perhaps we have a bad connection," Tidyman said. "You might remember that I was about to discuss a security matter. We must have got disconnected."

"Yes."

"What I wanted to let you know, Mr. Duffy, is that the problem could be fatal."

"I see," he said, now holding the phone in his hand.

He watched Marjorie step naked from the bed and move to the chair where she had piled her clothes. For a moment he thought that she was going to dress and leave. But she was reaching for the cigarettes in her purse.

Something seemed odd about that. Duffy realized what it was. She hadn't smoked until now and this suite was on a non-smoking floor.

He was starting to feel hungover now. The room-service cognac hadn't damaged his performance the way Marjorie had told him it would, but he knew that he would pay for it all tomorrow.

"Fatal?" he said into the phone. "What do you mean, fatal? You said something about our security." He saw the woman look around for an ashtray, then give up and flick the ashes into her open palm.

"Yes. I suggest to you that your security is all but non-existent. That could result in serious harm to your own people and perhaps some customers, too."

"Listen, fella, you try anything and you'll be surprised to see how good our security is."

"Good heavens," Tidyman said facetiously. "I track you down to a hotel where you're not supposed to be with a woman who certainly isn't your wife, and you don't think we—"

"We—?" Duffy tried to cut in.

"—can penetrate any little nook and cranny of your world we choose to?"

"You said *we*," Duffy persisted.

"I don't work alone, if that's what you're wondering. That's how I know that, unless you take steps to protect the good name of your firm, people are going to be hurt. Lots of people."

"And how do you figure this is going to happen?"

"Your whole operation depends on students," Tidyman said. "Students and part-timers, all working for minimum wage and less."

"Shit," Duffy said softly. The pain in his head was getting worse. His left temple throbbed against the phone. He just didn't know how to handle the guy. Now the girl was wandering around looking for a place to butt her cigarette.

Marjorie Brooks dumped her handful of ashes into the drawer of the bedside table, crushed the butt against the plastic liner and closed the drawer with a slam. There was an acrid smell as she bounced off the bed and made for the chair. This time, to Duffy's dismay, she began stepping into her clothes.

"If you were an easier man to deal with, Mr. Duffy, a great many lives could be saved," the voice on the telephone told him. "If only I didn't have to convince you."

Marjorie was pulling her slacks on and looking around for her silk blouse. Just a few hours earlier, when he had peeled it down over her shoulders, Duffy had, for reasons that now escaped him, whirled it over his head and flung it across the room. It might have landed behind the television set.

Duffy made up his mind. He switched quickly to his office voice. "Pal, you're not telling me much. I want to know precisely what you expect from me. I want to know what you think it's going to cost. And I want to know it now."

Tidyman seemed surprised by Duffy's new stance: several seconds passed before he answered. "I'm afraid it's not that simple. There are services we can offer. Services your company will need." Marjorie was on her hands and knees behind the television set. She found the blouse and started shaking out the wrinkles. Tidyman droned on. "Once you see what—"

"The bottom line!" Al Duffy growled. He saw Marjorie jump and drop the blouse from her fingers.

That was when Tidyman decided to give the son of a bitch the number right between the eyes. "Thirty-seven million dollars—"

"No deal, pal," Al Duffy barked into the phone.

He hung up before Tidyman got off his final two words: "—a year."

It took all of Al Duffy's considerable power of persuasion to convince the shaken Englishwoman that it was okay, just some crank. "Guy in my position gets crap like that all the time. Assholes who never work a day in their life looking for a fast, easy buck."

"I'm frightened, Mr. Duffy."

"Hey, come on, now. We were getting along so well."

She was still there at six a.m. when Al Duffy made an urgent call to his New York office, and in full detail, recited to the person on the phone all the forthcoming activities in which his restaurants might be vulnerable to funny business.

Marjorie Brooks, listening with her eyes closed, concentrated on memorizing names, dates, and numbers.

CHAPTER 9

Brattleboro, Vermont, August 18.

Penzler had given him more than a day to get back, so Harry had taken the interstate east, then jogged north to Biff's place, a red brick pile above the Connecticut River. The builder had been the mill-rich scion of a family that had gone into collective catatonia during the Great Depression. The house had subsequently been bought by a girls' school, which had gone into a depression of its own during the sexual revolution of the 1960s. Biff had liberated the building and spent grandly restoring it.

Harry had been there often since his return to America, usually taking a problem with him. His old professor and recruiting agent helped keep the hardships of readjustment in perspective.

Gisele, a six-foot, talcum-dusted woman of indefinite ancestry, opened the door. Behind her came an old man in a wheelchair.

"Harry!"

"So how are you, Biff?"

"Still mobile, thanks to this marvelous rechargeable technology borrowed from golf carts. I am able to hear you thanks to microcircuitry that originated in the Bell Laboratories. And I still get to piss into a plastic bag. How are you, Harry?"

"Better than you, Biff."

Biff twisted the joystick and headed for his den at high speed. He raised his voice over the whining motor. "I've had them do a few demon tweaks on it since you were here last. We rewound the motor with plastic-based magnets. I can get eighteen miles an hour now on the straights." Harry jogged in Biff's wake. "And I'm getting significant G-forces on the corners: maybe a half a G. It can take me from one place to be bored to another place to be bored in half the time it used to take. Hurry up, Harry."

Harry reached the den in time to see Biff skid to a stop in front of a cabinet topped with a draught beer tap. "Smithwick's on draught, Harry. Most of my other needs are still indigenous to the area. For conversation, I have frequent visitors from the School for International Training just up the road. For a randier range of topics I can call upon my neighbors at the Holstein-Friesian Breeders' Association and learn the newest approved technique for jerking off a bull. And of course I take special comfort in knowing that the resources of Brattleboro Retreat, one of America's more distinguished asylums, is just a short ride away in a padded wagon. But the Smithwick's I have to have flown in. Had to get a special tapping tube for it—not at all like the North American arrangement. Need an oxygen tank to pressurize the kegs, but I usually keep a few of those around the place in case I feel the need to breathe."

Biff tapped the beer lovingly into a thick glass stein. He handed it to Harry and watched him drink with the eyes of a puppy on a young boy with an ice cream cone. "Tell me how good it is, Harry. I'd have one myself but my colostomy bag has its limits."

"It's very good, Biff. You'd like it."

"Nice of you to lie to me, Harry. We need more people of your tender years with manners. The stuff's syrupy. Sweet. Even when I chill it, which of course you're not supposed to do. I inflict it on people for old times' sake, or at least I think I do. Sometimes I have trouble remembering if I really enjoyed Smithwick's, or whether I drank it because there was nothing else available at the time."

Harry knew that Biff's "old times" were during Churchill's crusade against a darkened Europe, when Biff had been some kind of sidesman—his description—to a group of merry High

Church men who put refugee Poles, French, and Dutch aboard black-painted Lysander aircraft and sent them winging back to their motherlands with radio transmitters.

"Ah, you remember, Biff. You told me you used to drink a gallon a day of this stuff."

Biff smiled into the distance. "Where we were it was rationed. But we had an excellent printing department. Having them print the coupons was a quality-control exercise. Excellent practice." He did a little spin in his wheelchair. "So, Harry. How can I be of service on this lovely afternoon? I'm afraid the old fart's network grows older these days. To the point of extinction in some areas. And I really know very few of the young farts, except those who ask to come and see me so that they can write in their memoirs that they've seen me and basked in the reflected light or heat or whatever."

"Biff, what I want to know is why somebody is trying to poison beer drinkers."

When Harry finished his recitation, Biff stared, an old frog in an old pond. He opened his mouth once and closed it. Then he pushed aside the Hudson's Bay blanket on his legs and lifted a plastic drainage bag from a chrome hook near the armrest. "It's the new Curity model: carries two liters. You can tell your throughput by the markings on the side of the bag." Biff shook the bag. "About two-thirds of a liter. I wish they'd put one out marked in pints. It would add to the symmetry of everything. I think, however, that you could safely draw me half a pint."

Harry drew him a beer. "So what the hell is the Jacamar Corporation? More to the point, who's behind it? The PLO? The Wiseguys? The IRA? The Weathermen? Students for a Democratic Society? Another beer company? The Women's Christian Temperance Union?"

"Oh, I'm sure it's nobody you know, Harry, if that's a comfort." Biff touched the joystick and twirled, heading toward an antique rosewood secretary. He opened the front. Inside was a computer terminal, a monitor, and a telephone. He flicked a switch and the monitor lit up, casting the same kind of amber light that Harry remembered from kerosene lamps in the field.

The light reflected in Biff's face and gave him a mummified look, the color of old leather.

Biff tapped some keys, waited, then tapped some more. The screen flickered. "Our old friends, the newspaper databases of America. I wonder if they think that poisoning beer drinkers is fit to print." He entered the word "Jacamar." The screen remained still for several seconds, then suddenly began to fill with words, a display that looked as if it might hold some promise.

Biff ran a twig-like finger down the lines and dropped his hand in his lap. "Nothing. Nothing." He busied himself again at the keyboard. All it tells us that the Jacamar is a tropical bird, colorful, with a prominent beak. Hmmm, this is interesting. The Jacamar is one of only two known species with the courage to feed on that most industrious insect, the honey bee. Do we see a little symbolism there?"

"Feeding on industry," Harry said quietly.

Biff kept reading. "A slender, noisy bird with spectacular plumage. It's sounding more and more like my own dear daughter. Perhaps you'd care to draw another beer for yourself. And get another half for me while you're up."

Harry walked over to the cabinet and took out two fresh half-pint glasses. Tilting the glasses at the tap, he drew a pair of almost headless draughts.

Biff took his beer in two hands and raised it slowly to his mouth, a bishop taking communion. He swallowed and sucked his upper lip. "The Jacamar portfolio being in a Mark Cross binder is an intriguing angle, Harry. In my day, such communications were wrapped around a brick and hurled through your window. The upwardly mobile are taking over. Lucille and the plastic-man would eat it up, I'm sure."

Lucille was the daughter whose affectionate ministrations to Harry had been curtailed by Biff. The plastic-man was Biff's epithet for the boy Lucille had begun to date in Harry's semestral absence, and had subsequently married. Biff rarely missed an opportunity to remind Harry that the two were perfectly matched. The inevitable corollary was that Harry should thank his lucky stars for Biff's help in getting him out when he did.

Biff parked the glass on his wheelchair tray and lifted his plastic bag again. "It would be nice if they had remote digital readouts." He rehung it. "The fact that the newspaper databases are not aware of a Jacamar cabal is also of interest. Most political action groups like to have their story told. Normally, after an atrocity, they're on the phone to the newsroom, dutifully retching out details. Recognition is what most political groups are after. It justifies their masters' funding. Thus, what we have here is either a new kind of political action group—or the Wiseguys."

"It just doesn't sound like the Mafia," Harry said.

"I agree. Not their line of business. They'd break heads: 'Whack some guys' in the jargon of the day. So that brings us down to two possible conclusions."

"Two?"

"The first being that this is an entirely new kind of political action group. They don't want the splendid publicity the others are forever seeking. They simply want cash, in continuing amounts."

"The second conclusion?"

"Is that we're very possibly wrong about the first conclusion." Again Biff twirled his chair to face the computer. He stretched his hands out on the keyboard. "It's a very nice information system. But it's so very quick. It hardly lets you digest something before it stuffs more information into you again, like ramming food down the maws of geese to make the foie gras taste better." Biff began tapping keys. "The other disadvantage is that we used to have girls to do this work, and some of them were young and some of them were pretty and some of them were willing."

The beer was taking hold of Biff, just a little. He kept hitting keys. "This is the database of a London-based security firm. If someone wants to locate a plant in Bolivia, it can tell them what the odds are that guerillas will kidnap their executives or blow up their factory or, even more frightening, set up a union. No, I'm pulling your leg about the unions."

"What else are you doing there, Biff?"

"Just crawling around in the bowels of their computer. I am a subscriber. Or, more correctly, I can use the service free because I have helped them in their inquiries at one point or another." Biff touched a final key and waited.

"Their data bank knows nothing about Jacamar or Jacamar Corporation," Biff said at length.

"Oh."

Biff's fingers did an arthritic adagio on the keyboard. He waited. "No, Harry, I'm afraid your little mob has yet to lose its maidenhead, at least in the big leagues of international terrorism. That could be good or it could be bad."

Biff rotated to face Harry, who was now slumped on a leather couch. "Perhaps we should chance another beer?"

Harry drew the beer, this time keeping the glasses more vertical. More head in the glass would leave more brains in Biff.

"How could it be good and bad?" Harry asked.

"It could be good in that you may indeed be up against nothing more than regional amateurs. People with a taste for careful research and methodical presentation, but of modest scope and ambition. After all, they didn't chase after Miller High Life, even though the champagne of bottled beer might have been a more lucrative target."

"But the way they set it all up," Harry said. "Very professional. Very thoughtful. Only some of the bottles and with a potion that just caused enough discomfort to put across a message."

"That's one reason I lean toward the bad half of the equation, Harry. It could mean you are up against heavyweights venturing into a new arena. They may have the resources and the time and the money to do it right. You might consider bringing in your FBI friend—the one with the Admiral's name . . . "

"Nimitz," said Harry taking a pull on his beer.

"Nimitz, yes. Talk to him generally about what the FBI would do in a case like this."

"What the FBI would do in a case like this would probably have the brewery going down the tubes. And I don't think I could talk to Nimitz generally. He'd be all over me for particulars. Start subpoenaing Hanover's records, that stuff. I mean Nimitz's a nice guy but he's still FBI and . . . "

"What do you know about Billy the Kid?" Biff asked. He started playing with his joystick until the chair was going in a slow continuous circle.

Harry waited and watched.

"Billy started out by killing people he didn't know, people beyond his kith and kin and class. But as time went on, his craziness became profounder, fuller, more robust. Eventually, his social universe—his circle of friends—became smaller. Not because they didn't like Billy any more, but because Billy didn't like them. He began defining more and more people as his enemies, as not being within his universe, until he started thinking that his very close friend, Pat Garrett, was on the outside of his universe. He tried to kill Mr. Garrett."

Like some electric figure skater, Biff kept moving in slow circles around the room. "I'm not an expert in this, Harry."

Harry recognized the beer-driven storm front of what usually turned into a drizzle of false modesty. "Yes, you are an expert at this, Biff. I've worked with you. Worked with you against God knows how many Billy the Kids."

Biff stopped the chair to face away from him. Harry stared at his shoulder blades and thought back a lifetime ago to the time when Biff had offered him a job, a bribe to get him away from the future bride of plastic-man. That year the group had been funded through the American University in Beirut and it had been called The Study Group on Non-governmental Policy. Eight months later the money had flowed to them from the Paris office of a multinational advertising agency to whom they sent invoices for transcultural research. Five months later, Harry's pay cheques had come from a freight airline for "security procedures evaluation."

But it didn't matter where the cheques came from, Biff had been right: the work had mostly been trying things on. One lovely autumn day in the late 1970s, Harry had been driving with Rachel through the south of France when he noticed a group of pigs sniffing for truffles under oak trees. After that weekend, Harry had put the question to Biff: if pigs were better than dogs at sniffing out truffles, might they not also be better at sniffing out other substances?

Explosives, for example.

Less than a year later, Biff handed Harry a photo of an immaculately dressed German border patrol. The men were standing at rigid attention beside their trained police pigs. That earned a hearty and liquid commendation of approval from Biff. Several drinks into the commendation, Harry found the nerve to put forth his second brainwave.

"If we want to find terrorists why don't we advertise for them?"

Within weeks, classified advertisements appeared in local newspapers throughout Europe, the Middle East, and the Orient. The carefully worded messages invited "true patriots" to join the enduring struggle. Hundreds of ardent hopefuls responded. They were sent a follow-up mailing that requested biographies and photographs so that "documents" could be made up before the start of the "mission." The library of photographs and biographical detail of young men and women willing to kill people at random ultimately resulted in the arrest of thirteen terrorists, nine of whom were later exchanged for kidnap victims.

Harry's third claim to fame was the shipment of explosives and arms to various liberation fronts. Harry delivered automatic rifles with metal fatigue near the loading mechanism and plastic explosives that proved highly unstable in storage. For a short time, Harry was a weapons supplier for three major fronts; all three were quickly transmogrified into minor fronts. When he got on a roll, Harry came through.

Unfortunately, he rarely knew when to leave well enough alone. After Rachel had died, killed in the explosion a block from their Paris apartment, he had found it all but impossible to leave things alone. It had never been determined if the bomb had been meant for Rachel or whether it was like most other bombs set in Paris that summer: random violence to punish the French for selling arms and fighter planes to Israel. Three weeks after the funeral, Harry had been at Biff's with his daughter in tow. Fleur had been sent to the kitchen to take comfort and cookies with Gisele. And Biff had listened with his head cocked as Harry let the words trickle slowly out.

"I am causing other people to go out and kill other people," Harry had said. "That's like a chicken farmer sending his chickens out to be butchered. The farmer admits the inevitability of the chickens dying. But he will not do the deed himself. It puts the chicken farmer in a class with Adolf Hitler. He only gives the orders. I only give orders."

Despite Biff's assurance that his complaint was symptomatic of the loss of Rachel, Harry took it further, insisting on—and getting—a more personal role in the struggle. Unfortunately for Harry, he had trouble distinguishing the good Lebanese from the bad ones. Eventually, he had been let go, brought home for good, and offered the job with Hanover Casualty.

"I don't know what would persuade any violent group to sponsor something like the Jacamar Corporation," Biff was saying. "The idea of stooping to poison is foreign to the milieu. They like guns and bombs. Poison is too sissified. Perhaps it's a plot to take over the world."

"Nobody plots to take over the world, Biff."

"Don't kid me, Harry. Don't kid yourself either. Did you never tuck yourself into bed with pre-sleep dreams of what you would do if you ran the entire world? I did when I was your age. I still do, though it's a much different world I dream of running now. Your Jacamars, or whoever's behind them, have dreams of running the world. But you'll remember what I've said. Their universe is shrinking. And as it shrinks they'll become more violent."

"What do you mean?"

"They will kill. And they will kill a lot of people."

The Smithwick's was taking charge. Harry hurried. "And what do I do?"

"I'm not sure that you should do anything, Harry. Despite the brewery's fear of bad publicity, and despite what you say about your friend Nimitz and the FBI, I think the proper authorities should be notified. You need to go at the Jacamars with more resources than even your agile mind can muster. We have government agencies to handle domestic scenes like this. I would avail myself of their services, post haste."

"Be hard to do that without having King Kohl beer turn up in your newspaper data banks, Biff. You have to keep in mind that both the Kohls and my employer have vetoed even my efforts at peeking around here and there."

Gisele suddenly filled the doorway of the den. She took in the row of empty glasses and strode over to Biff. She lifted the edge of his blanket. "That's three bags full today." She wheeled him away down the hall.

"Yes ma'am, yes ma'am, three bags full." Biff called back to Harry, "Whatever you decide, my instincts tell me you're up against people who are bad, and good at it."

CHAPTER 10

Hanover, New Hampshire, August 19.

Morning television:

"This weather is one son-of-a-gun for the people in the northeast, Susan."

"Meanwhile, in Kuwait, David, new reports indicate that Palestinians are taking the jobs—and homes—of refugee Kuwaitis."

"What is today's America really missing in sex? And does it have anything to do with the levels of artificial potassium that scientists have been noting?"

"Shit storms and scattered urine," Harry said to his face. He bit his lower lip to stretch the skin and give the razor a chance to come closer. "And what's coming up next, Harry?" he asked himself through the shaving foam. He gave himself a television smile before answering his reflection. "Well, next, Harry, we have a chat with Harry Bracken, who'll be coming to us live from Hanover, New Hampshire. Harry, as you know, is the insurance investigator who found that foreign substances on beer bottle caps can play absolute havoc with the digestive tract. Who do you suppose is behind this rampant sabotage, Harry? Well, Harry, I'd like to tell your listeners that we're still working on that one. But unfortunately I can't do that since, as of yesterday morning, no one seems to give a shit, figuratively speaking. You sound as if you're a tad on the bitter side, there, Harry. Oh, I don't think I'd go that far, Harry; met a good woman, though, and it's not often you get to do that. Hmm, sounds good, Harry, you old dog, you; so what's next on that whirlwind agenda of yours? Well, my next assignment, Harry, is a real humdinger: I'll be going after another one of those bad asses from the third world who keep trying to rip off our large New England insurance companies. Sounds swell, Harry, and I'd like to hear more of that insurance talk but I see it's time for us to skeedaddle outa here."

But by the time he reached Penzler's office the news had changed again. Wolfgang Kohl had telephoned Penzler himself.

"Told me that he'd figured it out overnight," Penzler said. "The only reason that dink son of his, as he calls him, wants to do business with this Jacamar outfit is to keep a pretty face on his brands and sell the brewery to one of the nationals when Wolfgang turns it over. Found his son had already made up a pro forma share offering. Big family fallout over that."

Harry nodded, slowly.

"Fact is, Harry, Wolf is dead right to re-open the investigation. And it's in our own interest to help him along. Whoever it was that did this thing could hit again, and maybe next time the victims will do more than bellyache, if you catch where I'm going with that thought. This insurance company looks at it as a moral responsibility."

Returning west along the interstate, Harry thought about the problem with getting one or two things right: it gave people high expectations. He had come through in Miami and quickly too. So what if he hadn't been supposed to? He had even used his deductive powers to figure out the reason why he wasn't supposed to solve the case—and ruined Penzler's morning in the process. Two good deductions in a row. Then, with just a couple of days in Buffalo, he had done what the entire world of Science and Discovery had been unable to do: he had solved the Case of the Contaminated Caps. Three things he'd found out, and didn't life move in sequences of three? So why are you putting all these miles on your car, Harry, when this time all you're going to put an end to is your blind streak of luck?

He'd left a note, five twenty-dollar bills, and a credit card for
Fleur, telling her to do some back-to-school shopping. He'd
repacked his bag with his last three clean shirts, phoned the
travel people, and found out that going by air would involve at
least four terminals. Four airport terminals meant four airport
bars. So he'd climbed in his Plymouth again.

This time he drove a little faster. He still remembered the look
in Alex's eyes when he told her how the Jacamar Corporation
had done it. It's been a while, Harry, since a woman looked at
you like that.

CHAPTER 11

Los Angeles, California, August 19.

"What if it falls out?" the Mexican wanted to know.

Marjorie Brooks sighed and took a deep breath, starting over again. She knew what deep breaths did to her blouse and she knew he was watching. "It won't fall out. It will stay in there with the Velcro tabs the same way that the flotation cushions all stay in there with Velcro tabs. Right under the seat. All you have to do is take out one of those flotation cushions when you clean the plane. Put the new little cushion up in its place. That's it. That's all."

Zap fingered the new little cushion. It looked just like the real thing, a real airplane flotation cushion, only smaller, maybe just a quarter of the size. Plenty small enough to fit inside his shirt. As long as no one looked there. As long as no one was there at the airport looking for drugs.

Drugs. She had told him right out that it was drugs. That was something, at least. She was an up-front lady, didn't hold anything back, leveled with a guy, even though he hadn't known her that long.

Still, Zap wanted reassurance. "Have you thought this thing through?" he asked her. "All the way? What happens if the drug guys use one of their dogs to sniff through the cabin? Those dogs are good. Rodriguez, he says the dogs get a percentage of the drugs they find, keeps them interested in the job." He laughed.

"The dogs are overworked, Zap. They save them for high-risk flights: incoming from Colombia, Jamaica. You know that. They don't give a damn about the plane you're working on. This plane's been set up with all first-class seating like the MGM plane that just travels between New York and L.A. and back. All it does is fly executives and television stars and that sort of person back and forth to Trinidad and the poncey resorts. That's how I latched on to it—a story in *Traveler* magazine about an aircraft for high rollers. If the kind of person who takes the Platinum Trinidad flight is packing drugs, it's for their own use, not for dealing. And Customs is interested in dealers' quantities: they don't mind if some corporation executive does a few lines."

Zap studied her from behind his shades. She did that kind of shit so well. Made a guy feel like a jerk for even bringing the subject up. He wasn't even looking for an angle. He was happy enough to have a union job with the independent all-first-class airplanes that traveled on dedicated routes. She was talking easy money here, but there was something just a little strange. Least a guy could do was make sure she'd considered the downside.

But he knew she was right. No one was going to find anything he shoved up under a seat.

"Would you like a drink, Zap?"

"Yes. You got scotch?"

Marjorie went to the kitchenette and opened a cupboard. Scotch. Mexicans drinking scotch. Did Zap think it made him a real American? All the Americans she had met in California drank tequila. Zap seemed to be striving for an American Mid-West look with his polo shirt and khaki trousers.

Zap took the drink. "So I have to put the stuff on board. Then what? I was pretty drunk last night."

She lowered her eyes. "You did all right."

"Yeah. Everything was working but my ears. But why Trinidad?"

"Zap, Trinidad is not one of your usual tourist and banana places. Trinidad is near Venezuela and, like Venezuela, they have oil. And they have money."

Zap held up a hand. "But it's in the Caribbean. All of those places, they're dope factories. It's where they invented the stuff. Who'd want to haul dope to the Caribbean? Like taking beans to Mexico, for chrissake."

"Zap, listen to me. Suppose, just suppose for an instant that we painted you black."

Zap looked up quickly. Another angle. She was always coming at him from an angle.

"Suppose I were to paint you black," she went on, "and put you on a beach down there and give you all the money you needed for a car and for beer and"—slowing down a little here—"for the ladies. Trinidad has money. No one wants to work there and making drugs is hard work, Zap, like picking cotton or turning melons. You wouldn't want to pick your own drugs, Zap."

He studied her and tugged on his mustache.

"The other thing is that people of a certain class will always prefer things that are imported. It's why some Americans drink scotch instead of bourbon."

Zap examined his glass. He wasn't sure he liked being tagged as a person of a certain class.

"Think it through, Zap. Even if you had all the cocaine you could handle down there, it would be nice to have something that's a little more fashionable. People are always looking for the state-of-the-art narcotic."

"So why not just bring it up from South America? Lot closer than L.A."

She took his glass and went back to the kitchenette. Fucking Mexicans. Goddamn bus boys. She made him another scotch and poured herself a weak one just to have something to hold on to. She counted to ten, took another deep breath, and walked back into the living room. "Look, Zap. You work at the airport. You know about the war on drugs. You've seen what happens now when a plane comes in from Colombia or Peru full of people who've been on packaged tours. The kind of people who take packaged tours are the kind of people who can be talked into taking packages of drugs home ... The Customs people have dogs all over the place, sniffing the plane. They're even making passengers take off their shoes. But a plane full of corporation executives, high rollers, maybe some politicians coming in, who would check that? You ever seen the MGM plane checked?"

Zap let it go. He knew she was making a point and maybe for a foreigner she was making sense. He didn't know.

"And Trinidad. Who would ever think of smuggling drugs from Los Angeles to Trinidad?"

He knew where she was going, but he didn't know what to do next. He wished for a moment she were more like his wife so he could give her a quick backhand with the knuckles across the mouth, nothing serious, maybe draw a little blood, little pain in the morning to remind her she didn't have all the fucking answers. It worked with his wife, but he just couldn't see it here somehow. He thought for a second about walking out. Just setting down his drink and hauling his ass out the door. That would make some kind of statement, sure enough. But you don't walk out before you know exactly what you're in.

He made his point quietly. "Look, what I'm saying is I've got a job, you know, and a wife, and a car. That may be no big deal where you come from but in California, for a Mex, it's pretty good."

"Does your wife know where you were last night?"

"Just be quiet, okay? My fucking turn. What I'm saying here is that if they catch me with this stuff, they put me in jail. They don't put me in jail, they still take away my job. And if they take away my job, my wife will go back to her mother and turn Catholic again. So what I'm saying here is that they could really fuck me around." He listened to how that sounded and didn't like what he heard. It sounded a little desperate. He tried again. "So what I have to know is why I should do this for you."

She watched his eyes shifting from her to the corners of the room. She knew she had him now but she had to be careful how she reeled him in. "Super Platinum has three flights a week to Trinidad, Zap. For that you'd get two thousand a week."

He worked out the numbers in his mind. Two thousand a

week, and none of it taxed like the rest of his pay. Take two weeks off for vacation and you're free and clear a hundred thou a year. He looked out across the pool to the dusty hills. Don't get greedy but stick with it, say a year and a half. That would be what, a hundred and fifty? Ask for more, see what she says. "Maybe you're getting more than that," Zap said quietly. "Maybe you're getting more than two thousand."

It took her a full thirty seconds to answer. When she did she sounded angry. She waved her arms at the rented apartment. "Sure. I could be making a million dollars a package, Zap. Take a look around this place. Does it *look* as if I'm making a million dollars a package?" She was really raising her voice now.

Zap shuffled on the couch.

"But do you know something, Zap? It doesn't matter if I'm making a million dollars a package or not. Because you're getting two thousand a week for doing next to nothing."

Zap put his hands up. "Okay, look, I'll tell you what."

She waited.

"I'll tell you what," Zap said again. "Two thousand a week works out to six hundred and sixty-six dollars a parcel—"

"—And sixty-six cents," Marjorie cut in, letting loose a little smile. She was enjoying this now, getting into the game.

"Fuck the sixty-six cents, okay?" Zap was breathing harder now, not sure she was taking him seriously. "Fuck the six sixty-six and call it eight hundred a package. That's what, a hundred, hundred and thirty-four dollars difference? Which is no difference at all."

She could see him doing the figuring in his head, adding it up. She could picture him doing the addition: four hundred a week, times fifty, made it twenty grand more a year, tax-free. "So you'll do it."

"I never said I'd do it."

"All we're doing now is arguing about the price."

"Okay, we're arguing about the price." He had picked her up—what?—only three days before? He had been drinking in the Dead Stick Landing, a bar just outside the airport, where the cleaning crews and baggage people went after work. The drinks were cheaper than at the airport bars and they gave you an honest shot. He usually just had a couple of scotches, bar brand. Keep expenses down. He didn't want to spend the next twenty years being a jet janitor. The pay was good but what kind of man spends his whole life vacuuming ashtrays? Put some money away and you could buy something of your own.

At the Stick she had tried to climb up on the bar stool two down from his. He and Rodriguez had watched her. She had tried to get herself up onto the stool but made a funny move as if something had given that wasn't supposed to give and she'd ended up falling on her ass.

He and Rodriguez had moved in together but Zap had spoken first. "You okay?"

She had looked at him closely, not even noticing Rodriguez. She put a hand on Zap's arm and gave him an embarrassed little smile. Rodriguez went back to his bar stool. "I think so," she said. "I did my back in last week playing squash." She put her hand at the bottom of her back and frowned. She tried to squeeze the frown into a smile. "Maybe I won't sit. Maybe I'll stand."

"You okay? Really?"

"Could you get me a—what's that you're drinking?"

"Scotch." Zap waved at the bartender. "Chivas for the lady. My tab."

But yesterday she had told him that she hadn't fallen off the stool, that she had been looking for him on purpose. That she hadn't hurt her back at squash, had never played squash in her life. At first, it was to have been a straight business deal, and she was going to try and get him for a thousand a week. But now, there were these feelings. Now, she felt that she could have a real relationship with a man.

A real relationship and twenty-four hundred a week. Zap decided it was time to seal the deal.

He left earlier than usual on his Honda Gold Wing to pick up the package from Marjorie. She met him with coffee laced with sugar and scotch.

She handed him the package. "Be careful. The big thing is just to get it done. And remember: the exact seat number I wrote down. That's where they'll be looking for it at the other end." She kissed him as he left. He thought she might cry, but she shook her head and told him to go. Zap eased the package into his jacket. "Okay," he said. "I'll call you, let you know how it goes."

"No." She opened the door a little wider. "Don't phone me. It's better if we're not seen together for a while. Meet me outside the Dead Stick Landing after your shift. Out back in the parking lot. Leave your motorcycle in front so I'll know you're there. I'll swing around and give you the money and tell you where we'll meet."

Zap pulled the flotation cushion from under the seat. He pushed the package up and felt the Velcro tabs take hold. He took the cushion he'd removed and put it in an overhead bin halfway down the plane on the other side, under a stack of blankets. He started cleaning out seat pockets and tried to figure how much he had just made: eight hundred dollars in thirty seconds was how much an hour? The numbers started to roll around together. It was sixteen hundred a minute, times sixty. That was, Mother of Christ, almost one hundred thousand dollars an hour. Who made that kind of money? Did Barbra Streisand make a hundred grand an hour? Tom Cruise? Zap didn't think so.

Later, behind the Stick, he thought maybe a guy who made a hundred grand an hour shouldn't have to hang around parking lots to collect it. Garbage cans all over, old bottle cartons stacked against the door.

He wondered what he would do now that he was earning this kind of money. He'd need a new car. Maybe one of these Infinitis with a pewter paint job. A Firebird wasn't going to be good enough for him, he could tell that already. He needed something foreign, something reserved.

A fat Toyota four-by-four with knobby ground-pounder tires

and a thick bush bar eased into view. The driver turned on the lights just as it made the corner. It looked like Marjorie but he didn't think she owned a four-by-four.

Suddenly the engine went from a soft burble to a throaty shriek and the Toyota lurched forward. Zap wondered for half a second what was happening, and then he knew. He started moving to his right. But the half-second had been too long. The bush bar caught him on the knee and he went down banging against the side of the Toyota before he hit the ground.

Marjorie braked. There was a little grind as she threw the gears into reverse. She put her foot on the gas and drove over his heart.

"Nobody should be a pedestrian in Los Angeles," she reflected.

Ismail Gezmis watched Tidyman talking on the phone. The man's color was rising and muscles were stretching in his face. But the sound of his voice stayed the same. He spoke almost entirely in monosyllables: "No. No. Yes." And then, "I'll be there tomorrow. I'll phone you later and tell you what I need." Tidyman put the phone down without saying goodbye. He looked at the small black meter beside the phone.

"Where the hell do we get these no-hopers?" he asked Gezmis. Gezmis stared back.

"Abdel Saddam. First thing I told the guy was he wasn't supposed to phone here. Ever. Rule number two, I tried to beat into his horny little skull was not to leave tracks. He must have left tracks. Guy's got the I.Q. of a fencepost."

The living room of the Beverly Hills house was almost forty feet long but it seemed small with Tidyman pacing up and down the middle of the floor. "So he phones. Here. Me. Asks one of the students was I here. Asked for me by name. You talk about dumb. If there was ever a tap on the line we'd be in trouble." He looked at the device beside the phone. It would detect the extra impedance of a bug on the line; Tidyman was relieved to see that the meter hadn't left the green zone.

"How about your person at the brewery?" Gezmis asked.

"That's how the dizzy little shit's supposed to stay in touch. Through the contact at the brewery. That's how we know what's going on there." He shoved his big hands into his pockets. "So first we hear that everything's fine. They're going to pay us. Then some jerk from their insurance company comes snooping around. I don't know what they've told him. And I don't know what he's told them. All I know is that the old man has changed his mind. Doesn't want to pay. Now Saddam's getting all uptight because he thinks they're going to bring in the cops."

Gezmis listened, hands folded on his lap, a picture of calm. "And you don't think they will do that?"

Tidyman looked hard to see if Gezmis were serious or not. Gezmis was okay, a good enough guy to work with and, for a foreigner, pretty bright. But sometimes you just had to wonder with these people, you really did. "Number one," Tidyman held up a finger. "Number one, Saddam and I and Marjorie are the only ones who know how we did the beer thing. Marjorie is here now. So unless Saddam's been mouthing off to some bimbo in the sack, the only way he's going to get nailed is if he walks into a police station with his hands on his head. Okay? Number two. Number two is that no one from the brewery is going to go to the police because if they go to the police they kill their brewery. Especially a little place like that. If you're the size of a Johnson & Johnson when they had that problem with loonies fucking up their Tylenol, you can maybe get away with it. But a Kohl's just can't buy back beer drinkers the way you buy back headache-pill customers. You'd be talking years before you got those people back. That was the reason I wanted to start with a brewery. They're vulnerable and they know it."

"I see," Gezmis said. "So if not the brewery, would anyone else alert the authorities?"

"The insurance guy might. Harry Bracken. Our brewery contact says Bracken was told right up front there wasn't a problem. Told to go home. Just about shoved out the door. Next thing you know he's checked himself into a hotel and starts wandering around asking questions, as if he might have to pay a claim out of his pocket. Finally, Matthew Kohl gets on the phone to

Bracken's boss, tells him that the only way there's going to be any claim made is if he doesn't pull his man the hell out. So Bracken was gone."

Gezmis looked down at his hands for a moment, waiting for Tidyman to continue. But Tidyman stood there shaking his head. Gezmis prodded gently: "But now Bracken is back."

"Better he should be dead. And if he's dead, it also sends a little message to the Kohls: that we're serious. We can reach out and hurt someone. It'll get them off the pot, get them moving, sending those cheques in. Both things make it important that Mr. Bracken shouldn't be walking and talking any longer. But I don't want to take any chances, so I'm going there to put things right myself."

"If you terminate Bracken, the insurance company might send someone else," Gezmis suggested.

Tidyman sighed. "Why would they want to do that if their client isn't making a claim? The insurance company wouldn't have any further interest. None."

"I don't know, Felix, I must admit that this is not going quite as smoothly as I had hoped. The aspect of the insurance company didn't come up in our earlier discussions."

Tidyman threw his arms out to his side. He was working hard at keeping control. "It didn't come up because it's not a fucking issue." He paused. "Forget it, Ismail. We whack Bracken, that'll be the end of it."

"We?" Gezmis said.

"Figure of speech. I meant I. Me. I'll go up and whack him."

"You could take a couple of the students. They need the experience."

Felix tried to wave the idea off. "I know the ones you've got in mind. Forget it. Can't use them."

Gezmis believed that Tidyman was as violent a person as any he had known. But the American's violence was of a different brand, more dispassionate, more methodical, more cold-blooded and efficient than that of his people. If the young men were to ever become useful they would need to acquire these traits. If not, they might still serve a purpose: a warning to the rest.

"Those kids are fundamentally lazy, not very bright, and I just don't think they have the balls for a job like this," Tidyman said.

Gezmis held up a hand to stop him. "Felix, I have a proposition. You take Tariq and Mahmoud. If they're able to help, they're able to help."

Tidyman waited for the second shoe to drop.

"If not, I don't believe we can use them back here. With what they have seen, what they know, they could do us more harm than good."

Tidyman considered the offer. Another thought struck. "And what about the other little shit, Abdel Saddam?"

Gezmis's smile turned hard. "I would like you to bring Abdel back here. He and I have another little matter to discuss."

CHAPTER 12

St. Catharines, Ontario, August 20.

Harry and Alex told the receptionist at Canada Caps who they were. In less than a minute, a slightly overweight, nervous Chinese man in a hard hat and smock pushed through a door to shake their hands. "Mr. Jarrett's in Montreal today, but he asked me to help in any way I can. I'm Walt Wong, the plant manager."

Wong led them down a hallway toward a soundproof door. He stopped at an alcove to hand them hard hats, steel-rimmed glasses and what looked like yellow plastic ear muffs. "We have to wear the safety gear inside," he said. "It's clean in there, but it gets pretty noisy." He tapped at the lens of his safety glasses before he slipped them on. "And of course we work with metal."

Wong steered them through the whole production line, from raw metal stamping, printing, and crimping to insertion of the plastic cap liners. Almost everything appeared to be automated; the caps moving down lines, past control stations where men sat at large consoles, occasionally checking digital read-outs and making slight adjustments to controls. The constant, high-pitched metallic jingle sounded like sleigh bells gone wild.

Harry leaned over to shout at Walt Wong's ear protector. "How could anyone get at your plastic liners?"

"Mr. Jarrett asked the same thing. Called me last night to ask the same thing. I'll tell you what I told him. They couldn't. You can see for yourself. The liners come in here in sealed plastic bags. Mr. Jarrett, he wondered if the problem was maybe with our liner supplier; but I said, Mr. Jarrett, how come it's only on the liners we put on the Kohls' caps? We make caps for four breweries and seven soft-drink bottlers. Anyway, Mr. Jarrett didn't know what to say to that. There's no way you could get at the caps here without shutting the line down. And when the line shuts down a bullhorn sounds and everyone, including me or the night boss, comes running out to see what's going on. It's all automated, here. World-class. Look at that, see that little beam over there? It's checking to see that the King Kohl name goes on straight. If the printing's out even a little, the caps are tossed out. They go right into that recycling bin and back to the steel plant. We got seven different lines; they all work the same."

"What about after the caps leave the line?" Alex leaned in to ask.

"Come on over here. That's where they leave the line. What do you see?"

Harry and Alex walked over to where the bottle caps spilled into waiting cardboard boxes. As soon as each box filled, the flow of caps automatically halted until the full box moved away and an empty one moved in to take its place. The flaps of the full box were immediately machine-sealed before continuing down another line to be stacked—automatically—on a waiting wooden pallet.

They followed the pallet into the shipping area and watched as it was snatched up by the fingers of a fork lift and shuttled into the back of a transport truck. When Walt Wong asked if they had seen enough, Alex and Harry looked at each other and nodded yes. They followed Wong back through the acoustic doors and pulled off their safety gear.

"Anybody else you'd like to talk to?" Wong asked. "I mean, I'm biased. I think we've got a pretty foolproof set-up here, better than a lot of the ones you have in the States. But maybe you'd like to get some more opinions. What do you think?"

Harry thought for a while. "There is someone I'd like to talk to, Mr. Wong. The guy who worked over in the packing area where the caps go into the cardboard cartons. Youngish guy. Wasn't here too long. Quit just a little while ago."

Wong rubbed his chin with his hand. "Youngish guy, just quit, oh, you mean Abdel. Abdel Saddam." He looked at Harry, surprised. "You know him?"

Harry shook his head. "No, but I was pretty sure there was someone like him."

Alex searched his face for a trace of smugness but didn't see it. "Okay, Harry, what is it?"

Harry said, "Mr. Wong, most plants like this are not designed to protect themselves from their own employees. Someone who comes to work to deliberately sabotage your product could do it easily enough. Especially doing it the way these people did, just a few caps at a time." He reached into his jacket pocket and pulled out a handful of bottle caps.

Walt Wong and Alex stared at the caps in his hand. "How'd you get those?" Wong's eyes showed real alarm.

"Look, I'm not saying this is how it was done. I just want to make the point that it could have been done this way. And, the way I see it, someone working near the packing end of the line would have had a better chance than most to pull it off."

"Pull *what* off, Harry, what are you talking about?" Alex wanted him to quit the nice-guy business and get to the point.

Wong snapped his fingers. "The discard bin?"

"Yeah. But if I worked here I'd have a dozen other opportunities."

"But discards aren't supposed to leave the plant. Mr. Jarrett goes crazy if he sees a crooked design on a cap."

"But once the caps pass that magic beam of yours, who's going to notice a slightly off-center brand name? The brewery's bottling plant is automated too, and there's no need for them to check the esthetics, because supposedly that's been done here. So let's say that Mr. X or, more likely, Abdel gets a few of these caps, coats their plastic liner with the contaminant, then, when no one's looking, drops a handful of them into the shipping carton at the end of the line."

"But the liners come in here in sealed plastic bags. They're literally untouched by human hand," Walt Wong protested. "Besides, you saw it out there; can you really picture a guy standing around doing all that without someone getting curious?"

"Mr. Wong, you're an honest man." Harry's tone was almost apologetic. "But if I worked here and if I were dishonest, I might simply scoop up a handful of caps on Day 1, take them home and do my business with the plastic liner—"

"But—" Walt Wong started to protest but Harry was having none of it.

"And if, as you suggest, I couldn't get my hands on liners here, I'd buy a few dozen beers from my friendly neighborhood beer store, peel off their liners, and glue them into the borrowed caps. Then I'd stick the nasty stuff on the surface, and take them back to the plant on Day 2. In fact, now that I think of it, I might prefer that option even if I could get the liners I needed here. Less exposure."

Walt Wong shook his head. "But the way you zeroed in on Abdel—"

"No, no, you did that. I just threw out a few things I was fairly sure of. I said he was young, because it's the kind of job that young people do better than old people. Since the people we're dealing with are professionals, it's unlikely they'd have taken a chance on winning over one of your staff. They had to have one of their own, so that meant he'd be a fairly recent arrival. And I said he'd just left. That was easy. His work was done, so why would he stick around?"

"Mr. Jarrett is not going to be a happy man," Walt Wong decided.

"What can you tell us about him?" Harry asked. "Abdel, I mean."

Wong looked hard, as if deciding how to answer. "You want to know the truth? The guy was a yo-yo. A real turkey. Good enough worker, which was the only reason I kept him on after the three-month trial they all get. He was here four, four and a half months, I guess. Did his job, but always coming on to the women. Women in the office, women in the plant, couldn't keep his mouth shut. Always making cracks, you know? Liked to get them blushing, and, let me tell you, you have to go some to get the girls in this place to blush. Had one he lived with, too, so I don't know what he had in mind."

Harry looked surprised. "You know anything about her?"

"No. I really didn't know much about the guy, either, tell you the truth, except this thing he had, always coming on, you know, to the women. So when I heard someone say hey, Abdel, what would so-and-so say, you carrying on like that, I was, you know, kind of surprised that he had a girl at home."

"You don't happen to remember a name?"

"No. Didn't know much about the guy. Or want to know." Wong gave a crooked little smile. "He had this very strange necklace he liked to wear."

Alex said, "A necklace?"

Wong looked quickly at Alex, then at Harry. To Harry, he said, "It was kind of, ah, naughty."

"Mr. Wong," Alex said sharply. "I can handle naughty. I work at a beer plant, remember?"

"We prefer the term 'brewery,'" Harry reminded her.

Walt Wong followed their exchange, hoping they would keep it up or maybe ask him about something else. No such luck. The banter stopped and they both stood quietly waiting to hear about the necklace.

"I made him take it off in the plant," Wong stalled. "Too much machinery. Thing like that could catch on something and strangle a guy."

"Thing like what?" Harry persisted.

Wong took another look at Alex, and finally shrugged in resignation. "Had a small gold sculpture on the end of it."

Silence.

"Of a couple," Wong continued.

"Couple? Couple of what?" Harry asked. "Couple of kids? Couple of beers?"

"No, no. A couple. Man and a woman."

More silence.

"Doing it."

"On a necklace?" Alex couldn't keep the incredulity out of her voice. Clearly, she'd been spending too much time on the job, not keeping tuned to the galloping advances in artistic self-expression.

"The sculpture was in two pieces." Walt Wong, having leaped the first hurdle of discomfort, was finding the rest of the tale slightly easier to deal with. "With parts that fit together, if you get the picture."

Alex looked off down the hall to let him know she'd got the picture.

"Lunch time, he'd stand out by the Jiffy Wagon embarrassing the girls with it, you know moving the little parts in and out, in and out—"

"Perhaps, Mr. Wong," Alex cut in with a little more edge to her voice, "you could give us the guy's home address."

"A photocopy of his job application would be helpful, too," Harry said, smiling to himself.

The superintendent at Abdel Saddam's apartment building was even less flattering in his recollections of his former tenant. "The guy was a complete jerk. Always hitting on women. Even hit on my wife. You never seen my wife, but I'll tell you a guy's gotta be a jerk to try that. I'm a jerk."

"Did he leave anything behind?"

The superintendent shook his head. "They didn't really have a lot of stuff. You know, not like some young people, where you wonder how they ever found time to buy it all. His wife moved out before he did. I saw her get into the cab. She only had maybe two small suitcases, that was it."

"His wife?" Harry said.

"Had some real loud fights so I just assumed it was a wife, not a live-in. English girl. Sounded English, anyway. Might have been Australian. I have a hard time telling the difference."

"These fights, what happened?"

"You know, the usual stuff. Lot of noise, throwing things. Last time it was kind of late; I had to send the wife up to settle them down. My wife's a big girl. The woman pulled out the next morning. I saw her get into the cab myself. Good-looking woman. They both were."

"Both?" Alex asked.

"After the English one left, there was another pretty girl. She was from Niagara-on-the-Lake."

"And how do you know that?" Harry asked gently.

"After he left she came here looking for him. Left me her name, address, number, in case he showed up. Said I should tell him she wasn't pissed off at him or anything."

"Still have it?"

"The letter? Somewhere in the drawer there, I might still have it."

"Swap you a twenty for it," Harry said.

After they left the superintendent, they went upstairs and banged on doors near Saddam's apartment. Then they went down the street to a bar that looked as if it might have been a likely hang-out for a young beer-cap maker in heat. Everything they learned there simply confirmed what they had already been told. The only lead they were left with was the name and address of the girl in Niagara-on-the-Lake.

It took them half an hour to drive there, only to learn that the girl had gone out for the evening. "I really couldn't say," an older woman told Harry, when he asked when she might be back.

"I've been rolling up a lot of mileage on my expense account, lately," Harry said to Alex as they climbed back in his car. "But I might be able to spring for a hotel room. We should maybe stay over here and try Abdel's girlfriend in the morning."

"A room?" Alex asked, heavy on the *a*.

"It's a nice old hotel," Harry said, looking up at an elegantly restored three-storey brick building. "Old hotels like that usually have very big rooms. I can't see why we'd need a pair of them."

"Two rooms, please," Alex said to the man behind the desk.

The bellboy decided there was only one reason a guy would be traveling with a woman like Alex and want a room of his own, and the kid wanted no part of anything like that. He handed Harry his key at the elevator and pointed down the hall. While Harry fumbled in his pants to find a coin small enough to make a statement, the bellboy took off with Alex in the opposite direction.

Harry's room was clean, even romantic, with a large rustic pine double bed. Harry thought about which side he would sleep on. He could sleep in the middle. He could sleep crossways. He could sleep with his feet to the headboard. He wondered if George Washington had ever slept here, and if he did how did he get through Customs? Did George sleep alone in all those places? And if not, did he start off by sharing a romantic dinner for two? Harry checked his watch. She had said to meet her in the dining room in fifteen minutes.

"What are you going to have?" She was already giving the menu a rigorous going-over when he sat down.

"Maybe George Washington ate here. I wonder what he had."

She put the menu down and looked him in the eye. "Look, Harry, I was up in my room asking myself just exactly why we're here, and what we think we're doing."

"Very philosophical. I have some Kant in my room. Perhaps later on we could check what he has to say."

"And what do we *do* if and when we find Saddam? Torture him into revealing everything? And when we find out who's behind all this stuff, what do we do then? Write a letter to the editor? What I'm saying here, Harry, is that perhaps this isn't our job." She fished a dark brown bun out of a basket, broke it apart in her fingers, and started to nibble at the edges. "I mean it's been fun, but now that our man has a name and a description—"

"—and a necklace," Harry cut in. "You can't forget the necklace."

She shook her head, as if she were trying to forget the necklace. "What I'm saying is that it's suddenly very real to me. And it strikes me that this isn't my line of work. I mean, you're so suspicious of everyone and everything it's making me suspicious of everyone and everything. Paranoid. I want to take up smoking again. Even that man over there, I guess just because he's sitting alone, but it makes me nervous now."

"You want me to call the FBI?"

He could tell what she was thinking: call in the FBI and make the headlines. That could cost her her job. She smoothed her napkin.

"I say, let's have a nice dinner on our respective companies' accounts, call it a night, and sleep on it," Harry suggested.

The dinner was even better than their first one together. They started with a creamy pâté, and washed it down with a soft red wine from Hillebrand Estate, a winery that the waiter said he cycled past twice a day, to and from work. Harry guessed the waiter was in his sixties.

A second bottle of wine was uncorked just before the pepper steaks were presented with a well-deserved flourish. They said no to desserts and when the waiter suggested a liqueur, they said no to that, too.

"I might try a cognac from room service just to put me to sleep," Alex said after the waiter had gone to bring the bill. "But if I have any more now I'll never make the stairs."

"Would that be cognacs for one or cognacs for two you had in mind up there?" Harry asked.

"I think cognac for one would be best, Harry. Oh, I don't know. I think I'm a little frightened and I don't want you to stay with me just because I'm nervous. If I wanted you to stay with me, I'd want you to stay with me because I wanted you to stay with me. Understand?"

"Of course, I understand," Harry lied.

"So tomorrow I'd have no way of knowing if I'd wanted you to stay with me because I was jumpy, and I don't get into these situations as often as some people do, Harry, so I really need to know what it is I'm doing. So I think cognac for one would be best. Yes. I do."

Harry sat on the edge of his bed alone. Maybe he should phone down for a woman. Did Canadian hotels have that kind of service? Maybe he should have straightened the bellboy out right from the start; bellboys can be helpful with that sort of thing. Maybe he should have been more charming at dinner. Maybe he should have brought a good book.

Maybe Alex was right. What are we doing here? They now had a name for the guy who'd done the job: maybe it'd be the right thing to phone Nimitz, turn it over to the FBI. Maybe Nimitz would cut a deal. Maybe the whole thing could be blamed on the cap company and maybe there were other cap customers involved and maybe if the bad news was spread around enough, the damage to Kohls would be minimized and Alex . . .

Piss on it.

There would be a Gideon Bible in the night table drawer: it might have something pertinent to say. Did George Washington have a Gideon Bible in all those rooms he slept in? And did we ever clear up whether he slept alone? And if he slept alone so much, how did he get to be the father of his country?

The phone rang. Harry let it ring three times before he picked it up.

"Do you have a woman in your room?" Alex asked.

"George Washington was the father of his country. Did you ever wonder why?"

"I just checked with room service. That is, I would have checked with room service if room service existed past 10 p.m., which it doesn't. I didn't make a scene with anyone because I've always believed that Americans should behave themselves on foreign soil, but I would like a little sip of something all the same. And then I said to myself, old Harry Bracken likely has a little something in his suitcase, and perhaps he'd have a bit to spare."

After he hung up, Harry looked at himself in the dresser mirror. "You've been spending too long between dates, Harry," he told the undapper reflection. He adjusted his tie. He squared his shoulders in his jacket. He pulled at his cuffs. He turned from the mirror and took a deep breath. Maybe he should phone her back, tell her to get the goddamn bellboy to bring her a drink, play hard to get, gain a little respect.

"Then again, maybe not." He picked up his bottle of Hundred Pipers scotch, opened the door, and headed for the ice machine.

CHAPTER 13

Niagara-on-the-Lake, Ontario, August 20.

Sitting at the wheel of the rented station wagon, Felix Tidyman smiled as Harry Bracken and the good-looking woman checked into the hotel.

It had been a long day. As soon as they had cleared Canadian customs at Pearson International Airport, Tidyman had gone to the Avis counter. From there he could see where Abdel Saddam was waiting. He didn't acknowledge the man, but signed out a brown Ford wagon and, as they'd arranged on the phone, drove out of the terminal alone. Then he circled back to pick up Saddam and the two Palestinian students who had walked upstairs to wait for him on the Departures level.

"Bracken and the girl will be at the cap plant tomorrow at ten," Saddam had told him, as soon as he climbed into the front seat.

Mahmoud and Tariq got in the back. They'd assumed elaborately casual expressions, as though they set out every morning to murder someone. With bored gestures they pointed out the sights on the airport roads, which to Tidyman's eye looked just like goddamn airport roads anywhere else.

Saddam pointed with his thumb to the pair in back. "Mr. Cool and Mr. Cool, right?"

Tidyman shrugged and looked for road signs. No one spoke to him again until he drove past the ramp that would have taken them to downtown Toronto.

"We need guns," Mahmoud said.

Tidyman sighed heavily and wondered how this new generation could possibly be so ignorant. These two would have charged downtown, looking for a store that sold handguns, just as if they were in Houston or Philadelphia. Next thing you knew, they'd be sitting in a cubicle talking to curious policemen. Tidyman wanted to grab them by the neck and tell them that they should have done their homework; then they'd have known about Canada's pantywaist gun-control laws. Instead, he said, "No, we're going to build a bomb." To Saddam he added, "You find what I asked for?"

"I found a place, but there's a dog."

"What kind of dog?"

"Doberman. Big fucker."

"Doberman's no problem." Tidyman had guessed that if there were a dog it would be a Doberman. Construction bosses were partial to Dobermans.

He followed Saddam's directions to the depot, and rolled down a window. He stopped a man in a white hard hat with Steve printed on the front. "I'm looking for Nicholas Muller," Tidyman said.

"Never heard of him," the man in Steve's hat said.

Tidyman swung the car door open suddenly and stepped out. "Our records show he worked here, and that he left his last address owing sixteen thousand dollars to our finance company."

The man in Steve's hat took another look at Tidyman and the carload of strangers. "But I could be mistaken," he said quickly. "Check with Hazel in the office; Hazel, she keeps all the records."

Hazel, who had seen the big man talking to Steve out front, thought nothing of it when the man walked into the office, said, "Hi, Hazel," grabbed a hard hat off a wall hook, and kept on walking out into the yard. That was when Tidyman saw the Doberman. And the shed that had been built too far away from any of the other buildings to house anything but explosives. It would be easy, thanks largely to the dog. Trained Dobermans, he knew, went right for your throat with a minimum of noise. Once you caught them in mid-flight with your knee, knocked out their wind, and broke their neck, you could take your own sweet time, because no one would know you had been there.

That was exactly how it had gone later that night, when they returned to the yard and let themselves in with bolt cutters. The only noise was a short high-pitched squeal when Tidyman snapped the dog's neck. They left with a handful of blasting caps and a 50 lb. case of C.I.L. ditching dynamite, a straight nitroglycerin brand with a velocity of 17,500 feet per second. Tidyman estimated that sixteen eight-inch cartridges, along with the nine-volt batteries and the model airplane controls he'd brought with him, would do the job nicely.

Later in Saddam's motel room, he explained to the students how the joystick control sent a radio signal to the transmitter packed in with the detonator and the dynamite. The students kept their expressions of concentrated cool, but he was pleased to notice a little sweat as he made the connections to the dynamite.

At nine-thirty next morning, Tidyman parked the brown Ford wagon on the street in front of Canada Caps, where they had a clear view of the visitors' parking area. Half an hour later, a Plymouth with New Hampshire plates pulled up. Abdel Saddam caught a glimpse of the woman with Harry Bracken, and said, "Hey, too bad. Too bad."

One hour later, they saw Bracken and the girl get back into the Plymouth. They followed them north across town. "Hey, I used to live around here," Saddam said, surprised.

Tidyman was surprised, as well. How had Bracken connected the caps to Saddam? Or was Saddam just one employee that Bracken was checking? Or had Saddam somehow made himself so conspicuous that the insurance dick couldn't help but trip over him?

They followed the couple all day, saw them take time out for lunch in a little bistro, then make the rounds of bars in Saddam's neighborhood, asking questions everywhere. But there was no opportunity for them to trot out the bomb.

Tidyman wasn't worried. As the day wore on, he knew he'd have his chance. Something in the way they had acted in the bistro, the way he looked at her, and the way she tilted back her head when she laughed told him that, whatever else they were up to, these two were in no hurry to split up and head home.

And he had been right, although the Palestinians doubted it at first. When Harry headed out of St. Catharines and onto the Queen Elizabeth Way, Mahmoud saw road signs for the U.S. border, and became uneasy.

"They will look into our car at the border." Mahmoud waved a hand toward the back of the stationwagon, where the bomb and the remote control were sitting under a motel towel.

"No one's going to the border," Tidyman said.

"No, they're not going to the border," Saddam said. Tidyman looked over and saw that Saddam was smiling to himself. "You any idea where they're going?"

"They're going to turn off up here," Saddam said. The exit sign said Niagara-on-the-Lake.

Tidyman followed Harry's car around the cloverleaf. "How did you figure that one?"

"Maria. My sweet Maria. She must have come looking for me at my old apartment. Must have left her address for me there. She was hot for me all right. Now they're looking for Maria. It's okay. She don't know anything."

Tidyman followed the Plymouth to a house that Saddam said must have been Maria's, even though he'd never been there. They watched Bracken and the girl get back in their car and drive to the Duke of Cumberland Hotel. Tidyman pulled up across the street and parked. As the couple climbed the steps to the hotel, Tidyman felt his first flash of regret; she really was a nice-looking woman. But the feeling passed quickly. "I want two of you in the car at all times," he said.

Tidyman waited a few more minutes, then looked at his watch.

"I'm going into the hotel. If either of them leaves the hotel, I want one of you to follow and one of you to come and get me. Do you understand that?"

"When do we get to . . . " Mahmoud let his voice trail off. His eyes shifted back to the shape under the towel.

"We get to do it tonight," Tidyman said.

He had blessed them each with a smile, which he held all the way into the hotel. He peeked into the dining room as if he might be meeting a friend there, and saw them at a corner table. They looked as though they were settling in for a long meal. Tidyman turned and walked down the hall to the reception desk. A fiftyish lady with a hair style that went with the Victorian decor looked up. Tidyman reached into his jacket. "Hi. I've got an envelope for Mr. Bracken." She took the envelope with two delicate fingers, as though she'd been handed a sardine, turned, and slipped it into the mail slot for room 214.

Tidyman walked past the dining room again and followed the signs to 214. He checked the door and smiled. Then he paced off the distance from the room to the end of the hall.

Outside, he paced the same distance back and glanced up at the window above him.

Back at the stationwagon, Tidyman pulled his lanky body into the front seat of the car. "Okay, here's how it's going to go. Bracken's in room 214. Mahmoud and Tariq, you go up. You'll have no problem with the lock. Saddam will keep the nice lady at reception busy, asking about their winter-rate package for a family of nine. Anybody else asks where you're going, you're going to Mr. Bracken's room, and ain't that the truth? When you're in the room, shove the box under the bed. Give a quick look to see if he's left any helpful papers laying around, but I don't want you in the room longer than a minute. Then you close the door and walk *slowly* back to the wagon. Simple?"

The three nodded. Mahmoud said, "Yeah, sure, no problem." Tidyman nodded with them, somewhat warily: "If it's simple, then repeat what I just told you. Tariq?"

Tariq licked his lips and managed to get it out, slowly, but in the right order. "And you will be waiting right here?" he concluded.

Tidyman let his eyes roll up to the ceiling of the stationwagon. "Yes, yes. I'll be checking the building from the outside, in case

there is anything that you should know about upstairs. I will
have the car running and ready to get us back to the United
States border. From Buffalo we'll take a flight to Chicago and
from Chicago we will take a flight to Los Angeles. Now, is there
anything else?" His voice was a treacle of sarcasm. "In that
case, kindly fuck off and get your job done."

But Tariq wanted to be sure. "So you will be here?"

"I will be right here. Now take the package."

"Take the package now?"

"Take the fucking package," Tidyman roared.

After they had left, he started the car and turned on the radio.
Blue Jays winning. He shook his head. America's national sport
and here was a Canadian team made up of Dominican million-
aires leading his Yankees by sixteen games. He punched at the
tuning buttons and found nothing else but rock and cowboy
music. He wished he'd brought one of his Sinatra tapes; he liked
songs that told stories you could understand.

Minutes later, Saddam and the students came walking back
as if they were part of a funeral march. Tidyman sighed. Tell
them, walk slowly, they turn into snails. He rolled down his
window and waved for them to move it along.

They hurried up a bit, jostling each other as they climbed
back into the wagon. Tidyman waited until the doors closed.
"What's going to happen is that we're going to watch the third
window up there. We're going to watch until the light goes on.
That will tell us that Bracken and the girl are in the room. Then
we're going to watch until the light goes off. That will tell us
Bracken and the girl are in the sack. And then we'll wait exactly
three minutes just to make sure that someone's not still going
wee-wee. Then we'll play with the remote control."

It was an hour-and-a-half before the light in the third window
went on. Tidyman spent part of the time thinking about what
Bracken was eating. Probably a good steak and some nice
boiled potatoes and a few crisp carrots. Then there was that pie
he'd seen displayed on the dining room trolley. Tidyman was
getting hungry picturing it. Maybe when they got across the
border they'd have time for a meal before their flight.

When the light went on, Tidyman looked at his watch: 10:20. He kept glancing from his watch to the light. Buffalo was famous for chicken wings. About three dozen of those and some fries would go good.

Then the light went out. Tidyman waited three minutes, then gently moved the joystick in his hand.

When the blast came, it surprised even him. That was the great thing about a straight nitro dynamite. It didn't need a tight space to do what it was paid to do. Shook the whole fucking car. Felt good. Other cars stopping now right on the street, people running, everyone wondering what's going on.

Saddam spoke casually, trying to out-cool the two students in the back seat. "We got 'em," he said, studying the confusion around the hotel. Onlookers were crunching through the glass that had blown out of the window. It was unlikely that anyone in the room would have lived.

Which was why he was so startled to see Bracken and the girl running out the side door without their shoes.

CHAPTER 14

Niagara-on-the-Lake, Ontario, August 20.

Harry strolled with his Hundred Pipers down the hall, stopping briefly at the ice machine. Then it was past the brass sconces with flickering bulbs where there had once been gas lights, past a military figure scowling down from a painting. Harry squinted at the brass plate in the frame and learned that the man in the painting had routed the Americans from a place called Queenston Heights in the War of 1812.

Excuse me, Harry, but why are you standing here in this broadloomed hall with your ice cubes melting and your scotch getting warm in your armpit? She's waiting, old boy. And you know this kind of opportunity doesn't knock on your head every day.

That was the problem. Harry was so unused to being pursued he didn't know how to play it. And now that he was finally at her door, staring at the number, he couldn't decide how to knock. Should it be a furtive gentleness: the kind of soft tapping that once resonated along the upper halls of Victorian country houses? Perhaps a brusque, businesslike tap: an actuary come a-wooing. Or maybe something with a snappy little rat-a-tat-tat that said hey, sure, I know it's late but don't think for a minute this boy's sleepy, ho no.

What would she be wearing? Something careerist and tailored, something very Today's Woman? Did young ladies buy filmy peignoirs anymore? Or was there now a version done up in

114

leather with chrome studs where the lace used to be? Alex wouldn't *have* a filmy peignoir on, because she wouldn't have packed it, because if she'd packed it that would have meant that she meant to get herself into a situation where a peignoir was . . .

She opened the door before he knocked. "I was wondering if you'd gotten lost or something." She wore jeans and a sweater.

Harry looked around the room and saw that although it had the same antique theme as his room, the individual pieces were quite different. An antique pine highboy sat in the corner holding a tray with glasses.

He splashed scotch over ice cubes and handed one glass to Alex. "You want water?"

She shook her head and sipped. Then she smiled. Maybe, thought Harry, she just likes my scotch. Maybe that's what this is all about. We're going to sit here and drink scotch. Get with it, Harry. It's perfectly acceptable these days for one businessperson to invite another businessperson to a hotel room for a little business drink, genders notwithstanding. Done all the time.

She took another sip, walked to the edge of the bed, and sat.

Harry stayed on his feet and took what he thought were two genteel sips. But when he looked at his glass it was empty.

He poured another and looked for somewhere to sit. Her coat was on one chair, her purse on another. Harry wondered if she had blocked off those seats for a reason. He was still wondering when she patted the quilt she was sitting on, inviting him to sit beside her on the bed. Harry sat. Then three things happened in quick succession. First Alex took Harry's glass and placed it next to hers on the bedside table; then they both kicked off their shoes. And then a bomb exploded down the hall.

A large gilt framed mirror fell off the wall and crashed into the top of the dresser. The highboy in the corner groaned and shook. There was the sound of a bottle breaking and Harry didn't have to look to know that his Hundred Pipers had tumbled to their death. He jumped off the bed, yanked her by the arm, grabbed her purse from the chair, and pulled her along the hall to the stairway.

"Harry, where are we going? Harry, you're hurting my arm. Harry, my shoes!"

They were down the back stairs and out the side door before he spoke. "That brown Ford. Over there. Two guys in it. It was parked outside Saddam's place."

A mysterious car. A big boom from the general direction of Harry's room. And now Harry pulling her over to his car, unlocking the door, and trying to push her past the steering wheel into the passenger seat.

"Harry, stop!"

He paused, the car door handle in his hand.

"Is it those men in the stationwagon?"

"Yes. Get in." Harry pushed but she refused to squeeze past the wheel. He heard the Ford start up.

"Get in the other side," she shouted. "I'm driving." She snatched the keys from his hand and started the engine. Harry ran around and climbed in the passenger door.

Alex dropped the car into low, and tore out of the lot, heading north, the opposite direction from the border. The Ford pulled out to make a cumbersome U-turn.

"Say what?" Harry said.

"When we were talking about my dad teaching me to shoot and arm wrestle, I should have mentioned that I've been driving since I was nine. One of the benefits of hanging around a body shop. You get to learn on other people's vehicles." Ahead, a dark-colored Buick nudged out of a side street. Alex moved the wheel slightly and stepped on the gas. The Plymouth swerved out against oncoming traffic, then fell neatly back into its original lane.

"Jesus." Harry recognized a beautiful maneuver. But behind them, the Ford was gaining on the straightaway. "Only thing he never taught me was how to outrun a V-8 with a four. Harry, I've got to talk to you about your taste in cars."

"Jesus," Harry said again.

A sign warned of an intersection ahead. A gravel road ran off to the left. Alex waited until the last possible second, braked sharply, pulled down on the wheel, and hit the gas. The Plymouth fishtailed, then chewed into the gravel and straightened out. The Ford, Harry was relieved to see, missed the turn and had to back up. But as soon as it got behind them again it began to gain.

"These roads are too damn straight," Alex said. "And dark. Aren't these roads dark? Talk to me, Harry."

"Dark," Harry said. "Very dark."

"What's that sign say? Can you make out what it says?"

"Winery of some sort. Might be the one we had for supper."

"The one? I thought we packed a pair of them away." She watched the headlights of the Ford grow in the mirror.

"Thank God we did," Harry said. "I'd hate to be doing this sober."

"We've got some nice little wineries in New York State, Harry. A lot of them aren't far from Watkins Glen, where I go to work on my driving now and then."

"I was having such a lovely evening," Harry said.

"You know the thing about grapevines is that they have to be far enough apart for a tractor to go up between them. For spraying. Do you think they spray their grapevines in Canada?"

"I'm not sure," Harry said.

"Good. Because if they can get a tractor between those vines, we should be able to squeeze your gutless little Plymouth between them."

"Jesus, I don't know. They'd make it in the Ford."

"It's a wagon, Harry. Those things oversteer. Put one in a tight corner and you find your back end in the ditch. Lots of corners in wine fields. And I bet a front wheel drive like this little Plymouth could do great bootleg turns. I think we might lose them in there, Harry. What do you think?"

"We're going cross-country, is that what you're saying?"

She jerked the wheel to the left and the Plymouth crunched bottom twice. It sailed up a grade and made contact with a dirt track between two rows of Pinot Noir. "Hang on."

Harry hung on to the bottom of the seat, but his head still hit the ceiling. The wheels of the Plymouth sank into the soft soil, but Alex gave the accelerator just the right amount of encouragement to lurch free. She snapped off the lights and they vanished between the rows.

Harry looked back. "I don't think they're going to try it."

Alex turned left at the end of the row and shut off the engine. They sat in silence, watching from the darkness as the Ford prowled back and forth for a couple of passes, then finally disappeared.

"Hug me, Harry." She fell away from the wheel and into his arms.

Harry kissed her lightly on the head. They stayed for an hour, listening to each other breathe.

When Alex finally closed her eyes, Harry got out and walked around the car. He gently moved her over, climbed behind the wheel, started up, and, still driving without lights, found an exit onto another road, about a mile behind the one they had turned off. Then he snapped on the lights and headed for the Queen Elizabeth Way and the Fort Erie bridge to the U.S.

Alex opened her eyes. "No."

"No?"

"They'll expect us to go back over that way. Stay on the back roads. Cross over at Lewiston. It's longer, but we'll lose them."

Harry followed the signs reading "Lewiston and Bridge to U.S.A." Seconds later, they passed a darkened service station lot, and the rearview mirror filled with high beams. Harry could make out the shape of a stationwagon behind the headlights. "Oh, shit."

Alex turned to look back. "I was sure they'd think we'd take the other way."

He rammed the accelerator to the floor. "If these guys are professionals, they will know who you are and where you live. They might have guessed that you'd know about the Lewiston bridge."

"Of course they would. I'm sorry. I've really screwed it up, Harry."

He turned down a side street, hoping to make up in maneuverability what the Plymouth lacked in speed. But he lacked Alex's magic at the wheel. "Don't be sorry. It sounded like a good idea to me. Which way would you turn here?"

"Left. The border's not far."

Harry entered the intersection as if he planned to drive straight through. At the last second, he turned the wheel left. The Plymouth careened on two wheels and scraped a parked pick-up truck. "Excuse me," he said to the truck.

A sign told them they were two kilometers from the border. "Decision time," Alex said.

"Just what I was thinking. These men behind us: if they want us bad enough they're not going to let a customs officer get in the way."

"They'd have more than one customs man there," Alex said. "Lewiston's not a big border crossing, but they'd have more than one guy at U.S. Customs, even this late at night."

"The trick is going to be for us to get over and leave them behind." Harry checked the mirror. The Ford had eased back, following at an inconspicuous distance. Alex reached across to the phone and tapped out the number for information.

"What are you doing?" Harry asked.

"Reaching out to touch someone." Into the phone, she said, "What's the number for U.S. Customs, Lewiston, New York?"

She moved her lips as the computer voice told her, pressed the END button, and tapped in the number. "Ah, excuse me, sir," she said, when a live voice answered, "my husband and me were having a little argument here, nothing serious, but we were wondering. Well, wondering about this drug we're always reading about in the paper, these days, this crack, I think it's called. Some boys in a brown Ford stationwagon filled up at our service station a few minutes ago, and I overheard them talking about it. Said they were going to cross the border into New York State at Lewiston."

She paused.

"Their license number? Ah . . . "

Alex turned in her seat. "H, something, something, one four three. No, I'd rather not give my name. We got the daughter-in-law coming tomorrow and I don't want to get involved in any foreign courts."

She hung up just as Harry slowed down for the Customs booth. Suddenly, the whole area came to life. Uniformed men ran toward the one open lane of cars. They quickly waved on the car ahead of Harry, glanced inside Harry's car and waved him on too. Then they descended in a group on the Ford wagon. Harry drove through, then slowed to turn to Alex.

"Who says there's never a cop around when you need one?" he said, smiling.

CHAPTER 15

Brattleboro, Vermont, August 21.

Okay, Harry, now you've got it, he told himself as he drove through the night. You've uncovered a subtle clue and it intrigues your subtle mind. Somebody subtly tried to blow you up into small subtle pieces. A large explosion in a room you would have been occupying if you hadn't been occupied yourself. Didn't that have to be a clue? It would pass right by most people, but not you, Harry.

Let's work on it. Be deductive. List reasons. Why would someone try to blow you up? Usually terrorists blow up people they don't know: schoolchildren, people in subways or on airplanes, people shopping in department stores. But these terrorists took care to blow up one particular hotel room. That suggested they knew the occupant. So there must be something personal here, or at any rate something more personal than a random terrorist act.

Yes, indeed. You seem to have drawn some attention to yourself. But how? Up to this point you've been more or less ineffective. You've drawn attention to yourself in the same way Edsel drew attention to Ford. Why would they put that much explosive in your room? Unless they've mistaken you for someone who knows what he's doing. Unless! Secretly! Yes! You've been doing something right!

But what?

Harry was tired and fed up. He was forty. He had had a lot to drink. He had not been made love to. He had been almost blown up. He was probably a fugitive. He had been followed and now he had been driving in his socks for—how many hours? They were almost back to Vermont, to Biff's Georgian folly.

Beside him, Alex had not been sleeping well, certainly not the sleep of innocence.

Perhaps the bomb had upset her?

Why should the bomb upset *her*? It wasn't in *her* room. It was in *your* room. Somebody tried to blow *you* up. Because you've secretly been doing something right.

Perhaps you should have tipped the bellboy after all.

She had woken up once near Schenectady to ask him what the plan was. "What's the plan? We have to have a plan. What are we doing? Where are we going? What about my job?"

Harry had made up a plan because it seemed important for her to have one. "The plan? Yes. The plan is that we go and see a friend of mine called Biff. He has a computer, which may or may not tell us more about this. Then we go to New Hampshire and I'll see my boss and tell him what happened. A bombing has to convince him that these people are worth our serious consideration. You should perhaps phone Wolfgang Kohl and tell him what happened. Tell him you think you may be a target and you're planning to spend some time with friends. If he asks you where, don't tell him."

Alex was tired enough to believe that was a plan. She put the heels of her hands over her eyes and slumped forward in the seat as Harry pressed on through the night. When they pulled into Biff's circular driveway, the crunch of the gravel woke her.

"Wah?"

"We're at Biff's."

She sat up and with automatic motions started to straighten out, running fingers through her hair, smoothing fabric and looking for the shoes she had left in her hotel room. "Coffee."

"Yes. Biff will have coffee."

He got out, walked around the car, opened her door, and offered her his hand. She took it and pulled herself out.

"Coffee."

"Yes. You mentioned that. Come on." He guided her up the stairs to the black-lacquered door with its polished brass knocker: a huge duck that rapped on a lily pad. Harry wondered if it were too early to use such an instrument. He looked at Alex.

"Coffee."

Harry grabbed the duck's head and banged it on the lily. It sounded like an anchor striking the bow of a garbage scow.

They waited. Just as Harry was wondering if he should swing the duck again, the door opened a crack. The housekeeper, Gisele, stared at them, rumpled and shoeless.

"Coffee," Alex said.

"Come in, please. He's not up yet. He doesn't usually get up until seven. You could wait in his den. I'll bring coffee."

"Just bring one for my friend, Gisele," Harry said. "I'll draw myself a beer."

Twenty minutes later Biff announced himself with the sound of tires doing a power turn into the den. "Ah, a beer! Ah, a woman! Harry, old son, if you had a hot chicken pot pie, you'd have all three essentials of life in this one small room." He started toward the tap, but Gisele strode into the room, intercepting his chair to put a cup of tea into his hands.

"Ah, tea. Thank you, Gisele. Thank you very much. Yes."

"I'll be in later with some toast and cottage cheese."

"Thank you." Biff watched her leave the room. "I only keep her around so I can humiliate her by overfilling my bag. A small revenge, but all I am left with. And you, my dear, who would you be this early in the morning? Some nymph come to decorate my dawn?"

"This is Alex. She's in product management."

"Only a cover story, Harry. What she has not told you is that she is Botticelli's Venus Rising reincarnate. She is looking for a secret prince so that she may step with him back into the sea and live a life of endless orgasm. Sadly, I doubt the prince is you, Harry. I am profoundly sadder it is not me."

Alex smiled. She looked up on the wall at a picture of a younger Biff in an unidentifiable uniform. She looked back at Biff and smiled again, this time showing her braces.

"You've been keeping the lady up all night, Harry, doing whatever it is you young people do without your shoes on. What I'd suggest—and I'm sure she would agree—is that she go and find Gisele, who will show her to the guest suite and find her a soft downy comforter."

Alex nodded, and rose. "Endless orgasm?"

"My dear, if I were four years younger."

"And if I weren't so tired."

"But such is life. Gisele is likely in the kitchen, curdling the milk for the cottage cheese. I've been told the kitchen is toward the back of the house."

She nodded slowly and left. Biff watched her and sighed. "A splendid argument for heterosexuality. And why does she look so bedraggled?"

"Last night she really felt the earth move."

Biff reached into his cold teacup and picked out the quarter slice of lemon. He sucked it for half a minute, then threw it into the fireplace with surprising force. He put his chair in motion toward the desk with the computer, flung the door open, and flicked a switch. Waiting for the terminal to boot up, he jerked his chair back and forth with small movements of the joystick. It was like a man with sensate feet tapping his foot.

Biff keyed into a database. He ran his finger down the screen and noisily smacked his lips. He tapped more keys. Biff rooted through the information, making chewing noises with his mouth, snorting occasionally through his nose. In the pauses, when his computer waited for another computer at the end of the line, Biff's hand fell automatically to the joystick and tapped it back and forth. Harry saw him feeling the pockets of his Irish tweed jacket, looking for the cigarettes he had given up twenty years ago.

Then, as though he were praising a well-mannered dog, Biff patted the monitor, turned his chair to Harry, and rolled across the room. At the last moment his chair veered to the tap. He opened the cabinet, took a glass, and began to pour.

Gisele appeared in the doorway. Biff looked at her. Gisele left.

"Well, Harry." Biff spoke with a low, hoarse cheeriness. "According to available data, you're fucked."

Harry rubbed one red eye.

"The first thing is that you're a fugitive. Think about it, Harry. For the first time in your life you can feel wanted. In this particular situation you're wanted in connection with a bombing at the Duke of Cumberland Hotel in Niagara-on-the-Lake, Ontario. It seems that the police in Canada are expressing interest in a dead male found outside your door: a bellhop."

Harry listened in silence.

"You have been reported as having left the country. The license number you gave the hotel was traced to the border crossing point at Lewiston, New York. A reception clerk—no name mentioned—reports you as 'behaving suspiciously.' The young lady is also wanted in connection with the event, which may have something to do with an investigation into a crack-smuggling operation. Busy, busy, Harry. Perhaps we'd do well to have your car put away in the garage, away from the eyes of the neighborhood."

Harry nodded.

"What all this means is that not only do you no longer have a solid lead, you're a fugitive from justice to boot. It also means that some force other than the judicial system is after your sagging buttocks, and that you have involved an innocent young lady in international machinations, the depth of which can scarcely be comprehended. All of which adds new meaning to the term 'Baby, this thing is bigger than both of us.' And gives me pause for thought."

Harry stood and wiped one hand against the other. "God, I wonder what I'm going to do *today*?"

"Assuming, of course, that you did not put the bomb in your own empty room, who did? And how did whoever put the device in your lodgings know where you were? Have you been scattering breadcrumbs behind you?"

"No."

"Did you leave a detailed itinerary with your press agent?"

"No."

"Or do you have somebody with you who has been phoning in your whereabouts? Hmm?"

Harry sighed. He remembered that once, in a fit of whimsy, he had written "nuclear physicist" on an application for a visa to the Soviet Union. All over Leningrad, he had been made spectacularly welcome. In bars, he had been bumped into by magnificent women, anxious to talk about cultural and other exchanges with the West. A tawny-haired ballerina from the Bolshoi had told him how demanding her art was, but that it had compensating benefits, such as one's own apartment with one's own double bed.

Harry had treated the whole thing as a training course in how not to be manipulated by women. He had noted the variety of approaches and was surprised at how attracted he was, even though he knew what was happening. He was also surprised at how genuine their disappointment appeared when he gently turned them down.

The experience had left Harry with the dangerous conviction that he was immune to being fooled by women.

"But, Biff, she invited me to her room."

"Hell, that's no criteria. My daughter invited you to her room, and there's a woman robust with malice. There are a number of reasons Miss O'Connor might have done the same thing. She could have simply been assuring your absence from the room so that the bomb could be placed. Or she might not have known that that was the night the deed was to be done and have invited you to her room for—let's call it a last supper. Or, to grant her some innocence, she might not have known that your death was being planned at all. She may have unwittingly helped the perpetrator or perpetrators, believing they were only intellectually interested in your meanderings across the continent. We'll call this last one the National Geographic theory."

"Look, Biff, I'm not tremendously good with women. But I think I know when one is on my side. And I think this one is on my side. So I must have been followed some other way."

"How?"

"Just be quiet for a second. Let me think."

"You wouldn't rather keep playing to your strength and continue blundering across the landscape?"

The only scenario Harry could devise that made any sense at all was that someone had broken into his room, left a bomb on a very short timer, and when the bellhop, wandering nearby, had come to investigate . . .

"What I think," Harry said, "is that we are not yet in a position to think logically. We do not have enough information."

"Meanwhile," Biff observed, "your pursuers—both the good guys and the others—appear to have information in abundance. The question is, which of them has enough to find you first?"

"Hey, she got those guys stopped at the border, Biff."

"Hmm."

"You're always so suspicious."

"But I'm still alive, Harry. Most of me."

CHAPTER 16

Cupertino, California, August 21.

The reception desk was a clear plastic slab with chrome-plated legs. Behind it sat two tall plants and a blonde girl with a California tan. When the woman and the Arab guy walked up to the desk, the girl flashed the Arab an almost perfect smile and said, "Geez, you must just be roasting in that watchamacallit." Then she winked at the woman to let her know she was just being nice to foreigners, not coming on to the guy or anything like that. Just in case it mattered. Around this place you never knew. The woman smiled back and said in a clear English accent that they had a meeting with Mr. Nunni.

"Sal?" the girl asked. The question seemed to show that everyone here was on a first-name basis rather than to distinguish Sal from untold other Nunnis. "He knows you're coming?"

The woman bristled at the suggestion that she would ever cut in on someone's morning without an invitation. "He does," she said, dropping her smile.

The receptionist spoke briefly into her headset. "He'll be right out. I have to ask you to wear these visitors' badges. They're pretty ugly, I know, but we're kind of high-security here. Oh, and I got to get a business card from each of you. For our records."

Ismail Gezmis and Marjorie Brooks were handing her their cards when Sal Nunni entered the reception area. He was a short, thin man, in his late thirties, with dark curly hair that started high on the forehead. The receptionist thought he seemed rattled, a little unsure about whether or not he should shake the Arab's hand. Yes, Sal was a little disoriented, all right. Or maybe just tired. The hours these guys put in, she didn't know how they did it. She shrugged and looked at the logo on the visitors' business cards. "Cute-looking bird," she said, opening a drawer beside the table.

Sal Nunni led his guests through a labyrinth of hallways to a large, glass-walled office. His desk was also a clear plastic slab, covered with papers strewn around a pair of computer terminals. The chairs in the room were of cherry red tubular steel. A bench along one wall and an easel in the corner held schematics of electronic circuitry with pencil marks on them, as though the circuits had been graded by a teacher.

Nunni motioned for them to take chairs, then perched himself on the edge of a cherry red stool. He glanced back at the diagram on the bench—clearly the one he had been working on that morning—and made a production out of turning the paper face down. A pencil fell off the bench and rolled toward the chair of Gezmis, who made no move to pick it up.

Nunni jumped off the stool to retrieve the pencil. He held it near the eraser and wagged it between two fingers. "I'm going to be very, very honest with you," he said. "I don't think I'm going to be able to help you this time."

The woman crossed her legs and smiled at him. "Poor Sal. You haven't got it yet. Don't you realize who this is?"

Sal sucked on the end of his pencil, then pointed it at Ismail Gezmis. He smiled a little smile. "Not Sheik Omar Kamal?"

The woman nodded.

Sal Nunni, flooded with relief, jumped from his stool to pump Gezmis's hand. Then he shook his head and pointed a naughty-naughty finger at Marjorie Brooks for shaking him up like that.

The first time she had called on him at work—how long ago was that, eight months? maybe nine?—he had also told her very,

very honestly that he didn't think he could help her. That time she had been with Felix Tidyman.

"Help *us*, Mr. Nunni?" She had leaned hard on the us.

Nunni had fidgeted then, sitting between her and Felix Tidyman.

"You know, what you mentioned on the phone. I don't think I can help you with anything."

The woman had listened with a frown. Suddenly she broke into a smile of understanding. "Oh, what we talked about on the phone. The evening I called you at, ah, Brian's."

"Yeah, I still don't know why you'd want to call me there. I mean, Jesus Christ."

"At Brian's, you mean?" The woman blinked sweetly. "You don't know why I called you there at Brian's?"

"Well, yeah, I guess I know, all right." Nunni had played with his pencil on that day, too, wiggling it in and out of his mouth, pulling his lower lip down with the eraser, giving them a flash of pink gum. "You want me to do something for you and that's your way of letting me know that you know something about me." The sentence was garbled by the pencil in the lower lip. What he said next sounded like, "Or think you know something. About what was happening at Brian's place. Which it wasn't."

He gave them time for one or the other to confirm or deny their understanding. They said nothing. He tried waiting them out a little longer but realized he couldn't take the silence. "That kind of thing really isn't a very big deal, you know. It really isn't. Not any more. Not in California. Not today."

"You called it Brian's place, Mr. Nunni," the woman had said. "But it's not *really* Brian's place is it?"

Nunni had taken the pencil right out of his mouth to answer, and he had spoken more loudly than he had to. "Hey, sure it is. He lives there. You've been asking around; you should know that."

"He lives there with his parents," the woman had corrected. "It's actually Brian's parents' place, but they weren't home that evening, were they?" She looked at her hands and waited for an answer. When it seemed that none was coming, she lifted her head and blinked again, an unnerving little-girl look of studied innocence. "Mr. Nunni, how old is Brian?"

Nunni perched forward on his stool, in danger of tumbling right off. He pasted on a smile and moved his gaze from Marjorie Brooks to Tidyman. "Hey, what is this, how old? I mean, what kind of question is that? Like, what are we getting at here? Brian's nineteen. No, twenty. I think he turned twenty last month. What do you mean, how old? You don't think he's that old?" His mouth kept moving, but the size of his eyes revealed that Sal Nunni had crossed over from discomfort to fear.

Felix Tidyman recognized his cue. "This work you do, you've done it for a while, I understand." He waved a vague hand toward the schematic diagram on the easel. "Your specialty's automotive electronics, I hear."

Nunni had stared at him, wondering if he'd just been asked a question. Two questions, maybe. He looked at the woman for help but found none there.

"I'm afraid all that is well over my head," the woman said. "I look under the hood of a car and have no idea about what's going on there."

Tidyman shaped something close to a smile. "Guys like Sal here have made it damn near impossible for any of us to work on the car in the driveway any more. Can't even change a plug any more without running it through a computer."

Moved by professional pride and a hope that the conversation might be lapping against a friendlier shore, Nunni had felt some of his confidence surge back. "Unless you really like the idea of greasing up your clothes, you're a lot better off just leaving the power module alone. I mean, what's left to do? You've got electronic sensors that pick up on any sign of trouble, ICs that automatically advance or pull back your timing, adjust the airflow into the engine, control the pumping of your air out to the manifold ... " He trailed off, wondering if they wanted more.

"What are 'eye sees'?" the woman had asked.

"ICs. Integrated circuits," Nunni explained with a disdainful little shake of the head that belied the fact that, a few minutes earlier, the woman had almost turned him to jelly. "You want to pay the money, you can get computer-controlled springs and never feel a pothole again." He let all that sink in and felt pleased to see the two visitors looking at each other and then back at him. He thought he sensed a new respect.

"I've been working on this stuff ever since California passed its environmental control laws," Nunni continued. "There are people who'll tell you those laws went in just to make jobs for our computer industry. 'Cause that's exactly what happened. Before the emission-control legislation, the only electronics in the family car was in the radio and eight-track tape deck. Remember eight-track? Anyway, when California decided we had all the smog we needed for a while, Detroit started looking into ways for ICs to control the spark plugs and the timing and the airflow and give you a cleaner running engine. A great big lift for the semiconductor industry, I don't mind telling you."

"Semiconductor?" the woman had said.

"ICs, microchips, same thing. You want to know what I'm proudest of in all those years? When I was with ITT, I worked on the chip for the first electronic antilock braking system. I mean the very, very first. So what do the absolute neanderthals in Detroit do? They let the Germans get it first. Can you believe that?" Nunni shook his head, scarcely able to believe it himself.

Felix Tidyman had pressed on. "Driving up here I was trying to explain to Marjorie the basic principles of automotive micro-circuitry. I might have oversimplified it a little—"

"It certainly didn't seem like oversimplification to me," the woman interrupted. Nunni wondered if she were going to start batting her eyes and tell him how women were so helpless when it came to that sort of thing.

Tidyman said, "I tried to explain to her how specific instructions are now programmed into the microchip, so that if a certain thing happens—like your example of the foot hitting hard on the brake—the circuitry will respond in one way. And if something else happens, then it knows enough to do something totally different."

Sal Nunni had thought it over for a moment. "Well, you've certainly simplified it, that's for sure." He permitted himself a quick smile, then gave his head the same kind of shake he had just used in describing the kind of stupidity that gave the Germans the jump on anti-skid braking.

Tidyman ignored the theatrics. "So a microchip can be programmed to respond to signals and to control whether or not the car stops or goes, how fast it goes, that sort of thing?"

Sal Nunni wasn't sure why, but he was starting to feel uneasy again. It would just be a matter of time, he knew, before they got back to that business with Brian.

"I know this might sound a little dippy," the woman cut in, without sounding dippy in the least, "but must those signals that the chip receives have anything to do with the specific function that is being controlled?"

Nunni had studied her hard. "Excuse me?"

Tidyman cleared his throat and climbed to his feet, aware of the effect that always had, particularly on shorter men, who were nervous already. "What Marjorie is wondering is, could your ROM—I think that's what they call it—be programmed so that the microprocessor responds to a sequence of unrelated activities?"

Nunni waited for more, jiggling his left knee up and down on his right.

Then the woman had taken over: "Could your IC thingamajig be programmed in such a way that if, for example, a motorist happened to tap the brake three times within a certain time span of, say, two and a half seconds and then shut off the engine, the little chip in there would tell the engine to respond in a particular way?"

Nunni had blinked at the question and the unexpected exuberance of the delivery. Wary now, "Like what?"

The woman had paused, pretending to consider the question. Looking coyly at Tidyman, "Tell him now?"

Tidyman had said nothing, just stood looking down at Nunni. Suddenly he broke into a warm smile. He reached into his jacket pocket and pulled out a photo of Ismail Gezmis, complete with robe and burnoose, standing between two Rolls-Royces. They had snapped the photo at a Beverly Hills dealership the day before.

Sal Nunni had studied the photo.

"Before we tell you anything, you have to understand a little about the mentality of the Arabian potentate," Marjorie said.

"The who?" Nunni kept staring at the photo.

"The wealthy Arab. And I don't mean wealthy in the sense that you and I might use the word. I mean the kind of wealth that staggers the imagination. For example, do you know how many cars this gentleman owns?"

Nunni had shaken his head.

"Forty-three. Seventeen of them are Rolls. Can you imagine anyone owning seventeen Rolls-Royces?"

Nunni had looked up and said, "No, I can't imagine that." He went back to staring at the photo with a blank expression.

"His friend, Sheik Kamir Rajat, the one who's always playing jokes on him, purchases mostly North American cars. Cadillacs, Lincoln Town Cars, and the new SX-E sports sedans for which you're doing the electronics."

Sal Nunni had squeezed his eyes at the photo. Here it comes; he could feel it coming now.

Marjorie Brooks had continued, "What you and I will find difficult to fathom, Sal, is the intense and utter boredom that comes with an income measured in the tens of millions. To want for nothing is its own kind of hell. You're sensitive. You could understand that."

"So you end up looking for different kinds of diversions," Tidyman said.

Christ, they were taking turns on him: tag-team harassment. Marjorie climbed through the ropes again. "The practical jokes these people play on each other are just unbelievable. Kamir once actually had a shot filmed and edited into an existing Hollywood movie, a little shot it was, a close-up of the actress. You can hear a male voice off-camera say, 'What do you think, Barb?' That line is in the movie. But in the part that Kamir Rajat had redone, the actress, and this is Bellamy Wright I'm talking about, not some little bit player but Bellamy Wright herself, she now answers the question somewhat differently. She now says, 'What do I think, Harv? I think that of all the world's great penises, the greatest of them all hangs between the legs of Rajat Kamir.' That was all; the rest of it was the original movie. But he went to all this trouble to get Bellamy Wright to do her hair and make-up the way she did in the movie, he paid lighting people and sound men and a cameraman; and even though Bellamy Wright didn't charge, just did it for a laugh, he still spent over a hundred thousand American dollars, all for a five-second gag. Then he had to spend a few dollars more to get the man who looks after Omar Kamal's film library to switch it with the original so it would just come out in the middle of a screening one night."

"This is the kind of thing these people do all the time," Tidyman threw in. "I think it's pretty sick myself, but I guess if you've got the money and nobody gets hurt, why not? A chance to spread the money around. Which, by the way, is why we're here."

"To spread money around?" Nunni looked interested.

"Hell of an idea Sheik Kamal's come up with," Tidyman said. "He's pretty sure he'll end up buying four or five of the cars you're doing the integrated circuits for. What he was wondering—I guess what all of us were wondering—was if your circuit there could be specially programmed. Programmed so that with a designated sequence of activity, like tapping the brake three times within a period of say, two and a half seconds, then shutting off the key, well the next time the guy starts it up, the car would just take off into the desert. I think that'd be pretty amusing, I have to admit." Tidyman chuckled to show how amusing.

Sal Nunni swallowed. "You mean the car would take off without the driver controlling it?"

Marjorie's turn again: "Only if you happened to know the combination of activity that made it do that. I mean, the average motorist certainly would never hit the brake three times in two and a half seconds and then shut the key off. It just wouldn't happen. And just the idea of this fat old Sheik taking delivery of these brand-new cars, and every time he gets in he goes roaring off into the sand dunes, I mean it is pretty hilarious when you stop to think about it."

Nunni stopped to think about it. He didn't look as if he thought it was hilarious. He looked as if he was sharing his office with crazy people.

Marjorie pressed on. "It wouldn't be like the sort of thing that was happening to that German car a while back, the Audi. I mean, no one would get hurt or anything."

"Someone taps the brake three times in two and a half seconds?" Nunni was losing his last vestiges of composure.

"You're worried about someone getting hurt, forget it." Tidyman was beginning to lose patience. He couldn't keep this up much longer. "Out on the desert. Nothing to hit. Just a few rich people having some laughs."

"And spreading their riches your way," Marjorie had added.

"But why would anyone want to do a thing like that?" Nunni had asked, his voice a little higher than before.

The woman had stared at him then, eyes blazing. "But why would anyone want to do a thing like that?" she mimicked. Then softer: "I wonder if young Brian's parents will ask that question?"

"Hey, now, hey, come on," Sal Nunni had said.

"I wonder if your wife will."

"Hey, whoa."

"Your three lovely daughters . . . "

Felix Tidyman, still standing, had reached into his jacket pocket. He unfolded a sheet of paper and began to read. "Jennifer Nunni, aged seven, Marta Nunni, aged nine. Both leave for school between eight-twenty and eight-thirty-five a.m., both walk south down Miller's Grove, turn east on—"

"Hey, hey, hey, hey, hey," Sal Nunni said. He wiped his brow with his shirt sleeve.

Tidyman folded up the paper and replaced it in his pocket. They had waited quietly for Nunni to pull himself together. While they waited, they'd been shocked to see the man go into a pantomime, moving his lips to each detail of their proposal, punctuating every point with an elaborate opening of the hands and a nodding of the head. Finally, they had heard: "It's a joke? Turning millions of cars into missiles?"

"Not missiles. It would only work if someone primed them by tapping the brakes three times then shutting off the engine." Tidyman sighed, not wanting to have to keep repeating himself. "An idea for a gag, that's all. If you say no, you say no. I just thought you'd have a little more respect for your family, that's all."

"Jesus, Jesus," Nunni said.

"And little Brian's family," Marjorie said. "Let's not forget Brian."

Nunni sat, head down, reflecting his options. After several moments, he looked up and smiled. It was a smile of relief. "I won't do it. I'm very, very sorry. I just won't."

Felix Tidyman had sighed and reached inside his pocket for the sheet of paper. "Sarah Nunni, aged thirteen—"

"Oh, Jesus, Jesus, Jesus," Sal Nunni wailed.

Nunni had since blocked out that day—and the changes he had made to the microchip circuitry as a result of that conversation. He had buried it all away in the deep folds of memory reserved for life's dark moments. Buried it so far that he didn't make the connection between the Arabian guy in his office and the photo of Sheik Omar Kamal standing between two Rolls-Royces.

Now the Sheik, who had taken his own sweet time letting him know that he was here on a mission of peace, was standing with an arm around Nunni's shoulders. "Mr. Nunni, I cannot begin to tell you how much pleasure our little prank has brought me at Kamir Rajat's expense. I could not resist taking the opportunity to thank you personally."

Nunni found himself stuck for words.

"I shudder to think of the lengths Rajat will go to get even, if and when he discovers what we have done," the Sheik guy was going on. "But the look on his face each time I have someone 'prime' one of his new cars. The mechanics he has flown in from Detroit to find the problems . . . "

Gezmis started to laugh and found himself swept up in the humor of it all. Marjorie Brooks began giggling along.

"So much pleasure. So much pleasure," Gezmis continued. "It seemed only fair to give a little in return. Marjorie, you have the photo?"

Marjorie opened her purse and pulled out a color photo of a Caribbean villa on a lush green hillside.

"What is it?" Nunni asked, less guarded now.

"Yours," Ismail Gezmis told him.

Nunni blinked hard at the photo, looked at the woman, then at Gezmis to see who was pulling his leg. When they both smiled back and nodded, he wondered if the offer might be real.

"It's on the island of Tobago, near Trinidad," Ismail Gezmis told him. "My company has some dealings there tomorrow. If you would care to fly down to L.A., then on to Tobago with one of my employees, we could close the transaction immediately."

"Unfortunately, because the trip is so sudden," Marjorie added, "you won't be able to take Brian." She smiled as she said the name.

Nunni sighed. It was obvious he'd have to go. He'd invent an illness for the office, a business trip for his wife. Still, it wasn't all bad. He'd seen pictures of the Caribbean, the beaches, the sunsets, and the lithe black boys.

CHAPTER 17

Brattleboro, Vermont, August 21.

Noon. Harry was climbing into bed for the first time in thirty hours. He wanted sleep with the same pervasive yearning that someone who has just quit smoking wants a cigarette. Naked under the cover of a pencil-post bed, he resisted for a while.

What was it, a week, a week and a half ago, Harry? You were down in the Florida sunshine, merrily examining dental records. And just a couple of days ago you were merely a man with a mortgage and a daughter and a rose bush. Regular meals, regular bowel movements, regular sleep. Now there are people wanting to blow you up, people wanting to chase your car through vineyards, and people in uniform in two countries who would like to have long talks with you. And in the next room, a beautiful woman who may be assisting in some or all or none of the above.

Not a mean set of accomplishments for a forty-year-old man who works for an insurance company. But look, Harry, we've got to resolve this stuff. You're just not set up to be a fugitive. For one thing, you've still got a quart of milk in a refrigerator in Hanover, New Hampshire, and it's getting past the date on the carton. Your car insurance is due. The ficus in the bathroom needs watering. Your daughter's coming home from school and wanting milk and cookies. Or Pepsi and burritos: Fleur had made the transition to America with a vengeance.

You are investigating a claim. Somebody's spiders have all

died. The owner explains this over and over again. Her spiders are dead. She tells you the names of each spider, but you can't remember them all. Now you are driving through a moonlit field full of wine bottles. The woman with the electric teeth sits beside you and tells you the names of the spiders again. There is a bulldozer behind you. Your car is going slower and slower. The bulldozer is catching up. The bulldozer has bright lights. You get out of the car. You step around the bottles. You raise the hood and discover that someone has stolen the engine. Meanwhile the bulldozer keeps coming and you can not remember the number of your automobile club. In place of the engine, there is a mattress. You are looking at it from above. Now you are falling toward it, and you land with a soft bump. And when you wake up, there's a woman climbing into your bed. "Hi," she says.

Harry woke up. "This is not my wallpaper," he told her.

"No. It's very nice, but it isn't you," Alex said.

Harry looked at the face on the other pillow. "Do you raise spiders?"

"I could try." She gave him a long kiss that tasted a little like toothpaste.

Harry wondered what his own mouth tasted like after the nap. Then he stopped wondering and put his arms around her. That was when he discovered that she was dressed in a bath towel.

"Checking out of hotels quickly does have its drawbacks," she said. Harry moved his hands inside the towel and felt the sudden warmth of her skin. "You were lucky to find something in your size," he said.

"Now that you mention it, it feels a little snug." She pulled the towel open and tossed it on the floor.

Harry continued to stroke softly. Then he began to kiss where he had stroked. "I don't remember you declaring these at the border," he said.

"I hid them up under my shirt."

"I'm afraid that I may have to seize them."

"Oh, yes," Alex said.

*

He awoke to hear her padding back from the bathroom with a wet hand towel. From the way she was moving it from one hand to the other, he guessed that it was hot.

She dropped the towel where he had hoped she would. Yes, it was hot.

"Oh, dear," she said, peeking under the towel, "I seem to have woken up your friend."

Harry was amazed at just how wide awake his friend was.

"This is something I read about in *Popular Mechanics* once."

Harry gave a soft moan as she pulled away the towel and planted a kiss in its place. Then she stopped kissing.

Harry, believing that one good turn deserved another, turned around to face the opposite end of the bed. As soon as he found what he was looking for, Alex let out a series of gentle exclamations.

That was when the intercom phone on the wall began to buzz.

Harry stretched out as far as he dared onto the floor and yanked at the suspended cord. The receiver fell to the floor, and Harry dragged it to his ear.

"Dinner will be in forty-five minutes," Biff said, as Alex brought her teeth playfully together.

"Yee-ow," Harry yelped.

"Yes, I thought you'd be pleased," Biff said. "By the way, Harry, here in Brattleboro we dress for the dining room."

"Eeee-yiiii," Harry squeaked.

"Splendid," said Biff. "Perhaps you would be so kind as to give Miss O'Connor a buzz and let her know? Her intercom number is 12."

"Yes."

"Till then, then."

"Yes."

"Good boy."

Harry turned to her. She was smiling at him. She had just pulled the sheet up to her nose but he could tell that she was smiling.

"Biff says dinner's in forty-five minutes. He says that they dress for the dining room."

"How very Vermont of them."

"And that I should give you a buzz."

"If you think we have time," Alex said.

Twenty-five minutes later she tucked herself back into her towel and opened the door, peering both ways along the hall before she tiptoed out.

Harry showered and dressed and started down the stairs. He was halfway down when Biff's wheelchair skidded to a stop by the newel post at the bottom. "Ah, thought it was you. The whole house creaks, Harry. You can tell where everybody is at any given moment. Very handy, very handy. The house is in harmony with my body. I have creaks too. I can tell where every nerve end is. Currently receiving message from my liver. It needs a little more abuse today. I have some white port, which is execrable but doesn't discolor the product in my outbag. To the port room?"

Biff led the way to a small study, filled with leather chairs and a buffet. A fire crackled in the hearth. "I've arranged the house so that I can tell what I'm drinking by the room I'm in," Biff explained. "Wine in the dining room, scotch in the gun room. Or rather, guns in the scotch room. I'm feeling very refreshed, Harry. Had as nice an afternoon's nap as I can recall. And yourself?"

"Fine nap."

"Good, good. The port's on the buffet. Best pour three: I hear Miss O'Connor coming."

"I don't hear anything."

"I have the advantages of microcircuitry, Harry. Good evening, my dear. Harry has poured you a port, which of course is not nearly good enough for you."

She sipped. "You seem very cheerful, Biff."

"He has the advantages of microcircuitry," Harry explained.

"Even better than that, we have chicken pot pie for our meal," Biff said. "Gisele makes it with little pearl onions, which are infuriating to peel, and wild mushrooms that are very difficult to find, and red wine that is too expensive to use for cooking. It's magnificent, and she's thoroughly irked, and I have a plan."

"A plan?" Harry said.

"It's a very nice one too, Harry. It leaves me with the girl, which is just the kind of story I like. Aha! The dinner bell. No shop talk at the table, now."

Alex watched Harry eat as Biff talked: "Harry used to be quite involved with my daughter. Toffee pulls, bobsledding, charades. You know what youth gets up to. Met at university, where I was pretending to teach and Harry was pretending to learn. That was before I sent him away to raise swine for the German border guards. I saved him, you know. Lucille's puppy paws turned into tiger claws and Harry went on to better things. There was a time when he ran a temporary staffing service for the terrorist industry, and a time when he had a very interesting photographic business: very *cinema vérité* and highly regarded in some circles, though not without its critics. Lucille, who is, or was, my daughter, ran off and married a man made entirely of polyvinylchloride, and I get Christmas cards from them, usually decorated with imitation Wyeth. Can you imagine Harry sending out Wyeth-type holiday greetings? Can you imagine Harry sending out greetings at all?"

"Temporary staffing service for the terrorist industry?" Alex remembered how quickly Harry had reacted to the sound of the bomb.

"Actually, I misphrased it," Biff said. "It was a staffing service for people who were very temporarily terrorists. Harry ran any number of those kinds of businesses. A news service. An electronics company. Can't keep a job. Always picking on the wrong Lebanese." Biff lifted the skirt of the tablecloth to check his bag. "Dessert? More wine? If you want scotch, we'll have to go to the gun room. There are filberts there, too. Freshly roasted."

There was only one gun in the gun room: a small .22-calibre mounted on green baize in a mahogany frame. The blaze in the tiled fireplace smelled of apples. On a pie-crust table sat a slab of pale cheddar and a bowl of filberts next to a basket of grapes. "They're not seedless," Biff said. "Can't stand seedless grapes. Nothing to spit into the fire, and if you can't spit into the fire, it's not really your own house."

"So what's the plan, Biff?" Harry asked.

"So where's the scotch, Harry?"

Harry poured one single malt and handed it to Biff. Biff took the glass and swirled it slowly at eye level. "Low in volatile oils." He looked Harry in the eye. "Harry, the plan is not to plan."

Harry's expression didn't change, but Alex's did. She had been expecting something more.

"You've been doing exactly the right thing by instinct, Harry. Logic wouldn't have worked. Consider the opposition—whoever they are. If you'd reacted as a professional, reacted as you had been trained to do, I truly believe they would have mounted a superior force against you. However, suspecting you of being a bungling amateur, they saw fit to send rather inferior people. The 'set a thief to catch a thief' idea. Your Jacamar Corporation has done everything else extremely professionally." Biff paused and swirled his whiskey again.

"Now of course they must suspect one of two things. The first is that they were simply unlucky in not getting the bomb to the right place at the right time. Or they may suspect that they are dealing with someone professional enough to change rooms and escape. Frankly, I doubt that, but in either case the outcome is the same. They will come looking for you with better people. As with any bureaucracy—and the scope of their operation convinces me that it is large enough to have its own bureaucracy—one feels compelled to make good on something one has promised one's superiors. They will use better people next time."

Harry poured a whiskey for himself. He looked at Alex, who shook her head.

Biff went on: "My opinion is that we have a terrorist group here, one that is very well run, very violent, and very much in need of money. Those facts do not narrow down the field substantially. Terrorist groups have their mitts extended for money as often as Lucille. Last time, I recall it was absolutely necessary for her to have a cedar gazebo, but she had run plastic-man out of funds that month."

Harry could see that Biff was doing the whole act for Alex's benefit.

"Similarly, the IRA constantly needs money because we Americans have cut off most of the funds that they used to send over with vacationing New York City policemen. That romance is very much over. The IRA now gets a good part of its cash by running taxicabs. They ensure a growing market for their taxis by bombing the Belfast bus fleet. They deal in slightly gentler ways with competitive cabbies. They also have opened some nightclubs. Lord knows what they'll do next: perhaps a theme park."

"IRA World," Harry suggested.

"A possibility," Biff agreed. "But rest assured, my young bucko, they will do something next, because guns and explosives cost money, and so do safe houses and lawyers."

"And undertakers," Alex chipped in.

"It's the same elsewhere," Biff went on. "Colombian guerillas finance their continuing revolution with cocaine. The PLO is in the hashish trade, and also owns shoe factories and airlines. They need the money for arms and for those wretched refugee camps. Perhaps they've decided America is an untapped market for their business style. Or the whole thing could be an Iraqi initiative using the PLO. The leader of Iraq is a little short of money and has been quoted as saying he is very interested in visiting his country's problems upon our country."

Harry smiled. "You said you were napping this afternoon. What were you really up to?"

"I've been on the phone here and there to some of the old farts. I've managed to learn a little. Evidently, the bomb damage to the former bellhop was considerable. Although he was outside your door, the force of the blast was sufficient to drive the doorknob into his temple. I hate people who listen at doors, don't you? As to the bombers, we know they were not guests. Which means we don't know whether they were Irish, Basque,

Armenian, Iranian, Tamil, Sikh, Turk, Mohawks, Quebecois, or whatever."

"Nor if they were the same ones who were chasing us in the stationwagon," Alex said.

"Which brings up your other problem, Harry. The problem of your being a wanted man, an international criminal. During my communications, I learned that the Ontario Provincial Police are dusting much of the Niagara peninsula for your smudgy little fingerprints. The FBI could also regard you as terrorist-connected, and anything terrorist-connected gets their noses sniffing. They are required to keep people with bombs out of the country, and although they're very tight-lipped, they must know by now that you are back inside the country. I had Gisele move your car."

"Thank you," Harry said.

"Of course, you could consider giving yourself up," Biff suggested. "Just walk in and say you're sorry. We've seen Germany let terrorists go. And I understand that France is not all that anxious to arrest terrorists, because arresting them prompts other terrorists to leave explosive devices in department stores. When I talk to the old farts, I find they are becoming increasingly frustrated by what their political masters tell them they can and cannot do with terrorists. They say that the press is being quietly urged not to keep bringing up the subject of terrorism, in the hope that, deprived of the sunlight of the media, it will wither away."

"Worth a try," Harry said, but he looked dubious.

"Yes. And it may explain why we hear so little news of domestic terrorism here in the home of the brave and the land of the couch potato."

"The thought has crossed my mind a time or two," Alex said.

Biff studied her carefully. "Well, we've never really been given the whole story on such matters." He thought for a moment. "Suppose a police department in, say, San Diego, were to find, oh, say, an oil refinery bombed, with little pieces of time clock scattered hither and yon. Would the San Diego police force announce this as a terrorist bombing or as a case of human error? And if there is a telephone call to a newspaper or a television station, claiming that the deed was done by the People's Front for the Liberation of This Week's Fashionable Cause, what would you wager that the police describe that call as the work of a crank? Would you wager a dollar? Ten thousand?"

"I'd put some of my money on it," Harry said. "No city government wants to frighten the public or scare away investors."

Biff clapped his hands together, a proud teacher witnessing a breakthrough in class. "Nor do they want to see the terrorists get the kind of publicity that glorifies their cause and draws other loonies out of the woodwork. No, they want to demonstrate to the People's Front of Whatever that screwing around in their city doesn't garner much attention or reward."

"So where does all this take us?" Harry wondered.

"I honestly don't know," Biff said. "Your natural reaction—to flee—was likely correct. I don't know. As I say, I was talking to the old farts, not the new farts. Some of the things the new farts do are quite insane. Selling arms to one place where they're not supposed to be selling arms to raise money to buy arms for another place where they're not supposed to be sending arms, for example." Biff shook his head sadly.

"So what do we do?" Alex asked with an edge of impatience in her voice.

"So you don't want to go in and see the authorities? The final argument for that attitude is that it isn't necessary, and if something is not necessary to do, it is probably necessary not to do it."

"Yes," Harry said.

"I still think the plan is not to plan. I think the plan is to go to bed and sleep on it. Something will turn up. My tentacles are extended, my ears perked, my various wires plugged in. Something will turn up."

CHAPTER 18

Los Angeles, California, August 21.

The stretch Continental pulled to a stop, and Alistair Duffy stepped out of the back seat. Reading from the instructions he had written on an index card, Duffy entered the park and strode directly toward the tennis courts. Just before he reached the first one, Ismail Gezmis fell into step beside him.

"Mr. Duffy?"

Duffy kept walking, a believer in taking command by setting the pace. This wasn't the guy who had called him at the hotel. This guy was a foreigner; he hadn't expected that. "I'm Duffy," he snapped, not looking up or changing pace. On the path ahead, a man who looked to be in his early thirties walked hand-in-hand with a boy and a girl, neither of whom came up to his waist. The boy wore jeans with deep cuffs and was running his free hand along the bamboo rails that lined the path.

"Ah, the Saturday father," Gezmis observed. "One of the sadder traditions of today's America. Wouldn't you agree, Mr. Duffy?"

Al Duffy walked on, seething in silence. What was going on here? Foreigner comes over, shakes down the president of one of the country's most respected restaurant chains, then buggers around talking sociology.

"A suffering child is a pitiful sight in any part of the world," Gezmis went on. "I am from Palestine. I know whereof I speak."

Duffy glared at the pathway. *Whereof*? What the hell kind of word was *whereof*? Where did these people learn their English?

"A child's suffering in America is different, I suppose. The broken home. The weekly visit with a father who squeezes in the time for a walk through the park on Saturday morning. Then cheeseburgers at one of your beloved restaurants. Then back to their mother's to spend the rest of the week wondering what they did to deserve it all. Notwithstanding your financial interest in the system, I put it to you, Mr. Duffy, it is sad."

Notwithstanding? Duffy slowed. "Look, you went to a lot of trouble to get me here. And you only got me here because you seemed to know a hell of a lot about my plans."

"I also know that Flight 603 is not likely to get to Trinidad," Gezmis said.

Al Duffy stopped walking. Thirteen of his executives were booked on Flight 603 for the company's annual Performance Club Brain Stormer. He put his hands on his waist and faced Ismail Gezmis eye to eye. "What are you saying?"

"I'm saying that your people should make alternative arrangements."

Duffy shook his head. "No, you people wouldn't try that kind of shit here. C'mon, now. Seriously."

"You may choose to send your people, anyway. I have no way of knowing what benefits that might entail in terms of corporate life-insurance policies."

Duffy reached out with both hands and grabbed Gezmis's lapels and started shaking. "You miserable sonofabitch. Don't you *ever* judge me by your own sick standards."

Gezmis's punch to the stomach was so quick that Duffy doubled over before he felt the pain.

The little girl, watching from the far side of the pond, tugged on her father's shirt. Now the three of them were staring at the two men who seemed to be scuffling.

Gezmis grabbed Duffy's shirt front and tie in his hand just below the collar and pulled him upright. "People have been underestimating our resolve for years, Mr. Duffy. It disappoints me to find you among them."

Duffy, gasping for breath, noticed the Saturday father and his children taking short, cautious steps toward them. He tried to regain his composure, even put a smile on as he straightened up.

Gezmis relaxed his grip just as the family reached their side of the pond—three puzzled faces keeping their distance. Gezmis bent his hand and flapped a friendly greeting.

Duffy tried to compose himself, straightening his tie and trying to wipe the wrinkles out of his shirt. "What precisely do you want from me?"

Gezmis studied the family coming toward them: two children sucking thumbs; a part-time father not sure if he should mind his own business or run off and look for a cop. Gezmis guessed he would choose not to get involved. Americans were like that. To Duffy he said, "You represent American business. Some of us feel that, so long as America is causing people to fight and to die, their business ought to share the cost."

Duffy expressed astonishment with hands on hips. "I run a restaurant chain, for Christ's sake. What do I know about fighting? What do I know about dying?"

Gezmis turned to face him and cracked his knuckles just inches from Duffy's face. "Harvey Firestone was just a man who made tires. When the vote to partition my country was taken in the United Nations in 1948, the small nation of Liberia was prepared to vote against it. Harvey Firestone, tiremaker, personally told Mr. William Tubman, president of Liberia, that unless Liberia changed its mind, Firestone would not be developing its rubber acreage in Liberia. Firestone tires never sold well where I come from, Mr. Duffy."

Duffy threw his hands out to the sides. "I'm just trying to understand what you want. Honestly, I'm really trying. But, so help me God, I don't have the faintest idea what's going on here."

Gezmis's face lit up in a smile. "Quite simple. Our group believes it can provide you with certain services. As evidence of that, we have just saved the lives of thirteen of your key employees. Call it a demonstration of our ability to deliver a continuing and valuable service. The cost of this service is thirty-seven million dollars."

"You're crazy."

"A year," Ismail Gezmis added.

"Jesus Christ Almighty."

The Saturday father, having decided that he'd witnessed nothing more than the over-exuberant greeting of lodge brothers, was leading his children away.

"What do you think?" Duffy asked. "Do you think I'm going to walk out of the park, call up my board and say, 'Guess what, ladies and gentlemen: our company has been asked to allocate thirty-seven million dollars a year to an outfit that wants to provide us with certain unspecified services'?"

Gezmis studied him with mild amusement. "Unspecified? Mr. Duffy. I have saved the lives of thirteen of your finest employees. How dare you call that unspecified?"

"And that's another thing. You've as good as told me that you're going to blow up a commercial aircraft. With Americans on it. What am I supposed to do? Quietly pull my people off the flight and keep quiet about it?"

Gezmis seemed shocked by the question. "That information was given to you in confidence. If we find that we are not able to trust you, we may be unable to supply you with more confidential information. And we may have to take further action."

They started walking again.

"What are you suggesting, you might do a number on one of my restaurants?" Duffy suggested, a few steps later.

Gezmis feigned an expression of disbelief. "One? You have more than nine thousand. Why on earth would we settle for one?"

Duffy winced and shook his head.

"What would it take to get through to you, Mr. Duffy? An attack on three dozen restaurants in different communities, all on the same day? Wouldn't that be extraordinary? People would then know that you were under attack by a serious organization. And I can't imagine anything more detrimental to your business than people knowing that. Can you?"

"You couldn't do that," Duffy said, with no conviction.

"Your principal vulnerability as I see it is that you have made your money by exploiting students as part-time workers."

Duffy walked on in silence.

"Students. You will remember that it was students who took over the American embassy in Iran."

"Not our kids. That's not the kind of kid we—"

"Nevertheless, I suggest that you are extremely vulnerable, simply because of your size and your inability to be totally certain of the students you trust with your good name."

Duffy coughed and tried to get his form back. Once, he had been able to silence the spokesman for 150 angry southeastern franchisees with a perfectly-delivered, "Bruce, I think you ought to go back and re-think your position." He tried now to summon that timbre to his voice. "Listen, I'm not denying for a minute that your people, or any other gang of, ah"—groping for the word—"fanatics could do our company some temporary damage."

"We could destroy you in less than a month," Gezmis said quietly.

"You could do us some damage. At considerable risk to your own—"

"The real pleasure in working with fanatics, as you term them," Gezmis interrupted, "is that personal risk is rarely a factor."

Duffy took deep breaths, now content just to keep his voice from cracking. Finally, "But even assuming a worst-situation scenario, thirty-seven million dollars a year, I mean . . . " He shook his head to demonstrate that the sum was out of the question.

Gezmis gave him a look of understanding. "Everywhere I go in the United States I keep seeing that commercial with the dog. You know, the one where the children pester their father for money so that they can go to your restaurant and their spaniel—"

"Terrier," Duffy corrected.

"Spaniel, terrier, whatever—the dog follows the children to your restaurant, where of course it is not allowed inside. I remember vividly the shot of the children wolfing down french fries while the dog is left outside in obvious hunger. Coming from Palestine, one relates to hunger, even a dog's. When the children finally leave the restaurant, it looks as if the dog has been forgotten; but in the last five seconds of the commercial one little girl pulls out a paper napkin and gives the pet a little something she has saved from her meal. You must remember the one I mean?"

Duffy said he did.

"Well, our people have done some research, which reveals that your company spends approximately three hundred million dollars a year on advertising."

"Two seventy-five," Duffy corrected.

"And let's say you run, what, ten, twenty commercials like that a year? And that one with the spaniel has been around for several years now. My colleagues and I, doing rough calculations believe that your company could have spent thirty-seven million dollars showing just that one commercial alone."

Duffy started to speak, then held it back.

"You may think of us as barbarians, Mr. Duffy. But we have children who have been eating dogs so they can stay alive. And here you are spending thirty-seven million dollars to put dogs in commercials."

CHAPTER 19

Aboard Flight 603, August 22.

Saddam was tired. It had been three in the morning when Tidyman had finally talked their way out of the jam at Lewiston. The customs people had taken the car apart, ripped linings out of suitcases and strip searched them all, despite Tidyman's story about a "practical joke" and "student hazing." Then there'd been the drive to Buffalo and the long flight to the coast. He'd only had an hour to pack after Gezmis had told him he had to be on this flight. But being tired wasn't going to get in his way.

As soon as the meal trays were cleared away, he opened his third little bottle of cognac, eased the seat back, and figured out his chances.

The bad news was that the two were sisters. In Saddam's experience with sisters, the only way you got to one was to have a friend along for the other. The only person he knew on the plane was the man he'd been told to accompany, Sal Nunni, and Saddam guessed that it would take two young brothers to get a rise out of him.

The good news was that God in His infinite wisdom had left the seats across the aisle from them empty. On his way back from the can, Saddam had slipped into the aisle seat and started a conversation with Jo-Anne.

All through the extravagant dinner he'd been stringing her along about his villa in Tobago, right on the sea near Rox-

154

borough. "I should show you my agoutis," Saddam had suggested, just loud enough to draw a look from the sister over in the window seat as if she thought he was suggesting something dirty. Then, when Jo-Anne asked what agoutis were, he said they were a little short-eared rabbit type of animal, cute as hell. They had all kinds of them around his villa; she should come up and see them.

Jesus, what was he doing making up this shit? If he really wanted to impress her he should tell her about the project he'd been on before he drew this escort junket. But there was just so much you could tell a stranger on a plane, even one you're trying to haul into your private Mile-High Club. And Mr. Gezmis had warned him about talking.

For a while there, he thought Mr. Gezmis might have been mad at him for the misunderstanding he'd had with Marjorie Brooks. But instead of giving him hell, Gezmis had given him this plum of a job, taking Sal Nunni to Trinidad. He had even bought him a present: a diver's watch, and told him to take a few days off while he was down there.

Saddam had been surprised at that. But then, when he thought it over, he had to agree that he'd been working hard. Now he was working hard on Jo-Anne. He'd made a good start, telling her about his life in a country that he'd never been to, except by reading *Fodor's Guide to the Caribbean*.

"Sounds like we'll have some fun," she said. Abdel found that encouraging, until he thought about it a little more and wondered if she'd been referring to her sister in that "we." After dinner he bought them both cognacs, and stuffed a few extras into the seat pocket.

That proved to be a good move. Even the suspicious-looking sister by the window thanked him, more or less, with a reluctant little tilt of the crystal that Super Platinum served its French wines in.

There was something in her look, he decided, a little uppityness or something, that made him wish for a minute that she was the one he was trying to sign up for Mile-High membership. See if he couldn't show her a thing or two while the rest of the plane snoozed off and the flight attendants all sat at the back, complaining to each other.

Suddenly, both girls excused themselves and took their carry-on bags with them to the toilets. They came back wearing bright, tiny sundresses, all giggles and secrets.

"Excuse me," he whispered across the aisle as soon as it looked as if the uppity one by the window was dozing off. "Is your sister asleep?"

Jo-Anne glanced to her left, then gave him a smile, a little one with just a hint of mischief. "Looks like."

"I was going to write out a list of the places you should see while you are in my country." That was good. Sound sincere, whatever it took. Just get her over here under the blanket.

"That would be nice." The "nice" came out a little slurred. Thank you, cognac.

Saddam stretched his neck out into the aisle, making a big production out of looking back down the plane. "It seems as if a lot of people are sleeping. Perhaps you could come and sit beside me so we can speak more quietly." He said the last part in a whisper, in case she missed the point.

Now it was her turn to look over her shoulder: another quick peek at her sister. "I guess I could. For a while."

Scrunching in his legs to let her squeeze past, Saddam could smell the cologne or bath soap or whatever she'd splashed on herself back in the can. "Here, let me swing the arm up so you can get your feet up there, be a little more comfortable. That's it. Here, put the blanket up over you, keep nice and warm."

He was a little surprised when she started taking charge. First there was a long, cognac-flavored wet kiss and then she was guiding his hand up under her tiny dress and suddenly her panties were on the floor next to her shoes. By the time he realized how it would work, she had his zipper undone and was straddling him on the middle seat, not caring a whole lot about the blanket that had tumbled on top of the panties and sandals.

Abdel Saddam leaned back with a mystified smile, his hands on her pumping hips like someone trying to steer a machine that had taken off on its own. Dreamily, he flopped his head to one side and was startled to see her sister wide awake and taking in the show, grinning away like an Oldsmobile hubcap.

What the hell was she up to now? He tried to lean forward to see, but the way Jo-Anne was rocking up and down, it was difficult to move. The sister was holding up her hand: two fingers in the shape of an upside down V; now a finger across to make it an "A". A for Abdel?

Preoccupied by the turbulence on his lap, it took a while for him to get the point. She was scoring his performance. Old Abdel got an A. There's another finger, what's that, a 1? Sure, she thinks old Abdel's an A1 guy. Well, all right!

But by the time that message clicked in, she was holding up more fingers to shape the last part of the message. This time it looked like a capital D.

First an A1, now a "D?" What was that supposed to mean? Sure, he wasn't doing a whole lot to help old Jo-Anne along here, but he was in an airplane seat, for Christ's sake. No, not even that uppity bitch would have dropped him to a "D" for performance. What's she doing now, wiggling her finger like an S. A-1-D-S? A-I-D-S?

The news had just come crashing home to Abdel Saddam when the transmitter that Ismail Gezmis had implanted inside the brand-new diver's watch gave a barely audible click. Three rows ahead, inside the flotation cushion beneath an aisle seat, a tiny receiver imbedded in a half-pound bar of Czechoslovakian-made explosive triggered a spark from two lithium wafer batteries.

The hole that was torn by the explosion through the side of the aircraft sucked out pillows and newspapers and three nearby passengers who had not been wearing their seat belts. The first was a small boy, who went through like a bullet. The second was a chubby banker from Port of Spain. His fat body filled the hole for almost two seconds, stopping the rushing noise of the wind before he was extruded with a pop at twenty-one thousand feet. The third one sucked out was Jo-Anne.

Moments later, the rest of the aircraft dropped into the sea.

CHAPTER 20

Brattleboro, Vermont, August 23.

Gisele was always glad to see Harry. As Biff's political history student, he had been the young man who walked into chairs and newel posts and ate enormous amounts of anything she served. She had once seen him put away three servings of her mashed potatoes while he argued with Biff about whether diplomacy had ever really been anything but a continuation of war by other means. Harry had eaten five farmers' sausages that night and three pieces of her strawberry and apple pie. Later, when they got down to Theodore Roosevelt, they had eaten popcorn. Yet when he left that night, his clothes hung loose. The food had merely fueled the fervor of his arguments.

Gisele had gone with Biff to visit Harry in his Paris days. She remembered watching Harry eat there too, seeing him discuss the trout with the chef, asking where the fish had been caught, and whether the flesh would be firm enough from that particular stream. He had questioned the provenance of the peas, the genealogy of the berries, and the history of the champagne. The chef had enjoyed that discussion and, while they ate, Biff had enjoyed discussing Harry's premise that the terrorist groups of the world should all band together. "The increase in size would cause them to choke on their own bureaucracy," Harry had claimed. He had been earnest then, even when proposing the creation of an organizational guide for urban guerillas. The guide would insist that everything be done by committees.

"Everything, Biff, everything. If they wanted crayons for their peace march signs, the book would tell them to form a committee and work out a consensus on which brand to buy. We'd tell students that that's how it was done on the Long March, and in front of the Winter Palace, and in the Cuban mountains. We could sell the kit in campus bookstores around the world. And all these students would start to believe that before you struck a blow for freedom you'd have to have an operational control system. If we made a convincing enough case, we could get them all down to the speed of the Indian government."

There was still no fat on Harry then; he was just a little thicker, more strongly boned than he had been as a student. But now, as he stood against the stone wall in Biff's New Hampshire garden, she wasn't quite sure how he looked. She peered into the viewfinder. Under the eyes, he seemed almost bruised. There were laugh lines—or were they furrows? His flesh was looser on his face. It had been stretched by strain and had lost some of the elasticity it needed to pull itself back tight on the skull. Too much like Biff.

The camera was a twin-lens reflex, the kind used for passport pictures. She didn't think there would be enough time to prepare a passport before he left, but she would be ready for any documents he might need in the future. This time it would probably have to be a birth certificate from Canada. Easy to produce, needed no picture, and it would get him into St. Lucia. Gisele nodded dismissal at Harry and went off to check her inventories of miscellaneous documents.

"St. Lucia?" Harry had said, when Biff dropped the news in the gun room.

"Discovered by Columbus, as all those islands were. I forget whether it is a leeward or a windward island. I have tried to keep myself ignorant of sailors' jargon, which keeps me from having to talk to people in blazers and deck shoes. It's about halfway between Cuba and Venezuela, and appears on my map to be the size of a smallish ladybug, in contrast to Puerto Rico which appears to be about the size of a largish locust."

"Oh."

"Evidently, there is a body of St. Lucian water known as Rodney Bay, named after an Admiral Rodney. He was an Englishman who, if memory serves, won several key battles against the French in the Caribbean."

"Yes." Harry wouldn't be baited. He wouldn't ask. Biff would have to tell him.

"Last night an aircraft bound for Trinidad from Los Angeles fell into the sea near Rodney Bay. The final communication from the pilot suggested that there had been an explosion in the passenger compartment. All aboard are presumed lost."

"Yes."

"I had previously put a little tickler in my terminal, a stern command to wake me if it found in any of my regularly frequented databases a whisper of the name Abdel Saddam. This morning the device was tapping my shoulder to tell me that it had indeed located the fellow. The name appeared on a certain passenger list."

"Yes."

"Ah, fuck it, Harry, you're no fun. You used to be fun. Is it being a hunted man that's giving you that hunted look?"

"Yes."

"Shall we play a little game in which we guess what passenger list Mr. Saddam was on?"

"He was on the passenger list of the plane that crashed near Rodney Bay," Harry guessed.

"His name was listed as being on that very flight. We won't know if he was actually on it till they sift through the wreckage. If it isn't in waters too deep for that. If the great sharks don't gnaw the passengers like so many crustless sandwiches at a church tea. So. Gisele will soon have your identification for you. Since we may presume that the authorities are looking for you at all of the New England airports, I have arranged for a friendly local pilot to whisk you to Chicago. There is a direct flight from Chicago to St. Lucia. You can mess about down there and find out what there is to be found out. You will also be hidden from the various bands of men who seem anxious to accomplish your destruction or incarceration. Gisele is arranging tickets now. First class. You'll be safe in first class, Harry. No one would think to look for you up there."

"No."

"Harry?"

"I'm not going to go, Biff. I'm through with this. I just can't keep going all over the place chasing people when I don't know who's playing on the other side. I mean, this could go on forever. I want to go home. I want to give my daughter milk and cookies. I want my own fridge. I want to have my own medicine cabinet. I want my own chair and toaster and toilet seat."

"Harry, you're getting crotchety."

"And my own brand of mayonnaise on my own peanut-butter sandwiches."

"So you're going to go to the authorities and 'fess up? Make a clean breast of it? Suffer the consequences, head held high?"

"Yes. I'll start with Penzler. Find out what he knows. Maybe something more has happened at Kohl's."

"Not according to my databases."

"The police will have been to see him. He'll know what their attitude is, if they think I've done it or if they've written me up as just a missing witness."

Biff sighed. "You're turning into a dreadful bore, Harry. Next, you'll be taking up golf and bragging how you almost birdied the twelfth. It would be best if you made your call to Mr. Penzler from your car phone. Less traceable—if anyone cares."

It took, on average, four separate phone calls to get through to Bill Penzler. This time it took just one, and Harry barely had time to say hello before Penzler launched into a gush of words delivered with the breathless enthusiasm of a sports announcer. "Harry, Harry, good to hear from you. Okay, I think we've got things under control here. I've had about three visits from three different kinds of cops. They're all the same. They don't really want to know. I pointed out to them that you had no motive for blowing up a Canadian bellboy. They thought you might be under contract to Israel. One set of cops knew about your previous job and their version of the truth is that you certainly would know how to blow somebody up if you had to. I told them you were dependable, straight, and that the people who fired you had fired you forever. I didn't tell them about how you're always ending up in places where you're not supposed to be, or screwing around with jobs that are supposed to be over. I pointed out your record of service to the country, but they argued that a bomb blew up in your room and that you had disappeared. I told them they were taking a very simplistic view of things."

"I appreciate that, Bill," Harry said quietly.

"But we've got it all organized here, Harry. I don't want this company to get the sort of reputation it would get if they pin this thing on you. We've got a lot of old money invested in this place and old money is nervous money. So I've signed on Hartisson and Gregg for the legal stuff. You remember Rambler Hartisson, got the Southside Strangler off last year? He's standing by, and he's been in touch with a legal firm in Canada. Good man, Hartisson, a Baptist."

"Yes, well—"

"What I want you to do is get yourself here, Harry. But first phone Hartisson direct. What I'll do is phone Hartisson now and tell him you'll be calling and to keep himself available. Right? Where should I say you'll be phoning from?"

"Right," Harry said, and hung up gently.

"And what did Mr. Penzler have to say?" Biff asked.

"He was making very caring, loving statements. Hiring me lawyers. Asking after my health. Begging me to come home."

"How nice."

"It makes me nervous. He never gave a fuck before."

"Isn't it wonderful to be wanted?"

"Last week he would have fired me."

"Good judgment prevails."

"Why's he changing?"

"Perhaps he wants something from you, Harry?"

"What?"

"Your location?"

"Why?"

"Perhaps he's feeding it to the bad guys."

"Why doesn't he just fire me and take me off the job?"

"Perhaps he knows you don't stay fired. Perhaps he thinks that it's better for you to be turning in occasional reports than to be fired and not turning in reports at all. This way he can keep track of you." Biff stuck his thumb into his beer, brought it out and sucked it.

"If they're keeping track of me like that, I must be important. I'd rather not be important because I'd rather go home and sit on my own toilet seat. And I wish I knew why I was important. I can't see it, really. Do you think Penzler might want to know where I am so he could tell the Kohls?"

Biff removed the thumb from his mouth. "It's all very interesting, isn't it? Actually, there's a way to find out more about the resources of all these people who are following you about."

"How?"

"Go to St. Lucia. Alone."

"Then?"

"We'll see if anyone follows you."

"And what about Alex?"

"There are reasons to think carefully about Alex, as well as Penzler. After all, she was at Kohl's; trouble came to Kohl's. She was in the hotel; trouble came to the hotel. She is here now—"

"I brought her here, Biff. For all we know, they could have been after her, not me. They could have just assumed she would be in my room—"

"You flatter yourself, Harry—"

"But she'll be safe, here. If she's the target, I don't want her going back to Kohl's."

"She's welcome to stay," Biff said. "And if you go to St. Lucia alone, without telling her where you're going, and trouble does not follow you, then that will tell us something else, won't it?"

"I leave her here?"

"For a while. I'll chat with her."

Harry had seen Biff chat with people. Trying to keep track of those conversations was like watching one mosquito in a cloud of mosquitoes. A subject would come up, be dropped for an hour, come up again, be transmuted into something else while a new topic was raised, dropped, and transmuted. There would be humor in the conversation, whimsy, jokes, quoted poetry, spurious logic coldly applied, real logic hidden, continuous cross-referencing. It was a shell game, three-card monte, therapy, and interrogation all in one.

"And then?" Harry persisted.

"Then I will make a judgment," Biff promised. "I may even send her down to join you."

"Or?"

"I may not. Gisele is putting the finishing touches on your Canadian birth certificate. She's found you some shoes: a pair of mine. Hardly used. Really for display purposes only. Our local pilot is waiting and Gisele will drive you to him. Finish your beer."

"I have to call Fleur."

"I've called Fleur. She has a place to stay: the Bagnols. You know them? She has forged your signature on the car insurance cheque. She asked my opinion on red camisoles. Nothing to worry about."

To Harry, sitting in the front seat of the small plane felt like being back in his MG-TD. It was a Mooney 20, and everything was squeezed together, there for a purpose. The plane seemed solid enough until the pilot yelled over the engine that a lot of it was built out of plywood. "Just like you use for pingpong tables or doghouses. Better stuff than that, really. Close-grained laminated spruce."

The pilot's hands seemed everywhere at once: on the throttle that stuck out of the dashboard—did they call it a dashboard?—on the wheel, on a little knob here, on the radio there, on a lever that pulled up the undercarriage. "It's got the 180-horse Lycoming instead of the 150. That gives us a max of 190 but we'll cruise at 160 unless we pick up some wind."

The aircraft was climbing. Harry looked out the window; it seemed alarmingly thin. A small wooden airplane, going three miles a minute? He hoped there was no wind.

"You got a map there?" the pilot yelled. "Should be on the floor there somewhere." Harry looked under his feet and found a small book of maps. "Look up Chicago," the pilot shouted.

A small wooden airplane going three miles a minute and the pilot didn't know where to find Chicago?

Four hours later they found it just about where Carl Sandburg had left it.

During those four hours, Biff had his chat with Alex. The discussion was fueled by champagne. "I have to tell you first of all, my sweet, that I am worried about your physical and mental condition. You've been bombed and you've been chased and, even worse, you have been overlong in Harry's company. Acting as your doctor, I have telephoned your company. I have informed Mr. Kohl senior that you will be taking a week off, possibly longer."

She started to say something but he shushed her.

"Really, you do need a mental health week. Besides, I find the idea of your company very fetching. Here we are left alone together in the house without our dear Harry."

"Where is Harry?"

"I suggest we seek consolation in champagne. In my youth, which was a period of time somewhere between the Neolithic and three years ago, champagne was considered an aphrodisiac. Much the same way people think of vitamin E these days, but of course vitamins don't tickle your nose. I would be pleased to send for vitamin E and tickle your nose manually, if you wish. You might prefer manual stimulation. Blink your left eye for the champagne, your right eye for manual stimulation."

She blinked her left eye. Biff poured.

"Now you must tell me everything about yourself, my witch. How's Harry in the sack?"

She hiccupped.

"Thought so. Taught the boy everything he knows, of course. Just wanted to make sure he remembered. Now, why would a nice girl like you go into the beer business instead of getting married? Dislike of ruffly aprons? Can't clean a stove? More champagne?"

Later, the questions became harder. The escalation was imperceptible.

"What did you think of Ronald Reagan, really?"

A second bottle of champagne. Tattinger. Alex noticed that unless she focused carefully there were now two Biffs. One was enough. What was he asking now?

"What sort of clubs did you join at university? I myself was in a sort of thing where we studied William Carlos Williams, but I'd guess that would be very out of place these days. What clubs were you in? Sewing? Birdwatching?"

She told him, and then told him more. About her father. About her roommate, who was the only person in the entire dormitory to keep things neat, and then about the man she had met and almost married. About her braces.

Alex stuck her tongue in the champagne and felt the bubbles. "But about clubs, I never liked clubs. Clubs are all full of people who join clubs. I like people who do things, you know? I like Harry. Harry does things. Did Harry ever join clubs?"

"Just the one, just the once."

She listened to the champagne, her ear next to the glass like a maid at a keyhole.

"Why isn't Harry still working at his old job?"

"Harry killed the wrong Lebanese. In revenge for the wrong Arabs killing the wrong woman."

"Which woman?"

"His wife."

"Oh." Slowly she started to cry. She didn't snuffle or sob: it was just tears rolling down her face.

"You ought to be careful with Harry, my dear. He keeps old letters in his bedside table. He saves theater stubs. Has the carnation from his last prom pressed in his diary. He's only ever known about four women in his life. The world's biggest boy, really. He could grow awfully dependent and if you don't want that, you'd better be careful."

"You have more champagne?"

"Certainly. I have champagne to launch a thousand ships. Did I ask you how Harry was in the sack?"

"I like Harry. He has a sweet potato face. What have we done with Harry?"

CHAPTER 21

Detroit, Michigan, August 23.

Felix Tidyman pulled into the visitors' parking lot and found a space beside a three-ton truck with colored stars and "Film by Flynn" painted on the side. As he walked past the truck, a man was yelling through the back doors, "He wants more light. Wants the president 'absolutely glowing'. Glowing, my ass. We're gonna have to go with the H.M.I.s."

"Ah, shit," a voice inside the truck came back. "These ballasts weigh a ton. How many's he want?"

"He says four. Wants a lot of light. I'd take five, save another trip. You should see the size of Petrelli's office. Must land his fucking Lear Jet on the desk."

"We're gonna need the cart, then. Better give me a hand in here."

Tidyman pushed through the glass doors of the car manufacturer's main entrance. Inside, a uniformed guard stood with his hands behind his back, looking bored. With a TV commercial production on the premises, there were all kinds of people coming and going, too many for the guard to take an interest in. Tidyman guessed this would make things easier than he'd thought.

He turned back to the two men who were struggling to push their equipment through the doors. "How we doin', guys? Usin' the H.M.I.s today, huh? Must be one hell of an office." Tidyman threw his briefcase up on the cart and took charge. "Here, you get the far door, you get this one, I'll hold the lights and pull you in."

The two men had done enough TV production to know that you never questioned a stranger with a suit and a briefcase.

Nor did any of the seventeen other people who had taken over the president's office to capture eighteen seconds' worth of executive sincerity. No one paid the slightest attention to the tall guy in the suit. Employees from the car company, the advertising agency, and the production company all assumed he was with one of the other two firms. Tidyman decided to look busy and wait for his moment. He found a wingback chair in the corner, sat down, pulled out a pen and notepad, and started writing.

He had been writing for just over half an hour, waiting for something to happen, when the room filled with light and a man in tight black leather slacks who appeared to be directing things walked over to an older man who was standing at a tripod. Perched on the tripod was a video camera aimed at the president's chair behind his desk. The chair was empty. The director looked through the eyepiece of the camera and both men nodded at each other. The older man called out to one of the kids who had been stringing cables between the lights and told him to go and sit in the president's chair for a minute, so they could check the lighting on his face. The kid sat and made a big deal about pretending he was president of one of the world's largest car companies. A man with a long beard came up and held a light meter to the kid's face and got a few laughs by telling him, "Keep still, Mr. President, or I'll have to kick your ass."

"Ready with the prompt, Betty?" the director asked. In a louder voice he shouted, "Okay, tell Mr. Petrelli we're ready to go."

The kid scooted out of the chair just as Petrelli came through a door behind his desk. He was taller than Tidyman had pictured him from his other commercials. He glared at the kid, squinted at the lights, sat down, then squinted again at the teleprompter. He looked as if he had done it all before.

"Quiet, everyone, please." This from a nervous-looking man holding a clipboard. The room quietened immediately and the director said, "Roll sound."

"Sound rolling," someone said.

"Roll camera."

"Camera rolling," the older man called out.

"Slate."

A man in blue jeans and a T-shirt held up a black and white clapperboard in front of the camera and clicked it shut. "New spirit, desk shot, take one," the man called out, then jumped out of the way.

"Whenever you're ready, Mr. Petrelli," the director said reverently.

The president stopped squinting and gave the camera a curt nod and a chief executive's version of a smile. "As I travel throughout America, I sense a new spirit building, a spirit of pride, of self-worth, a spirit that says, 'Hey, we can do it here in America.' Well, my friends, we can't do it here in America, and look what we're doing for you."

"Cut. Good, that was very good, Mr. Petrelli, very good," the director said. "I want to try just one more, and can I get you to maybe jab your finger out like this when you hit the words 'doing for you.'"

"Like this?" Petrelli jabbed his finger as if he were punching the button of an out-of-service elevator.

"That's perfect. Just try that when you say 'and here's what we're doing for you.'"

"Look what we're doing for you," a woman with a stopwatch corrected.

"Yeah, whatever," the director said.

"Did he say 'can't?' I'm pretty sure he said 'can't' instead of 'can do it in America,'" a nervous young man in a suit asked. "It's supposed to be 'can do it in America', not can't, isn't it?"

"Jesus Christ," the director sighed. "Okay, Mr. Petrelli, it's 'can do it here in America,' not 'can't,' okay?"

"What did I say?"

"You said 'can't.' They think you said 'can't.' Okay, everyone? Quiet, please. Roll sound."

"Sound rolling."

"Slate."

"New spirit. Desk shot, take two."

"And, Mr. Petrelli."

"As I travel throughout America, I sense a new spirit build-ing, a spirit of pride, of self-worth, a spirit that says, 'Hey, we can do it here in America.' Well, my friends, we can't do it here in America. And look what we're doing for you."

"Cut."

"How was that with the finger? Was that all right?"

"He said 'can't' again. 'Can't do it in America.'"

"The finger was fine, Mr. Petrelli. I really felt you were involv-ing me there when you did that. We, ah, think you might have said 'can't' though, instead of 'can.' It should be 'can do it in America.'"

"Here in America," a woman with a clipboard said.

"Fucking hell," Petrelli snapped. "Can't you edit it out or something?"

"No, I'm afraid we can't."

"They can dub seven hours of *War and Peace* from Russian, you can't take out one little 't'?"

"Let's just try one more."

The president got it right on take five. Tidyman moved in immediately, but by the time he got around the desk, a gray-haired woman was there, holding up her wrist to show him he was running behind.

"Fine job, Mr. Petrelli," Tidyman cut in. "I believed every word."

Petrelli looked up, momentarily puzzled, then looked back at the gray-haired woman. "How long they been waiting?"

"Over an hour. They mentioned a flight back at seven."

"Jesus."

Tidyman leaned down to hand the president his card. "I'm Felix Tidyman, Mr. Petrelli, The Jacamar Corporation. I wrote you about your security, put together a fairly detailed presenta-tion about how your company could avoid the sort of fiasco the Audi people had, you know, getting bad coverage on *60 Minutes*, getting sued by customers who don't like the car taking off on its own. I mentioned that our company might be able to help."

Petrelli looked at the card still in Tidyman's hand, looked briefly at Tidyman, then turned back to the gray-haired woman. "See if you can hold them for just ten minutes more. Gardiner's had a dealer delegation waiting for me since nine. I've got to stick my head in there, then I'll be right down."

"Mr Petrelli," Tidyman said to the president's back as it vanished out the door.

Tidyman picked up his briefcase and wondered at the maze of scurrying bodies. Everyone seemed busy with familiar roles: taking light stands apart, rolling up cables that had been strewn across the floor, comparing clipboard notes, packing cameras, lenses, and sound gear into metal trunks. Tidyman stood at the president's desk, arms folded, stunned by the human effort that had gone into filming three sentences. He lifted his briefcase onto a corner of the desk, and decided to do the rest of it just the way Gezmis had planned it.

Gezmis's plan had been inspired by the January issue of *Car and Driver* magazine. There was a feature on the new SX-E sports sedan, written by a guy who had visited the company's Michigan test track and interviewed someone named Foster Styles from Product Development. One of the photos showed the writer and Styles looking over the new car.

Tidyman picked up one of the president's three phones and dialed the switchboard. "Get Foster Styles up to Mr. Petrelli's office right away, please. We need him in on this thing."

In less than five minutes, Tidyman recognized a puzzled Foster Styles standing at the main door of the president's office, gaping at the scruffiest people he had ever seen on the executive floor packing things away in metal cartons. Tidyman walked over, looked down at the man, and wrapped an engaging arm around his shoulder. "Hi, Foster, I'm Tidyman. We've got a problem on the SX-E. Petrelli asked me to fill you in."

"Which department you with, Tidyman?" Styles wanted to know. He was still looking around the room, trying to find Angelo Petrelli.

"Jacamar Corporation, industrial security. We've got a problem here. Let's get a car. I'll show you what's going on."

"The SX-E?"

Tidyman kept his arm around the man and steered him to the elevator.

"We don't have any SX-Es back there. We finished our work on them months ago."

Tidyman pushed the elevator button, playfully trying to imitate the action Petrelli had used to convey to Americans what he was doing—just for them. "Yeah, well, that's what the problem's all about, Foster. We're not talking a production fix here. We're looking at a potential recall—quite possibly the line."

"Oh, no." Foster Styles looked up at Tidyman, eyes pleading for him to say it wasn't so.

"Looks like. Unless your people have an idea or two. Petrelli was so pissed off when we told him about it, he stomped off out of the room."

"Was that what the camera crew was all about? Don't tell me *60 Minutes* is after us."

"Not yet, they're not." Tidyman gave a grim chuckle as he steered Foster Styles into the elevator. "Now you were going to see about getting us a car."

Foster Styles led the way to the parking lot and unlocked his own SX-E. It still had the smell of a new car. Tidyman said he would take the wheel and show him the problem. He turned on the ignition. "So far so good. We didn't go anywhere we weren't supposed to go."

"Is that what this is about? Unwanted acceleration? I thought Audi had proved that was impossible, that all those people were just hitting the gas instead of the brake."

Tidyman put the car in gear and steered it out of the lot. "I don't think so. Almost all of the Audi incidents happened while the car was standing still. If it were just pedal confusion you have to ask yourself how come it didn't happen more often when they were driving. Things get more confusing when you're driving."

"No, no. When you're driving, you've got a better reference point for your feet to work from than you have when you first get in the car," Styles argued. "Listen, Tidyman, I've got no love for anyone at Audi but I can tell you all those stories just never happened the way people said they did. I mean, all due respect to *60 Minutes*, but this is a matter of physics. You idle an engine at 3,500 rpm—even 4,000 rpm—your throttle's hardly open at all. Now drop it into Drive and you've got one hell of a load all of a sudden and your engine speed drops right down to next to nothing. The car will damn near stall on you. The only way it's going to leap forward the way those people were talking about is if it gets a sudden surge of gas, and the only way you're going to get a sudden surge of gas is for someone to thump down on the accelerator."

Tidyman steered into the parking lot of the Westlands Mall, and headed for an open area at the back. He waited for Styles to glance away then he quickly gave the brake three light taps. He let the car coast to a stop and shut off the key.

"Sounds to me like birds of a feather flocking together," Tidyman said. He handed Foster Styles the key.

"It has nothing to do with that," Styles snapped. "Come on, Tidyman, you went to high school, took a little science—"

"I must have played hooky the day they covered throttle linkage. You try this thing." Tidyman said. He jumped out of the car and slammed the door.

Styles slid over to the driver's side and opened the window. "What you just said, you're referring to that theory about the Audi throttle linkage, right? Dirt getting in and clogging the transmission control valves? Building up hydraulic pressure and pushing the throttle linkage? Instead of pulling it? That's supposed to send the car shooting forward no matter how far you've got the brake pressed down, right?"

"I once heard that offered as a possibility," Tidyman said.

"Okay, okay, here's what I'm going to do. Come on, get in, I'll show you it doesn't work that way."

"You're going to fuck around, I'll watch from out here."

"Fine. That way you'll be able to see the brake lights and see exactly what I'm doing."

"What exactly are you doing?" Tidyman asked, stepping back from the car.

"I'm going to turn on the engine. Then I'm going to rev it up to 4,000. Then I'm going to put my left foot on the brake and drop the car into Drive. If you want, you can put your foot right under the front wheel, because as long as my foot is on the brake this baby is not going to budge."

"Maybe you should put your foot on the brake before you start the car," Tidyman suggested.

Styles stared out the window as if he were addressing a visitor from outer space. "Tidyman, the fucking car is in Park, okay?" He turned on the engine. "Now I am putting my foot on the brake and, as you can see, it's not going—"

Tidyman guessed that Styles had meant to say "It's not going anywhere," or "It's not going to move." He never found out because as soon as Styles dropped the car into Drive, the big SX-E surged forward with a squeal of tires and a startled Foster Styles trying to wrestle it under control. It went about two hundred feet, brake lights glaring all the way; then it suddenly stopped.

Tidyman loped over with long strides. Foster Styles was out of the car, keys in his hand, and staring at the hood as if the vehicle might be cursed. The smell of burned brake lining was intense. "That didn't happen," he said.

"It happened," Tidyman insisted. "Look at your tracks."

"Goddamn idle stabilization valve. Only thing it could be. I had to turn it off with the key."

"Yep," Tidyman said.

"What I don't understand is what your role is in all this, Tidyman? Who'd you say you worked for?"

"Jacamar Corporation Security. Industrial security specialists."

"Hired by Petrelli?"

"I talked to Petrelli just this morning. In his office."

"That's not what I asked. I'm getting a cab back to the plant, see what's going on here."

"Your car should be okay to drive back."

"Yeah? And how would you know that?"

"It's consistent with our experience."

Styles stared at him. "You've had some experience with our cars, is that right?"

"Why don't you drive me back and we'll talk."

"You know so fucking much, you drive." Foster Styles threw him the keys.

Styles remained silent all the way back to head office. If there was something funny going on here, and it was pretty obvious that there was, he didn't think badgering the big sonofabitch at the wheel was his responsibility. Back in the parking lot, Styles took his keys, locked his car, and said to Tidyman, "I think I'd like to meet with our own people, talk to Mr. Petrelli, see what's happening here. Give me your card. I'll get in touch."

"I'm from out of town," Tidyman protested. "I should really come with you when you talk to Petrelli."

"I thought you already talked to him. You said you talked to him in his office. That mob scene back there. Or was that a crock of shit? I mean, what's going on is what I want to know. Give me your card. I'll get back to you."

Tidyman handed him a card.

"Where's your phone number? There's no phone number. No address. What kind of card is this? What the hell's going on here?"

"I move around a bit."

Styles looked him up and down. "I'll just bet you move around a bit. I'd like to know where you've been moving around here, that's what I'd like to know."

"Tell Petrelli we have to talk contract," Tidyman said, heading toward his own car. The film company truck was still there.

Foster Styles, drawing closer to the safety of his building, was feeling bolder. "You're such good friends, why don't you call him yourself?"

Tidyman spun around, and for a second Styles feared he was going to come after him. Tidyman roared, "I'll be calling. And you people better listen when I do. Otherwise, you could find this place closed down."

"Yeah, I'll tell him you said that," Styles muttered. He took the steps two at a time, waited until he reached the other side of the glass doors before he added the word "asshole" under his breath.

Tidyman checked into the Sunny Times Motel on Woodward and waited until next morning to call Petrelli. He called once an hour and was told each time that Mr. Petrelli was unavailable. In the early afternoon, he started calling Foster Styles. The woman who answered Styles's phone kept asking Tidyman his name, even though it was clear that she recognized his voice after the first few calls. Every time he told her, she said Mr. Styles was in conference.

Tidyman kept phoning until 6 p.m., when the company line was automatically routed to the security desk, and a male voice said to call back tomorrow.

Instead, Tidyman phoned Ismail Gezmis in Los Angeles. Gezmis listened to what he had to say, hung up, and immediately dialed the number of a Palestinian safe house in Paris. He asked for twelve good men to be in Los Angeles by Thursday. Good men, he emphasized, who would be eager to make their presence felt.

CHAPTER 22

St. Lucia, August 24.

Harry read all the early newspaper coverage of the crash, and found nothing that surprised him. He knew that airlines had departments that looked after these "incidents." Sometimes they were called Public Relations, sometimes Corporate Affairs. But Harry knew that whatever name they went by, they brought out the same thick book whenever there was a crash. The book told them who was to say what, how to treat the next of kin, which press releases to send out, and in which order.

The book said that, after a crash, you never put the name of your airline in the first sentence of a press release. You could open with the name of the aircraft manufacturer, as though the make of plane might have had some bearing on its going down. You could mention the weather, unless of course the skies were clear and sunny. You could start with the place of departure or the destination, especially if either place had a record of civil unrest. But never the name of the airline.

None of the newspapers he saw had any articles about himself, and that vaguely disappointed him. What was the use of being a fugitive if you didn't get recognition? He was feeling everything a fugitive feels: a sense of loss, a feeling of impending doom, and relief at still being free. But the world wasn't sharing his feelings. Harry didn't understand.

The flight from Chicago to St. Lucia took almost six hours.

That was time enough to watch the movie, eat the dinner, reread the papers, and think.

Think about Alex O'Connor. Harry had got women wrong before, just as surely as he'd shot the wrong Lebanese. But he thought he had it right this time. What could be wrong with a woman who drank beer and enjoyed it, and even ordered it before she asked what you were having? How could a woman who knew how to back up a car without biting on her lower lip possibly be telling him lies?

At St. Lucia, Harry showed a tired black man his Canadian birth certificate and the visitor's card that the flight attendant had told him to fill out. Then he walked outside to look at cars.

The heat was remarkable. It hung in the air with a tangible presence, like high noon in Beirut, but softer somehow. Harry felt the muscles in his neck start to loosen like a starched shirt going limp.

He looked for the most expensive-looking limo he could find, not just for its air-conditioning, but for its driver. Wherever he went, Harry found that the driver of the most expensive limousine seemed to know things: the key politicians, the important legal figures, all the good bars and hotels—and the better local gossip.

The flip side could be equally useful. The driver of the most expensive car would also know the local criminals and the hotels that didn't ask to see your passport.

Harry's theory had proven itself in Belgium (a stately Bentley and a driver who had once worked for the OAS), in Sweden (a Volvo Turbo and a driver who manufactured a superior variety of moonshine aquavit), and even in that most foreign of all possible places, New York City (a Mercedes driven by a former police sergeant). Here in St. Lucia, the car was an aging white Rover, whose driver said please call him Junior, although he looked well over fifty.

"I want you and the car for three days," Harry said.

"Yes, sir."

"I want a hotel within walking distance of Rodney Bay."

"Yes, sir."

"And I want you to drive me to the nearest cold beer."

"Yes, sir."

"And could you please call me Harry?"

Junior didn't answer that one. He picked up Harry's bag and put it gently in the trunk. Then he walked around and opened the rear door for Harry. Harry pretended not to notice and climbed in the front. Junior shut the back door silently.

The nearest cold beer was at an Italian restaurant near the airport. Junior pulled the car up to the entrance as if he were docking the Queen Mary.

"Perhaps you would care to join me for a beer?" Harry asked.

"That would be fine."

Harry noticed the missing "sir." He also noticed that Junior walked into the place ahead of him, and that he moved with more dignity than the pope. Harry suspected that he was somehow being put in his place.

A waitress who could have been descended from Queen Nefertiti looked up from where she had been polishing a table. She saw Junior and began glowing. "Junior, sakafet?"

"Sava," Junior said.

"Moi aussi," said Harry.

Junior blinked and Nefertiti looked at Harry as though she had had her privacy invaded. White sweaty people in wool suits were not supposed to know Creole, not the way they spoke it in St. Lucia. But Harry could remember long dinners with a farm girl from Languedoc, and if you could understand the French there you could understand it anywhere.

"Two Amstel," Junior said and pulled out a chair.

Nefertiti brought the beer with cold glasses from the refrigerator.

"You had a plane crash here." Harry took a sip of his beer as punctuation. "What I'm looking for is something that was on that plane. Right now, your government people and our government people are bringing up wreckage from the sea. Somewhere on this island they're labeling the pieces and trying to put it back together so that they can figure out what happened. They would have some local help to do this."

Junior studied Harry's face and counted the lines: the worry lines, the thinner laugh lines, and the two clefts on his forehead leading down to his nose that meant that Harry did a lot of thinking.

"You have any identification, sir?"

Harry was "sir" again. He pulled out his wallet and handed the whole thing across the table to Junior. He had thought of telling whoever he hired that he was looking for something that had been smuggled on the plane, something illegal. But Junior had been handling things well enough so far that Harry thought he might as well try the truth.

Junior went through the wallet a piece at a time: dry-cleaning receipt, driver's license, Hanover Casualty identity card, picture of Fleur in her French school uniform, social security, four credit cards, and a matchbook cover with a phone number on the back that Harry couldn't place any more. There was also a telephone calling card and seven hundred and twenty-three dollars in cash. Junior seemed disappointed.

Harry sat watching and came to the same conclusion. Maybe he ought to keep a condom in his wallet or a picture of somebody dark and beautiful inscribed with "Ah, those nights of safe sex in Ankara!"

Junior handed back the wallet. "You want another beer? Beer doesn't taste the same on planes, does it?"

Harry nodded. Junior raised two fingers about an inch from the table and let them fall. Nefertiti was over in seconds with more frosted glasses and two more Amstel.

"My aunt's son, Clifford, he works for the government here on the police boat," Junior said. "He's helping them bring in the bodies from the wreck. But he's going to be working till ten tonight, so I'll drive you to a hotel. I'll pick you up about ten-thirty and we'll go meet Clifford. You have some sleep first. You want to be awake when you meet Clifford."

The small white stuccoed cottage Junior delivered him to was one of forty identical buildings surrounding a central restaurant and pool. Inside was a galley kitchen, a table, four chairs, and a bed. Harry hung his suit in the closet and fell onto the bed. Canada to Brattleboro to Chicago to St. Lucia to sleep.

CHAPTER 23

Boston, Massachusetts, August 24.

It was Betty Sue Myers's turn to be on fries. That was fine with her. On fries you got to move around more. It was almost as good as being on the counter, but she hadn't been there long enough to go on the counter yet.

The new guy, the cute one Mr. Beresford had shown around the place yesterday, would almost certainly begin as a go-fer. All the guys did. He would take the frozen burger patties over to the grill, then bring the frozen chips over to her frier, maybe say something to her when he did. She liked his kind of looks. Dark brown eyes, like that old guy, the actor her mother used to go on about, Omar something or other.

Not that Mr. Beresford would give him much of a chance to talk to her. Mr. Beresford was always saying, "Chitchat on your own time, children." What a turkey. Calling them children. And there wasn't one kid there who was under fifteen.

Betty Sue sneaked a look at her watch. That was another thing Mr. Beresford didn't like to see, the kids always checking the time as if they couldn't wait to get out of there. And here she had just started her shift. Twelve minutes after eleven. She wondered about the new guy. She was pretty sure he was supposed to have started at eleven, too. Maybe she was wrong. She hoped so. She couldn't see Beresford letting a guy off with coming in late the first day on the job, even if he was pretty cute.

Betty Sue lifted the basket out of the grease and gave it three hard shakes, the number of shakes Mr. Beresford had said always to give the fries. She dumped them into the holder.

Then she heard the woman scream. Betty Sue ran up to the counter and looked over at the first row of tables. The woman was kneeling down beside a little boy. The boy's mouth was covered with blood and he was clawing at his tongue.

At the far side of the room, another woman, older than the first, started screaming, too. She was standing beside a man who appeared to be gagging, hitting him on the back.

Now another man, a big guy in denim coveralls, was on his feet, his hands up to his mouth. There was blood at the corners of his mouth, and he sounded as if he had a speech impediment. The man seemed to be trying to talk and hold onto his tongue at the same time. Betty Sue had never seen anyone try that before. She wondered if the world was going crazy.

Mr. Beresford started saying, "Okay, okay easy now," trying to calm people down, but she could tell that he didn't know what was happening either. A woman with three kids suddenly caught onto what was happening, and started yelling, "Don't eat it! Don't eat it!" She was reaching into the mouth of the nearest kid, pulling out the food, telling the others to "Spit! Spit!" The kids looked at each other, bewildered, wondering if their mother really meant that they should spit right on the restaurant floor.

Suddenly, Mr. Beresford was behind the counter, yelling at all the kids who were just standing there gaping out into the restaurant. "Quick, go around to all of the tables, get all of the burgers back. Move. Move. Move."

Betty Sue now figured she knew what was going on. It was the burgers, something in them. It was cutting people up. She wondered why Mr. Beresford hadn't yelled out for people to stop eating, instead of just telling the kids to go around and grab the burgers back. The kids had gone, too, no questions asked. Now all the customers who had been standing at the counter waiting to be served had stopped looking at each other. They were looking at her, wanting someone to please, please tell them what was going on here.

Well, couldn't they see what was going on? Betty Sue was only sixteen years old and she had figured out that there was something in the meat. What was the matter with people? What was the matter with Mr. Beresford? The big guy in the denim coveralls was going over to him now, grabbing him, spinning him around, gurgling through his tongue, pointing to his mouth. Mr. Beresford was trying to get away, but now the big guy had both his hands around his neck.

Betty Sue knew what she had to do. She ran to Mr. Beresford's office and dialed the emergency number. When the lady asked what service she wanted, she wasn't sure what to say. Then she heard another woman screaming in the restaurant, so Betty Sue said an ambulance, for sure. Maybe two ambulances, she couldn't be certain. "And I think we should maybe have the police here, too."

She went back out and looked into the restaurant. The big guy still had hold of Mr. Beresford.

Well, that was something, at least. If the cute guy showed up now, Mr. Beresford wouldn't notice he was late.

CHAPTER 24

St. Lucia, August 24.

It took about ten minutes of increasingly impolite knocking on Harry's cottage door to wake him. "You missed the manager's rum punch party," Junior said.

Harry nodded and threw his suitcase on the bed.

"You missed happy hour at the pool bar."

Harry tried to find the zippers on his suitcase: somewhere in here were Biff's old khaki pants and a polo shirt.

"You missed the seafood barbecue."

Socks? He didn't need socks. This was the tropics: just fourteen degrees from the Equator.

"And you missed the limbo contest down by the pool. Sonja won."

"Sonja?"

"My niece. She works here. They call her Sonja, because her mother saw one of those films where they skate on ice, and the name of the star was Sonja. Are you ready now?"

"Where are we going?"

"Down the coast, two, three miles. To a town called Gros Islet. The whole town is bars except for some fishermen. Clifford, he'll meet us at the German Bar."

The town was a ten-minute drive down a skinny, pock-marked road that passed for a highway. Gros Islet was a cross between Dodge City and a Caribbean fishing village. In the middle of town, every second house was a bar or a restaurant, or both. The bars were open to the crowded street and every place had a radio or tape machine playing different music from the one next door. Every second bar had black men playing dominoes as loudly as they could, slamming the pieces down with solid overhands that made the tables bounce. For every two men playing, three more watched. In each bar there seemed to be an average of one person drinking.

The German Bar didn't look the least German. It was a two-storey heap of clapboard and Victorian gingerbread painted in nine different colors, none of them colors found in nature. Junior braked slowly. All the heads in the bar turned toward the car, then in unison back to the dominoes.

"Clifford, he's that big one in the yellow shirt," Junior pointed out. "Some people call him Warrior but I don't think that's right. I think he's only big."

"Are you coming in?"

"I don't think you need me. If I'm around, Clifford won't behave like he usually does, and I think you want him behaving like he usually does. If I'm around he'll be too quiet."

Harry tried to digest that. He nodded and got out of the car. There was a porch three or four steps higher than the street. He took the steps carefully, walked slowly across the porch, and through the open doorway. Nobody stopped talking when he entered. Nobody hiked at their belt. Nobody stared. This was not *Gunfight at the OK Corral*; this was *The Invisible Man*.

Harry put himself in front of the bar and resisted the impulse to order sarsaparilla. When the bartender looked up, he said, "Amstel."

The giant in the yellow shirt glanced over, studied him briefly, then turned away.

What are you going to do now, Harry? Ask if anyone's seen a stranger in town? Inquire if they need a good cowhand? See if they want a fourth for dominoes? "I'm looking for a man named Warrior," Harry said to the big man's back.

Silence. The domino players stopped to take it in.

"Who be lookin'?" the giant said at last, without turning around.

"I be lookin'," Harry said, and immediately wished he'd chosen something a little less flip.

"I'm Warrior." The big man turned slowly. He was under twenty-five and over six-foot-three, and black as a hearse. The yellow shirt was stretched tight over muscle.

Harry took a pull at his beer. Good move that, Harry. Keep the giant off balance. "Your Uncle Junior said we might talk a little business."

"Might want to talk. Might not." Clifford the Warrior passed a smirk to the domino players who grinned at each other and watched.

"Ah," said Harry. He put his glass down and looked the huge boy over. "I see." Wait the bugger out.

Clifford didn't like that game. "What do you want?" His hand went up and fingered a gold chain. Hanging from the chain was a small gold sculpture of a man in sexual congress with a woman.

Harry remembered where he had heard about a necklace like that. How would he get Clifford talking? Money? Might work, but with money he wouldn't know if Clifford were telling the truth. Threats?

"Clifford, you might not want to be seen talking to me. Maybe we should take a little stroll."

Harry reasoned that Clifford would figure he was safe in the dark. There were no secluded alleys in Gros Islet, but a three-minute walk down a reggae-raucous side street took them to the waterfront. Harry could sense Clifford tensing up. Something in the way he was walking.

Harry felt curiously easy. He had a beer in his left hand. It was a tropic night, full of cheerful, humming bugs. A soft wind was coming off the sea.

The moon lit up Clifford's face as Harry hit him in the throat. Clifford made a series of small strangling noises and put his hands to his neck just as Harry hit him again, smacking the palm of his hand into Clifford's nose. Harry didn't put much into it, just enough to start a trickle of blood. Clifford's hands went up to his nose and Harry backed away and kicked Clifford hard in the testicles.

Clifford had run out of hands. He kneeled and rolled over on his side. He made a noise like a faraway gull.

Harry shifted his beer to his right hand. Hadn't spilled a drop. A nine-day course—when?—must be fifteen years ago or more.

Harry sat on the ground beside Clifford and watched the boy's mouth contort. He felt good. People had been bombing him and chasing him. Now he had hit back and someone was paying attention.

"Clifford—you don't mind if I call you Clifford? I told you that you wouldn't want people to see you talking to me."

"Jesus."

"There are a couple of things I want to know."

"Jesus."

"First of all, I want to know where you stole that little medallion with the two people screwing."

"Fuck off."

Harry leaned forward and took a short hard slap at Clifford's nose. It had been bleeding a little; now it started to spout. Harry winced a little himself.

"Jesus."

"Answer the question, Clifford. I should tell you I'm not with the police. Maybe your Uncle Junior already told you that. So you can talk."

Harry leaned forward again. Clifford flinched and Harry could tell that even flinching hurt.

"Wait a second, man, wait a second. You pound my throat and . . . " A voice strained through gravel.

"Your little necklace, Cliffie, where'd you get that?"

Quietly: "I'm taking the airplane pieces off the boat, the boat the divers use when they go out to dive for the plane."

"Do those pieces include the bodies, Cliffie?"

Clifford rolled on his back, a beached black shark. "Yes."

"Just keep talking. Just keep telling me the story."

Clifford paused. Harry could see he was thinking. He thought he knew what Clifford was thinking about. He reached over and pinched Clifford's nose and wiggled it.

"Jeee . . . sus."

"Does sort of focus the mind, doesn't it, Cliffie? The human nose is chock-full of nerve endings. Keep telling the story."

Clifford's breath was coming in short, shallow pants. "They take the bodies from the fuselage. They bring them up to the boat. They put them in bags. They take the bodies to the old dairy building to keep them cool. I drive the van. They keep me going all day."

"You checked some of the body bags."

Clifford nodded slightly.

"You found the necklace."

Another short nod.

"What else? What else did you find in the same bag, on the same body?"

"Wallet. He had a wallet on him."

"And where is the wallet?"

"Home."

"Where's home?"

"Here. Gros Islet."

"Take your hands away from your face. Let me see it."

Clifford looked up at him, deciding. Then he slowly lowered his hands. Harry sounded gentler now. "Didn't break your nose. You just lie there for a second."

Harry got up, took out a handkerchief, went to the water, and dipped it in. He came back, kneeled beside the boy, and carefully wiped the blood off his face. "No scars. I didn't leave any scars on you. Sorry about that. They might have looked good on you, made you look more like a warrior. Think you can walk?"

"You hit me when I'm not looking."

"Best time for it. Otherwise you might have hit me."

Harry stood and stuck out his hand. The boy looked at it, then he took it. Harry eased him up onto his feet. "Trying to stand up straight can be a chore after a good kick in the balls," Harry said sympathetically. "But at least wipe the mud off your pants."

Clifford flicked at the front of his pants.

Harry tossed the bloody handkerchief into the water. "Can you walk? Come on, walk. Imitate yourself walking."

Clifford took a few steps, then managed something like his normal stride.

"Come on. We'll go to your place. We'll pick up the wallet."

"Then what? Police?"

"No, Warrior. You give me the wallet and then I'll buy you a beer."

The house was a living room and bedroom. Clifford went into the bedroom, and Harry heard something heavy being moved. Clifford came out and handed Harry a wallet. Harry opened it under the light of a hanging bulb. Inside were two condoms, prelubricated with reservoir ends, three hundred and seventy-nine U.S. dollars, a passport-sized photograph of a plump woman with dark hair and small eyes, a motel receipt, and a note written in somewhat childish handwriting that said, "S. Nunni."

Saturday, Nunni?

South Nunni?

See Nunni?

There was nothing else in the wallet but a small, folded advertisement that began, "Anita likes her phone calls hot and heavy. Major credit cards."

"Did you look at the guy when you took the chain off him and borrowed his wallet?" Harry asked.

"Didn't look at his face: it was pretty smashed. But somethin' was funny. He had his fly open and his thing was out, but they didn't find him in the toilet."

Harry thought that over. Could Saddam have died in the saddle? That would fit in with what the bottle-cap plant guy and the super had said. How *did* people do that five miles up?

"Maybe we should go have that beer now." Harry handed Clifford the money from the wallet, then stuffed the wallet in his pocket. Clifford looked at the money, then at Harry, and wondered what the deal was. He decided that the deal was that Harry was crazy. Clifford shrugged and checked a well-polished wall mirror to see that his face was in one piece. Then he led the way out.

The German Bar had picked up business: there were now two people drinking and four playing dominoes. Clifford asked the man behind the bar for two Amstel and handed one to Harry. To the bartender he said, "This is Harry. He's cool."

Harry finished his beer and ordered a banana daiquiri. He considered getting drunk. Someone once claimed that Hemingway had consumed thirty-two double daiquiris in one day in Cuba. Harry wondered what he would have done here, where according to the guide book they grew a hundred and twenty-seven kinds of bananas. He ordered another and thought about who might have blown up Abdel Saddam and where South Nunni was.

Three daiquiris later, Junior loomed up with a girl who looked like Whitney Houston, but more buoyant.

"This is my niece, Sonja," Junior said.

"She's cool," Clifford said.

"I'm cool too," Harry told her. He drained the last of the daiquiri—his fourth? His fifth? "Isn't it nice to have so much in common so early in our relationship?"

"My *niece*," said Junior. "Come on, I'll take you home. You're tired."

"Passenger manifest." Harry looked at Clifford. "I need a passenger manifest and the seating plan from that plane."

"I don't know about manifests. I'm just moving bodies from one place to another place," Clifford said.

"Need a manifest. Need a seating plan," Harry said.

Sonja patted Harry on the arm. "I'll get you a manifest. I'll get you a seating plan. Tomorrow morning."

"Yes?"

"My girlfriend is working down in the airline offices on Brazil Street."

"You know what flight number? You know—"

"I know all that. Everybody knows what you want, Mr. Bracken." She patted him on the arm again.

Good, good. Fine, fine. At home, everybody knows where

you are, Harry. Here, everybody knows what you want. And they've got one hundred and twenty-seven kinds of bananas.

He got to his feet and looked at Sonja's hand on his arm. It was surprisingly large for a nice slim girl. Hairy too. With a muscular forearm. It took a while to register that it was Junior guiding him out to the car.

Harry woke on top of the covers, fully dressed. He wiggled his toes. He had remembered to take his shoes off. Or somebody had remembered to take his shoes off.

He checked for other vital signs. His right hand was tender from hitting Clifford. He wondered how Clifford's face and neck felt. His armpits smelled like armpits. Who had paid for the drinks last night? He raised his arm. Sonja had patted him on that arm twice. There was no imprint and it didn't glow but he knew where she had patted it.

He raised his head. It felt clear. No hangover. He felt curiously cheated. All that money he—somebody—had invested in his liver last night and no hangover.

The bathroom mirror told him his eyes were a little bloodshot but his teeth were unfurred and his tongue was a fetching shade of pink.

Biff's shirt was wrinkled. Biff's pants were wrinkled. Wear the wool worsted? There was a store here, wasn't there? Beside the restaurant. Souvenirs and noisy shirts. He padded barefoot into the living room and opened the sliding glass door. Where had he put the key? It wasn't in his pocket. All he had in his pocket was two wallets.

The morning was fresh and quiet. Walking back from the store, he could see the Caribbean behind the other cottages. Three men in a green and red dugout were paying out blue fish netting. A hummingbird was tonguing a flower on the shrub beside the window.

He was back in his kitchen chair, drinking coffee when Sonja arrived. "I'm Sonja, Junior's niece."

"I remember."

She smiled slowly. "I was just checking. Uncle Junior said to remind you I was his niece."

"You want some coffee?"

"No, thank you. Did you get that shirt in St. Lucia? Very vulgar."

"I got it at the store here. I thought it was bright and tropical."

"It matches your eyes. Blue and red."

"The saleslady didn't mention that."

"I brought you the manifest and the seating plan. My girlfriend at the airline office says you shouldn't tell anyone where you got them because the airline hasn't notified all the next-of-kin yet, and she could get in trouble. And I brought you the newspaper so you can read about the crash. It's a regional paper they publish in Antigua."

Harry looked at the tabloid. The headline read "Lucky 13! The men who didn't fly Super Plat!!!" There was a color picture of one happy smiling executive above a story that told how he and a dozen other food executives had canceled their flight to Trinidad at the last moment because of an emergency meeting in New York. "Reg DuVall of Santa Barbara and his 12 colleagues are probably the only people happy about the flight," the story said.

"Lucky Reg DuVall," said Harry.

Sonja sat on the corner of the table. She had on a green skirt and a matching green shirt. She crossed her legs. It seemed to take forever.

Harry took the seating plan, a photocopy of the original:

A. Saddam, seat 34C.

S. Nunni, seat 34B.

A person.

He stood up and walked to the window. Another humming-bird was tonguing another flower. The red and green dugout had been pulled up on the beach. There was a far-off sound of a lawnmower.

So who was S. Nunni?

He walked back to the table and spread out the manifest.

There it was: S. Nunni. So. How did that help? How lucky *was*
... Reg DuVall? What was going on?

"You beat up Clifford last night?" Sonja asked.

Harry looked at her. If Sonja were Junior's niece and Clifford
was—what?—Junior's sister's whatever, then Clifford and
Sonja were ...

"It's okay that you beat him up. He's a good boy, but sometimes he does bad things. I think it's educational that he knows
that muscles aren't everything. He spends two hours a day
lifting weights and then he's down at the beach whenever he can
get off work, showing the muscles to the tourist ladies. That's
too easy a life."

"Oh."

"I make my living going around to the hotels teaching tourists
how to limbo. That's too hard a life. I'm using the money to go
to computer school."

Harry had just started to wonder how she got all that body
under the pole when a shadow fell over the table. He looked up.
There was Junior. Behind Junior was Alex.

"Good morning, sir," Junior said.

"Anybody want coffee?" Harry tried to stay calm.

"Black," Alex said.

"Just take a second, if you don't mind instant. This is Alex.
She's a product manager. This is Sonja. She's Junior's niece and
goes to computer school."

"Instant is okay," Alex said.

"Cool."

Later they walked along the beach in the shade of coconut
palms. Ahead of them, land crabs scuttered into their holes.

"Interesting shirt."

"I bought it this morning. I think they have sizes for ladies."

"I talked a long time with Biff. He said I should come down
here."

"I'm glad you did."

"Sonja didn't seem glad I was here."

"Sonja? Oh yes: Junior's niece."

"The one at computer school."

"I'm glad you came down here."

"These cottages here, what do they rent for?"

"Single or double?" Harry asked.

CHAPTER 25

Phoenix, Arizona, August 24.

It wasn't working out as well as Larry had hoped. At least, not yet. Last week, when he had been promoted from counterman to assistant manager, he had thought it might put Horst Mohr in his place once and for all. Not that assistant manager was prince of the heap or anything; Larry was just one of three. But it meant that when Mr. Todd was out, as he was now, Larry was in charge of the restaurant. Larry figured that would give him an edge in terms of respect. He had seen the way the young girls looked at Horst, and the leering look Horst gave them back. Larry couldn't stand the guy, even hated the way he walked. Not so much a walk as a swagger.

And Horst Mohr wasn't tall enough to swagger: five-eight, five-nine at most. Larry was damn near six feet with his shoes on. Girls liked taller guys; everyone knew that. He couldn't see where this Horst guy got off, thinking he was such a ladies' man and all. And, really, some of the girls, he thought they would have more sense than to put up with a guy coming on to them like that. Especially Jennifer, who had always struck him as being more level-headed than the others.

Larry stood behind the staff at the counter, watching. This was their peak time of the day, and it was a feather in his cap that Mr. Todd had left him in charge.

Oh, oh. He didn't like the look of these fellows: four bikers, mean-looking guys. Except they weren't really walking much

197

like bikers. Most bikers that Larry had seen walked like Horst Mohr or, more likely, Horst Mohr had copied his walk from the bikers he'd seen in the movies. But these guys, even though they wore all the bad-ass biker gear, just didn't walk like real bikers. They looked a little neater, too. No pot-bellies or long beards or scruffy hair like a lot of the bikers in Phoenix.

Hey, they can't do that! Knocking plates on the floor. Pushing people around in their seats. What's that big guy trying to do, turn the table over? Doesn't he know all our tables are bolted to the floor? Where are these guys from, another planet?

Larry moved closer to the counter, but didn't go around the other side. He noticed some families edging toward the door. "Excuse me," he called out as loud as he could.

The biker who had been trying to uproot the table looked up. The other three walked between the tables, swiping food onto the floor.

"Excuse me. Look I don't know what your problem is, fellows. But it's only fair to warn you that I have just called the police. They'll be here within thirty seconds, so I suggest you clear out now." Shit. Why did he say a dumb thing like that? Thirty seconds? He was always exaggerating things; that was one of his faults. Whenever he told a story, even a good story, he had to color it up somehow. And it always had the opposite effect he hoped for. Even now. He could tell from the way the cretin at the table was looking at him that he didn't believe the cops would be here in thirty seconds.

Over near the window, a customer who had just seen one of the bikers push his wife in the chest stood up and pushed the guy back. Dumb, dumb, dumb, Larry thought. Now one of the bikers had a chokehold on the guy and another was punching him in the stomach. The third guy was squeezing the guy's wife's tits, really making the husband look like an asshole now. The fourth guy, the one who'd been trying to rip the table out of the floor, was heading over there, too, looking to join the fun.

Larry knew it was time to take action. Mr. Todd had driven that point home when he had given him the promotion. He explained that ninety-nine percent of the situations he'd run into were covered by the book. But it was that last one percent that made the difference between a guy with true management potential and a guy just going through the motions.

Larry didn't really mind having this chance to prove his full management potential his first week on the job. If nothing else, it would show Jennifer and the others that he was in a whole different class from Horst Mohr.

He knew exactly what he had to do. He walked directly to the cash register and leaned into the cashier's microphone. He turned up the volume, heard a loud squeal of feedback, turned it back a touch and spoke.

"Excuse me. If you four gentlemen would come over to the cash register, I have something that may be of interest."

The bikers looked up as if they had never heard a speaker in a restaurant before. Larry wondered if they might even be from another country, despite their gear, which was so obviously American. As the men approached the counter, Larry hit the No-Sale button on the register and scooped all the money from the upper trays, placing the twenties on top so the pile would look more substantial. When Mr. Todd got back, he would be pleased that Larry had the presence of mind not to touch the fifties and hundreds under the cash tray.

The smallest of the four, the one who had been throwing punches into the belly of the customer, grabbed the money out of Larry's hand. Then all four vaulted the counter. The jerk who had been grabbing the woman's breasts leered at the young girls all bunched together against the food-prep counter. Larry caught Jennifer's eyes. She wasn't crying. She was watching, waiting to see him take charge.

He heard a loud crash behind him and spun around to see the cash register on the floor. One of the bikers, the one who had tried to yank out tables, was waving Horst Mohr over to the register.

Larry couldn't believe what happened next. Horst Mohr, the short-assed, swaggering dolt, just stood there in a trance. "You, here," the biker was yelling. But Mohr couldn't move, just stood as if someone had planted him there. Behind him, two of the other bikers burst out laughing. There was a puddle on the floor and a stain on Horst Mohr's trousers. God's gift to women had pissed himself.

The two laughing bikers joined the third at the cash register on the floor, trying to kick it open. By now Larry was convinced. Biker gear or no biker gear, these people were not of this world.

He heard a familiar voice: "Larry."

The fourth biker, the one who had roughed up the woman in the restaurant area, now had his arm around Jennifer and was moving her hair away from her face.

"Kiss. Kiss. Kiss," the pig was saying. An accent.

"Lar-ry," Jennifer called. It was all so suddenly clear. She knew who the real man was, the guy with the future.

Larry was not about to let her down. The three at the cash register had succeeded in getting the drawer open and were scooping out the fifties, hundreds, and traveler's cheques. If he could make a good showing here, prove he wasn't a guy to knuckle under, there was a chance they'd take the money and run.

The animal with Jennifer was stroking her shoulders now, letting his hand drop down to the top of her breast, making animal noises.

All Larry needed was something hard and heavy. He saw it under one of the shelves, a forty-pound pail of lard.

After that he didn't stop to reason. He picked up the pail, moved in behind the biker with Jennifer and raised it over his head. The biker must have seen her eyes shift, because he turned just as Larry brought the pail down with all his strength.

But the full force of the blow caught the biker on the side of the head, and he fell in a heap at Jennifer's feet.

The other three looked over, saw the man collapse, saw Larry still holding the pail.

They moved in as a unit. One wrapped his arms around Larry's feet; the other pinned his arms behind his back. The third, the big man, punched at Larry's face.

Larry heard the girls screaming in sympathy and, with dazed satisfaction, realized that one of the screams was Jennifer's.

Then the punches stopped. Larry opened his eyes to see the big man looking past him into the food-prep area. He was smiling.

The other two were looking back there too. Larry wondered what was going on. He couldn't imagine what could be so interesting. The only thing back there was the vat where the French fries were cooked—overcooked if they'd been left in all this time.

Suddenly, Larry was up in the air, his arms and legs still pinned. The big man went into the food-prep area and lifted the wire basket of burnt fries out of the fat.

The other two tipped Larry down head-first. I will not scream, Larry promised himself. They are doing this to make me scream, to make me look silly in front of the girls. But I will not scream.

Larry did not scream. Not even when the bubbling fat was just a few inches from his eyes and he realized that they planned to do more than embarrass him. That was when he smelled something like the smell of hair on fire.

But it wasn't his hair; it was his eyebrows. And still they were pushing him down.

CHAPTER 26

St. Lucia, August 25.

"You sleep around," Alex said.

"What?"

"I mean, first you take me up to Canada to sleep there. Then we go to Biff's to sleep there. Now we're in St. Lucia and we're sleeping here. You sleep around. Where's it going to be tomorrow, Harry? Cleveland?"

"Have you noticed that most of the time we've been sleeping around, I haven't been sleeping?"

"Old people don't need as much sleep."

"What time is Junior coming to take us to dinner?" Harry asked.

"Seven. It's six-thirty now."

"Perhaps a rum and something before we leave." Harry had bought the rum at a shed with a tin roof beside the road. It cost half of what rum cost in New Hampshire and was twice as strong.

Alex got up and stretched. "Perhaps we should get dressed before we leave. Perhaps we should shower before we get dressed. I noticed a sign in the reception area that says the island's having a water shortage and we're being asked to conserve. Perhaps you'd care to join me in the shower. So we can conserve."

"I'm very old, you know," Harry pointed out. "And if I get into the shower with you, we'll end up playing hummingbird

202

again. I don't think I can play hummingbird five times a day. All this needing less sleep is making me tired. I think I'll just have the rum and try and restore my precious bodily fluids."

"Have a double."

Harry did, with grapefruit juice, out on the patio. Life was fine. Fine afternoon nap. Fine rum: it snuck up on you, but you knew it was going to sneak up on you, just as you knew when a small boy was coming at you tippytoe from your blind side, getting ready to say "Boo." Fine young lady scrubbing herself down in the next room, washing off fine sweat. And a fine evening breeze off the mountains. Looked as though they were going to arrange a fine sunset tonight. In all, a fine tropical island: the kind of place God would go if he ever had time for vacations.

Yes, Harry told himself, you did very very well to arrange all this. It took careful planning to arrange for that bomb to throw the young lady into your arms and give you an excuse to take her away to this tropical paradise, but it was worth it.

She came out and joined him on the patio, a towel around her body, her hair still wet. "I can't stand rejection," she said.

"All right. Okay. If you're going to whine about it all night, just throw in the towel and I'll be in in a moment."

Harry yawned. In mid-yawn he discovered a tongue in his mouth that wasn't his.

"Mmhmmph," Alex said.

"Excuse me. You want me to come back at seven-thirty?"

"No, that's all right, Junior. I just had a piece of mango caught in my back tooth and Miss O'Connor was trying to get it out."

"Think I got it." She smacked her lips. "Yup. Mango."

"Where would you suggest for dinner?" Harry asked.

"We could go up the mountain and you could eat with the tourists, or I could take you down along the sea and you could eat chicken with the chickens. My wife's cousin Nelson, he runs a chicken place. He barbecues them. You eat outdoors and he's always got chickens running around the place. Like eating oranges under an orange tree."

The restaurant was a series of small tin-roofed huts about twenty yards from the sea. One of the huts held a pool table and five small boys, who were trying to be cool by pretending that the game they were playing wasn't the most exciting thing they had done all day. Another hut held a six-man bar. The six men were watching satellite television and explaining the game of lacrosse to each other. A third hut was the kitchen; it held a small grill and a large woman poking at pieces of chicken. Occasionally, a small piece dropped on the floor, where it would be fought over by the late fowl's next-of-kin, profligate nephews haggling over a will. Between the huts were tables, all of them full. Harry and Alex were the only white people in the place.

Over the meal Harry explained to Junior how they could franchise the concept in the United States. "We'll have to make adjustments, of course. Not every one of the places could be by the sea. But with rear screen projection and an audio tape of waves lapping the shore we could get pretty close, even in Kansas. I don't know about having real chickens running through; the health codes might prove a little sticky on that. But perhaps with robotics . . . The thatched roof is a good idea. Miss O'Connor will make a note to get on to Dupont or Monsanto; they ought to have a good durable polythatch. There are a couple of other things we're going to have trouble with, though. First of all, this beer's too cold. The cost of that extra refrigeration multiplied by, say, two thousand outlets could make a heck of a dent in the quarterly dividend. Make a note on that, Miss O'Connor, and send a copy to engineering. As to the food product itself, I got a problem. Two problems. First, there's an utter lack of portion control here. And I have a problem with this being a free-range chicken. Can you imagine the cost of the range we'd have to free up for two thousand outlets? So what I'm thinking is that we can do a demi-free range bird. Maybe something we let out on a rotational basis for half an hour a day. How's that sit with you folks in Operations, Alex?"

Alex wiped her mouth with a paper napkin. "Mmm. Were you saying something?"

A boy of about fourteen came and whispered into Junior's

ear. "Excuse me," Junior said, "I'll be away a minute." He got up and walked to the beach where two black men were waiting.

Harry put down his fork. "That's all it is, then. You don't listen to me when I have ideas. To you I'm just some sort of sexual plaything."

She reached over and rubbed his thigh.

"A sexual plaything to be used over and over and over again," Harry muttered.

"Mr. Bracken?" Junior motioned for Harry to follow him to the beach, where he said, "Tell him, Clydey."

The smaller of the two new arrivals looked at Harry. "A man at the airport. He asking about you. Asking one of the luggage guys who said you go with Junior. He asking where. Luggage guy say he heard Junior take you maybe to your hotel. Luggage guy just young and he don't know you don't tell peoples what Junior do, don't tell anybody what anybody do if they're strangers. The man gave him some monies."

"What kind?"

"U.S."

"What did he look like?"

"Young. Twenty and a bit. Clear."

"Clear?"

Junior spoke up. "What Clydey means is not black like me. Not brown like Sonja. Lighter, but Negro. Clear."

"Not Negro, Junior," Clydey said. "The man's skin clear color, but he look like maybe some Italian. Only darker."

"Where did he go after the airport?" Harry asked.

"I look for him after I talk to the luggage guy about what he told, but he already gone in a taxi. I found the taxi man. He told me where the man stay."

"What was he wearing? What kind of luggage did he have?" Harry asked.

Clydey closed his eyes to bring the man back. "Like a safari jacket thing. Lots of pockets. He carrying a suitcase about this big." He moved his hands to indicate a two-suiter.

Harry reached into his pocket for some money but Junior put a hand on Harry's arm. "My thing," he said. He spoke to the two men in rapid Creole—too rapid for Harry. Clydey spoke back just as quickly. Junior nodded. The two men both said a quiet "Good evening" to Harry and left.

Junior said, "Maybe I should talk to you a little while we're alone, Harry."

Harry noticed it was Harry again. He nodded.

"People in St. Lucia come to me and tell me things. And I tell people things. And I do some things for people, and people do some things for me. It makes things happen easier."

Harry nodded again.

"So I looked at you when you came to the airport and I saw a man who has maybe had some troubles in his life. Then you asked me what you asked me about the airplane, and I saw that you are probably still having some troubles. I don't think you're a man with big troubles with the police. That kind of man comes down here a lot. Up in Cap Estate we had a man who used to live there in a big house and he would go home to Germany and rob a bank every little while. And there are men who come down here thinking they can get some drugs. I drive a lot of these people in my car. They dress different than you, and their faces look as though they're trying to look smart. You don't look that way. But you still look like you have some troubles. On this island, a lot of our troubles come in through the airport, so I tell my friends to listen."

Harry's face lit up, surprised.

"Then we get this man today. He doesn't sound like a policeman. Policemen don't pay like that for information. And a policeman would have asked for our police to meet them. So this man is not with the police. And this man is not your friend. Your friend would know where you were. So I wondered if maybe you had taken money from this man and he has come to get his money back. But I don't think that either. I think you don't worry a lot about money, and it would have to be a lot of money or this man wouldn't have come all the way down here."

Harry felt something cold and wet being pressed on his forearm. Alex had brought him a bottle of beer.

"Are you guys telling jokes over here? Masculine humor? I

don't really mind being left alone, except that so far nobody's made a move on me. It's either my advancing years or they're all afraid of Junior."

Harry took the beer. "I've got some bad news."

"What?"

"The plan we never had is working."

Over coffee, Harry explained the situation to Junior. A group of men had tried to take some money from a company. Harry and Alex had found out about it, and because they had found out about it, this group had tried to blow them up with a bomb. Harry had traced one of the group to the crashed plane, and now there was a man here who would try to do Harry and Miss O'Connor some harm. The plan was to get hold of the man and then somehow—Harry smiled and shrugged—get hold of some information.

Junior nodded. "You got information out of Clifford. You did that pretty quickly. He came to me to confess what he had done and what he had told you."

"He told you about that?"

"They confess to me. Confession is good for the soul. Besides, I would find out about it anyway. But this time I think you need some help. Clifford is one thing. From what you have told me, this man may be another. And I would like to help. I don't know what you do at home, but this is not the kind of man we want on our island."

Sonja, Alex, Junior, and Harry walked past the dance floor to Reception. The man had a room on the third floor, the reception-ist told Junior. Harry thought that the receptionist was perhaps the first person Junior had talked to who wasn't related to him directly or by marriage. But there appeared to be some other connection: the receptionist giggled throughout the conversation.

Upstairs, they walked past the man's room to the nearest stairwell. Sonja adjusted her beaded dress to show a little more

Sonja. She slung her oversized purse over her shoulders, winked at Harry, took a deep breath, and walked back to the man's door. She knocked on it softly.

The door opened just far enough for a head to peer out.

"Yes?"

Sonja put on a puzzled look. "I'm here."

The man said, "What?"

"You told the taxi driver you were looking for some company."

The door opened wider. Brown eyes traveled down Sonja's body, then up again.

"Twenty-five dollars, you told the taxi driver. American," Sonja said.

Harry listened from the stairwell. What would you do if you were the guy, Harry? Twenty-five dollars? Sonja? Even though you hadn't told a taxi driver anything? Harry had asked himself this a dozen times since they made the plan. Harry guessed that the least a guy would do would be to ask her in to talk things over.

The door opened wider. The man stepped into the hall and gave a quick glance each way: he was about twenty-five. He gave Sonja another appraisal, this time almost counting the beads on the dress. "Yes. The taxi driver. Yes. Come in." He stepped aside to let her in the room. That was when she let her purse drop. Brushes and combs and bottles of makeup scattered across the terrazzo. The man bent down to help her pick them up. That was when Harry, with the ease of an All-Conference place kicker, took three quick strides to the doorway and kicked him in the head. The man was propelled neatly into his room.

He woke up minutes later, bound by electrician's tape to a bamboo chair, his mouth full of tissue held in place with more electrician's tape around his head. His room was full of strangers.

Downstairs, some of the tourists began to sing "Yellow Bird" in German. Harry decided he was glad he had equipped their border guards with pigs. Then he decided the thought betrayed prejudice. He wondered if Junior were prejudiced. He wondered if he had prejudiced Alex by roughing up the man.

"It's quiz time," Harry said. "I wonder if you ladies would

excuse us." He took the bedside lamp, switched it on, and unscrewed the light bulb. The man in the chair began moving about, shaking his head frantically, and drawing up his knees to guard his crotch. Harry guessed he'd heard about the trick. He was thankful for the noise the band was making. "What we want to know about is a lucky man named DuVall and an unlucky guy called Nunni," Harry smiled.

Sonja backed out of the room, eyes and mouth wide open. But Alex walked out quickly, facing straight ahead.

The door closed loudly behind them.

Harry emptied the man's pockets. American passport, made out to Gregory Bent. Only one stamp: St. Lucia Immigration. Today's date. Airline ticket from Miami. Today's date, with an open return and made out to Gregory Bent. Paid cash. Economy. No credit cards. American cash: $804. Driver's license: Gregory Bent. A nice consistency there. No photos. He put the wallet in his pocket, bringing his billfold collection up to three. He pushed the man's head forward and tore the label out of his shirt. Eighty percent cotton, twenty percent polyester, size, medium. Hell of a clue.

He removed the man's left shoe. Florsheim 8½. Newish.

In the luggage were three new shirts, one new pair of cotton twill pants, a new Bic razor, one can Gillette Foamy, three pairs of socks and three pairs of Fruit-of-the-Loom. He'd planned to stay three days tops. No weapons. Junior checked the toilet tank, the backs of the drawers, under the mattress, and in the medicine cabinet. Nothing. It didn't make sense.

Until the second man, the one with a 9 mm Browning in his hand, eased the door open said, "Don't do anything or I will shoot you. Could you all please lie face down on the floor?"

Right, Harry.

Bad thinking.

These people never travel alone.

Next time you'll remember that. Perhaps if you had a little mnemonic device that'd help bring it to mind.

"For every Tweedledum, there'll be a Tweedledee," said Harry.

"Shut up," said Tweedledee, closing the door quietly. He held the gun a little unsteadily as though he weren't quite used to it. It wavered slightly as the man stripped the tape from Tweedledum's head.

Tweedledum winced but didn't talk, even after the tape was ripped from his mouth so he could spit out the tissues. Harry knew that the man was staying silent because he'd been taken. He had failed. Tweedledee, unfortunately, had everything under control.

"I like to do a bed check on my friends, Mr. Bracken. Make sure they are all tucked in and comfortable. Everybody in their proper place. Almost everybody. We're missing your friend, Miss O'Connor. Perhaps you could tell me where she is? Or perhaps you would like me to shoot this older man? I could start on his foot and work my way up. You'd talk before I hit the navel." He was trying to sound cool, and he was almost making it.

Harry guessed that with the band downstairs, no one would notice a gun shot or two. He could barely hear the knocking on the door.

Jesus Christ, knocking on the door?

"Would that be Miss O'Connor?"

Harry prayed to God it wasn't. He prayed that Alex had been picked up by a rich Greek and taken by yacht to Tahiti. He prayed that she had gotten so pissed off with him that she was back at their hotel throwing things in a suitcase.

Tweedledee stood with his gun behind his back and used the other hand to inch the door open.

Alex reached in with an aerosol can of oven cleaner and sprayed it directly into his face.

The man screamed as the caustic hit his lungs and his eyes. Alex shoved on the door with all the muscle she had. The man was trying to wipe his eyes with one hand and bring the gun around with the other. Junior jumped up and caught him with a body check that sent the gun flying across the floor.

Tweedledum was leaping out of the chair as Harry tackled him. The man fell with his knees on Harry's face and Harry heard a quiet snapping sound that could have been made by somebody cracking a turkey bone. All the colors he could see were suddenly red. The room was red, Junior was red, and Alex was red and crawling for the gun in the corner of the room. She picked it up in two awkward hands and shot the man who had his knee in Harry's face. And then shot him again.

Then she shot Tweedledee, who had just slugged Junior and was scrambling for the door. She shot him once more as he fell. Scanning the room with wild eyes, she was looking for more people to shoot, feet properly positioned, gun held in an overlapping grip, body crouched to present a smaller target.

Harry didn't see it. All Harry could do was listen. He remembered thinking that the gun was not making much noise. He took that information through his back files, where he found a distant reference to the armorer's practice of taking bullets apart, dumping half the powder and putting them back together. Very useful in situations where you wanted the accuracy that a silencer couldn't always give you, but still wanted to keep the noise down. Interesting data. Then he fainted.

Harry woke up. It was hot. Sun was bleeding through the curtains. His head was full of pieces of glass that somebody was stirring with an iron spoon. This was his room, and that meant he could get up now and urinate in the privacy of his own toilet. But could he get up? Maybe if he did it slowly, first rolling slowly on his side and then easing himself up with his arms. Very slowly or else the person with the iron spoon would start to whip those shards again.

Now inch across the room toward the bathroom. Then slowly sit down even though that's not your customary position. What was it you were doing? Yes. Flush and then stand up, and let's get over to the bed again. We're doing about half a mile an hour in the straights here, Harry. Slow down for the corners though. He felt for his nose. God had done this to you for hitting Clifford in the nose. God evens things up. Somebody had taped something there.

She's there. She's giving you a hug and now she's looking at your nose.

"Don't ever tell me to leave the room again." She said it quietly. Then she turned and walked out, slamming the door.

Harry sat down on the edge of the bed. He lowered his body and put the head full of glass shards on his pillow. Well, yes. Shooting people always did make you cranky. Police officers involved in fatal shooting nearly always reported feeling anger at the person they'd shot. And then depression, Harry. And you've done something wrong, he thought.

When he woke up, Junior was banging on the door. Over a beer, Junior told him what it was. "She thought that she was more a part of this thing. You started excluding her and she didn't like that. So she stayed around. She sat on the staircase, and heard the other man go into the room. She ran down to the kitchen and got the oven cleaner."

Junior took a sip of beer. "She is disappointed in you. And she thinks she is as involved in whatever this thing is as much as you are. I think so, too."

Harry thought about that as Junior told him the rest. "We put them one at a time in the laundry hamper. Took them down to the car. Spread plastic in the trunk. Took the sheets. Cleaned up the room. Went to my wife's aunt in housekeeping, gave her a hundred dollars of the money we found. She gave me new sheets. She will be very quiet. I went to the other man's room and took his luggage out. I went to the room clerk, Mr. Shaughnessy. I gave him five hundred and sixteen dollars to pay their bill and told him the men had left on a cruise to Martinique. Then Clifford and I took the bodies to my cousin's boat. We took them out to where the plane crashed. There are a lot of barracuda there these days. What are you going to do now?"

"I don't know."

Half an hour later he walked out to the patio where Alex was sitting. "Okay," he said, "I'm sorry. And this time *you* can make the fucking plan."

CHAPTER 27

Calais, Maine, August, 26.

Because a regional carrier had bumped him from his scheduled flight, he arrived one day late. But it probably wouldn't matter. Jamal knew that his mission in Calais was not intended to inflict serious damage on the enemy. It was really an afterthought, a whim of Ismail Gezmis to give the operation some sense of geographical symmetry. The strikes would then have run coast to coast, from Seattle to the Maine-Canadian border.

Jamal guessed that if he didn't come back alive, none of the Palestinians would care. He was an Iraqi and, like all the Iraqis on this mission, he was being treated as an outsider, disposable. His death would only enhance the status of the Palestinians.

He had thought at first that even his assignment was demeaning. He was to walk into the restaurant, ask to see the man in charge, then put a bullet into his head.

One man. One bullet. Jamal considered it a poor use of his time and his courage.

But when he saw the size of the restaurant he realized it would be a challenge after all. The chain had moved quickly in response to the attacks of the day before. Two armed security guards stood outside. He guessed there would be others inside. And the restaurant was bigger, much bigger, than he had expected it to be. There would be a very large staff, and the manager might be difficult to get to.

Jamal parked his rented car in the street beside the parking lot. To one side of the restaurant, a bulldozer was moving back and forth, grading a terrace. Jamal looked at the man at the controls and felt a twinge for the old days, when he had worked on construction in Baghdad. He got out of his car and walked over to watch the machine at work.

Three minutes later, the customers sitting near the windows noticed something strange. The bulldozer left the terraced slope it had been grading and crashed through the low wooden barrier onto the restaurant parking lot. It kept on coming right into the side of a BMW 320i, which it pushed into the car beside it. Soon, three cars were being shoved, one into the other, and the whole collection moved toward the side of the lot. The security guards took their guns out.

Jamal maneuvered the big yellow machine around the lot with remarkable agility. He raised the blade just high enough to catch the side mirror of a Volvo stationwagon and peel it away.

Jamal then spun the machine around and drove back into the side of the Volvo, pushing it into the Buick beside it.

A man at the restaurant window cried out, "That's my car!" and ran into the parking lot, only to be chased back inside by the lumbering bulldozer.

The two outside guards discussed the situation with the security man inside, who also had his gun out.

Some customers were standing with their palms pressed against the windows. They surged back from the glass when it seemed as if the bulldozer were going to crash right through the wall into the restaurant. But the huge machine veered away at the last instant, to push around more cars in the lot.

The customers moved back to the window, only to scatter again when the bulldozer came their way. At the last moment, the huge machine turned.

When the bulldozer careered toward the window for the third time, the experienced onlookers knew the game and held their positions. So when it crashed through the window and kept on coming, crunching through benches, tables, and people, only those on the fringes of the crowd were able to jump to safety. The bulldozer continued through to the serving counter, which splintered beneath it, and then into the food preparation area. Finally, it turned, and rumbled back out through the window.

That was when the guards opened fire. Only two of their eighteen bullets hit Jamal, but they were enough.

Seven other people died under the treads of the machine, and a child was crushed in the stampede to the exit.

The tenth casualty wasn't found until later that afternoon, when Calais police found the body of the original bulldozer operator in the shrubbery at the edge of the terrace.

CHAPTER 28

St. Lucia, August 26.

There is no way to nurse a broken nose, Harry soon discovered. It just sits there in the middle of the face, right between the eyes, and it aches. He'd been right when he told Clifford that it focused the senses. The bandages impinge on the eyesight. The bones grate on each other with any attempt to chew. Smelling becomes an optional extra.

Harry's universe was turning around his nose. If he wanted a glass of rum, he had to first ask his nose how it felt about the idea. If he wanted to stand up, he consulted his nose. At one point he thought about asking Alex if she would help him take his mind off his nose, but quickly reconsidered when he realized how he looked. Sneezing he didn't consider.

Then there was the other problem: the brain wound. Harry had seen Alex shoot two men. Twice each. Harry had killed people, but they had died in the conscious act of preparing to kill somebody else. There didn't seem to be much blame that could be wrung from that. For a time there had been the problem of Harry's shooting the wrong Lebanese, but he couldn't even feel bad about that any more. The Lebanese had had a gun in his hand, appeared guilty, and was in fact guilty of being where he wasn't supposed to be. That he was the wrong Lebanese was a matter of ill fortune, not ill will. Or so you say now, Harry.

But she had killed two men and . . .

Granted she had first been attacked by one man, seen another man attack you and leave you with blood geysering out of your face, Harry. And all this just a few days after she had been bombed, chased, and gone from being a product manager to a fugitive on the run from most of the world. She had reacted naturally enough. She simply shot everybody in the room she didn't know. There was nothing personal in that. It was like spraying the beach for sand fleas.

"You feeling better?" She entered quietly, looking down at the bed.

"There are elephants resting on my nose. I'm ignoring them. But there are whales sitting on the elephants. That would be okay if they didn't wiggle."

"Your nose will look better broken. You were too pretty before."

There was no lightness to her voice. He waited.

"Do you want a drink or something?" she asked finally.

"I think I'll just lie here with my nose. It's probably God's way of reminding me that I shouldn't have belted Clifford."

"I'll get myself a drink then. I'll be back in a minute."

Harry listened closely. He heard light footsteps across the terrazzo, a fridge door opening. There was the sound of a bottle being opened and a short pouring noise. He could hear the cap going back on, and then the cap coming off another bottle. He heard a fizzy liquid pouring and a bottle being replaced on the refrigerator shelf. The refrigerator door closed. Then the quiet feet came closer again.

"I've got a plan, Harry."

He looked at her face. It was hard to see because the last light of day was streaming behind it, making her a gray silhouette.

"Junior's been helping me. I think because he likes you. He thinks you're some kind of blood brother. I told him the whole story and he drove me down to Brazil Street to the airline office and told Sonja's friend there to tell me everything she knew and he sat there while she told me. And I read the newspaper on the 'Lucky 13.'"

Harry tried to sit up but quickly changed his mind.

"The first thing she told me was that the plane was only about half full," Alex said. "That suggests that Mr. Saddam and Mr. Nunni checked in together, since they were originally seated side by side. Then we have Mr. Nunni's name on the slip of paper in Mr. Saddam's wallet. According to the airline office in New York, where they are putting together data on the passengers for the insurance people, Mr. Nunni worked for a company that develops electronic systems for cars. His body has still not shown up. And then there's the fact that the blast came from the passenger compartment, right about where Abdel Saddam should have been sitting. Which makes me wonder if one or both of them had been ordered to sit in that part of the plane. That would also explain the piece of paper with S. Nunni's name. But Saddam wasn't sitting there at the time of the explosion because there were no blast effects on his body. And then there are those thirteen people who never got on the plane at all. Now you think all that over for an hour or so and I'll come back and tell you the plan." She went back out to the living room leaving him staring at the ceiling and trying not to think about his nose.

An hour later she was back. "How's your nose?"

"I wish you'd quit asking about my nose. My nose is a pain in the ass."

"I mean, can you walk and talk and things like that?"

"It's like a permanent hangover. An Ouzo hangover with retsina and banana liqueur."

"So you can walk and talk? That's good. This plan calls for you to walk and talk. You go to New York. Get the story on those restaurant executives. I'd start with an Alistair Duffy."

Harry recognized the name. "Why Duffy?"

"Thirteen of his people were booked on that flight. They canceled. Does that suggest someone knew something?"

"It could suggest that."

"At least one person on board was involved with the Jacamar Corporation. The bomb went off near that person's reserved seat. Does that suggest that Jacamar is involved in the bombing?"

"It could suggest that," Harry agreed.

"Could it also suggest that the Jacamar people told Duffy or someone in his company that the plane was going to be bombed?"

"It could also suggest that," Harry said.

"Duffy's chain serves food and beverages. Kohl's sells beer. It could also suggest that the Jacamar Corporation is concentrating on food and beverage companies. It makes sense. It's easy to adulterate what people eat and drink, and to do it in a way that's hard to trace."

"Explain the airplane."

She thought for a moment. "Could be they wanted to make a point with someone. Or get rid of someone. Who knows?"

"Abdel Saddam," Harry said.

"Or S. Nunni."

"Maybe both."

"Yes. But right now Duffy's organization is all we've got," Alex said. "Besides, I made a short call to Mr. DuVall's office in Santa Barbara. He not only didn't make the Trinidad flight, he never made any flight to New York."

"So I go to New York and talk to Duffy. How do I get to New York? The immigration people likely have my picture taped to their counters."

"I thought about that," Alex said. "It's part of my plan."

"And why me? I was getting the impression this was some sort of joint venture."

"Because you lie better. You lie better than any man I've ever known, and that's the truth."

She sat on the edge of the bed. There was a low hum from the air conditioner in the back wall of the room.

"Is that why you love me?" Harry wanted to know. "Because I can lie?"

"I'm not sure I love you."

After an awkward pause she put a hand on Harry's shoulder. "Maybe," she said. "Possibly. I don't know if I want to love somebody that people keep trying to kill." She moved her hand from his shoulder and rested it gently on Harry's stomach. "You have a nice stomach."

"For an older man."

Harry put his hand on her thigh. "You have a nice thigh."

"For a younger woman."

"I'm not sure I can make love," Harry said.

"Headache?"

He tried to think it through. What things were possible with a broken nose? His hand moved on her thigh. "It would be impossible to do it like the Eskimos, for one thing. No rubbing noses."

"I've always thought nasal sex was overrated." She moved her hand.

"Then, you know, there's my mouth here. It's located pretty near my nose. In fact, it's probably nearer my nose than it used to be."

"Are your fingers working?"

Harry showed her that they were.

She twisted her body, and very gently lay down beside him.

"Say, I'm counting eleven fingers, here," she said.

Harry moved his head to look. Moving his head still hurt. "You could give me a French kiss if you had a very long tongue. Gently."

She did it, gently. "That takes care of the French and the Eskimos."

"There are more than one hundred and fifty member countries in the United Nations," Harry pointed out.

"Abyssinia," she said. "We'll start with Abyssinia."

"Abyssinia? How does Abyssinia work?"

"Well, we can't do the whole thing because we don't have the pony. But first you take off your clothes. Then you take off my clothes."

It took three minutes to ease off Harry's T-shirt without getting it caught in the bandages. He yelled just once.

"How does this Abyssinian thing work?" he asked again.

"'The Abyssinian came down like the wolf on the fold.'" She recited it in singsong fashion.

"Wasn't that the Assyrian?"

"Shut up."

"Which fold?"

She showed him.

"And how do you do it like a wolf?"

"You huff. And you puff. And you blow."

"Oh, *Abyssinia*," Harry said, smiling.

"In all the old familiar places." She started to sing.

It hurt when he laughed, so Harry stopped laughing and Alex stopped singing. An hour later, they started to cover Albania. By then he had almost forgotten about his nose and all the dead people. But it kept coming back to him that she was doing the killing and she was doing the planning and all he was doing was the talking.

CHAPTER 29

New York City, New York, August 27.

Latimer had woken up that morning trying to think of a new way to keep his brain from pouring out through his ears. He had been at this job for fourteen years: look at the face, look at the passport, check for glaring differences between the face and photo, check country of departure stamp and unusual immigration stamps. Check name against hot list. Ask "Business or pleasure?" or "How long will you be staying?" Listen to their answer. Decide if they sound too nervous, too calm, or too aggressive. Make a decision. And through it all keep the line moving.

Latimer knew that the guys who screwed on the gas caps at General Motors had a more interesting job than this. At least the gas caps changed every year.

At Latimer's desk at Kennedy Airport, all you saw were assholes. And if you went on one of those vacation packages full of sun and fun, Latimer, you'd be an asshole too by the time you got to this desk, he told himself. You'd be half pissed, three-quarters sunburnt, and absolutely sure you were going to get that extra bottle through.

To keep the volume of assholes from causing his brain to melt and pour out through his ears, Latimer played games. Some days he passed everybody whose name began with F, asking absolutely no questions. Some days he held up all women who had had their hair corn-rowed. One warmly remembered Sunday, he had stopped all men who wore gold chains. A search of their luggage turned up two kilograms of ganja in eighteen separate lots. "That's spottin' 'em, Latimer," his supervisor had beamed.

Today he was giving a hard time to every eighteenth person. The Nicks had just dropped it by eighteen to the Lakers, and Latimer had dropped an even hundred to his supervisor.

But he knew that despite these little distractions, the assholes at his desk were eventually going to melt his brain and it would leak out through his ears. Seventeen assholes had gone by when the lulu showed up, nose all covered in a bandage. Likely fell down after drinking for six straight days in—where?—St. Lucia. Nope, only been away three days. Something odd there. Guy's name: Gregory Bent. Not on the hot list. Photo not a great likeness, but who could tell with all those bandages and that steel thing on the nose? The guy had two black eyes.

Latimer raised his eyebrows.

"Fell on a diving board," Harry said. "Fat Kraut pushed past me and I fell."

"Nasty pair of shiners."

"Fuck every place but New York," Harry said.

Latimer waved him through. The guy had trouble enough.

Harry stopped at Macy's long enough to buy a new shirt and slacks, which he changed into in the men's wear department. Downstairs, he bought a clipboard and a stopwatch and walked five minutes east.

The building that was home to the restaurant chain was sixty-one storeys of pale marble and mirrored glass, one of the newest buildings in Manhattan. Harry walked over to the bank of eighteen elevators, took out his pen, and clicked the stopwatch each time an elevator door opened. He wrote numbers down on his notepad.

It took the security guard about three minutes to come over; he was winding up to say something when Harry spoke first.

"Number three's getting slower, am I right? I've got my doubts about five and nine too. People been complaining to you?"

"Well, sometimes."

"It's the electronic controls on these things: they just haven't got them right yet. They're done in the same factory that makes the cable converters. You having any trouble with your cable converter?"

"Sometimes, yes."

Harry peeked at the name badge on the man's slightly sunken chest. "You're Luce, right? Security, right?"

"Yes, yes, I am."

"Let me make a note of that. L-U-C-E?"

"Yes."

"What percentage of people have been complaining to you about this problem, and how long has it been going on?"

"It's been going on, I guess, maybe a month."

"He figures longer." Harry jerked a thumb toward the ceiling. "Oh?"

"He figures he's lost two thousand man-hours on these elevators, which would put the expenses in time lost up there around fifty-sixty thousand bucks. You know Al Duffy: he'd have that stuff figured out."

"Yes."

"Then he figures in his own lost time and he's telling my boss that's maybe worth another sixty thou." Harry began riffling through the blank pages of his notepad. "Which one is Al Duffy's floor again?"

"Sixty."

"Yeah, here it is, sixty. What do you know, they got that right. Look, I'd appreciate if you'd let me know if you hear any other complaints. I'll be around again in about a week if I don't get blamed for all this and lose my job. Ha, ha. Just kidding. But seriously, if I were you, I'd take that cable converter back and get a new one. They know what the problem is, they're just not making it public."

*

The sixtieth floor had been done up like an English country manor. But where the portraits of the gentry should have been, hung three large oil paintings of Alistair Duffy, all by different artists. Beneath them was a row of plaques commemorating his generosity to worthy causes.

"Yes?" the receptionist said.

Harry clicked the stopwatch and wrote down the time. "Where's your security badge?" he demanded.

"I don't wear it any more. It's got, you know, this really stiff clip and it sort of ruins the fabric in your blouse."

"Luce didn't tell you about the new imitation gold chains you can hang your badge from?"

"Luce?"

"Security, downstairs."

"No. Nobody told me that."

Harry said the word "Luce" aloud, and wrote it on his note-pad, frowning. "No wonder they've got him down there check-ing the elevators. You gotta follow up every little bit. Been having a lot of trouble with those clasps on blouses. Lot of complaints. That's why we went to the chains. You don't sound as though you've been through a security drill before."

"I just was transferred last year. Just before Christmas."

"Didn't think I'd seen you here before. Just let me jot down your name: I usually get it from the badges."

"Emmy Knowles."

"That's with a 'K' right? Any relation to Knowles down in accounting?"

"No."

"That's fine. What I want you to do over the next few days, Emmy, is go over the security procedures book again. They're just not putting enough emphasis on that. Nobody gets enough time to really study it. But you never know when I'll be back here checking on things." Harry turned to page four of his blank pad of paper. "Station Forty 'F' is through that door, right?"

"Station Forty 'F'?"

"Really. You should take the time—even take a night off from your other stuff—and read the book. Forty 'F' is Mr. Duffy's secretary."

"Oh yes. You mean 'F'. Yes. She's right down there, down the hall, second on the left."

Alex was right. He *was* really good at telling lies. Harry stood and took deep breaths for half a minute, an old engine gathering steam. Then he headed down the hall, taking note of every door and clicking his stopwatch regularly. Two people passed him, striding purposefully. Harry quickened his step. By the time he got to the desk of Duffy's secretary he had warmed up to the role.

"Yes?" she said.

"Station Forty 'F'. Good, but not good enough. He'll want the reports soon. Don't say I didn't warn you." Harry turned and strode purposefully into the private office of Alistair Duffy.

Duffy looked up, disoriented for a second, but then he was smiling, rising from his desk, and putting out his hand to be shaken. "Ah—so there you are. Been too long, hasn't it? What's happened to the old nose there? Jealous husband? Take a seat. Take a seat and tell me what's happening."

It hit Harry that Duffy didn't know who he was, and was just assuming that Harry was an appointment he'd forgotten. "I'm here about the Jacamar Corporation," Harry said.

Duffy leaned back in his chair and folded his hands on his stomach. He tilted his head and watched Harry for a while. Harry watched back. Duffy's face became blanker.

Harry tried again. "The Jacamar Corporation?"

"Who the fuck are you?"

"I'm the guy who's going to save you."

"And what the fuck is the Jacamar Corporation?"

"The people who are threatening your restaurant chain."

"With what?"

"You know what."

"I don't have one fucking idea what the hell you're talking about, friend. Not one."

"I have information—solid information—that indicates that you have been threatened. That these people are going to disrupt your business unless you pay certain regular sums. I want to know precisely what they threatened you with and how much you are paying them." Harry played his ace: "Must cost a bit for services like warning your executives off the Super Platinum Flight."

Duffy sat, head still tilted, but now his blank face had become a tight-lipped smile. It was the smile of a guy who knew he had a full house to Harry's three eights.

"You're not government, friend. Government would have had seventeen pieces of I.D. out by now. I don't know who you are, but I don't think you're officially anything at all. I think you're fishing. And you're in the wrong pond." Duffy stood. "The media? No, I don't think so. Hell, you don't even know what's going on." He reached into his wastebasket and snatched out that morning's *Daily News*. He threw it to Harry. "In fact, if you even read the newspaper, you'd know that it wasn't my restaurants that were in trouble. It's the friendly folks down the street—the we-never-freeze-our-meat folks."

Harry picked up the tabloid. Page one. Full-width head, three-inch-high type: "Fresh meat: mayhem in burgerland." Duffy's major competitor. He saw the picture of a bulldozer. He saw the words "rape," "poison," and "murder."

"I've never heard of the Jacamar Corporation, friend."

Harry clicked his stopwatch. It had taken Duffy just two minutes and eight seconds to find out Harry was a jerk. Talk about efficiency.

When he got off the elevator on the main floor, Luce told him there had already been two more complaints about slowness. Harry handed Luce the stopwatch. "Keep checking it. We're changing the rectifiers now." He walked past the marble and the mirrors and left through the revolving doors.

CHAPTER 30

Los Angeles, California, August 28.

Maxie Schneider leaned back in the passenger seat with his arm around the back of the headrest and wondered what to make of the guy at the wheel. If this bozo was for real, he was going to make Maxie's day. Hell, if this guy was even close to being on the up-and-up he was about to make Maxie's month.

But how do you figure it? Fairly slow Friday morning and you're in your cubicle doing follow-ups, calling to see if people are happy with their new cars, no big deal.

Maxie Schneider had made President's Circle nine months out of twelve last year, and he owed that to the referrals he picked up on calls to see if his customers were happy.

But this morning, all he had reached were secretaries and goddamn answering machines. Christ, he hated answering machines. He wasn't all that big on secretaries, either, when you got right down to it, especially the old ones who weren't happy with just taking down your name and number, but had to ask what company you were with and what the call pertained to. The last one who asked him that, he had been about to suggest she take a big bite out of his rosy red patoot when he suddenly remembered he had already given her his name. So he had just said never mind the message, he'd call back later. Then he'd gone out to the coffee machine, and that's when he'd seen the guy with the burnoose walking into the showroom.

Since he was having that kind of day, the last thing in the

world Maxie had expected was for this guy to tell him he was interested in four of the new SX-Es for his family.

"That must be some family you've got there," Maxie had grinned at him, figuring the guy had just been breaking the ice with a little humor. People did that sometimes.

But the Arab hadn't smiled back. Kept a dead straight face and said, "We are five. But my brother is partial to German engineering."

That had left Maxie's smile just sort of hanging on his face. He tried to recover, let the guy know that this was one of L.A.'s biggest dealers, and not the kind of joint place that would get all googly-eyed because some guy in a dress comes in and orders four cars.

"I'd have to say you came to the right place, sir. Not many dealers could give you instant delivery on that many vehicles. It's been a powerfully good seller. I can't remember seeing anything like it, and I've been selling cars for more years than I'd care to let on."

"My family saw the photographs in *Car and Driver*," Ismail Gezmis said to Maxie. "But none of us has yet had an opportunity to drive one."

"Good as done," Maxie said, almost tripping over his feet in his rush to grab the keys to the demo.

The Arab certainly took it easy on the test drive. Maxie guessed they didn't have traffic like L.A. traffic wherever he came from, and that he wasn't taking chances. The guy had told him where he was from when he had asked him, but it was a funny-sounding name; Maxie couldn't remember.

When they pulled back into the lot, Maxie was all set to steer the guy into his cubicle, pull out the order sheet, start talking options and good old casherooni. But the Arab just stood there, holding out the keys.

That convinced Maxie that the guy had been serious about the four cars, and now he was going to look at something else. He started to panic. The guy was heading for the street. Maxie ran after him. "What was it, something about the car?"

Ismail Gezmis turned back and studied the man's face for

long seconds. "The car is very nice. But I find the suspension a little, ah, tight." Gezmis smiled, and waited for the man to scramble together a comeback. The Jacamar program was going well, he reflected. The volunteers Majeed had sent were proving exceptionally versatile. First against the restaurants, now with the cars. Only the Iraqis he had sent to St. Lucia had failed. Not just failed, but disappeared without a trace. But apart from that, everything was moving to plan.

Now Maxie Schneider had his hand on the Arab's arm, anything to keep him from running off. He noticed that the guy seemed preoccupied all of a sudden, as if he was losing interest. Schneider glanced up and saw Jack Jennings coming down the steps from the showroom.

Jennings had bought the dealership on the commissions he'd made largely through his skill as a closer. Some of the guys still got Jack to close their trickier sales; Maxie hated to do it because the sonofabitch took ten percent of your commission, even though he was the owner.

But he couldn't let a four-car sale wander off down Wilshire Boulevard. "Sir, would you allow me to introduce you to the president of this dealership, Mr. Jack Jennings."

Jennings shook the Arab's hand and gave Maxie a smile that was quizzical enough to ask for a clue, let him know what the guy's area of resistance was.

"This gentleman is interested in acquiring four of the new SX-Es for his family," Maxie said. "But he's a little unsure about the suspension. Might be a little tight."

Jennings's reaction was immediate. Suspension he knew was so subjective that you could talk anyone into feeling a different ride from the one they were getting. He fixed Maxie with the look of a scolding teacher. "You didn't by any chance take him out in the blue one, did you?"

Maxie wasn't sure where Jack was going with this. Jack was quick on his feet, but sometimes too quick to keep up with. The blue one was the only SX-E demo they had. "Ah, yes I did, as a matter of fact."

"Maxie, Maxie, Maxie," Jennings said, shaking his head.

"You have to start reading my memorandums. The blue demo slipped off the ramp when they were unloading. I'm not surprised the gentleman noticed the ride. Compared to others it bounces around like a tank. That's why I asked you all to use the beige."

Maxie thought he knew what was coming next, but he couldn't be sure. With Jennings you never could. All he knew was that they had never had a beige SX-E in the dealership. "I ah, think the beige one got sold," he said.

Jennings was already shaking his head before Maxie finished. "I've never seen anything like it. This car is in such demand, we can't even hang onto our demos. Tell you what. Maxie, bring the blue one over here. I want to know exactly what the gentleman is thinking in terms of suspension. Because—and Max, I don't want any of the other boys to know I'm doing this—that car's suspension can be fine-tuned on the hoist. I'd be quite prepared to do that with the compliments of Jack Jennings Motors."

Ismail Gezmis watched with satisfaction as Maxie bounced away with happy steps to get the blue demo. He had watched Maxie's eyes during Jennings's performance, saw him feverishly try to catch up with the master salesman's peregrinations, and noted the pleasure in his face each time he caught up. Now he watched Maxie get into the car, the car whose brake pedal Gezmis had just tapped three times quickly, before turning off the key. As Maxie closed the door, the Arab snapped his fingers and said to Jack Jennings, "My umbrella. Foolish me," and began walking up the steps to the showroom. He turned when he heard the engine start up. The car shot forward and was already doing thirty by the time it got to where Jack Jennings was standing. Jennings bounced up over the hood and lay spreadeagled on the roof until the car bounced down the ramp and onto Wilshire Boulevard. Gezmis heard a squeal of brakes and the thud of a distant collision. As curious salesmen began to press their faces to the showroom windows to see what in hell was going on, Gezmis walked back down the steps and glanced over at the remains of Jack Jennings. "I think," he said to himself, "that I'll shop around a little longer."

CHAPTER 31

San Francisco, California, August 28.

Felix Tidyman was at the wheel of an SX-E sports sedan, metallic blue. Marjorie Brooks was in the bucket seat beside him. He gave her a mischievous smile and said, loud enough for the salesman in the back seat to hear, "I don't think so."

"What do you mean, you don't think so?" Marjorie Brooks shot back. She was feeling playful too. Everything had been going so well recently that they had finally stopped annoying each other with speculation about the team they had sent to St. Lucia.

The salesman behind them pretended that he hadn't heard. "A wonderful car, don't you think, ma'am?"

"I don't like the brakes too much," Tidyman said. "Big car like this, you expect a better brake."

"They seem okay to me," Marjorie Brooks said. They had agreed beforehand to get into an argument and stomp off in separate directions as soon as they got back to the dealership.

"How could they seem okay to you?" Tidyman snapped. "*You're* not driving the goddamn car."

"Moves like a dream, though, doesn't it?" the salesman said.

"Yeah, but the way the assholes drive in this town, a man's got to have a good brake under his foot." Tidyman changed lanes quickly and the driver behind leaned on his horn.

"Look who's talking about driving like an asshole," Marjorie said, pronouncing it "ahh-sole."

The salesman spun around in his seat to look at the angry man in the car behind and got a raised middle finger for his troubles. "The ah, turn indicator is on the steering column there. On the left."

"Guy was following way too close," Tidyman said.

"He wasn't exactly following, *dear*," Marjorie pointed out. "He was in another lane. At least he was until you cut him off."

Tidyman turned in his seat to catch the salesman's eye. "Women. What are you supposed to do with 'em, eh?" he grinned to the salesman.

The salesman gave him a nervous grin back. He hated it when people turned around while they were driving, especially when he was in the car. "Right, right," he said, hoping to sound noncommittal and keep the lady on his side. She seemed to be the only chance he had now, and that was certainly no screaming hell from the look of things.

Tidyman turned back to face the road. Suddenly he jammed the brakes down. Marjorie Brooks and the salesmen were both thrown forward. The driver in the car behind leaned on the horn again and, this time, kept leaning. The salesman took out his handkerchief.

"I guess the brakes aren't that bad," Tidyman conceded.

"No, they seem to be working pretty good," the salesman agreed, wiping the side of his head with his handkerchief.

"I don't know, though. It's a lot of money for a car," Tidyman reflected. He turned left without signaling. The driver behind, still leaning on his horn from the last offense, sent a string of obscenities through his window.

"That was a lot of money for a boat, last year," Marjorie Brooks improvised.

"You all said you wanted the boat," Tidyman told her. He saw the dealership sign ahead and pulled into the curb lane.

"Yes, but how often do the girls and I get to use it?" Marjorie was getting into it now.

The salesman was relieved to see they were back at the dealership. He hated when people started in on each other like this. You never knew how to handle them, and they almost always buggered off without buying. Still, he had to give it the old try. "Just pull over there, if you would, and we can go in and look at some of the color options. These people are doing some really exciting things in upholstery coordinates."

"You know that you and the girls are welcome on the boat any time you care to come," Tidyman said. He drove up the ramp, then turned the wheel sharply, as if he'd suddenly changed his mind. The car was now on the sidewalk, blocking it completely.

"Just pull right over there, by the door will be fine," the salesman said.

"Oh, yes, the girls and I are welcome any time," Marjorie mimicked. "You think I'd dare take the girls near that crowd of drunks you're always out there with?"

"Clients," Tidyman said. "They're clients."

"Just right over by the door, if you would," the salesman said. He noticed that pedestrians were having to walk around the car and were giving them dirty looks. That sort of thing didn't reflect well on the dealership, not at all.

"Any man who has to suffer fools like that for clients ought to take a good, hard look at how he earns his living," Marjorie shouted back.

"If we could just move the car—"

"It's a good enough living to keep you in decent clothes, and pay your club fees, your housekeeper, your shrink—"

Marjorie took a deep breath and glared at the salesman in the back seat, then back at Tidyman. She started pummeling his shoulder with her fists. "You are a despicable, wicked man." Suddenly, she stopped and jumped out of the car, bumping into a fat man, who already looked a little unhappy about having to walk around the car.

No, this sort of thing did not reflect at all well on the dealership, and the salesman knew that it could hurt them all. "Sir, if you could just pull the car onto the lot, maybe by that door there."

But Tidyman was now sitting with his head cradled into his arms against the steering wheel. "Why does this always have to happen?" he sobbed, while the salesman wished once again that he had stayed in school, maybe taken that degree in Chemical Engineering.

Without warning, Tidyman jumped out of the car and ran after Marjorie, yelling, "Wait!" The salesman sighed and swung open the door, almost hitting a woman who was wheeling a baby carriage around the car. He got in behind the wheel and turned the key.

With screeching tires the car bolted off along the sidewalk, just missing the woman with the baby carriage. Fighting for control of the wheel, and leaning on the brakes and the horn as hard as he could, the salesman steered the car down the next ramp and onto the road. As soon as he got the wheel straightened out, he reached to turn off the key.

But by then he was in the middle of an intersection and an oncoming truck smashed into the side of the car and sent it careening into the path of a brightly painted van. The van swung sharply to miss the collision, and bounced up onto the sidewalk, pinning two pedestrians against the wall of a convenience store.

CHAPTER 32

Brattleboro, Vermont, August 29.

Alex took a different plane back and cleared customs in Miami. As she stepped off the aircraft, she undid the top three buttons on her blouse. The immigration official studiously compared her chest with the head and shoulders of Mrs. Isobel Dunnin on the passport Alex gave him. He asked her cleavage a few quick questions, then waved her breasts through. "Thank God they passed," Alex murmured to herself.

Junior had arranged with a temporary maid at their hotel to borrow Mrs. Dunnin's passport. The resemblance to Alex wasn't remarkable but glasses, a scarf, and the three loose buttons got her through. She did up the buttons and looked for connections to New England.

Biff seemed relieved to see her, but she knew that he was worried about Harry. He had pulled the heavy drapes closed in the room where he kept his computer, and was sitting in almost total darkness in the early afternoon. Sometimes darkness nudged aside his worries of the day, he told her. But not this time. Biff had kept the terminal screen alive, looking for news. But there had been nothing about Harry, nothing about the Jacamar Corporation, and nothing more about Mr. Duffy's restaurant chain—just that bizarre streak of atrocities at his competitor's.

"I wouldn't worry so much about him, my little cabbage,"

Biff said, consolingly. "Harry, despite his appearance, does know how to look after himself. I particularly call to mind one fine evening in Naples when he flattened two Italian gentlemen who disputed his claim that pizza—real pizza—was developed in New York City, and that the Neapolitan edition was mere ketchup and crust. He flattened them while he was drunk, too. Quite drunk. I was drunk, as well. So were the Neapolitans. Fine evening all around, though it wouldn't have impressed Cholly Knickerbocker. Care for some wine? Not the plonk I pour for the Holstein-Friesian people, but some stuff I've had resting for a round dozen years."

Alex nodded. She walked to the wall and studied a painting of a haystack. Monet? A real one? Biff gathered air into his lungs and yelled for Gisele.

She appeared with an air of huge impassivity in the doorway.

"Wine," Biff said, "that stuff from St. Pauline."

"Where is Harry?" Gisele asked.

"Bring three glasses," Biff said.

Harry was still in New York City. He was rehearsing in front of a bartender, who was good at uncapping beer bottles. Harry kept emptying the bottles to see how good the bartender was. "Maybe we should just let the terrorists have it all; have you ever thought of that?" Harry asked. "Let *them* be the government. Let them run the airlines. Let them run the cruise lines. Let them have the whole fucking works, and then see if any airlines or cruise lines get blown up. Did I tell you that the PLO already owns three airlines?"

"Yes," the bartender said.

"Fucking well do, man. Fucking well do. And have you ever heard of those airlines being threatened? No. Guaranteed no. Not ever. So, you want a safe world, we just turn it over. Just give them the keys and the ownership papers and tell them to slip behind the wheel."

The bartender seemed unconvinced, so Harry took another beer and explained the whole idea to him again.

*

Biff also seemed unconvinced when Harry staggered through the door later that evening, wondering if Biff would cash a cheque for a three-figure sum. A Manhattan taxi driver in the doorway behind him was holding Harry's watch and insisting on cash payment for what had clearly been a long and memorable fare. The three faces that greeted him were too overcome with relief to object to his condition. Biff welcomed him back, said that it was time to put on his nighttime bag, and left. Gisele shook her head, then paid the cabbie with large bills extracted from the nether reaches of her pockets. Alex kissed him, held him long enough to make his shoulder wet. Then she put him to bed.

Next morning, over eggs and aspirin, he explained what had happened at Duffy's. Biff sat quietly, until Harry finished his entire report. "I am going to commune with my databases." He put his wheelchair into reverse, knocked over a Boston fern, and headed at flank speed to his study.

There was silence in the morning room. Finally, Alex said, "Okay, so my plan wasn't very good."

"I don't think it's because your plan wasn't good. It got us back to the States. But maybe we should just stop now."

"And if we just stopped, what would we do?" Alex asked. "The police are probably still looking for us. The Jacamar people are definitely still looking for us. Do we send them a note and tell them we've decided to just stop? Tell them we've re-evaluated our positions and decided to drop out?"

"Let's just stay home," Harry said.

"The thing is, these people are going around killing other people, too," Alex said. "It isn't just us. They're bombing planes and bulldozing restaurants."

"And there are people starving in Africa. We can't fix everything. I've checked. We're not qualified. Not in my résumé. Not in yours."

"Not my table," she said quietly.

"It is *not* my table." He threw a napkin down.

"So you want to resign?"

"We weren't hired in the first place. Did anybody hand you an application for Freedom Fighter? 'Woman required to combat forces of evil—typing an asset'?"

"I can't type."

"I can't combat the forces of evil."

"Speaking of which . . . "

"You're right. I should check in with Bill Penzler."

At noon, meandering in the garden, they heard the hunting horn, followed by Biff's reedy voice: "To horse!" Harry took Alex's hand and led her up to the porch, where Biff sat smiling, the horn across the blanket on his knees.

"Any squirrels out there?" asked Biff.

Harry shook his head.

"I've been spraying them with my colostomy bag to shoo them away from the crocus bulbs. Makes a dandy water pistol. I'm tempted to try it on encyclopedia salesmen." Biff paused. "I have half a plan."

"Half a plan?" Harry asked. "A whole plan would be nice, since as of this morning I don't appear to have a job."

Biff waved off his concern. "I wouldn't worry about Mr. Penzler. Come. Let's away to the scotch room. Warmer there. Right atmosphere for planning. Or at least plotting. When this was a girls' school I'm quite sure the girls used to do their plotting there. It reeks of prepubescent schemes."

"Is this plot prepubescent?" Alex wondered.

"Yes. Thoroughly boyish: a plot with scabbed knees. You'll adore it. So will I. Who knows? Brisk activity like this may delay my internment at the Home for Vague Oldsters down the road."

Looking down the hunting horn as if he were peering through a telescope, Biff told them what he had learned from the databases. "First, we checked out Mr. Duffy. Self-made man who unmade several other self-made men whilst making himself. One of his suppliers, fellow who sold him pickles, took a large loan to build up his production capacity on the basis of a contract from Mr. Duffy. Mr. Duffy found a loophole that allowed him to renege on the contract. The pickle man went broke. Duffy's bought his factory. Vertical integration, I think they call it. Mr. Duffy seems to have done quite a bit of it. His rivals have also suffered from his predatory pricing and selective regional promotions against specific competitive targets. All just within the letter of the law, all brilliantly effective."

"For some reason, none of this surprises me," Harry said.

"Everything we know about Mr. Duffy suggests that he would have no ethical reservations about dealing with low-lifes like the Jacamars," Biff said. "And the fact that his executive team escaped Flight 603 indicates that he is probably doing business with them. Also, we have no evidence that any of his restaurants has ever been disturbed."

Harry pulled at his ear. "You think Duffy paid them to pay attention to his rival?"

Biff nodded slowly. "An acceptable premise. I also asked my equipment to look into the affairs of Mr. Nunni. Through a human resources database established by the Society of Automotive Engineers, I was able to establish that a Mr. Sal Nunni was indeed an expert in automotive electronics, educated at MIT and interned for a short period at ITT. Now why do we have an expert in microcircuitry seated on a plane next to a man who adds potions to beer bottles that make people go woopsie? A common interest in stamp collecting or fern gardening? Clearly, the bomb on the plane was meant to extinguish Mr. Saddam at the same time. Perhaps their usefulness had ceased, assuming Mr. Nunni *had* some usefulness at one time. It's very interesting, my children. Just yesterday in California, there were a couple of bad accidents, believed to have been caused by unintended acceleration."

Harry and Alex exchanged glances.

"The curious thing is that, although these incidents took place in different cities, they both involved the same make and model of car."

CHAPTER 33

New York City, New York, August 27.

Sirhan Nassar was doing even better than Ismail Gezmis had predicted. Gezmis, when he had heard about the dealer convention in New York City, had guessed that, of those who would drive to it, a good number of them would show up in the new SX-Es. Gezmis had thought perhaps as many as eight or ten, but so far this evening, Nassar had parked fifteen, tapping the brake pedal on each of them three times before he shut off the key.

It had gone well from the start. Nassar had first shown up four days ago, asking for a job parking cars. Told there was nothing open right now, he'd struck up a conversation with Tony, one of the regular car jockeys. Nassar had come back every day since, quickly becoming a familiar face around the ramp. This afternoon, the supervisor had looked at him as if he were going to kiss him. "You're on. That jerk-off Tony never showed up today. Never even called in. And here we've got a fuckin' car convention."

The hardest part for Sirhan Nassar was trying to act surprised when he heard about Tony's absence.

Nassar took care to park the SX-Es where they would do the most damage when they took off. In the garage, he left them in outer aisles so that when they were started they would cover as much distance as possible, instead of just bumping into a wall or the car ahead of them.

He parked three of the cars on the entrance ramp to the garage and, after 8 p.m., he put all the rest above ground. The owners might have some trouble finding them but, Nassar guessed, that would be the least of their troubles that evening.

His only regret was that he wouldn't be around to watch the entertainment. The image of nearly new cars racing wildly through an underground garage, while others squealed up a ramp and bounced out into the streets of Manhattan was extremely appealing. But Ismail had told him to do his job and go directly to the airport.

CHAPTER 34

Chicago, Illinois, August 29.

The telephone room had been Tidyman's idea, but Gezmis had been quick to approve. The first part of the plan was to have fedayeen and students out priming SX-Es for self-acceleration right across the country. Students with the better American accents worked all day in a telephone room—a roomy suite with three phones at the Airport Holiday Inn. The students called newspapers, wire services, and radio and television stations across the country. By rotating their calls, they were able to call each newsroom several times to ask what was going on with these killer car SX-Es.

They had started phoning the Los Angeles media as soon as they got the signal from Ismail Gezmis that one of the cars had taken off on its own volition down Wilshire Boulevard, injuring several motorists and killing the owner of a large Los Angeles car dealership: ironically, a dealership that sold the killer cars.

Gezmis liked that phrase, "killer car." He told the telephone people to use it often, hoping to plant the term in the minds of the media.

When Felix Tidyman called in with his report from San Francisco, the telephone room staff passed it along to the Bay Area media, pointing out that a similar incident with a similar car had occurred earlier that day in Los Angeles.

When one of the phone room staff called the next morning to report that an automobile saleswoman had been seriously injured in Philadelphia, the story became national, and the wire services began to pay attention. Soon a rumor took root that a delegation of auto executives were meeting at a Manhattan hotel (true) to discuss the crisis (untrue); by then the New York media were familiar with the story, and itching for a strong local angle.

Which they got later that evening, when the first SX-Es started roaring up the hotel ramp and rocketing through the streets of New York City.

CHAPTER 35

Brattleboro, Vermont, August 30.

Harry was contemplating the way Biff had organized his library. Most people he knew did it by subject, although there were a few who went strictly by the alphabet. But Biff organized by color. All books with green covers went in one section; those with red covers went somewhere else, and blue covers somewhere else again.

There were a few exceptions: *How Green Was My Valley*, although it had a red cover, was in the green section, and *Red China Today*, black cover and all, was in among the reds. But the colors almost always ruled where the book was positioned, and the colors were arranged in the order of the colors of a rainbow. Harry thought the room was most attractive library he had seen, the two walls of books an almost perfect prism.

Gisele sat near the library door, contemplating Harry. "You are very like he was," she said.

"Who?"

"Biff. When he was young, he never knew how to wait, either. You look like a chicken chasing after ants, going from one book to another, never stopping, shifting from foot to foot. Biff was that way when we sent the people out. Always pacing. Or fooling with papers so that it would take days to get them back in the right order, or bothering the people in the radio room or asking the pilots again if they were absolutely sure of where they'd done the drop. Or going out and getting drunk. He was not a man of action physically. He was a man of action mentally, and I think that disturbed him. He didn't think that was fair somehow, with the war on. I think he dreamed about it. He was always thrashing around at night. It was very disturbing. If you have nothing to do, then you should do nothing."

A biography of Eugene Debs was in the red section although the cover was brown.

"How is your nose?" Gisele asked.

"Out of joint," Harry said. Biff was still in the study playing with his wonder box while simultaneously phoning around, a lightweight headset over his ears.

Biff had ignored Harry that morning and tucked himself into his electronic womb. Harry thought that Biff could live forever, fragments of his body replaced one by one by diodes, motors, and pumps, until the final, most important, part needed the ultimate repair. By that time science would have developed a brain to be inserted into the array of other pieces and Biff would be immortal.

Maybe it was wrong to depend so much on Biff.

Alex came into the library. "We could go for a walk," she said.

"Not right now."

"Would you like some coffee?"

"No, thank you."

"Would you like me to leave you alone?"

"I don't know. I'm sorry." Harry sat down and realized he didn't want to be sitting down. He stood up and walked over to the bookshelves again. *The Curse of Loni* in a white cover was in the black section. Why was that?

"He is like Biff was when Biff was a younger man," Gisele explained to her. "Biff once went three weeks without hearing from an agent, and it nearly drove me crazy. There were any number of things he could have done during the wait. He could have done other work, he could have taken up gardening, he could have written poetry, but he could do nothing during the wait, except wait. Like a dog waiting for someone to come home from school. When the person is late, the dog doesn't look for bones and doesn't chase doves; the dog simply waits."

In the white section there was a *Book of Common Prayer* with a black cover.

"What did you do with Biff during the war?" Alex asked.

"Helped him wait. But it didn't do very much good."

"Oh."

"It didn't do very much good. Between the waiting I would help him rush around. I was a dogsbody. Biff used to go for days without sleep. Three and a half days once. Just eating toast and drinking tea. It wasn't healthy."

"Why didn't you tell him to eat better? You should have just told him," Alex said.

"You have my permission to try and tell Biff anything he doesn't want to hear. You have my permission to tell Harry also. Impossible to live with."

"I recognize the type." Alex smiled in Harry's general direction.

"Not well enough." A warning from Gisele.

"Not well enough yet," Alex said.

"Maybe I'll go for a walk," Harry decided.

But he heard the electric whine and Biff was in the room, his lap covered with papers. "The Princes of Serendip went looking for something which they ended up not finding. But they found something else which was better. Hence 'serendipitous.' I like my library. The color scheme guarantees that you will never find what you're looking for, but you often end up finding something better. With my electronic effluvia I went looking for a somebody who poisoned beer, but ended up with a somebody you wouldn't buy a used car from. It all begins to tie together. Come, my children, and your Uncle Biff will tell you a story. May I have a whiskey?" he asked Gisele.

She nodded and walked to the buffet where the whiskey lived and poured him a very small drink in a large glass with a thick bottom, the kind of glass cheap bars employ to exaggerate the size of their servings.

"Once upon a time in a country whose name you would recognize, a group of evil men got themselves together around a table. And the leader of the evil men, whom we'll call Fred, told the other men in the Evil Men's Club that they were very short of cash. Donations had not been coming through, remittances were not being remitted. And due to the heavy expenses of the club—magazine subscriptions, the rising cost of thermite, the price of automatic weaponry—the Evil Men's Club was in a difficult position. They simply had to have more money. At this point I visualize that there was a lot of muttering around the table and shifty-eyed glances and blame-spreading. Then Fred told them that he'd been out duck hunting when an idea had struck him. He had noticed that when you went out to hunt ducks it was always best if you went to where the ducks were. Fred said there was a lesson in this and the lesson was that if you wanted money, you'd best go where the money was. To him that suggested America, where there was more of it than anywhere else. Everybody around the table nodded and said what a good idea that was."

Harry and Alex looked at each other.

Biff continued. "In America, Fred told them, there were things called companies that produced a variety of items like potato chips and ships and artificial fingertips. They also produced money. These companies produced money in direct proportion to the amount of confidence placed in them by the public. If they were to lose public confidence, they would lose the ability to make money. So Fred said, 'I propose that our organization go over to America and sell them confidence, or rather, get into the insurance business, and insure these companies against a loss of confidence.'"

"Who in his right mind would willingly go into the insurance business?" Harry mumbled more or less to himself.

"Well, Harry knows all about insurance," Biff said. "He will tell you that it is no good offering to sell insurance unless the intended buyer has faith that your firm will be able to deliver. So Fred and the Evil Men's Club, being new to the business, set out to prove their stuff. This they did first at Kohl's Brewing, proving with a relatively mild demonstration that they were worthy of their hire. Having gained good experience in the beverage business they decided to go into the food business as well."

Alex gave Harry a congratulatory pat on the arm.

"Alas," Biff sighed, "even the food and beverage business could not give them all the money they wanted. But Fred had already planned for that. He stood up in front of the Evil Men's Club and sprung his big surprise. Thanks to some brilliant preparatory work, they would soon be able to go where the big ducks splash around. They were going to introduce themselves to the biggest companies in the world: the companies that assemble automobiles."

"Sal Nunni," said Alex.

"You'll notice I use the word 'assemble,' rather than 'manufacture.' This is because companies such as Ford and General Motors buy little pieces of automobiles from thousands of factories and stick them together. To sabotage an automobile company—according to a large database given over to engineering matters—you no longer have to go to Detroit. You could do it by visiting a component plant in Des Moines or Cicero, Illinois. Or a plant that makes the computer chips that decide how fast a car will travel, and sometimes when. Say, a plant in Silicon Valley."

"Poor old Sal Nunni," Alex said.

"If you went to such a plant," Biff went on, "you would meet a very clever engineer whom Alex has correctly identified as Sal Nunni. At least you would have met him had you acted a few days ago when he was still alive."

"But how?" Harry asked. "All those cars. Jesus Christ!"

"At this point, we must interject a little automotive history. Over the years, a number of companies have produced cars that would occasionally take off without being directed to do so by their drivers. If we go back to the days of the Stanley Steamer, we will remember that it was a favorite trick of some of the owners of that marque to start the fire in the steam engine and then walk down the street in front of the car, knowing that the car would eventually start to follow as it built up steam. I myself had a 1939 Terraplane that had a sticky throttle that would occasionally stay open at awkward moments. Then there was that Audi business that was described on *60 Minutes*. And there have been accusations against some other brands as well."

"But where does it take us, Biff?" Harry tired quickly in history classes.

"Well, the important datum, dear youngsters, is this: in all of those cases the story evolved gradually. An incident would happen in one place one day, then someplace else a few weeks later, and then a third place perhaps a month after that. There was never a case in which sixteen cases of auto hyperkinetics were recorded for a single brand on a single day. But, as I pointed out earlier, there is such a case now, if you would care to browse through these printouts from the *New York Times* news service. I have since discovered that the computer chips in those cars are all from the firm that employed Mr. Nunni. Isn't science wonderful?"

By judicious balancing and careful control of his joystick Biff could use his wheelchair as a rocker. He was doing it now as he watched them read the news, grinning broadly, humming a tune from *The Pirates of Penzance*.

Harry looked up from the papers. "I'm going to Detroit."

"We're going to Detroit," Alex said.

"*I* have to go to Detroit," Harry said.

"We could all go to Detroit," Biff suggested. "We could take a picnic lunch of fried chicken and enjoy the whole cultural melange of the city. Cookie prize for first packed!"

"I am going to Detroit. Me. Alone. Solo. Unaccompanied," Harry said.

"There's an unnecessary redundancy there, Harry," Biff suggested.

"We are going. Us. Together," Alex said.

"It's too dangerous," said Harry, and saw too late that that was the most dangerous thing he could have said.

She began stabbing him in the chest with her finger. "Listen, Harry, if it weren't for me you'd be goddamn fish bait in Rodney Bay instead of pretending goddamn heroics here. If it weren't for me, you'd be goddamn Grade C mincemeat in Niagara-on-the-Lake."

"Alex, if it weren't for you I wouldn't be an international fugitive. I wouldn't have ended up in one hotel room where people were going to bomb me, or in another hotel room where they wanted to shoot me."

"Harry, I think I've demonstrated that my competence exceeds yours. In fact, what I'm going to do is go to Detroit alone, by myself."

"Me. I. Harry. I am going to Detroit. Alone. Period. End of story."

Biff loved it. "Why don't you children go alone together? I mean, you have so much in common: an ability to scream, to argue unintelligently, to gabble. Puts me to my mind of my dear, dead wife."

"Okay: she can go if she wants to. But she's not coming with me."

"You can't say that, Harry. I was going to say that. And look at your face. It's red. High blood pressure. You're too old to go."

"Good, good, children. I'll start keeping score. I think Alex's last remark counts for a three but I doubt the Romanian judge will give you any points for style. Gisele?"

"She reminds me of your wife."

"Yes. Doesn't she? I think they'd both better go." He kept the lightness in his voice but Gisele had made her point. Biff's wife had died in 1945 in Holland, but Biff had not been there. He had been home in England, waiting like a dog.

CHAPTER 36

Beverly Hills, California, August 30.

Ismail Gezmis walked out to the circular drive, as three olive-complexioned men in business suits stepped out of the limousine and marveled at the house. They looked a little jet-lagged: their flight across the ocean and then across the country had been long, even given the comforts of first class. But there was a sparkle of anticipation in the eyes of all three. They were like a management team from head office come to inspect the new branch plant.

"Very nice, Ismail old friend," Gamil Rashid gushed in Arabic. He was obviously the leader. "Tell me, do your neighbors know what you are up to?"

"My neighbors unfortunately are all entertainment people. Not an ideal situation, but with the shortage of good housing being what it is, one takes what one must take."

They laughed and Gezmis spread his arms to usher them into the house.

In the foyer, the newcomers greeted the four others who had arrived earlier that day. Felix Tidyman and Marjorie Brooks were there as well, with some of the fedayeen and students who had taken part in the restaurant raids and primed the SX-Es for unwanted acceleration.

"Ah, so this is the team of whom we have heard so much," Abu Salim, one of the new arrivals, trilled. "Ismail, Felix, my friends, you have done well."

Tidyman shuffled his feet and said nothing.

Gezmis shrugged. "We could not have done it without your men."

"From what I hear," said Walid Ibrahim, an Iraqi traveling on a Saudi passport, "this program was so well organized that it would have worked with recruits from the American Boy Scouts."

"Better, if I know the men I sent," laughed Gamil Majeed. "You would have spent less time rousting Boy Scouts out of brothels the night before a mission."

"Brothels?" giggled Abu Salim of the Islamic Jihad. "Well, it's comforting to know that there is at least one American business that it is still safe to patronize."

"Ahem," said Marjorie Brooks.

"Quite right, my dear. Gentlemen, please." Ismail Gezmis clasped his hands in front of him. "Perhaps you would care to refresh yourselves, and Felix and I will show you through the American headquarters of The Jacamar Corporation."

Rashid noticed the look that passed between Gezmis and the woman and smiled to himself. Well, well, after all this time.

The tour began in the basement where one of the students sat hunched over a computer terminal. Gezmis invited the visitors to lean in and look over the young man's shoulder.

"All I see are numerals," said Rashid. "One of the many gifts bestowed by our people upon the civilized world. But what do they mean, Ismail?"

"They mean that Antoine has coaxed a password from a disgruntled employee of the world's best known credit-card company. They mean that Felix or I will be making a proposition to that company early next month. They also mean that it doesn't really matter if they accept our terms for a security contract or not, since we are now able to open and close accounts at will, directly from this terminal. Antoine can persuade the computer to dispatch cheques in any amount he chooses to 'retail' outlets that are really just post office boxes in our control. All that remains is to resolve where those cheques should be dispatched to," Gezmis smiled.

The visitors stared as the young man at the console flashed his fingers across the keyboard and changed digits, randomly adding to and subtracting from the credit accounts of unsuspecting strangers.

"Can such a thing be possible?" marveled Rashid.

"We're not exactly pioneering in this," Felix Tidyman admitted. "College students, even high school kids, have been cracking into computer mainframes for years. It doesn't get a lot of publicity any more, largely because it tends to encourage other kids to break into bigger and better computers."

"But we have one or two advantages over students and other pranksters," Gezmis explained. "You see, for the 'hacker,' as such amateurs are known in this country, the challenge lies in making penetration."

"It so often does," murmured Rashid. The others laughed. So did Marjorie Brooks.

Only Ismail Gezmis remained prudishly straight-faced. He ignored the interruption: "The hacker is moved more by a sense of adventure than by out-and-out larceny. So he, sometimes she, is usually content to merely trespass through the files and leave the information unchanged. A few, of course, find it hard to resist leaving their signature, a kind of harmless, coded graffiti. I suppose it's the same sort of thing that motivates the youngsters of New York City to spray paint public buildings."

"Boys will be boys," smiled Marjorie Brooks.

Again, Gezmis declined to share in the laughter, which confirmed for Rashid that his relationship with Marjorie had indeed moved on to a new plateau. Remarkable. Ever since the death of Qatar, Gezmis had treated her more as an uncle might. He seemed to accept the need for her intimate roles with total strangers on a mission, but always made it difficult for anyone who sought a more conventional relationship with her between missions. Gamil Rashid had often entertained such a notion himself on his visits to Paris, but had always ended up taking his fantasies to professional women in heavily scented rooms.

Gezmis was still talking. "Also, should a typical schoolboy hacker encounter an obstacle, such as a password or code that cannot be deciphered, he will soon move on to something else. An amateur is not likely to resort to violence or coercion to get the information he requires."

The visitors murmured in agreement.

"On the other hand," Gezmis continued, "more ruthless criminals, who might be able to obtain such information by force, would have no idea what to do with it."

"We may be the only bunch capable of doing both," Felix Tidyman said.

Gezmis swung open a door leading out to a patio. A large table had been set with pitchers of iced drinks and Middle-Eastern snacks. Four young men in white kitchen uniforms stood by ready to pour.

"When I think"—Abu Salim's shoulders began to shudder with incipient laughter—"when I think of those New York Jews starting their new cars, then being jolted through the streets of the city. It is very funny, very funny. I should like to have a videotape."

"But not all of the attention has been desirable, has it, Ismail?" Walid Ibrahim asked. The Iraqi's expression didn't fit with the laughter around him. "There have been casualties, I understand. And you have been pursued."

"We have, it seems, attracted the attention of a small investigatory organization. An unofficial organization. Almost amateur," Gezmis conceded. He edged back toward the table and sampled a kibbee. "You must try these, Gamil."

Walid Ibrahim persisted: "They have caused a great deal of inconvenience, it would seem."

Felix Tidyman turned his head and spat a mouthful of pine nuts into the shrubbery. "More than inconvenience," he said, wiping his mouth with his hand. "We've lost a couple of people and the two assholes responsible are still around."

"Still around?" asked Ibrahim. "Around where?"

Gezmis silenced Tidyman with a look. "They were around Buffalo, New York. They were around Niagara-on-the-Lake, Ontario. They were around the northern part of St. Lucia. We have not yet succeeded in termination."

Gamil Rashid smiled curiously around a mouthful of borek. "I'm afraid I don't understand. We have bullied our way into major American businesses, received payments in the millions, inflicted all manner of chaos on American cities, yet we cannot terminate two men?"

"One of the men, I'm afraid, is a woman," Gezmis said quietly.

Now it was Rashid's turn to spit out food, but without the benefit of shrubbery. "A woman?"

"It is a different world, here," Gezmis said, fluttering his hand as if to ward off further queries along this line. "But Felix will confirm that they will both be dead within a week."

"Yes? And how can you make this claim with such confidence?" Rashid wanted to know.

"The two people we are talking about are fugitives," Tidyman explained. "And not just from us. The law is also after them, so there are only so many places they can go. Not only that, the man and the woman are now in the uncomfortable position of having to prove their innocence of things that were done by us. The only way they can prove their innocence is by nailing us. That's going to send them looking for us, and that's why they'll both be dead within a week."

"Please," Gezmis said. "We have many more items to discuss today. Sullieman, if you would . . . "

On cue, one of the four students who had been pouring drinks and serving food stepped smartly to a redwood patio shed, walked in, and emerged almost immediately, lugging an easel. He set it up in front of the buffet, went back to the shed and pulled out a large presentation pad and a pointer. He placed the pad on the easel and flipped the cover back to reveal the first page. Then he handed Gezmis the pointer and withdrew to take a position against the high wall of the patio, watching with the others.

"Thank you, Sullieman." Gezmis flipped back the cover of the large pad to reveal a crude illustration of a coffee cup, complete with wavy lines to indicate ripples of steam. "Americans enjoy their coffee as much as we do. Fortunes have been made upon America's passion for coffee. As with most things they do, they enjoy it to excess. This may be one reason that coffee has been linked to such ailments as heart disease. A growing part of the industry is dedicated to decaffeinated coffee, but most Americans are addicted to caffeine."

"Myself as well. Do you suppose that one of our young friends might arrange for a pot?" asked Rashid.

Gezmis looked at the boy next to Sullieman; the young man nodded and hurried back into the house. "It is on its way," Gezmis promised. "Although in a few weeks you might be a little more circumspect in ordering coffee in this country."

"Oh, dear, oh, dear," said Salim, eyes twinkling.

"One of our young colleagues at the Berkeley Medical School informs me that the amount of caffeine in a regular cup of coffee is sufficient to raise both the metabolism and the pace of the heart. He also claims that quantities of a chemical called Biosol added at any stage of production would cause the heart to accelerate to such a degree that eventually its vessels will explode."

"Ismail, you are incorrigible. Could we have a videotape?" laughed Salim.

"We have a number of options open to us here," Gezmis continued. "The large importers constitute one group. The major food companies that package the household brands are another. I favor the food companies myself. Some of them have spent prodigiously on building up not just awareness, but consumer trust. We have three of our people within one of these companies already positioned to act upon our needs. I thought we would begin with minuscule amounts of Biosol on a very limited scale. This would mean the death of a handful of heavy users, just enough to get the press at the ready, but not enough to destroy one of the more popular brands of coffee."

"How much do you think it would be worth?"

"Forty, perhaps fifty million dollars," Gezmis said. "At first I thought more, but the margins of profit on coffee are not extreme. There is, however, sufficient money being made to justify a contract with our group."

Gezmis flipped the page to another crude drawing that looked like a large cylindrical storage tank. On its side were the letters LNG.

He gestured at the page. "LNG stands for liquid natural gas. Scattered throughout North America in some very interesting locations are these mammoth storage tanks ... bombs just waiting to go off."

"Fuel storage containers?" asked Salim.

"To call a liquid natural gas tank a storage container for fuel, is like calling the Nile an irrigation stream. To begin with, you must consider the process of liquefying natural gas. By a process of refrigeration, its density increases to six hundred times that of the gas that is used in home heating and cooking. Now, as we all know, straight uncompressed cooking and heating gas is often enough to blow up a house and take a life or two. But can you imagine the devastation that could be created with a substance six hundred times as potent?"

"Surely the storage tanks would have been built only in desolate wastelands," Rashid suggested.

"Happily, no," Gezmis replied. "There are economic benefits in locating them close to major population centers. This makes their vulnerability doubly interesting."

The young man who had been sent to bring the coffee emerged with a tray, but no one took his eyes off Ismail Gezmis. He flipped to a new page on the easel: a group of stick drawings, resembling a man and a woman and two smaller figures. They were grouped around an item on legs that might have been a barbecue. Above them was what looked to be a cloud.

"A suburban family," Gezmis explained, "about to enjoy that great American weekend tradition, the family barbecue. Twelve miles away, too far for them to have heard the explosion, a liquid natural gas 'fuel tank' has just developed a massive leak. The liquid has turned into dense clouds, one of which we see floating gaily over the landscape. Floating until it makes contact with ... "

He flipped to the next page on the pad. The male stick figure had a lighter in his hand. " ... with a flame!" Gezmis continued. "Any flame. A cigarette, a pipe, a barbecue lighter."

He flipped the pad once more to reveal a comic strip formula explosion. Parts of the stick figures—legs, arms, heads—strewn randomly over the page.

"The Americans are curious people in this regard," Gezmis continued. "The news of a single disaster destroying one American neighborhood, or even a portion of that neighborhood, would have far more impact than the destruction of an entire city in our part of the world. Their concern, however, will play into our hands. I believe the energy barons would be most anxious to avoid any undue attention from the media to the topic of liquid natural gas, particularly since there are large ocean-going tankers—in effect floating firebombs—already jeopardizing sea lanes and world ports. I think they would like to believe that the potential they offer has not yet caught the attention of people in our profession. I think they would do business with us to ensure that things remain as they are."

Gezmis turned the page to reveal a drawing of an upturned hand. On one of the fingers was a small saucer-shaped object. "A contact lens," Gezmis explained. "Not a mass-market item, but it gives us a wonderful entree into a mass-market industry: the major U.S. drug firms. Several of them have products for contact lenses, which, knowing that vanity has few restraints, they sell at unconscionable mark-ups. Perhaps three or four hundred times the profit percentage on coffee. We feel they should be prepared for a little inconvenience if they wish to maintain those levels. So we are introducing an additive of our own. The name of the substance has more syllables than I am able to remember at the moment. The effect, however, is memorable indeed. It dissolves the cornea in the eye."

Tidyman could not help shuddering. As he looked around the patio, he noticed that some of the others were reacting, too. Sullieman, the young boy who had brought out the coffee, was shaking his head and screwing up his nose. Tidyman clearly wasn't the only one who considered tampering with the human eye a more gruesome prospect than death.

"I won't go into any great detail on the rest of these," Gezmis promised, flipping to the next page, which showed a magazine advertisement with a smiling baby, a spoon in its hand. "Our coffee is ready so let me just skip directly to our critical path."

Gezmis revealed the final page, a three-year calendar linking dates to events. "Not all of our programs will occur at once. We do not want a sudden flurry of unrelated disasters that would unite the American security apparatus. Instead, carefully, quietly, we will get the country used to perhaps one disaster a month." He smiled. "They are almost used to that now."

CHAPTER 37

Detroit, Michigan, August 31.

Gezmis was right: Felix Tidyman had no trouble getting through the team of presidential secretaries and reaching Petrelli on the phone. Petrelli had already talked to Foster Styles. He had been waiting for Tidyman to call.

"Perhaps you'd like to get together," Tidyman suggested. He had always enjoyed the way that powerful people played games with understatement.

"Of course I want to get together," Petrelli snapped. The president's tone was a country mile away from understatement. That unsettled Tidyman for an instant. Just when you thought you had the bastards on the ropes, they came back swinging. But Petrelli quickly sensed it was the wrong approach. After three or four seconds of silent line, he added in a softer tone, "If it's okay with you, Mr. Tidyman."

"Well, then maybe we should get together," Tidyman said.

This time, when Tidyman walked through the glass doors of Petrelli's head office, he saw a smartly dressed young woman talking to the pair behind the reception desk. She looked at her watch as he approached. "Mr. Tidyman?"

Tidyman assumed she had come to escort him to Petrelli's office, but when the elevator stopped at the presidential floor she steered him in a different direction. Partway down the hall she led him into a huge room paneled in oak. In the middle of the room was an oak table with two dozen blue upholstered chairs.

At the end of the table sat Petrelli. To his right sat Foster Styles. The other chairs were filled by twenty total strangers.

Petrelli jumped up to shake his hand. Tidyman was still looking at all the faces turned his way like twin banks of lights along the length of both sides of the table.

"I thought we were going to talk alone." Tidyman was visibly unsettled.

Petrelli studied his face for a moment, then took his arm and tried to nudge him toward an empty chair. Tidyman stood fixed. Petrelli nudged harder. Tidyman shook him off. "I thought we were going to talk alone," he said again.

Petrelli shrugged and made his way back to the end of the table, a skipper more comfortable at the helm. "Under the circumstances, I felt it best to bring in my colleagues from the various departments that this ah, situation, will impact upon: Tech Services, Customer Relations, Corporate Affairs, Legal—"

"No, I don't think so," Tidyman said.

It had been a long time since anyone had cut off the president in his own boardroom. "You don't think so?"

"I think that you'd be more at ease talking with a crowd around than I would," Tidyman said.

"Could save a lot of time," Petrelli persisted, "yours as well as ours."

"If I wanted to save time, Mr. Petrelli, I could just walk out that door and save myself the rest of the afternoon, couldn't I?"

Petrelli walked back and touched his arm again, as if that might keep him from heading for the door. "Okay. Fine. We'll talk. You and me. Let's go down to my office and we'll talk."

He steered him out of the room by the elbow, leaving the twin rows of lights bobbing in confusion.

"You'll have a drink, Mr. Tidyman?" Petrelli sat down and spun in his chair to a cabinet behind his desk.

Back to a one-on-one situation with a half-a-foot, fifty-pound advantage, Tidyman was suddenly more at ease. "No, I don't believe I will. Thanks all the same."

"Then you don't mind if I . . . " Petrelli let his voice trail off under clinking ice cubes. He splashed bourbon over the cubes, held the drink up to the light, reflected a moment, and poured in some more. He lifted the glass in Tidyman's direction, took a long swallow, pursed his lips, and studied his visitor as if he were seeing him for the first time. He pressed a button on an intercom. "Audrey, no calls," he said, then snuggled back into his chair.

"Well, I have no idea who you are or what the fuck you're up to, Tidyman, but I'll give you this much: you handle yourself like a pro and I have to take my hat off to you. I'm a businessman and I like to see business, even one as shitty as yours, done with a certain élan."

Tidyman didn't react.

Petrelli swirled the liquor in his glass. "But what I can't figure out is, Why me?"

"You don't know? You really don't know?"

"I really don't. It can't be our profits."

"The difference is you."

"Us?"

"No, no. You personally. You go on television, talk to people like you really give a shit, like we're going to see a human being get in there and turn things around. 'New spirit of America,' shit like that. When all you're after is a bigger bottom line."

"Hey now . . ."

"You say to people that the old values still mean something, that hard work, management, sharp ideas can still get the job done. You could have shown some real leadership, helped get this country back off its ass. But instead, you just did what the other guys did. You pushed for government quotas to keep out your competition and to help you drive up your prices. And profits. Some people, a lot of people, think there should be something better, maybe a real new 'spirit of America,'" Tidyman said. "But you didn't deliver."

"I want you to know that if it was up to me you wouldn't get a dime," Petrelli said.

"But it's not up to you, right?"

"If it were up to me, you would have walked into a carload of

FBI people when you pulled in here this morning," Petrelli said. He stopped to give a little smile to show how that thought pleased him. "But some of my team are of the opinion that that would be playing into your hands by turning you into some kind of martyr."

"It wouldn't do your sales a whole lot of good, either," Tidyman pointed out blandly.

"I'd be prepared to bite the bullet on that. Take the heat from the dealers, the unions, the press. I can take that kind of heat."

"Yes, yes, you're one strong fucking soldier all right, Mr. Petrelli. But you're not going to take any heat at all on this, are you?"

"If it was up to me—"

"Yeah, yeah, you'd hang out your dick and wait for the 'gators. But you've let your team make your decision and the team's decided that you should keep your fly zipped up, isn't that right?"

"God, you're one sonofabitch, you know that?"

"I'm going to tell you exactly what I want," Tidyman said.

"And I'm going to tell you if you're anywhere close to reality."

"I want seventy-eight million dollars a year."

"And I want you to take a fast flying fuck, Mr. Tidyman. I'll close the joint down first. Believe me. I would close the fucking place down."

Tidyman stood up to his full height. He pulled back his shoulders and clasped his hands behind his back. He walked the length of the room, nodding to himself. Then he started to laugh. It was a rich, full-throated laugh and Petrelli thought seriously about going for the buzzer on his desk. He was about to press it when Tidyman settled down and started wiping his eyes with his sleeve.

"What's funny? Why do you find that funny?"

"It just hit me. You can't sharpen a fucking pencil without calling in the senior executive committee. You couldn't close the place down if you wanted to."

Petrelli started talking very fast: "Yes, well that's not what I meant, not what I was going to—"

"But I could," Tidyman cut in. "I could close you down. That's what hit me as funny. You're the boss. But I'm the one who can bolt the doors."

There was a light tap at the door behind the desk. The gray-haired woman opened the door just wide enough to say in a very soft voice, "I'm sorry, Mr. Petrelli, but there's a call—"

"Audrey, for God's sake—"

"For Mr. Tidyman," the woman added. "The caller says it's urgent."

Petrelli snatched up one of his phones and handed it to Tidyman.

Tidyman smiled into the phone. "Yeah? You're all set? Wait. Maybe I should write this down." He patted his jacket, and looked around for something to write with. Petrelli shrugged and handed him a pen. "Okay, go ahead. They're ready in Washington? Just a sec. Washington, Atlanta, yeah, Miami, St. Louis, New Orleans, Newark, Pittsburgh, Kansas City. Okay. What happened to Phoenix? Oh, yeah, okay. Just a sec. It might be a go. I just got told to take a fast flying fuck. No. It's just a figure of speech. Yeah, well I'll explain it to you some day. I don't know. Wait a second, I'll ask."

Tidyman covered the mouthpiece. To Petrelli he said, "One of my colleagues. They're all set to do some, ah, new car inspections in nine, no, sorry, eight, they've only got eight more cities. He doesn't think the cars are going to do very well, and he doubts that he'll be able to keep the media away. What do you want me to tell him? And don't tell him what you told me about taking, you know ... He's still trying to figure out what it means."

Petrelli's face went white. "What are they going to do?"

"You know, usual stuff. See if there's been any improvement in the SX-E's tendency to automate itself when least expected. Should be a lively afternoon."

Petrelli, the legendary thinking-man's manager, was breaking into a sweat.

Tidyman looked at the covered mouthpiece of the phone,

waiting. To Petrelli he said: "I don't want to rush you or anything but my, ah, colleague is calling long distance."

"Jesus Christ!" Petrelli lashed out and sent the stack of papers that Audrey had placed on the edge of desk flying to the floor. "Goddamn you people. Goddamn you all to hell!"

"Better hold 'em off," Tidyman said into the phone. "I think we're going to do some business here."

CHAPTER 38

Detroit, Michigan, September 2.

Policemen. Two of them. Headed his way. Harry turned back to the woman at the airport Avis counter who had just handed him his keys. The Avis woman had already started to process another customer, and the cops were almost at the counter. "Ah, just one more thing, miss," Harry cut in, "I'm looking for the nearest office of"—that's the way; time it so the cops are well within earshot when you let it drop—"the Federal Bureau of Investigation."

The two cops walked on without pausing, and Harry sighed in relief. But within seconds he realized what an idiot he'd been. Clearly, those cops had no interest in Harry at all. But what if one or both of them had recognized you from a photograph, Harry? What photograph? Well, how about the one that Bill Penzler would have handed over without thinking twice about it? The photo that Hanover Casualty took for your identification card, the one that makes you look as if you eat live babies for breakfast. Now let's say that the photo had indeed imprinted itself upon the memory cells of law enforcement officers here in Michigan. And just suppose they had decided to come and talk to you about it, no guns or anything, just two young cops casually strolling over, smiling and chatting to each other on the way, until one of them says, "Morning, Mr. Bracken. Patrolman Tom and I would like a quick word."

Even allowing for that unlikely slew of suppositions, would your asking for directions to the FBI really have sent them spinning away on their heels? Think about it. If you had legitimate business with the FBI would you be waiting until you got to the Avis counter to find out where you were going? Jesus, Harry, you really are amazing at times. Those old synapses and neurons must finally be turning into porridge.

Too bad, Harry. You used to be reasonably good at thinking on your feet, back when you figured the freedom of the Western World was riding on each move. Now that it's only *your* miserable freedom at stake, you're screwing up all over.

Bad enough that you got Alex drunk on Biff's forty-year-old cognac, last night, then tiptoed downstairs without your shoes on. What's she going to say when she wakes up and finds you missing? Thank you, Harry, for leaving me behind?

He had thought about Alex through most of the flight. He knew that they had only been lucky in Ontario and again in St. Lucia. They were both in well over their heads.

He found the Plymouth he'd asked for. He loved Plymouths because they were invisible. He threw his case in the back and climbed behind the wheel.

Then he sat there trembling. He was alone and scared and, although he didn't know why that mattered more to him now than it had mattered before, the cops in the airport—two guys likely just heading for their lunch—had really rattled him.

Thank God that he had something to take his mind off things. Thank God that all he had to do now was get in to see the president of one of the world's largest firms.

And just how do you get in to see the chief executive officer of a car company, Harry?

Mull that one over.

You could just go and sit in the man's reception area and refuse to leave until he sees you. Or wait until some strong young men in conservative suits come to guide you quietly to the parking lot or a police car.

Or you could just phone Petrelli for an appointment. Except a company like that, selling twenty-three billion dollars worth of cars a year, is going to have people who take messages for the people who take messages for its chief executive officer.

How else could you do this, Harry? Pretend to be a fund raiser for the Republicans? In this suit you'd never pass for a Republican.

What you need is a disguise: maybe dress up as a penguin and tell the palace guard you've come to deliver a singing Pengie-Gram. Then when you get into Petrelli's office you whip off your beak and tell him that you can help.

Or convince a secretary that you had once been in the navy with the man, and that he still owed you twenty bucks and wouldn't it be a heck of a gag if you let me into his office to surprise him?

Finally, Harry decided to drive to head office and ask to see him about some "urgent personal business." He parked in the visitors' lot and walked through the big glass doors. Two security guards looked him over but said nothing. Harry strode purposefully to the reception desk, where he noticed that not one but two matronly women guarded the portals.

Neither of them would buy Harry's urgent personal business line or anything else he might be there to sell them. Especially insurance. That's what did him in. When they insisted on seeing some I.D., Harry handed them his Hanover Casualty business card. The first woman turned the card over as if there might be something more relevant on the other side. Then they looked at each other, ready to burst out laughing.

"I can tell you for a fact that Mr. Petrelli is very well taken care of with insurance. You'd be wasting your time," the nearest matron told him.

The two security guards began strolling toward the reception desk, side by side.

Harry knew his time was running out. He tried the sincerest look he knew. "I have to tell you, it's a matter of life and death."

"Life insurance always is," the nearest receptionist said, and the other one tittered her appreciation. By that time, the security guards had reached the desk. Harry looked them over, and decided he'd leave and try something else.

He checked into a downtown hotel and sent Petrelli a telegram: "Your relationship with Jacamar Corporation about to be revealed to major networks and *New York Times*. Sender wishes to discuss options. No monetary demands. Contact Gregory Bent, Room 1608, Detroit Plaza Hotel." Harry wondered what the real Gregory Bent would think if he knew what kind of life his name was leading these days.

He expected he would hear from one of Petrelli's lackeys, someone assigned to "find out what the bozo wants," but when the phone rang less than one hour later it was the man himself.

"I won't do this over the phone, Mr. Bent. I want to do it face-to-face. Meet me at seven tonight, Old Giancarlo's. Your concierge will know the address. Give your name to the guy in the tux at the front of the restaurant. He'll show you to a private room."

As soon as he gave Bent's name at the restaurant, the maître d' led him directly to a room at the back. The floor was covered in red and black plush carpet; the walls were darkly paneled, and a crystal chandelier hung over an oval table that would have comfortably seated eight, but was set for only two. The maître d' stood at the door while Petrelli patted Harry down.

"Jesus," Harry said, "you don't think I'd go to all this trouble just to shoot you, do you? I'm not carrying a gun."

"So I see. Thanks, Jerry, we'll be okay."

The maître d' closed the door quietly behind him.

Petrelli waved for Harry to take the empty chair. "You want to order before we talk? The spaghetti is good: tastes like food. That's what they serve here. Real food. Not like those pseudo-wop restaurants: all chrome and potted plants and limp-wristed waiters. And they're not ashamed to have spaghetti on the menu. I like that. Pour yourself some chianti. I'll get us a waiter."

Petrelli leaned back in his chair and pressed a mother-of-pearl button on the wall. Seconds later a waiter opened the door, tapping lightly as he entered. He took their order for two plates of spaghetti and two salads with house dressing, then left.

"Talk to me," Petrelli said.

Harry poured a glass of wine and took a generous swallow.

"You were approached by a group that calls itself the Jacamar Corporation. They told you they could screw up your sales unless you paid them money. I don't know how much money, but if you told me a hundred million it wouldn't surprise me. You refused. Now they're screwing up your sales to demonstrate how well they do their job."

"Keep going."

"Yours isn't the only business they've gone after. They've also been rough on the burger folks and a small New York State brewery. What you want to know are their future plans for the automotive industry."

"Keep talking: I haven't heard you tell me anything yet."

"My group—" Harry began.

"Does your group have a name?"

"Several names actually. I don't think you'd know any of them."

"Right."

"My group can indicate to you which other automobile manufacturers will be affected and when."

"How much do you want?" Petrelli asked.

"Nothing."

"Nothing?"

"No money. What I want is information. We, my people, need to know more about the Jacamar operation. We have extensive information already and we're very close to making our move. But we need a few more details. I think you can help us. I think we can help each other."

"You with the government?"

"I don't think you should ask me that. If the Jacamar people ask if you've talked to the government, you want to be able to deny it. That's important because I know you're still vulnerable, very vulnerable, Mr. Petrelli."

"That dog won't hunt."

"You don't believe me?"

"Nope."

There was a knock on the door and the waiter brought in their spaghetti dinners. A second waiter followed with a bowl of salad. He was a tall man, and looked like someone Harry might have seen before. As soon as the dishes were placed on the table the waiters left.

Harry took another gulp of wine. Neither man spoke. Accordion music from the restaurant leaked into the room.

Harry blinked first. "I'm not with the government."

"Yup."

"Not directly at least. You remember when Howard Hughes built that big ship to mine the ocean for magnesium nodules? There were all kinds of stories in the papers about how undersea mining was the wave of the future. But the whole thing was just a cover for the CIA. The CIA got Hughes to build the ship so it could retrieve a nuclear sub that the Russians had managed to sink off Hawaii. When national security is at stake the government calls in other resources."

Petrelli reached for the bread knife and cut himself a slice of bread. "So you're really Howard Hughes, is that what you're saying, Mr. Bent?"

"No, no, I was just using that as an example."

"Keep talking."

"Actually, the less said the better. On that score anyway."

"Keep talking anyway."

"I guess really that's all I can tell you. I think the deal I've offered speaks for itself." Harry leaned over and cut a slice of bread, dipped a corner of the slice into his spaghetti sauce and tried it. He grunted his approval and spiraled spaghetti onto his fork. But he had a hard time fitting it into his mouth. He picked up his napkin and wiped tomato sauce from his chin.

Petrelli stared. "That's it? That's all you've got to say?"

Harry kept chewing and finally swallowed. "That's it. I think you're in a take-it-or-leave-it situation here, Mr. Petrelli."

Petrelli reached for the wall button and jabbed it twice.

Harry took another bite and was wiping away more sauce from his chin when the door opened again. The tall waiter who had looked slightly familiar came in and raised an eyebrow at Petrelli.

"You were right," Petrelli told him. "He knows dick-all."

Felix Tidyman nodded and put his hand under his waiter's apron. The hand came back out with a Walther 9 mm pistol in it. "Stand up, Bracken. Put your hands against the wall."

Petrelli waved him back. "It's okay. He's not armed."

Harry looked from one man to the other. "Mr. Petrelli?"

"Yup."

"Is this the new spirit that's abroad in America?"

"Get fucked, Bent."

"I'm not really Gregory Bent," Harry confessed.

"Come on, Bracken. Time to feed the worms," Tidyman said.

"Mr. Petrelli?" Harry hoped he didn't sound like he was begging. That wouldn't work on a man like Petrelli. "You don't want to pay these people."

"Let me ask you something, Bent. Bracken. Whatever. You ever had your balls grabbed hard? Huh? Can you even imagine some big hairy hand with a vise-lock on your nuts? Think about that for a minute and think about what you'd do if these were your balls in question. Do you think you'd run away?"

Harry thought he knew where Petrelli was going with this. He said, "No, I wouldn't run away. But listen—"

"You listen. You wouldn't run away. Fine. Would you yell for help and get the guy that owned the big hairy hand your balls were in all ugly and annoyed? Would you do that, do you think? See, what we're into here is a situation where our friend Tidyman and some Middle-Eastern buddies have got the vise-lock on my scrotum. And it's going to hurt a lot more to run away or yell for help than it is if I stand and give them what they want."

"You're going to be giving for a long time," Harry said.

Petrelli sighed. "Tidyman knows that if he squeezes too tight the balls will drop right off in his hand and there'll be nothing left to squeeze. Meanwhile, at least I'm getting something in return for my money, which is a fuck of a lot more than I can say for the money I send in to the government."

"What about me?" Shit. Harry hadn't meant it to come out like that. Petrelli would respect a tougher stand. Trouble was, the waiter with the gun—Tidyman, Petrelli had called him—looked as if he were getting twitchier by the minute.

"You still haven't told me who you are," Petrelli said. "All I know is who you're not. And you're not somebody who has to keep a business with half a million employees and a dealer network going."

"No."

"I don't even know your name. He calls you Bracken. You call yourself Bent. What am I supposed to call you?"

"You could call me Harry," Harry said. "And now that we're on a first-name basis, I'd appreciate it if you wouldn't let this salad waiter shoot me."

"I don't think I can help you there, Harry."

Petrelli opened the door and disappeared. Tidyman moved closer. "What we're going to do is leave the room. But instead of going out the way you came in, you'll turn right as we go through the door. You'll see a busboy. He's a colleague of mine. We'll walk out the back door to a gray stationwagon. You'll be going in through the tailgate and you'll be lying down in the back. It's a nice big car; you should be comfortable."

In the alley, the wagon—appropriately, one of the new SX-Es—was waiting with the tailgate down. Tidyman nudged Harry toward it. A man dressed as a busboy stood between Harry and possible escape through an untidy row of garbage cans. Two dirty pigeons were taking inventory of the spillage.

The back of the wagon had been hung with quilted blankets, the kind used by moving companies to protect their customers' furniture. Harry climbed in head first and lay on his side. He wondered if it felt like this inside a padded cell.

The man in the busboy's uniform got behind the wheel. Tidyman climbed into the back seat and devoted all of his attention to Harry. His left arm was slung over the back of the seat; the Walther 9 mm was pointed at Harry's belt buckle.

The wagon started with a lurch and Harry wondered for a moment if they were all going to be victims of unintended take-off. Wouldn't that be a riot, Harry? Someone turning the tables on the Jacamars. You'd really enjoy a move like that, wouldn't you, Harry?

You'd enjoy it even more if the fuckers hadn't brought you along.

CHAPTER 39

Route 94, Michigan, September 3.

North of Detroit the highway skirted small towns all lit up for the evening. Felix Tidyman stretched his long legs across the back seat and reflected on his day.

He had begun his afternoon profoundly disappointed with Angelo Petrelli. On the phone, the voice of the American Dream personified had actually quivered. Someone had sent him a telegram threatening to tell the world that the Jacamar Corporation was shaking him down. What the hell was going on, he wanted to know. Hadn't Tidyman assured him, absolutely *guaranteed* him, that this would never happen? *Could* never happen? Didn't Tidyman realize that this could put the whole company under? Here he was, Mister Media himself, stumbling on about how this could destroy him, and take maybe a couple million employees and dependents down the tubes.

Assholes, Tidyman thought. They spend half their life in school and the other half learning on the job, and they still can't make a decision under pressure. That was one of the problems with business today—and with the people in government whose job was to regulate business—they'd been hiding behind the skirts of group thinking so long they'd lost the art of making a decision on their own.

But Tidyman had done his homework. He knew Petrelli was a regular at Old Giancarlo's, and felt sure that for a spender like him they would do what was asked, which was to come up with a couple of spare uniforms and keep out of the way of an important backroom deal.

Tidyman's second disappointment had been when Aly had met him at the airport. Aly was a Palestinian student enrolled at Ann Arbor University. Tidyman had told him on the phone precisely what he needed.

But Aly had shown no initiative at all. When Tidyman had hurried Bracken through the back door of the restaurant, the boy stood picking his nose, watching a pair of pigeons haggling over garbage. If Bracken had been anything like the tiger his advance billing had indicated, he could have lowered Aly with a knee to the nuts, swung him around to shield himself from the Walther, and made a break for it through the trashcans.

But Aly hadn't done his job and neither had Bracken. People just going through the motions, one disappointment after another. Maybe Bracken just wasn't taking them seriously, didn't really accept that Tidyman planned to kill him.

Hard to believe a guy could have lived so long making bad decisions like that.

But with Aly driving as if he were going out of his way to attract a cop, Bracken might have got lucky after all. Brainless little peckerhead squealing out into the traffic like that; why didn't he just drive up the steps of the fucking precinct house?

No thanks to Aly, they had made it to Route 94. Tidyman had spent most of the time making sure that Bracken stayed where he was supposed to. The guy really did look helpless back there.

Of course, he hadn't looked all that impressive the first time Tidyman had seen him in Niagara-on-the-Lake. But then he'd had the girl with him, and the guy had seemed to at least have a little life to him.

This was the guy who had done Tariq and Mahmoud down in St. Lucia. Was *supposed* to have done Tariq and Mahmoud: at least the guys hadn't checked in yet. Had missed three check-ins. They'd better be dead or he'd kill them himself for screwing with procedures.

Now, stretched out in the back of the wagon, Bracken was more like a sack of old laundry than the man who had Ismail and the other Arabs so worried. Lately, Ismail had begun to wonder if Bracken and his people were getting some kind of inside information out of the Jacamar Corporation; he couldn't understand how Bracken always turned up where he wasn't expected. Tidyman wasn't sure what to think about that. But he knew that he was going to have to knock the guy around a little to see whether or not they had a leak.

Tidyman was feeling weary. He would have been just as happy to kill him and get it over with.

Suddenly, the laundry came to life. "Is Tidyman your real name?" it wanted to know.

Tidyman kept the gun steady. From the corner of his eye he noticed Aly turn his head to see what was happening. "Eyes on the road, asshole," he cautioned Aly.

"My real name's Harry," Harry said. "Harry Bracken. I'm in insurance. Hanover Casualty. It's actually a pretty good company. I'm doing rather well there if I still have a job. They care quite a bit about me. What I'm saying back here is that I think I could raise a hundred grand if you were to take me someplace, open the back door, hand me a mailing address and just drive on."

Tidyman shook his head in disgust. Not only had this sad-faced clown stopped fighting, he didn't have the first fucking idea of how to go about buying his way loose.

"Are you going to torture me for information?" the jerk-off was asking now. "I'll tell you anything you want to know. No need for anything physical."

Tidyman tested a little reverse psychology. "You don't know anything worth working up a sweat for."

"There are things you should know," the laundry shot back. "And there are things I should know. I think you're going to try and kill me. I'd like to know why."

Tidyman made a circling motion with the gun; he closed one eye and looked down the barrel.

The clown kept blabbering. "I think I should know why. That way, you know, if I'm going to come around this way again I won't make the same mistake. Don't you think I have a right to this information?"

Tidyman thought that over. "The reason I'm going to kill you is that I promised a guy in Los Angeles that I would kill you. Of course, if you tell me something that this guy in Los Angeles needs to know, I may not have to kill you. That's up to you. But I have to keep this man's trust. Other than that, I don't really have a logical reason. It's not as if you've really been hot on our heels or putting us in any real danger. It's the guy in L.A. I promised, and I can't see any way around it, so why don't you shut up and think about what it might be that this guy in L.A. might like to know."

The clown clammed up.

"That sign says New Baltimore," Aly pointed out. "Don't we want the road to New Baltimore?"

Tidyman sighed heavily. "If I told you I wanted to take the road to New Baltimore, then I guess that's the road you ought to take, Aly. You didn't hear me say we were taking any other road since then, did you?"

"I was just checking, that was all."

"Take the road to New Baltimore. Two and a half miles past the cut-off there's a road to the right. A very rough road. You take that road. Then you drive exactly three miles to a clearing, and then you stop the car. You got that or do I need to write it down for you?"

"I got it. You don't need to write nothing down."

Tidyman could see the side of Aly's face; he saw the lips moving. Dumb fuck was repeating the directions over and over to himself so he wouldn't forget them. Tidyman looked back at Bracken. He was still sulking. "Hey, Bracken, lighten up. I didn't mean to hurt your feelings."

The loser rolled over and faced the other way.

Aly pulled off the bumpy country lane into a clearing. He shut off the lights and killed the motor. "We are here," he told Tidyman proudly.

Tidyman looked around, satisfied. Not a light to be seen. Some kind of engine sound way off in the distance, a truck or maybe a farmer doing some nighttime plowing. That didn't matter; whoever it was wouldn't hear a thing.

That was how it went when you did your homework. Tidyman had spent an afternoon scouting the countryside on his first visit to Detroit in case he might need a place like this. You look after the little things, you survive.

"Aly, go around the back and open the door." To the sulking heap in the back, he said, "Aly is now going to open the door. I want you to get out. I want you to get out slowly."

"I'm going to stay in here," Harry said.

"Get out or I'll shoot you right there."

"You're going to shoot me anyway, so I think I'll just stay inside here."

"This is not my car. I don't care if it gets untidy."

"You said you needed to know things," Harry said. "And I don't think you drove all the way out here so they could trace you through bloodstains in a rented car."

The tailgate swung open and Aly peered inside. "I'm staying here," the ill-mannered captive told him.

"Drag the fucker out," Tidyman said.

"I'll fight. I'll boot you in the balls. Hard."

"Aly, get this asshole out of here."

Aly pursed his lips.

The prisoner tucked his knees into his stomach as if to get more leverage for a kick. "Aly, if you touch me, I'll kick them right off."

"Drag him out," Tidyman urged. "Just grab him by the feet and drag him out."

Aly reached inside for a foot. Harry moved farther inside the wagon. "I can't reach his feet," Aly said.

"Jesus Christ." Tidyman shoved open his door, stepped out, tucked the Walther inside his belt, and walked past the blanketed windows of the wagon to the tailgate.

CHAPTER 40

New Baltimore, Michigan, September 3.

Harry made his move as soon as Tidyman left the back seat.

From his fetal position he uncoiled and sprang forward just as Aly reached in to make another grab for his leg. Aly was so astonished that Harry had changed his mind about coming out that he didn't have time to react to the shiny steel object the man had in his hand.

Harry plunged Old Giancarlo's breadknife into Aly's left eye.

Tidyman had almost reached the back of the wagon when he heard the scream.

Aly jumped back, blood and other liquids gushing from the hole in his face. He staggered into Tidyman who was reaching into his belt for the Walther. Tidyman needed both hands to push Aly away, and that gave Harry the split second he needed.

First, he leaped from the tailgate and caught Tidyman with a flying shoulder. Then he slashed the knife across the side of his neck. Tidyman fell back, but on his way down he yanked the Walther out of his belt. He hit the ground just as he got the barrel aimed at where Harry had been an instant earlier. But by this time Harry had sprung to one side and placed himself in a perfect position to bring the heel of his shoe down hard on the fallen man's adam's apple. Tidyman started breathing in thick gasping heaves. The gun fell somewhere between his legs.

Tidyman fumbled for it with his right hand, moving his left hand to his throat. He was trying to shout something that sounded like, "Maaahaaa Faaahaaaker!" He got his right hand on the gun as Harry ducked behind the car.

Harry grabbed at the driver's side door and threw himself inside. Where the hell were the keys? Cruise control. Four-way flashers. Graphic equalizer. Trip computer. Where are the fucking keys? Where are the fucking *keys*? Of course. Right there between the four-way electric side mirror buttons and the sunroof switch.

Calm.

Don't fumble.

Turn the key.

Terrific. You're doing okay, Harry. If you could just stop your hand from shaking. Now turn the key.

"Your door is a . . . jar."

The voice was feminine, modulated. It reminded Harry of his great aunt: slightly insistent but never strident. It came out of a little speaker in the middle of the dashboard. The engine was slow to catch: goddamn pollution-control features. Harry was still wondering why his great aunt thought his door was a jar when the car took off like a bull from a chute.

Harry knew immediately what had happened. That bastard, Aly. He hadn't trusted Tidyman. Hadn't liked the way he'd talked to him on the way up here. So, if Tidyman had any plans to leave him here with you, Harry, he was going to get the last word in by priming the car to self-accelerate—a posthumous practical joke.

Now, bouncing all over the clearing, picking up speed by the second, you're the beneficiary of Aly's wary ways, Harry, even though he's still out there, still technically alive, staggering around trying to see.

He remembered an item he had once seen in an insurance report: in an emergency situation, most drivers don't remember to brake. They simply freeze. Harry thought, Good Christ, it's true. You simply freeze. You sit here and bounce your ass over the meadow, and you watch it happen. You simply lock up, even when you're heading toward a large tree at the edge of the clearing and continuing to accelerate.

"Your door is a jar."

A bullet flashed in through the open tailgate and exited near the map light switch on the ceiling. Another one exploded the driver's side outside mirror. Harry jerked the wheel around, sending the fat-assed wagon into a skid that narrowly missed the staggering busboy. But the open tailgate slammed into the salad waiter, throwing him fifteen feet through the air in a graceless arc. Harry yanked at the steering wheel again.

The car continued through the field at forty miles an hour. It was still gaining speed when he saw the entrance to the clearing.

Harry's foot found the brake. It helped a little but not much. The wagon bucked over a large bump and careened down onto the road, tailgate still waving. Soon he was doing seventy-five miles an hour on a trail that was suitable for four-wheel-drive trucks.

Harry reached for the ignition key, but quickly pulled his hand back. Turn off the car now and it might not start again. Then you'd be stuck. Worse, you might have to tell the police why you'd cut down enough restaurant employees to cater a small convention.

Harry's head bounced against the roof as another bump threw the car into the air. His spine slammed into the seat as the car hit ground.

He wished he had done up his seat belt. He wished that the car would slow down. He wished that he could stop being slammed around like a marble in a clothes dryer. How much farther ahead was the side road? And how far beyond that was the highway?

"Your door is a jar."

"Fuck yourself," he told his electronic great aunt.

Harry saw the side road. How do you make a ninety-degree turn at seventy-five miles an hour? Isn't the parking brake on these things a separate system? Harry rammed his left foot onto the little pedal. The car slowed slightly, and its rear end began to drift out. By the time he was halfway across the side road, the car was traveling sideways. Harry released the parking brake and the car lunged forward like a puppy off its leash. By keeping his foot lightly pressed on the wide power-brake pedal, he was able to keep the speed to seventy-five.

"Your door is a jar."

Harry ignored the tailgate and concentrated on keeping the car on the road. The linings smelled as if they were burning, so he eased up on the brake pedal.

The car was soon doing ninety, even with his foot jammed occasionally back down on the brake. Harry knew that at this rate, he'd wear the linings down to the metal. He took his foot off to see what would happen running flat out.

Next time he looked at the speedometer, it was closing in on 120. Dead ahead was the main highway interchange. Harry hit the brakes and entered the cloverleaf on two wheels. When the car righted itself, the tailgate slammed shut.

By the time he reached the outskirts of Sterling Heights just north of Detroit, smoke was coming from the brakes of all four wheels. He rammed his foot hard on the pedal and heard a strange metallic squeal, but the car slowed slightly. He angled onto the ramp, made it onto a road lined with fast food outlets, and shut off the key. He glided to a squealing stop outside a Taco Burger. The engine made a low hissing sound as he got out.

"A duck is not an elephant. A door is not a jar," he said to his great aunt. He slammed the door, leaving the keys in the car. Someone would find it; he didn't care who.

Harry started walking, savoring how good it felt to be in full control of his momentum. But before long, tiredness swept over him. He found a cab and went straight to the airport.

At the airport bar he quickly finished a double scotch and then another and then decided to call his FBI friend, Bud Nimitz. Enough was enough. If they couldn't solve this, at least it would be off his plate. If they wanted to put him away it would at least be quieter there. Nimitz.

Daytimer. Phone number folder. Pay phone. Phonecard.

Harry called Nimitz's home number. Nimitz wasn't home. It took three minutes to persuade Mrs. Nimitz that he *was* Harry. Finally, she gave him the name of the hotel he was staying in in Washington, D.C. Bud picked up the phone on the second ring. Harry explained it all, from the beginning.

Nimitz didn't interrupt. Didn't ask questions. Aside from

telling Harry a couple of times to slow down, Nimitz didn't make a sound until it was obvious that Harry had run out of story.

"Well, Harry," he said at last.

"Well, Bud?"

"Drug dealers," Nimitz said, gravely.

"Not drugs, Bud. These guys are terrorists. Drugs never came into the picture."

Nimitz sighed into the telephone. "There are a couple of things you should know, Harry."

Harry waited.

"The first is that there is no such thing as domestic terrorism in this country," Nimitz seemed to be choosing his words with care. "If there were such a thing as domestic terrorism in this country, the FBI would be doing something about it, Harry. We'd have established an active special unit, for one thing. But we don't have an active special unit, because there is no domestic terrorism."

Harry looked around anxiously, then said in an urgent whisper, "Bud, I've got two guys lying in puddles north of Detroit who are A-1, certifiable, guaranteed-or-your-money-back international terrorists." A small black kid walked by Harry's pay phone and turned around to stare with his mouth open.

"Take it easy, Harry," Bud said.

"What do you mean, take it easy?" Harry lowered his voice and turned his face away from the child who was still standing, still staring.

"Drug dealers," Bud Nimitz said firmly. "Some sort of criminal-turf thing. That happens a lot around Detroit. Yeah. I think it was a criminal-turf thing. Where did this happen?"

"East of New Baltimore, in a clearing beside an unpaved road."

"I'll pass that along." All business now.

"What are you telling me, Bud?"

"Two things, Harry. America has no terrorists. And it's time for you to go home. Go home to your own apartment, Harry, sit on your own toilet seat."

"*Sit on my own toilet seat?*" Harry shrieked so loud the black kid took a little jump backward before he turned and ran.

Harry decided that a first-class seat back to New England would be a good idea, a fitting reward for what he'd gone through. A serious flight attendant stared at his rumpled clothes and the soiled bandage over his nose.

"Mugged in Detroit," Harry explained. "I got mugged and they stole all my luggage."

This failed to satisfy the flight attendant, who knew that first-class persons did not go into third-class neighborhoods and get themselves mugged. Far too many of those who traveled in first class these days were not truly first-class. There were game-show hosts, television evangelists, even men who ran factory carpet outlets. It wasn't always easy to spot them, but usually the drink order sorted things out.

"Beer," Harry said.

"Any particular kind, sir?"

"The cold kind. The coldest you have."

And that settled that. This was not the breed of passenger deserving of the first-class canapes. The flight attendant saw him weaving slightly, heading for the washroom right away.

Not his own toilet seat.

Drinking usually turned Harry into a puppy. He became a little clumsy and sometimes too exuberant, but he always remained interested and happy. This evening he was becoming increasingly sullen. The tanned executive beside him wanted to chat about the aging of the population and the effect it was going to have on condo sales in the sunbelt. But he soon gave up and retreated into a magazine.

Harry was sullen because he knew that everyone was lying to him. Nimitz was lying to him. Petrelli had lied to him and had tried to have him killed. And if Biff hadn't lied to him directly, he had at the very least not told him the whole truth. Harry didn't resent the lies, but he hated the idea of people thinking that he couldn't be trusted with the truth.

It was obvious that Biff had been keeping somebody somewhere informed as to where Harry was and what he was doing, right down to the fact that Harry wanted to be at home with his own toilet seat. There was something unforgivable in that. That was personal information, something you disclosed only to a friend. Maybe he would tell Alex.

"Care for another? Sir?"

"Sure. Coldest one you got."

"They're all equally cold, sir."

"In that case, I'll have scotch."

"Any particular brand?"

"The oldest one you got." These days you had to keep serving people in their place.

Maybe he would tell Alex, maybe not. Had she been telling him everything she knew? Or had she been taking lessons from Biff? Maybe he would make up a little test to check on her: tell her that his favorite pickles were bread-and-butter when they were really garlic dills. Then a couple of days later he'd follow Biff into the kitchen and ask if there were any of his favorite kind of pickles around. If Biff wheeled to the cupboard and took out bread-and-butter pickles, Harry would know that Alex was passing on vital information. He would have them red-handed. They weren't the only people who could play the game of subtle manipulation.

"Your scotch, sir."

Harry sipped. "Just the way I like it, nice and old."

On the other hand, maybe Alex was simply what she seemed: a beautiful and intelligent woman, competent, hell of a shot. The trouble with that theory was that if Alex were all the good things she appeared to be, why would she have anything to do with someone like Harry? That was the tricky one. Maybe she liked losers. The attraction of opposites? Emotional self-flagellation? Maybe Alex had secret faults. Perhaps she nagged and would begin to insist on things, like Harry getting more fiber or taking up aerobics. Maybe she was a secret collector of Norman Rockwell commemorative plates.

"Today, we have a choice of beef wellington or rack of lamb," the flight attendant said.

"Could you see if there's any chicken left over in economy? I think I'm developing gout."

Get organized and get back to your roots, Harry. Simplify your life. Pare it back to the essentials. Stick to broiled chicken. You will be happier and less confused if you banish the extraneous. Get the frozen burritos at the store. Take them home. Have your daughter show you how the microwave works.

Then he was sleeping, dreaming of tree houses with ladders you could pull up behind you.

CHAPTER 41

Concord, New Hampshire, September 4.

By the time Harry landed, he had convinced himself that after all he had been through, he also deserved a limousine, and to hell with the cost.

"I'm not going home," he told the driver as soon as he had settled himself in the plush folds of the back seat. The driver nodded, looked in the mirror at Harry's bandaged nose and for the third time that day asked himself why he drew all the winners.

"First, we're going to a bottle store and then we're going to Biff's place in Vermont," Harry explained.

The driver studied Harry's shambles of a suit and the first-class boarding pass sticking out of the pocket where gentlemen once stuffed silk hankies. Since this was New England, the driver pegged Harry as old money: in-bred old money, for certain, but old money nevertheless.

Later, snuggled in the back seat with two cold six-packs, Harry stared out at the houses along the highway. Would he and Alex end up living in a house like these? Would they stay home at night? Would they have a family? And what would Fleur think of that?

And how would you provide for this family, Harry, old boy? You evidently don't have a job and, because you are evidently ill-regarded in your newly adopted field, are unlikely to get one. Your nose is a marshmallow. Yet despite all this, the girl of your dreams is showing extremely bad taste by liking you back. Why?

He pressed the window button and started taking in big gulps of air to clear his head. Someone had been spreading manure in the fields. The ammonia smell speeded the head-clearing process, but the driver kept looking in the rearview at him. Harry closed the window.

It was no use trying to think this through logically. It was too much of a mess. Instead of trying to take control maybe he would just continue to let things happen to him.

He had finished the fifth beer when the limousine pulled into Biff's lane. Harry paid his fare, added a fifty-dollar tip, and told the driver he could keep the rest of the beer. He got out a little unsteadily, pissed against a tree, and was heading up the steps when the front door opened. Alex rushed out and flung her arms around his neck. Harry put his arms under hers and carried her into the front hall. Alex started kissing his ear.

The driver watched. Guy in a suit like that, nose like that, with a girl like that and a house like this. Go figure.

In the hall she was whispering, showing worry, not anger.

"Where were you?"

"Biff knows."

"You phoned? Biff didn't say—"

"I didn't phone. I don't have to phone Biff. Biff has people who tell him what I'm doing. They even know about my toilet seat."

"What are you talking about? Take off your jacket and your tie and your shoes. What are you talking about?"

There was the sound of an electric motor from down the hall. Biff came into the light, his hair uncombed, his eyes sunken, a faint trace of drool on his chin. He had been waiting in his chair. "Can I get you a beer, Harry?"

"Maybe you should go fuck yourself, Biff."

"Some scotch then."

"You knew more about this than you told me."

"Vodka with a little tonic?"

"And you didn't even tell me that you weren't telling me. After all these years, maybe I wouldn't mind you not telling me if you'd only told me you weren't telling me."

"I'm having brandy and soda myself. Would you care for one, Alex?"

She blinked and looked at Harry. "I guess so."

"That's two, then. Care to make it a third, Harry?"

"Okay, for fuck's sake."

Biff shook his head. "So hard to get people involved or interested in the social niceties these days, and yet never were they more necessary than in today's bustling world. Shall we sit in the sitting room or would that be too obvious?"

"Get the fuck down to the sitting room, Biff."

"This way, then. Could you get the lights, Alex? I have to tell you, Harry, that Alex and I have been having another series of discussions whilst you were gone. Interesting, how our views gradually converged. Would you be mother with the brandy, Harry? You know where the glasses are and have such a deft hand with the soda."

Harry knew he was going to be beaten, but he decided to string it out a little, let Biff do the work.

Biff took the brandy from Harry. "Take off your jacket. And your tie and shoes if you wish." Did Biff listen at all the world's keyholes? Or did Biff simply share an interest in Harry's comfort?

"I'm quite comfortable," Harry said.

"If you're so comfortable why are you going up and down on your toes like that? Why do you keep cracking the knuckle in your thumb?"

"Aerobics."

"Fine. Be uncomfortable."

Harry crossed over to the couch and sat down.

"Give him his brandy, Alex," Biff said. "He's uncomfortable."

"Quit calling me uncomfortable. Of course I'm uncomfortable. Poking a busboy in the eye with a bread knife is very stressful work. Remember those psych reports on intervention teams? The guys who'd go off to shoot Arabs or Turks or Armenians or whatever we had on hand that week? Stress was so much on day one, so much on day two, three and four? All that bullshit? Knifing a busboy in the eye is a stressful situation. Very stressful. Figures don't lie." Harry took a sip of his drink. "Scotch doesn't cure it and beer doesn't cure it and I'm pretty fucking sure brandy and soda isn't going to cure it. So I'm stressed, Biff, and I'm uncomfortable, and you didn't tell me the truth."

"I never lied to you, Harry."

"You didn't tell me the truth. You're in touch with whatever group the FBI has that it claims is a drug enforcement unit. The one they have instead of a terrorist unit because we don't have terrorists in this country. You've been playing telephone footsie with them, telling them where old Harry's going to be next. What are you doing that for when you're not telling me you're doing it? That's stressful. That makes me uncomfortable."

Biff's chair started gliding around the room: crisp figure-eights, graceful parentheses.

"All along," Harry said, "I figured Bill Penzler was guiding the Jacamar heavies to where I was. But that's okay. That's fine. You expect that from Penzler because Penzler's the practical definition of unmitigated prick and he has to watch his ass. So he was likely passing on information as some sort of favor to a client. That's fine. That's okay. But you were supposed to be a friend. Out of friendship I stopped fucking your daughter, and now you treat me like this. I would have married the bitch and inflicted grandchildren on you if I'd known this was the kind of shit you'd pull. You deserve to be a lonely old prick in a wheelchair chasing squirrels with your piss bag."

Biff brought his chair to a sudden stop. "Harry, would you like me to memo you on the whys and wherefores of all this? Or would you like me to explain it to you now?"

"Get me another brandy. I'm thirsty. Stress causes thirst. That was in the psych reports as well."

Biff touched the joystick lightly and the chair crossed the room toward the decanter.

Alex looked at them both. Biff was less pink, less well-wrapped, more like an old man. Harry was different, too. She had never really imagined Harry with a capacity for anger or the ability to be intentionally, unreservedly cruel. Earlier, over fish bouillon, Biff had said marvelous things about Harry, told her how Harry had saved so many lives and had shown such a capacity for work and ingenuity. Biff wanted Harry to fight the good fight again, with him, this time at more of a managerial level. They could, as Biff had put it, all live together in the country and sing songs at twilight.

Biff poured the brandy, forgot the soda, and wheeled back to Harry. He eased to a stop with the snifter just out of Harry's reach. "Here's what I'll admit to you. I'll give you a list of four or five things that I never told you and then I'll tell you why I didn't tell you and then in a day or two you can add up the sum of it all and tell me what you think. Okay?"

Harry grunted.

"The first error of omission was that, during my conversations with you, I under-represented the magnitude of my current responsibilities. They are more extensive than I suggested. That should not sit badly with you because it is an omission that is fairly standard procedure in the trade."

Harry shifted in his seat.

"The second error was that when you became involved in all this I neglected to reveal exactly how interested I was in the outcome. I did try to show a boyish enthusiasm, but it was the sort of gusto that a fellow who ties fishing flies might have for producing a perfect imitation of the Crackbridgen Spring Bug. I tried not to be serious and I tried not to show that I was glad that you were becoming increasingly serious. It was heartening to me that you were taking these incidents more and more to heart. It demonstrated that you had left your boyhood and become an old fart, screaming against any change in society that discomforts. That's important, Harry. The world needs old farts."

Harry listened, his nostrils still flaring in and out, but with much less intensity now.

"You used to be a young fart. Immature. Your interest in what you did was not what I would have regarded as morally sound. You would have been as happy undertaking the same sort of activities for the Soviets or the Bulgarians, or perhaps even for the Syrians. But as an old fart you would not. That is a profound transformation. Witnessing this transformation, I was intrigued and thus committed my third error of omission. I neglected to inform you that I was interested in having you return to our nest again. The fourth error was in not telling you that I had suggested to my colleagues that we regard this project as a sort of trial to see if you were a suitable candidate or still the kind of young fart who would go around killing the wrong Lebanese. My colleagues include people in units of the FBI that do not exist."

"You even got Bud Nimitz in the fucking conspiracy."

"His seniors are my colleagues. Would you take this brandy? My hand is quite tired."

Harry took it.

"I did not plan the trial. You were already involved in an interesting situation. I simply turned it into a trial. Not so bad?"

"So I didn't pass."

"No, you passed fairly well. In the end, no one else had to help you."

"And what do I get now, a degree in knifing busboys and running down salad waiters?"

"Come on, Harry. At least this time you hit the right persons. And you'll be glad to know that we have arranged suitable, if not wholesomely legal, justice for young Matthew Kohl, who I am sure you've guessed by now was the link that allowed the Jacamar group to stay on your trail, at least in the early stages. Matthew was so anxious not to jeopardize the chances of a sale to a national brewery should Wolfgang pass away that he lost all sense of perspective. His father has since helped him to retrieve it. A recent revision to his will stipulates that ownership will pass to the employees on Wolfgang's death. There is also a codicil precluding the company's sale to any other brewer for the next ninety-nine years. Since Matthew is no longer an employee and would not likely be around in ninety-nine years even if he were, he loses out all around."

"Hmph," Harry snorted. "What about that prick Petrelli?"

Biff held his brandy to the light and watched the liquid roll up the side of the snifter. "Ah, yes, well, Angelo Petrelli, who would have cheerfully seen you chopped into a savory sauce for pasta, will, I'm afraid, be spending some time in prison. Since officially there never was a Jacamar Corporation, there is no way for Mr. Petrelli to give an acceptable account of the payment he made. A substantial payment, too, I might add; makes whatever John DeLorean did seem small by comparison. So Angelo Petrelli will appear to have been caught with his fingers in the till. Very tidy, very neat. Only Alistair Duffy leaves us with something of a loose end. Some of us suspect that he knew that Flight 603 was going to crash. We have therefore arranged for him to appear before the FAA to discuss that possibility. I think that by the time the press has gone at his testimony with its usual subtle savagery, you may see some rather negative public feedback reflected in the quarterly earnings of Alistair Duffy's business."

"The invisible hand." Harry smiled and tilted his glass Biff's way.

"And that, dear Harry, brings us to you. What do you get from all this? You get an offer of a position, slightly more senior than the one you had before. More involved with planning."

Harry looked as if he might be thinking it over. "I don't know. Last time you hired me there were a lot of things you didn't tell me. That wouldn't be good enough this time."

"It would have to be, Harry. You would have to trust me. I don't think that's an outrageous proposition."

"Is it okay if I say no?"

"It's perfectly okay to say no. What are you going to do instead?"

"Did Penzler really fire me?"

"You could have that job back. I think I can guarantee that. Penzler's behavior, like most of the business people in this affair, was far from commendable. He would certainly be ripe for a little persuasion should push come to shove. But why on earth would you want that? That's a boys' club, Harry. Come to where the old farts play."

"I'm going to bed," Harry said. "I'm going to simplify my life."

Alex followed, but not without a long look back at Biff.

"Was it very bad?" She spoke softly in the darkness of the bedroom.

"It wasn't very bad. Count no day unsuccessful in which you kill a surly waiter."

"Would you like to be hugged?"

"I could stand quite a lot of it."

"Do you want to talk about it?"

"No."

CHAPTER 42

Brattleboro, Vermont, September 5.

She came to Biff's house the next day, just as they were finishing dinner. Gisele went to the door.

Harry hadn't talked much through the meal, either about the lamb or about Biff's earlier offer. But the only irritation Biff had shown about his silence had taken the form of telling Harry, twice, not to play with his food.

Biff wheeled away from his chocolate ripple ice cream to go and greet the visitor. Seconds later, he and Gisele returned from the hall, followed immediately by the woman. She wore riding boots, jeans, and a Harris Tweed jacket with a brown leather purse over the shoulder. But most of her wardrobe went unnoticed by Harry and Alex, who were focussing on the gun the woman held with two hands.

"If you will all just sit at the table." A crisp English accent.

"Would you like some wine?" asked Biff.

"And be quiet," the woman said.

"Or some chocolate ripple ice cream?"

The woman raised the revolver, just a little. She wasn't dramatic with the weapon, just quietly confident. It looked large in her hands.

"Is there anyone else in the house?" the woman asked.

"You told us to be quiet," Alex said.

The woman sighed, took two slow steps forward and gave Alex a casual swipe across the side of the face with the gun.

Harry jerked forward in his chair but the woman swung the barrel of the gun around to his temple, and there was a click like the sound of a door locking as she thumbed back the hammer.

"Don't even think about it," she said. Harry eased his full weight back onto the chair. "Now, again, is there anyone else in the house?"

"There's nobody else in the house," Biff said.

"The old man appears to be telling the truth," said Ismail Gezmis, entering from the hall. Biff opened his mouth, then closed it. Gezmis looked at Biff. "We will want just a little more of that. The truth, I mean. Just the name of the person in our organization whom you have managed to win over. The traitor who has given you information at every turn. The moment we receive that person's name and how you succeeded in reaching him, we shall leave you to resume your meal."

Harry stared.

"And what we are going to do now, is get to that truth," said Gezmis, as a tall man with a bandaged neck appeared in the doorway behind him.

"Oh shit," said Harry. "It's the salad waiter."

"Ah," said Biff, "that explains why he didn't show up until dessert."

"Shut up," said Marjorie Brooks.

"We will take you each to separate rooms," Gezmis said. "We will see how well your stories match, one against the other. Consider that if the information you give us differs to the least degree, we will cause one or more of you considerable pain. Mr. Tidyman is very anxious to do that. Marjorie will take the young woman. Felix would like to be alone with Mr. Bracken. The old man and the servant woman will stay with me."

Marjorie Brooks was smiling as she opened the door to the library. She motioned Alex in with the gun, then stood aside to let her pass. She reached out to touch the welt that she had left on Alex's face, then moved her hand across the skin until she felt the softness of her hair.

"You're very lovely," Marjorie Brooks said.

Alex shuddered as the door clicked behind her.

Felix Tidyman stood well away from Harry as he followed him down the hall. Considering that he had clearly had the help of an infiltrator telling him their every move, Bracken hadn't done a whole lot with it. But he did appear to have moments of competence. The bandages over two broken ribs where Bracken had caught him with the open tailgate were proof of that. The fact that Tidyman had been obliged to walk wounded down a long dark lane before convincing a suspicious motorist that he'd been mugged and dumped by niggers was further proof.

But Tidyman didn't add the knife wound in his throat to Bracken's skimpy list of wins. If anything, that merely demonstrated the man's ineptness, his inability to finish off an opponent when he had the opportunity.

Bracken's most serious blunder had been in leaving a trail that a pack of cub scouts could have sniffed out. It had almost seemed too easy.

First to Bracken's Detroit hotel, courtesy of Bracken's telegram to Angelo Petrelli. In a side pocket of the traveling bag that Harry had left behind, Tidyman had found the boarding pass for Harry's flight from New Hampshire. From there it had been a simple matter of calling the airline and using invented credentials to persuade a reservations clerk to cough up the telephone number in Brattleboro that Harry had given when he made his reservation. Tidyman had then gone through the Brattleboro directory and matched the number to a house. All routine for a professional.

But the ultimate proof of his superiority was that he now had a gun at Bracken's head.

"Why don't we just go into this room here?" Tidyman peered into the thickly draped darkness of Biff's den and located the light switch. His voice was a rasping whisper. "And why don't you sit on that chair, shithead? And why don't you put this bag over your head?"

Harry sat down. He caught the black cloth bag that Tidyman threw.

Harry put the bag to his bandaged nose and wondered at the odor. Fried food? Fear? A little of each? He drew it slowly over his head.

"Now, you're going to give me the name," Tidyman said. "Give me the name and I promise to kill you quickly."

Ismail Gezmis looked along the dining room table at the old man and the servant woman seated at the far end. He studied the old man's face. It was as if a plaster dwarf had come to life. At a casual glance, the face might have belonged to a happily dull man. But with closer study, there were furrows that suggested study, thought, and guile.

"Your people were so clumsy that at first I thought they must be with the CIA," Gezmis said. "But the erratic behavior of your colleague suggests a private organization, probably right-wing and funded by multinationals."

"Of course, you're quite correct," smiled Biff.

"And some of that funding is being used to purchase information from one of our people," Gezmis continued.

"There, I'm afraid, is where our respective recollections change trains," Biff said.

Gezmis nodded and smiled confidently. "We will wait to see what your young colleagues have to say."

"I think you'd be making a mistake if you believed that they know everything that's going on," Biff said.

Gisele nodded.

Gezmis shook his head, almost sadly. "In that case, when you hear their screams, you may wish you had told them more."

With her free hand Marjorie Brooks reached into her shoulder purse and pulled out a pack of Virginia Slims. She tapped one out and put it between her lips. She put the pack away and pulled out a gold lighter. She studied Alex.

"First, I want you to remove your clothes. Then I want you to lie on the floor."

Alex hesitated. "How will removing my clothes tell you something I don't know?"

The Englishwoman bit her lower lip. "The alternative is to see how hard I can hit you with my gun on your mouth. Imagine suffering all that orthodontistry for nothing."

Alex began mechanically unbuttoning her blouse.

"My name is Harry Bracken. I'm in insurance. And I have to congratulate you on your skilled interrogation. We've been here less than a minute and you've already got the whole story out of me."

"You can probably tell that it hurts me to ask questions," Tidyman croaked. "But it's going to hurt you more if you don't answer."

"Actually, most of the money comes from the oil people, although we do get some from companies involved in defense technology," Biff explained to Ismail Gezmis. "These sponsors would rather not know exactly what we do, which relieves us of such burdens as submitting reports and overviews. It frees our time for more constructive things. There is a retired general of the Air Force who does an informal monitoring of our activities and assures them that their money is being well spent." Biff spoke in a casual manner, as though he didn't care whether he was being believed or not.

Gisele nervously fingered the cutlery on the table.

Alex stepped out of her panties and looked pleadingly at Marjorie Brooks. The Englishwoman took a long draw on her cigarette and made a lowering motion with her gun. Alex sat on the floor.

Marjorie Brooks reached into her purse again and tossed a length of nylon fishing line to the floor. "Now I would like you to tie your feet together."

*

"My name is Harry Bracken, and I work in insurance." Harry knew that they planned to kill them all, so he decided to tell the truth. That would leave his mind free to devise a way to kill the salad waiter first.

The bag over his head was a problem. But Harry knew why it was there. In a training course years ago they had made him sit in a light-tight chamber. After fifteen minutes Harry had forgotten that it was all a game. The isolation, the lack of light and orientation, had made him forget. After three hours in the chamber they had put a bag much like this one over his head and walked him to an interrogation room.

"William Penzler runs the investigation department at Hanover Casualty," Harry told Felix Tidyman. "At last count, there were forty-nine people working in that department. Most of them are really good people. Except for Jeff Brock. He's always getting buffaloed, which isn't a feature you want in someone who investigates claims for a living. But that's okay, or seems to be okay, because his wife is somebody's daughter. I remember suggesting that Penzler send Brock to Kohl's when the, ah, problems started there. If only he'd listened, everything would have worked out fine. You people would have done whatever it is you're going to do anyway. And I wouldn't be sitting here in the dark with a broken nose on my face and a bag on my head."

I have a bag over my head and no gun, thought Harry. Tidyman has no bag and one gun. How am I going to help Alex?

How have I ever helped Alex?

"As a brand manager at the brewery, part of my job is overseeing quality control—" Alex began. Her ankles were tied and the wooden floor was cold against her skin.

Marjorie Brooks was behind her. She kept the cigarette in her mouth while she tied Alex's wrists behind her back. She stood up and exhaled smoke through her nose, holding her eyes all the while on Alex's body. "They used a woman to infiltrate Qatar's people, as well. But of course you knew that."

"Since Mr. Kohl Senior is such a stickler for doing things right, there's never been much of a problem with quality control before," Alex said.

"When they told me that a woman was working against us again, I prayed it would be you. I prayed it would be the woman who killed Qatar."

Harry stood up.

"Get back in the chair," Tidyman wheezed. He brought the gun to his eye and looked at Harry down the barrel.

"What are you going to do? Kill me? You're not going to kill me. At least not yet. Not until you find the leak. You can kill everyone in our organization and you won't solve a thing until you plug that leak. I suppose if you killed everyone in your own organization, you'd plug it up, but that might be a little self-defeating. In any case, I don't think you're going to shoot me until the Arabian gentleman says it's okay for you to shoot me." Harry kept walking backward. Could he remember where the hell it was? He thought it was somewhere near the door, positioned low where Biff could reach it in his chair.

Harry kept improvising. "You people took an awful chance coming here today. I don't think you would have done that if you'd had any other choice. But the fact is, if you don't find out who's been sharing your innermost secrets with us, your whole operation is grounded. And you and all your chums are going to be looking over your shoulders for the rest of your lives, aren't you?"

Harry felt it rub against his lower back: the switch.

In a dark room, the blind man is king.

Biff put his hand under the blanket on his lap. Ismail Gezmis made a threatening motion with the gun. Biff smiled and held up his colostomy bag. Gezmis gave a look that was half-surprise, half-apology. Biff checked the level: about a liter and a half. That should be sufficient.

*

"I didn't know him," said Alex.

"Of course not. Not in the sense of *really* knowing someone. If you'd *really* known Qatar, you wouldn't have arranged to have him killed."

Her eyes seemed to be focusing on something beyond the room. Almost dreamily, she reached into her purse for another cigarette, and lit it from the one in her hand. With an easy, almost theatrical movement of her fingers, she flicked the live butt at Alex.

"Whoops, missed," said Marjorie Brooks. She blew the ash from the end of the new cigarette and studied the red hot glow. "Let's see if we can do better with this one."

Do you turn a light switch up or down to turn it off? Harry paused, then pressed his back against the wall and squatted. The hint of light that had been leaking through the bag was gone. The lights in the room were out.

He had expected the salad waiter to shoot immediately; so the instant he squatted, Harry rolled across the carpet as quietly as he could. Harry had *wanted* to hear the gunshot: in a room as dark as the heavy drapes made this one, the flash of the gun would, for a matter of milliseconds, blind the cones and rods in the other man's retina. Time enough for Harry to pull off the bag, the bag that would have protected his own eyes from the flash. Harry would have still had his night vision. He would have been the only seeing man in the room.

But the waiter didn't shoot.

He didn't yell either. Harry had half expected him to shout, to run about, to act confused.

He yanked off the bag, and was surprised at how black Biff's heavy drapes had made the room. But he knew that his advantage would hold only until the other man's eyes adjusted.

There it was, a shape near Biff's computer desk. Felix Tidyman had moved silently to his right.

Now he was standing, and listening, and waiting.

*

Biff put his hands back under his blanket and pressed the button on his watch that made it go "Meep."

"Excuse me," Biff said. He yanked the tube from the top of his colostomy bag, pulled the bag off the hook that held it to his chair, and lifted it to eye level. "Ah, yes," he said, "I do believe it's time."

For a second he admired the coloring of the vintage, shook his head, then placed the bag on his lap.

Marjorie Brooks moved in with the gun and cigarette.

Alex flinched. "Okay. Look. I'm afraid that I'm not very brave. You want the name of the person we've been using. I'll tell you his name. I'll tell you how much we've been paying him. I'll tell you anything you want, but please don't—"

Marjorie Brooks blew lightly on the ash. "They say that cigarettes are hazardous to your health." She brought it slowly toward Alex's breast.

"Saddam!" Alex blurted out the first name that entered her head. "His name is Abdel Saddam. A little greaseball type of guy. Wears a necklace with two people fucking on it. Biff's been paying him twenty-five hundred a week."

Marjorie Brooks seemed suddenly confused. She pulled back the cigarette and stared at Alex. She took a long drag. Saddam? She could still feel his breath against her neck.

Something to throw. Harry squinted at the wall behind him. He knew there was a picture there. He couldn't remember it exactly. Something with haystacks in a French winter field. A real Monet.

His hand found the frame. Heave it, Harry. Make a noise. Make him fire at the noise. Quick, do it now. Then while the echo's still ringing in his ears, move in and he won't hear you coming. Move in and whonk the fucker now.

He eased the picture off the hook and hurled it at the dim shadow of Felix Tidyman.

An electronic alarm clicked on the instant the painting was lifted from its hook. Metal bells ripped through the silence.

Tidyman jumped.

Harry wasn't ready for it either.

The bells startled Ismail Gezmis. He turned toward the hall.

Biff picked up his colostomy bag and cradled it under his arm. He yanked the small plug from the neck. Gezmis turned to see what he was doing. That was when Biff squeezed the bag as hard as he could between his arm and his body and directed the stream toward the Arab's face.

The urine caught Gezmis in both eyes. He threw his hands up to his face. Gisele chose that moment to pick up the carving fork still sitting beside the leg of lamb. She jammed it into the Arab's scrotum.

Marjorie Brooks jumped at the sound of the clanging bells.

"Qatar," she whispered.

She stood and whispered again. But this time it was, "Ismail," and she walked trancelike to the door.

The painting crashed against a table crowded with small photographs mounted on stands. Felix Tidyman whirled away from the sound of the bells to the sound of the clatter. But still he refused to fire his gun.

It took Harry less than a second to cross the four yards toward the tall shadow. At the last instant he leaped and his hands clamped on the gun. Tidyman pulled with all his might in the opposite direction. They struggled in the dark for possession.

Harry could feel his grip weakening. It was strength against strength, and Tidyman was proving the stronger.

So Harry let go of the gun. Just then it went off and sent a bullet tearing into the ceiling.

With Harry's sudden release, Tidyman pulled the butt back

into his neck, close enough to the knife wound to cause a sharp, distracting pain. Harry, with both hands free now, brought them together to form an oversize fist. He concentrated all of his force behind a blow into the rib cage, hoping to make contact near the injury from the tailgate.

Tidyman doubled forward with a gasp and dropped the gun. Harry was still feeling for it on the floor, when Tidyman made it to the door.

Alex sat bound and naked in the middle of the library. She tried to remember if during all of those times that her father had taken her out to find pickerel and bass, they had ever actually *untied* a nylon fishing line. No. You either cut the line or you . . .

She heard the clicking of the Englishwoman's heels fading away down the hall. Then she heard the gunshot. The bells of the alarm kept clanging in the distance.

Alex remembered the lighted cigarette butt on the floor.

The pain in Ismail Gezmis's crotch became the center of his universe. The bells seemed a part of the nightmare: somehow, the pain was making bells ring. Still holding the gun, he reached down carefully with his left hand. Defiantly but gingerly, he gripped the bone handle of the fork. Slowly, like drawing a spoon from cold molasses, he drew it out. It fell to the floor and he stared, still half blind from the pain and the urine in his eyes.

He tried to straighten up, slowly, painfully. Gisele hurled herself at him and hammered her fists at his face. Blindly, almost unthinkingly, he swung the gun at her head and she dropped.

Biff hurled his empty bag at him and missed.

With his free hand, Gezmis pulled up a corner of the table-cloth, sending dishes flying; he began to wipe his face.

That was when he heard heavy, plodding footsteps approaching the doorway from the hall. He turned and fired.

Felix Tidyman fell through the door.

"Ismail, you camelfucker." His croak was barely heard above the bells.

Marjorie Brooks stopped partway down the hall. She saw Tidyman fall forward through the doorway of the dining room. Someone inside had just shot Tidyman. Who? How? Why?

And what were those bells?

She brought both hands to her gun and raised it.

"Ismail." She mouthed the word.

She spoke his name again as she stepped over the long hulk of Tidyman and into the room.

Watching from the doorway of the den, Harry lowered Tidyman's gun. He knew that he had blown it. The Englishwoman had stood staring down the hall ahead of him for several seconds. Harry had drawn a perfect bead on the top of her spine. If she turned his way, or started to turn, he knew that he would fire. But he had not been able to shoot the woman in the back.

An inner voice had tried its damndest: The woman is armed, Harry. Biff and Gisele are in that room, quite possibly still alive. Pull the trigger, Harry. Squeeze it now.

But he had lowered the gun. You're a fuck-up, Harry, plain and simple. In the company of killers, you're the one who only kills in the dark.

Which is how you hit the wrong Lebanese.

And while he was thinking all that, he saw Marjorie Brooks step over Tidyman's body and turn into the dining room.

Harry bit his lower lip until he tasted blood. Where was Alex? And who had shot the salad waiter and left his feet out in the hall?

Alex rolled over and found the cigarette butt. She blew silently on it and prayed. But instead of glowing to life, it rolled away along the floor. She moved awkwardly and pulled herself into position to blow on it again. She kept puffing until it rolled up against the edge of a mat and stopped there. She blew again. The butt was still alive. She turned around and slowly brought her wrists down until she felt the heat against her skin. She knew that if she brought her wrists down hard, it would eat through the line with a minimum of pain. Any other way would be like peeling off a bandage one hair at a time.

Biff backed his chair away from the table. He watched the Englishwoman with the gun walk almost in a daze toward the injured Arab, calling his name, then touching him to make sure he was still alive. The Arab reached out his hand.

That was when Biff saw Harry in the doorway. Biff jammed his joystick down and the chair surged forward. It jumped at the table with enough power to start it sliding slowly toward Gezmis and Marjorie Brooks.

The Arab turned, pushed the woman aside, and aimed the gun at Biff.

Harry squeezed the trigger of Tidyman's gun. Once, and the Arab lurched around in surprise. Twice, and he began to slide to the floor. Three times and he lurched again on his way down.

The woman scrambled on all fours under the table, hidden by the long tablecloth until she surfaced beside Biff, grabbing his ear with one hand and shoving her gun against it with the other.

The room was suddenly still. There were just the bells now and even they seemed to be growing fainter, more distant. There were no other noises, except for short panting sounds from Harry, still standing with the smoking gun.

"Drop the gun, Mr. Bracken, or I will kill this old man." Marjorie Brooks pushed the gun into Biff's face.

"Gently, dear," Biff said.

"Even if you pull the trigger, I'll still get a bullet into his temple."

"Very gently," Biff said.

Harry edged forward. "What am I supposed to do, Biff?"

"Fire when ready, old son," Biff said.

"Drop the gun, Mr. Bracken, and do it now." Marjorie Brooks said in her best schoolmistress's voice.

"Biff?" Harry, still unsure.

"If you drop the gun, Harry, she will kill us all. Aim for the head. Gisele will get the house, though I trust she'll afford visiting privileges to you and your good woman."

"I don't want anything from you, Biff."

Harry looked at Gisele still lying on the floor, saw the agony in her eyes, the almost imperceptible movement of the head. He turned back to Marjorie Brooks.

"My last warning, Bracken," she said. "Drop the gun now."

Harry shook his head sadly and pulled the trigger.

Alex smelled her own skin burning. But she knew the ember was also melting the line around her wrists. She tried to pull her arms away from each other and, seconds later, cried aloud when the line finally snapped. She picked up the butt and burnt through the cord at her ankles.

She was out the door and into the hall before she remembered she was naked.

Harry pulled the trigger again, and then again, with the same result: a hollow click. There you go, Harry. Never play with guns, especially one you've borrowed from someone who didn't like you terribly much, and especially when you have no idea how many rounds are left in the thing. Although, admit it now, Harry, he gave you a hint as wide as a house when he showed such restraint from firing at you back in the den.

Only you, Harry, would give a man credit for a display of cunning, when the jerk was simply preserving his ammunition.

Marjorie Brooks allowed herself a flicker of a smile, then with an almost teasing slowness, swung her gun away from Biff's head and aimed it at Harry.

She pulled the trigger and Harry went down.

She turned the gun back to Biff. "Cheerio, old man," she said quietly, just before Alex ran naked into the room, screaming, "No!"

The moment froze. It was a dance in a Brueghel painting, a

photograph of a football scrimmage, a child's game of Statues. Everyone stopped halfway through a moment of motion. An arm that had been moving one way was instantly stilled. A leg about to begin a step was held awkwardly still.

Biff moved first and then only his lips. He spoke calmly to Marjorie. "My dear, go quietly. What you want to do now is to just back your way down the hall. You want to back your way down the hall because you know that we will all stay very, very still until you reach the door and take the knob in your hand and turn it and leave the house. After you go through the door, you will simply walk to whatever transportation you have and go away to someplace better. That is how it will work. Walk backward to the door. Take the knob in your hand. Open the door. And then you will leave and you will feel much, much better."

Marjorie Brooks considered. She looked from Biff to Gisele to Alex. She raised the gun again to Biff's head.

"No," Alex called out. "No." She indicated Harry, a motionless heap on the floor. "You've done what you came to do," she said in a breaking voice.

Marjorie Brooks looked around. The Bracken man, Gezmis, the servant woman on the floor, Tidyman. For an instant, she seemed awed by the carnage. Then the hardness returned to her voice. She walked to Alex and tapped the barrel of the gun lightly against the mark on her cheek. "Yes. I've lived without him now for three years and seven months." She was almost choking on the words. Alex was astonished to see first one tear, then another. Marjorie looked over at Harry, heaped on the floor. "Now you will see what it's like."

She walked down the long hall without turning back. At the front door she paused to put the gun in her purse.

She lifted the latch and she was gone.

Harry stirred and gripped his side.

Alex let out a gasp of relief and ran to him.

"Alex, my dear," Biff said, gently. "In Vermont, we dress for the dining room."

CHAPTER 43

Brattleboro, Vermont, September 9.

Biff's doctor was not impressed by the wound in Harry's side. He had studied it dispassionately, explored it, done something with a needle and syringe, wrapped it snugly, and written two prescriptions, one for an antibiotic, the other for a painkiller. The doctor was more impressed by the special reporting procedure he was told to follow when he called the long-distance number Biff provided.

The policemen who came to investigate the alarm bells were surprised to find two dead males, a tall, bruised woman, a younger woman with braces and a welt on her face, and a guy with a bandaged nose and a bullet in his side. All they'd counted on was another false alarm from the home security system.

They were even more surprised when Bud Nimitz arrived and gave specific instructions for the disposal of the bodies.

The ranking policeman at first balked at the order. Nimitz dialed a number and handed him the phone. By the time the cop hung up, he was red-faced and compliant.

Next morning, Harry woke to see her lying beside him, watching him, the sun a halo behind her head.

"How are you?" Alex asked.

"Well, I haven't killed anyone yet, today. Do you think I might need more bran in my diet?"

"Could be lack of bran. Could be the way you keep mistreating your body."

*

By morning, the tremor had gone from her hands. She had stopped playing with her lower lip. Her voice was no longer constricted. "I was thinking we should take a little time off. Get away and go someplace. Get acquainted. Go to the kind of place where you get up and go down for breakfast and talk about what you're going to do for the rest of the day until it's time for lunch and a nap."

"Sounds fine," Harry said.

"Where? You've traveled, Harry. Where?"

"There's a place in the south of Italy where they cater to that sort of thing. There are several places in Mexico. St. Lucia looked pretty. And we made some good friends."

"You could pick one at random."

"I could pick one at random. But what I'd rather do is get a map and whatever place I pick we'll move one or two inches to the right or left and that's where we'll go. Going anywhere I've planned for us to go always turns out badly."

"That's a good plan, Harry. Or we could just stay here. But we can only make it for a couple of weeks. Because then I think I want to go back to work."

"I have to call my daughter," Harry said.

By the second day, Harry felt strong enough to walk. Alex still cried occasionally, but it was getting better.

They were sitting down when Biff wheeled into the dining room. Before he could speak, Alex was on him. "Biff, I'm afraid we have some serious reservations about Harold's job offer."

"Harold? Harold? You don't mean our Harry."

"'Harold' seems better suited to a man in an executive position," Alex decided. "The name of a man on his way up. Anyway we have these reservations. There are a few things we want cleared up before we—he—consents to it."

"Yes."

"The first thing is that I'll be continuing my own career at Kohl's. He'll need a flexible schedule so that we could see each other from time to time."

Biff twinkled. "Harry's schedule has always had an elasticity that could send the Spandex company into fits of envious salivation. I can't imagine him changing now."

Alex pursed her lips and took that in. "Fine. Now let's move along to salary, pensions, dental plans for daughters and any subsequent offspring, and company policy vis-a-vis mates accompanying employees to the office Christmas party."

Biff grinned. "We always had mates at the Christmas party, my dear. If not when we arrived, at least by the time the stilton and port had disappeared."

"Good, good. And how about Harold's chances for advancement?"

"Not quite as good, I'm afraid," Biff said. "Just last week the doctor took samples of every fluid I have. I was amazed again to learn how many there are. He concluded that I was in astonishing vigor for a man run by batteries. That would all suggest that Harold does not have any immediate chance of promotion. Of course, if it would be of solace, we could change his title once a week. That way you could send postcards to fellow members of your Junior League on a regular basis announcing that Harold has another new title. Would that suffice?"

"That leaves only the question of Harold's country-club dues," Alex said.

"I believe we would be quite able to afford the dues of any club that would have Harold as a member."

Harry sat there listening. Sometimes it was better when you let things happen to you. Let Biff happen to you. Let Alex happen to you. Let it happen, Harry.

Anything else is like arguing with the weather.